SEBASTIAN'S JOURNEY

AND THE WOMEN WHO MADE HIM CARE

David Martin Guyette MD

Design and distribution by Bublish

ISBN: 978-1-64704-716-0 (paperback)
ISBN: 978-1-64704-715-3 (eBook)

BOOK ONE

1

Every life has a pivotal moment that alters each second that follows. Sebastian Alexander Williamson's pivotal moment occurred at sunset on July 3, 1926.

His day began waking up beside Pricilla Connolly in his family's guest cottage on Lake Winnebago. The forty-acre lake compound was just five miles from Fond du Lac's swanky neighborhood, where his parents' mansion dwarfed every contender. Great Grampa built the mansion after he bought two-thousand acres for a farm, added a grain mill, and then expanded three times before dominating textile manufacturing, the dairy market, and whole-sale beef sales from one end of Wisconsin to the other. Sebastian's dad took over when Grampa died. If you didn't work for Old Zeek, you didn't work at all.

Zeek was a fine old dad, as fine old dads went, but if ever there was someone thick as brick, it was Zeek. His wife, Elizabeth, called the shots. Zeek never knew what hit him, nor cared, as long as Elizabeth aimed her cheap shots in any direction but his. In truth, he had no idea what he was doing, he just liked doing it. You might say Sebastian followed in his footsteps, except the two of them did more tripping than stepping.

Mommy Elizabeth had a reputation for being the foul wind everyone pretended to ignore. She would strut, scowl, and berate the staff endlessly, with tone and timbre the town managed to tolerate.

"Get those damn shoes off, Zeek!" Elizabeth shrieked in a whisper. "You'll wake Sebastian and Pricilla."

"I'm not sure that's possible. Them two kids finished off my second jug of hard cider on the dock last night. I ain't been this sober in weeks."

Zeek and Mommy Elizabeth tiptoed out of the main lodge with its ten bedrooms, four baths, two dining rooms, and a stone sauna to warm bodies after winter ice fishing. As they closed the front door in slow motion, both looked up the central staircase. They expected, as usual, that Sebastian and Pricilla were upstairs sleeping in separate bedrooms—one on the second floor looking north over Brush Brook, and the other up another flight of stairs watching the sun rise over eastern white pines. Neither of the old folk ever caught the two youngsters sneaking out at midnight. It'd been Sebastian's idea; he always got his way. Pricilla hadn't bothered to blush; she liked the idea of keeping her gold mine as close as possible. She had no idea that very day Mommy Elizabeth would pivot Sebastian's life in her face.

Mommy Elizabeth never bothered with what she did not want to know, like the fact that no one in this life picked their own DNA, no one chose the time and place of their birth, and no one petitioned for parents of distinction.

According to Elizabeth, young Pricilla was not wise enough to have chosen a grandfather who loved money, power, and pissing on the world. Pricilla's grandfather turned over dirt, planted corn, and loved his family till the day he died. He believed that, like with nature, the secret of happiness was patience.

There wasn't one family for miles around who earned Mommy Elizabeth's stamp of approval. As regular as rain in April, she would mention the Andersons of Milwaukee, the Becher's stone castle overlooking Chicago, or the W ranch outside Madison, all of which, by no coincidence, were rearing daughters in range of wedlock. All of them also dragged a reputation for underpaying the help as they ignored the common good. All the better, thought Elizabeth, as she formulated her plan.

The guest cottages were named for the trees Gramps had cleared to build them. Evergreen sat on the other side of Brush Brook; it had a front porch facing lake sand and a back deck extending an elevated walkway beside the brook for fall-run fishing. There was also a mahogany, arched bridge connecting the cabin to the rest of the compound. To the south, the cottages were Oak House, Maple Pastures, and Birch Heaven, aptly named for what Sebastian found there.

Pure white birch bark reflected morning sun through the back windows just when it lit the sky on the other side of the deck connecting the dock to the boat launch. Trees were all that were seen from the most private spot on the lake, at the back of Beaver Cove, the deep water farthest south.

As eagerly as Sebastian rose in response to Pricilla's reclining beauty the night before, he rose from the bed at the spectacular sight of the lake's morning reflections. Earlier that century, when the Germans, French, and English were killing each other in Europe, in the Midwest they made love, had babies, and laughed—a lot. It's amazing what a change of scenery can do for you. Sebastian stood over six feet tall, with shoulders wide and grin appealing.

The prominence of the lake's seduction was fleeting and no match for a woman's beauty. Sebastian turned and gasped at the sight, then held his breath. He prayed that what was before him would never disappear. Pricilla smiled back, covered to the neck by a thin sheet that contoured her body so intimately that the thread count disappeared. Her Irish side lightened her hair and ever so slightly freckled a body as healthy as it was graceful. She slid her legs out sideways to join Sebastian standing before her. She didn't bother to take the sheet with her. Sebastian was glad. Her next three kisses made his day.

"Remember," she said, hip to hip, wrapping both arms around his chest, "today is the day you're going to announce our engagement."

"Why, of course," Sebastian replied, pulling back to look her in the eye, a move he expected would confer certainty but didn't.

"Now, let's make sure we're on the same page here, sweetie," said Pricilla silken sexy. "It took you years to tell your mom we dated in college."

"And when we graduated, I did tell her."

"Sure—after she walked into your bedroom and found us necking. Do you remember what she called me?"

Sebastian, as usual, had begun to move the day along, sideways to the icebox for juice and Danish. "Hey, she calls everyone that. You should hear the names she has for Dad when he's not around."

Pricilla put on a robe before she joined Sebastian chowing down at the table on the deck. The sun rose to burn off smoldering lake haze. There was one thing you could always say about Sebastian, he knew good when he saw it. He also knew happiness when he felt it. The morning was warmed by the day's fresh sun almost as much as the passion that made them one.

Which wasn't to say that Sebastian never had anything else on his mind, like who he noticed looking out over the deck. He saw the shadow of a young man coming around the bend at Bay Point, where the rope swing hung over the water.

Sebastian changed the subject and looked Pricilla in the eye. "Let's take my coupe for a ride around the lake to Oshkosh. It's a brand-new Mercedes! You can go shopping, and I'd rather be late."

"To your dad's birthday party?"

"The old fogies will tie him up. He'll be surrounded by bankers for hours. I'll hardly see him anyway."

"Now don't you say that about poor Zeek. He just had the vice president's office repainted for you. When are you going to work?"

"Never, if I can help it."

"What?" said Pricilla, paying too much attention. "The Murphy's house at the end of Edgewood Drive just went up for sale. You start working, we get married, and Zeek will buy it for us. I want that gazebo. We will be the envy of the neighborhood."

Sebastian softened his voice, hoping Pricilla would do the same. "Yes, of course, dear, absolutely. It's just that we're having so much fun and can travel and sleep late and kiss whenever we want."

With Pricilla's index finger on Sebastian's lips, kissing was a problem at that moment, but nothing detracted from his smile. "Okay, sure, anything, perhaps. Let's just get going right now."

Now wasn't soon enough. A splash was heard from the lake. Pricilla turned and saw nothing. Sebastian had walked her to the door and was almost out when Pricilla then heard what Sebastian had expected.

"Fishing... fishing? Fishing... fishing?" said a boyish voice.

Pricilla's smile deflated to a scowl. "Sebastian, you promised."

"I sent Jimmy home last night, just like you asked me to. So he came back, what's the big deal?"

"The big deal is that we need privacy. After we're married, you *do* know things will change around here, right?"

"Yes. It's just that he depends on me, and we have so much fun together."

"You are not his keeper! And his problem is not your fault. Children fall out of trees every day."

"He fell after he reached out and swung me over to a branch. My head would have been splattered on Big Rock. Jimmy saved my life and hit his own head so hard next to the rock that he didn't come out of a coma for three months."

"And hasn't been able to read or speak right since."

The conversation ended when Jimmy's eyes rose above the deck. He stood in a canoe, swaying back and forth as he barely hung on, his bright, wide-open eyes and skinny little body dwarfed by a smile that every day remained genuine and overdone. "Fishy... Seb? Fishy... Seb?"

"No, but pull up the canoe, buddy. We're heading back to town. The rumble seat is all yours."

"Oh, goody… goody… I love the rumble seat. And Pricilla, Pricilla… you can go ahead… go ahead and kiss… Seb. I don't… I don't mind. Kissing makes people happy… happy. People… people should kiss, kiss… all the time… time."

2

Sebastian stopped three times on the way to town: first to crawl beneath Jimmy in the rumble seat to see if the meteor-sized pothole on the access road had broken the rear axle, then to dust off his pressed-metal masterpiece when they reached paved city streets, and then finally to fetch Jimmy, who'd walked away at a stop sign to feed ducks.

The party was packed, the driveway full, and street parking jammed two blocks away.

The three laggards took their time straightening up after Sebastian finally settled for a space thirty feet from the nearest bumper. "The walk will do us good" brought out "yes, yes" from Jimmy and "not really" from Pricilla.

Before home was in sight, the trio passed two Ford Model A Deluxe Roadsters, three Packard Twin-Six Roadsters, a green Studebaker, and one Rolls-Royce Phantom. Waiting for them in the front yard were Sebastian's friends—tall Boyd, who volunteered for anything; brawny Giles, who would offer to help with anything and then do nothing; and Lawton, the brains of the outfit and hedonist perfecta. The three stood silently as they blocked the way.

"*Now*, gentlemen," was all Lawton needed to say to put his plan into action. Giles and Boyd stepped beside each of Sebastian's arms, lifted him off the ground with grips under his shoulders, and then walked him backward. "Pricilla, would you mind so terribly if we borrowed your beau for just a second?" said Lawton, bowing.

From ten feet and fading Sebastian added, "I'll catch up with you in five minutes, pumpkin," and then, turning sideways, "If my feet don't hit ground in three seconds, two hungry stomachs are going to feel the wrath of my fists."

Jimmy stood by, laughing, until Sebastian got serious. The second Jimmy, the butt of every town joke, caught Sebastian's mood change, he moved beside the gang, his diminished physique in no way compromising all-out warfare. Message received.

"Now hold on, guys," said Sebastian. "Before you sign me up for another one of your cockamamie schemes, there is something you must know. Pricilla and I are getting married. I'm going to make the announcement at the end of the party."

"Over your mom's dead body, you will," said Lawton.

"I'm her only child. She knows I'm spoiled. All I have to do is look depressed and pretend to get teary. She'll come around. And you know what? Sharing life with Pricilla is fun and really sexy."

Giles, Boyd, and Jimmy, bobbing his head in agreement, all faced Lawton, waiting for round two. Lawton stepped back, crossed his arms, and for a moment looked and sounded like their high school math teacher solving an equation. "Excellent point young man. Yes indeed, fine reasoning."

Group disbelief at Lawton's comment silenced the crew. Sebastian knew better. "And?"

"Well, you see, Sebastian old boy," Lawton continued, frisky, just short of a giggle, "the thing is you're not married yet. Technically speaking, you're still free."

"And?"

"The Canadians are back, and Adalene is asking for you."

Sebastian's eyes widened. "They're at the border?"

"With Estelle and Camille," said Boyd, as everyone's eyes lit up—except Jimmy's, whose eyes always sparked fun.

"The fishing is good, the woods overstocked with deer, and there is a coyote or two we must dispense with to protect the chickens. We—that is to say, we five—in your car."

"And with my money."

"Well, yes, but only because you have too much of it, and it's our job to make sure it brings you happiness. We'll simply disappear to your parents' hunting cabin for a few days and nights. You owe yourself one last fling. You're such a good boy."

Pricilla was out of sight. Jimmy had started humming the second he heard the word "fishing," and Giles and Boyd rubbed Sebastian's back as Lawton's steely eyes stared temptation straight through Sebastian.

"Well, you know," Sebastian said, half daydreaming, "Jimmy does love fishing, and I won't be able to spend as much time with him with Pricilla in the way. Perhaps it's the best thing to do."

When Sebastian walked in the front door, the roaring twenties were in full swing. Balloons hung from matching marble staircases at the far end of a hall lit by a Swiss crystal chandelier the size of a dump truck. To the left, a ballroom-sized living room was stripped of furniture for dancing to Paul Whiteman and His Orchestra. To the right was the main dining room, with floor-to-ceiling doors that opened to an Olympic-sized back patio next to an Olympic-sized pool sporting barbecued delicacies of every North American game mammal. It was almost as popular as the dueling champagne fountains. Mommy Elizabeth's orders were specific: the help was to continuously circulate hors d'oeuvres, and every twenty minutes a Charleston was to be played.

Total victory had ended the war to end all wars. In Europe, democracies flourished, and in America, stocks were up. Everyone was making money. No one was foolish enough to disturb the peace. Life was as good as it got, and the Williamsons were smack-dab center stage.

Whenever Mommy Elizabeth opened her mouth, Jimmy wanted to give her a hug. The way he figured it, she needed it more than anyone else in the room.

"Not now, Jimmy."

"Okay, Seb Seb."

Jimmy also possessed an uncanny sense for detecting when Elizabeth was scheming connivance. The look she gave the group entering was all Jimmy needed to grab Sebastian's arm.

"Were going in, Jimmy," said Sebastian. "Don't worry, everything will be fine."

"Okay, okay, I serve, I serve."

He had the smile for it, and it was a great way to say hello to everyone at the party. Jimmy spent the afternoon helping the staff circulate appetizers, with the rule that one per tray was all he was allowed.

Sebastian found Zeek talking to Leo Guyette, the pastry chef who personally assured quality control by sampling every product from his oven, which explained the space he took up on the other side of the table.

Half-sloshed with a full mouth, Zeek nodded agreement. "Yes, yes, my good fellow, that's just the kind of local business we support."

"It won't take much to start up three new bakeries from Oshkosh to Appleton."

"What are these yummy little golf balls? I'm guessing half-butter and half-sugar, my two favorite foods."

Leo reached over and dusted powdered sugar off Zeek's tux. "It's a bit more complicated than that, sir, but you're close. So what do we do now?"

"About what?"

"Getting money to start my franchise."

"You have my vote, but you gotta talk to Elizabeth. She's good at pulling strings and all that contract stuff. Her father taught her all he knew. I'm a heavy machinery guy, and I'm still trying to figure out why she picked me out of the lineup."

Leo and Sebastian chuckled at Zeek's joke.

"Now don't be modest, birthday boy," Sebastian said, putting his arm around his dad. "You were the most handsome foreman in town. No lady could resist you."

After a second of self-deprecating laughter, Zeek added, ever more jolly, "I know a bunch who did." Then, standing tall and appearing almost sober, he said, "And you know what? I can still repair a processor faster than any of the young upstarts scratching their heads over there. That's right. If you want the assembly line up and running, you just call me. That's right, you just call me. I'm your man."

At the end of every day, Sebastian was Zeek's son and Zeek was Sebastian's dad. They knew each other as each other and were just fine with that. They also had developed hand signals over the years to keep their plans their own. A finger sweeping down to point to the study communicated intent.

The only action the books lining the three walls in Zeek's father-in-law's study ever saw was their weekly dusting. The bar, on the other hand, was freshly stocked and well used, and the study was the best place to hide out on the property, possibly with an open volume for camouflage. Sebastian never liked sitting in Gramps's towering desk chair; it still smelled like cigars, but he humored his dad when Zeek pulled it out for him.

"This birthday has got me a thinkin', son. Every year, I get shorter and weaker. I'm not sure how long I'm gonna be able to look after the plant. It's time you filled my shoes—but you might want to ignore my habit of stopping by the pub on the way home every night. There have been weeks I don't remember half the days."

"You're everyone's favorite. No one could ever replace you."

"Well, you're going to have to, and damn soon. I haven't told your mother, but some mornings I stay in bed 'cause my back won't let me get up."

"You just need to take it easy and cut back on the hooch."

"Okay, okay. So, are you ready? I didn't paint the vice president's office for you. It's for me. I'll stay on as. . . what does your mommy call it. . . oh yeah. . . a consultant. The plant, four corporations, and more money than you can spend in five lifetimes is yours. Are you ready?"

"I wasn't yesterday, but I am today."

"Why's that, son? Don't get my head a-spinning."

"It's about Pricilla."

Zeek paved the way by opening up. He found the young lass a plea-sure to the eyes and a joy to share time with. Her figure reminded him of Elizabeth's years ago, although that part he kept to himself. In honest revelation, he told Sebastian that he knew very well what a powerhouse his mom could be but also that every night when he went to bed, he knew he lay beside a strength unequaled in brash courage. He felt safe, he felt cared for, and he felt loved in the strangest way.

"Your mom doesn't like Pricilla because she reminds her of herself at that age," said Zeek. "I like her because, like your mom, she could hold the entire world together with a rubber band. Now, I'm not saying that you and I and all the men on this planet really haven't the damnedest idea of what we're doing; it's just that we never know where the heck we're headed, and those ladies, by gosh, some days I'd swear on a cricket that each and every one of them was born with blueprints in their heads."

Sebastian stared and then spoke in disbelief. "You know, I feel that same way sometimes, Dad. It's like the sheds are painted, the cars pol-ished, the bills paid, and then I look around and say, 'Okay, now what do I do?' And then Pricilla comes along with this certainty of purpose, a package of how life should be, and she's so sure of every detail that it gives me a place to be and someone thanking me for it."

"Son, it's also possible that we're a bunch of saps. But if that's true, then I am also certain I'm pickled happy about it. If this is leading up to you marrying Pricilla, you know my blessing is yours."

The hug lasted longer than was required to cover up a tear and a sniff.

"Just one final word, my son."

"Yes, what is it?"

"That contentment, that singularity of purpose, that gratitude and accomplishment that we get from the ladies, don't expect it to last. Something ticks inside them that trips up both sexes. I don't know what it is, but the next day or the next month, by golly, the game changes and we men have to fight it out with the world all over again."

"I get the picture, Dad."

It was Sebastian's turn to raise then lower the pointing finger to the door. "I'll make the announcement later, Dad. This party is all about you and how much we all love you."

"I love you too, but don't repeat that. I don't want those grease monkeys I work with to think I've gone soft."

Jimmy's cognitive processing and verbal skills left a lot to be desired, but he retained coordination and the reputation for being one of the best dancers in town who never sat down until the orchestra left.

Mommy Elizabeth and Pricilla socialized around the room from opposite ends, each stepping a greeting closer as the afternoon wore on. Neither wanted to appear indulgent or, heaven forbid, of groveling status.

"Oh, there you are," said Pricilla, acting surprised. "This is a fabulous party you put together for Zeek."

"Well, thank you, my dear. I'm so glad you could come."

"And the flowers! Where on earth did you find that strange one?"

"It's called bird-of-paradise. I had them delivered by express train this morning."

"They're exquisite."

"Yes, indeed."

Elizabeth bowed politely and began walking off.

"Just one thing, if you don't mind, Elizabeth."

"Certainly, child. What can I do for you?"

"It's about Sebastian. He told me he wanted to have a talk with you later."

"I'll look forward to it."

"I hope so. And I do have a suggestion. For the future of our relationship—that is, yours and mine—I would suggest you take him seriously."

"Why, of course. The happiness of my son is the most important thing on earth."

"Why, of course."

3

Think of sunshine, remember Mom, and flower petals soften the way. Sebastian felt the connection, kindled by memories of looking up waiting for his mom to hand over the cookie batter bowl, of Christmas Eve waiting for Dad to come home to sing "Jingle Bells," of the night she stayed up till dawn holding his hand when pneumonia almost took him from her. He never forgot those tears and the love he felt.

Elizabeth also had her ways, many akin to the Wicked Witch of the East, like her social intimidation, uncompromising insistence, and misguided materialism. In part, her intentions stemmed from the desire to establish insurmountable barriers between Sebastian and the evils that knocked every day.

Hand signals never worked with Elizabeth, that afternoon neither did several requests by Sebastian for a private moment. She cited guest etiquette as she greeted or bid farewell to important visitors, an excuse that was half-true and half-fearful. She knew Pricilla was about to whisk her little boy away. The end had come. She would no longer be number one in his life and would soon slide to second, third, and then further when more children arrived.

Years later, Sebastian would look back on that night and the change of plans she brought about and wonder if her intentions put prejudiced aspirations above his happiness or that, somehow, she knew he was indeed destined to be more to the world than just the great-grandson of a cow herder, the grandson of a business tycoon, and the result of lovers who would never forget the haystack at midnight.

When the last guest closed the door, Elizabeth looked around to see Sebastian standing in the threshold of her dad's study. The sun was setting behind him. She knew it was time. Not a word was spoken as Sebastian closed the door behind them. Elizabeth's eyes never left his.

It was her turn to need a drink. It helped to pull off the plan she had formulated weeks earlier, and Elizabeth was a pro.

"Sebastian," she said, speaking with authority.

Sebastian was a step ahead, which he accomplished by stepping forward to hold her hand. "Mother, you know I love Pricilla, and yes, I also love vacations, boats, fast cars. . ."

"And fast women."

"Well yes, them too, I agree," said the smiling lad with genuine passion and who apologized for nothing. "But it's time. I'm twenty-three years old. You and Dad were married at twenty-one."

"Those were different days, long ago. And I never got to Paris."

Sebastian walked behind Gramps's desk, sat down, and pretended to light up and puff on a fat stogie. "How do I look?"

His wit overcame her. She couldn't hold the laugh that came out with, "Too young and too tied down. And you haven't been to Paris, either."

"There's time."

"That's what I said. So," she said, stepping back, "you want my blessing?"

"I am pleading for it, I am begging for it, and I am 'you're damn right' insisting on it."

Elizabeth's look confused Sebastian. Her response was slow and sentimental. "Oh my. . . just that second, you looked just like your grandfather, without the spittoon of course. Promise me you will never get one."

"I promise. . . do you?"

Sebastian rolled back two feet when Elizabeth walked around the desk and hopped up to sit on the edge of the desk, just like she'd done when her dad was in the chair. When she looked down on Sebastian, he saw a fear in her eyes of which he never thought her capable. Her words were soft, slow, and mournfully disarming. "We have a problem, and it's my fault. It's the business, and you can fix it. If you agree, I promise never to speak, gesture, or insinuate critical reflection on your marriage or Pricilla, who, I am certain, loves wealth and power just as much as she loves you."

"Something the two of you have in common. So, what's the deal? And I want no fine print in the contract."

"It's the stock exchange. A couple of years ago, a slick New Yorker talked me into subdividing everything we own to float stock, which did go up, but then went to buy several companies in Europe that looked promising."

"Which means?"

"We don't own the plant or any of the other companies my dad built."

"So, we own a hell of a lot of something else overseas?"

"On paper our wealth doubled, but there are problems. The brokers gouged us, someone is extorting funds, and no one is buying our products overseas."

"Which means?"

"If the companies go under, then we go bankrupt, and they sell off everything we own, including this house. The entire town will end up on the unemployment line."

Sebastian's eyes widened as he took a deep breath before exhaling slowly. "That would be Pricilla's folks and Jimmy's dad! How could you do such a thing?"

"Money is a madness. There are always risks. I was out of my league. I saw dollar signs."

"Oh my God. And all this time, all I was doing was playing!"

"And your dad knows nothing about it. You can't tell him."

"So, what's next?"

"It gets worse."

"How is that possible?"

"There are new laws limiting foreign transactions overseas. One of us must go to Europe to get those businesses to make money, and then to Spain to sign papers. That's where you come in. But I swear, two or three months will be all it will take, and it takes that long to plan a good wedding anyway."

"What about Jimmy?"

"He can go with you. And your uncle, Javier, is over there."

"The priest? Oh, that should be a lot of fun."

"One of our holdings is a luxury hotel on the Spanish Riviera. You stay in a suite, you get carte blanche, a beach, boats, and nightlife. And also a chance to visit Paris. You can send me a postcard."

"And what are these companies that are losing money trying to sell?"

"Steel, explosives, and armaments."

"Are you crazy?" Sebastian said, stamping his feet as he stood up. "You invested in weapons in the middle of peacetime?"

"That's why we got so much so cheap."

Rubbing his forehead, Sebastian walked to the corner of the office and spun his dad's globe. He let it slow to a stop before turning back to face Elizabeth.

"Oh, Mother… oh, Mother… yes, Europeans have taken turns killing each other for the last two thousand years, but the kings and queens are gone. No one is going to send their children out to be slaughtered so royalty can settle a grudge or make a profit on the slave trade or add another bedroom to the castle. There *is* a limit to stupidity!"

Elizabeth wiped her cheek and calmed down.

"Okay, I get it. I may not be the best at business after all, but I'm also a mother, and you're a good person, Sebastian. Somehow, I managed to raise an intelligent and companionate son."

"Thank you, Mom, but holy crap," Sebastian said, disgusted and sarcastic. "Now all I have to do is catch a train to New York, spend a week at sea, stay up half the night for months going over books, and then figure out how to kill people faster to keep Fond du Lac out of the poorhouse. Am I missing anything?"

"Yes. No matter what happens, I will always love you."

Sebastian sat back down in Gramps's chair, looked around feeling ten years older, and then said, "And I will always love you too. So don't worry, I can do this. Everything will be fine."

4

The next stop in Sebastian's life was the train station. Zeek offered to drop them off. He was an innovator. "If a big coal fire can steam up a locomotive to pull a mile-long freight train, then a small garbage fire can damn well get us down the street." That was followed by an expression repeated with an accent. "Indian make small fire. . . keep warm from fire. . . white man make big fire. . . keep warm from getting wood."

Zeek's recycling was ahead of his time. He'd discovered that once his Stanley Steamer glowed hot, he could keep it moving by firing up a second chamber burning leftovers. Sebastian's car backfired. Zeek's farted. The neighbors learned to hold their breath every time he drove by. The steamer got the family to the station smoking potato skins.

Jimmy loved trains. The first thing he packed was his American flag. On every trip, he would make straight for the last car, step out on the rear observation platform, and wave the red, white, and blue at folks when they passed through towns, a habit he picked up watching Woodrow Wilson whisk by years earlier.

Sebastian, of course, insisted on luxury accommodations. He reserved space in the executive lounge, where swivel chairs larger than Gramps's monster were placed eight feet apart and a waiter stood by to serve food and drink. Life was easy when other people did all the work. Sebastian had a lot to learn, and no choice.

They had an hour to walk Union Station in Chicago, a masterpiece of engineering that was only one year old but already required workmen to shovel two feet of smokestack soot off the roof. The man in the newspaper stand had no hair, a drooped face, one eye shut, walked with a limp, and wore a purple heart pinned to his shirt. He said he was one of the lucky ones who made it back.

Coal fumes were everywhere. Jimmy coughed once a minute. As soon as their sleeper left the station, he felt better opening the window in their private compartment. He loved watching birds fly away; they knew better. The night was long and noisy, the tracks went bumpety bumpety bump bump screech screech bumpety. They were glad to get to New York. Jimmy said it felt like he was inside a giant tin can.

There was a layover. The two went straight to Central Park to rent horses. Being surrounded by trees felt like home. They missed home. When a policeman trotted by on a horse, they asked him where the most expensive place to eat was in town. He said the mayor's house and laughed. Sebastian and Jimmy had hot dogs with sauerkraut but didn't understand why the sauerkraut was there. Jimmy said it was the most fun day of his entire life. He repeated the comment a dozen times over the next month.

That night, as they waited at the back of an endless line waiting to board the ship, Jimmy asked where all the people were going. Sebastian said the same place they were and that by the time they got off, each one would be five pounds heavier. Jimmy said it was because they sat in water too long and wondered why they didn't take the salt out.

Once again, Sebastian insisted on the finest first-class two-bedroom stateroom. Wealth is its own calling card. The Williamsons were still listed among the richest one thousand families on earth. Seb, as everyone began calling him after hearing Jimmy repeat the name in duplicate every other sentence, was invited to dine at the captain's table. He and Jimmy accepted.

Jimmy knew just what to do. Rule number one was to refrain from eating until Captain Fitzroy put food in his mouth, which explained his tick-tock eye movements as soon as he and Sebastian sat down.

The evening began with sautéed mushrooms, petite cheese samples, and small talk.

"The weather is perfect for our crossing," said the captain, a well-tailored, burly hulk whose favorite subject was atmospheric conditions.

"I dare say, after a month of negotiating oil prices in hot, dry Texas, I'm looking forward to wet London fog," said Sir Baggerly, whose favorite subject was self-aggrandizement.

At the captain's table was also Cabal Armond, representing the French fashion industry. His specialty was men's suits that looked disappointingly similar to last year's collection and the prior decade. He turned to Sebastian at his side. "Monsieur, last month the Paris *Chronical* printed an article that cited your family as one of the richest on the planet. They also listed every one of your holdings. Are you planning to go to war?"

Sebastian grinned resolute. "When it comes to warfare, we Americans know very little compared to Europe's penchant for apocalypse."

"Brash wisdom from someone so young, Mr. Williamson," said Captain Fitzroy, tipping his hat.

"I agree completely," said Shauna O'Sullivan from the other side of the table, with a hint of Irish brogue and all its beauty.

Sebastian smiled, grateful for the support and the kind looks Shauna gave Jimmy every time he stared uncomfortably long at the reddest hair he had ever seen.

"My plan," Sebastian continued, "if you must know, sir, is to covert as many plants as possible to peacetime production."

"A wise choice," huffed the overfed Sir Baggerly, a perfect example of aristocracy living off the labor of others. "We thrashed the German beasts in the war. They know their place because we put them there. There will be no more wars, and thanks to the Maginot line, not one German soldier will ever set foot on French soil again or dream of overrunning London. We got them good."

Cabal Armond scanned the table for support as he said, "I'm afraid I do not share your optimism, sir. History is a comedy of errors, without the comedy."

"From what I learned in college," Sebastian added, "the only thing Europe never runs out of is cemeteries and grieving families."

"What if the Maginot line is outflanked?" asked Cabal directly to Baggerly.

"Our tanks will make sure it isn't."

"Unless *their* tanks disagree."

"Are you a traitor?"

"No, I'm a realist and a student of human nature. Your assertions disturb me."

"Pure poppycock," barked Baggerly, interrupting his dissection of a T-bone steak the size of a frying pan. "England didn't get where it is today by losing to anyone."

"No," said Shauna, "England got to where is today by stealing from Dublin, exploiting the ignorant, and silencing those who disagree."

"Now, now," interrupted the captain, who had heard it all before. "Eight years ago, the good guys beat the bad guys, and everyone at this table pulled together to make it so. We are all in the same boat, and you are on *my* boat. Let's forget past differences and enjoy the night." Then, standing and raising a glass, he said, "I propose a toast to the next one thousand years of peace that will replace the last two thousand years of suffering."

There are those who stutter endlessly through a simple request for a cup of coffee, but when both cerebral hemispheres work together, for singing or reading poetry, words flow freely. For months, Sebastian had noticed Jimmy looking at books, sometimes for hours, often the same page. Sebastian was curious. Jimmy's behavior was a mystery until everyone sat down and Jimmy remained standing. Slow and somber, Jimmy stumbled through, "Only the dead have seen the end of war, and those who cannot remember the past are condemned to repeat it."

"Wow," exclaimed Cabal, "Plato and Santayana in one sentence. I'm impressed. Any more?"

Jimmy moved upturned eyes back and forth as if searching his brain for words. "Hickory dickory dock, the mouse—"

"That will be fine," said Sebastian, who was already standing to give Jimmy a hug, having in all the years since the accident seen not one instance of hope for improvement. After a moment of silence, both sat back down.

"Did someone drop him on his head?" asked Baggerly, half as guttural and one-third less offensive.

"Yes, I did," replied Sebastian. "Right after he saved my life."

"By Jove, I'm dreadfully sorry. Please except my apology, deepest regret, and sincere respect."

Thereafter, the evening went well. Captain Fitzroy and Baggerly shared classical music memories while Cabal and Shauna debated proper thoroughbred training. Jimmy and Sebastian mostly kept to themselves and excused themselves before dessert was served, Jimmy to check out the ship's library and Sebastian to walk the deck, which ended with him leaning against the stern rail looking back. He was alone until Shauna showed up.

"Are ye missing home? Maybe your momma?"

"Yes, on both accounts."

"That be funny. I miss home at the bow looking east, and for you it be west."

"Do you see those shimmering lights off to the right?"

"You mean the northern lights?"

"No, oh no, those aren't the northern lights. Those lights come from the barn dance at the Sokal Camp, where my buddies are right now."

"And what be they doing there?"

"Well, dancing of course, or some kind of wiggling, and drinking beer, and kissing our Canadian friends who come to visit."

"Oh, so you kiss girls, do ya?"

"I've been known to lean in that direction."

"And that leaning of yours. . . just how far over do you get?"

"Far enough not to tell and smart enough to try again."

"Well aren't you a bag of trouble, with all your money, good looks, and broad shoulders."

"Look who's talking. Your hair lights up a room, and your eyes know damn well there's not a man on earth who can resist you."

"Would that also be you?"

"It wasn't yesterday. . . but it is tonight, and that's only because I have no choice."

"You sure are blarney slick for a farm boy."

"In my defense, college ruined me. Ever since sophomore year, all I do is think, and it keeps getting in the way."

"In the way of what?"

"I haven't the slightest idea. Would you do me the honor of walking the promenade by my side?"

Shauna did better than that. She crossed elbows in classic fashion.

"Seb—do I call you Seb or Sebastian?"

"Which do you prefer?"

"Sebastian. It sounds more like gold coins hitting the floor."

"Something I've been told to enjoy while I can."

"Anyway, the pool is steam pipe heated. Would you care to join me for a moonlight dip?"

"I would be honored."

"Then one last question."

"Shoot."

"Have ye ever kissed an Irish lass?"

"Is that a possibility?"

"Perhaps."

5

The first day at sea, the view from their stateroom was blue water, blue sky, and white seagulls. The second day was just the same but without seagulls. After that, the view never changed. Jimmy asked Sebastian if they were going somewhere or just making circles.

Back home, there had been nights, afternoons, or entire days when Sebastian would tell Jimmy that he needed to comfort a friend, privately. Thus abandoned, Jimmy would keep to himself or go home early. What Jimmy didn't understand was why every night, from New York all the way to London, Sebastian had to comfort Shauna.

Meanwhile, back at home, Elizabeth didn't waste a second. After requiring sworn secrecy, she informed Pricilla of the family's impending bankruptcy. She also told Pricilla that the mess would take years to clean up and that she might never see Sebastian again. Of course, Pricilla didn't believe her, so she left to visit a college girlfriend in Chicago, whose dad happened to head the largest bank in the state, who also made millions on inside trading and who had a son stepping into his Rolls-Royce.

The money moles confirmed Elizabeth's warning. Andrew, the lawyer's son who informed Pricilla off the record, consoled her over dinner, then comforted her by dancing at the Triainon Ballroom, where they were entertained by Rudy Vallee and his Connecticut Yankees.

The night ended with additional comforting in his dad's private city apartment.

When Sebastian left, Pricilla promised to wait for him. What she didn't say was that it would be for thirty-six hours. Following a rare exercise of conscience, she wired Sebastian on board with a story about how depressed she was and so therefore had to move to Chicago to start a new life. She realized the two of them weren't meant to be. She left out the part about feeling better after sex and then even better after a weekend on a yacht.

Years later, Sebastian got a letter from Mom finishing the story. Within three months, Pricilla married, then six months later delivered a baby boy who was instantly heir to more than the Williamsons pre-folly empire. A year after that, when twins arrived, hubby began drinking.

At sea, the atmosphere at dinner changed with the longitude. Sebastian no longer felt guilty about his infatuation with Shauna, but she became less enamored when Sebastian and old fart Baggerly teamed up.

"I tell you," Sir Baggerly would insist, with Sebastian backing him up, "without management, labor would starve to death. Management offers jobs, decent wages, and the self-respect of contributing to the country that gave us birth. Without management, labor is nothing."

With arms crossed and brow wrinkled, Shauna had her say: "Without labor, *management* would be nothing, have to get a real job, and actually make something and contribute to the general good instead of sitting back and collecting money behind a desk—money that you stole from carpenters you cheated out of fair wages, something you can get away with because your family was given land by the king, who was told it was his by the pope, who said God told him to. It's an open-and-shut case of grand larceny."

Cabal Armond, sitting next to Shauna, true to his pensive nature, said, "Unbridled consumerism competes one against another all the way to solitude and despair. Karl Marx was right: the productivity of capitalism engenders antagonisms. We stop liking one another when we don't work together as a team, and then feel legitimate anger at being bossed around by those who are in control by no other merit than a birth order or street address."

"Total nonsense," asserted Baggerly. "My family worked hard to build our empire, and we deserve to do with it as we wish."

"Your family," Shauna said, "rented out land that wasn't yours in the first place and then used that money to force starving people to build factories so you could put half of whatever they made in your back pocket."

"Ridiculous, young lady! Read the Bible. God clearly handed over ownership of all of Europe to five families, and those families rule in his place. Just ask the pope."

"Oh yes, the robed conspirator, whose predecessors just happened to get anything they wanted from those kings in return for turning an entire continent of free laborers into white slaves. Aristocracy and Vatican gold, one hand washes the other, while both hands work the common man to death."

"My dad always finds work for anyone needing it and pays a fair wage," said Sebastian.

"In the woods surrounded by cows, perhaps yes, but in the real world, I think not, laddie," Shauna continued. "Constant unemployment is the threat that allows rich folk like Baggerly to pay no more than bare subsistence."

Cabal attempted to intellectualize the economic state of world affairs. He began by pointing out that the idea of debt is a curious one since at any given time humanity produces a limited amount of goods and services and, as a whole, the human race consumes what it produces. But there's the rub: the servings are not equal and in no way proportioned to production or the principles of Christian sharing, which the rich ignore to justify themselves.

When Jimmy heard the name Karl Marx, he began stuttering sentences that popped into his head. "All history involves class struggle. . .

patrician and plebeian. . . lord and serf. . . oppressor and the oppressed. And you know, and you know. . . the ideas of every age. . . just. . . just happen. . . to. . . have been the ideas of the ruling class. . . orchestrated and enforced by religion. . . the opium of the people."

Shauna was astounded and grateful for the support. Perhaps it was her hand on his that got Jimmy through his finale without hesitation. "When commercial capital occupies a position of unquestioned ascendancy, it everywhere constitutes a system of plunder."

"Yes, yes," mocked Baggerly. "From each according to his abilities, to each according to his needs. We've heard that before. Actually before, during, and after millions of Russian peasants were murdered. Apparently," he finished with a down-home nasty chuckle, "what they *needed* was a huge cemetery."

"In all fairness," Captain Fitzroy corrected, "we all know Russia is a dictatorship that has nothing to do with fair play or the best interests of their own citizens. And, if you don't mind an old captain's opinion, if Christians were truly Christian, there would be no starvation, warfare, or fights at this table."

When words failed to snuff politics, Captain Fitzroy brought out his secret weapon—trays of apple pie, carrot cake, tiramisu, baked Alaska, and white chocolate cheesecake. It worked.

After dinner, the passengers split into three groups—the readers, the drinkers, and the lovers, unless you added a third category, the book lookers. Jimmy kept busy in the ship's library while Sebastian and Shauna strolled the deck, bow to stern. Later, after Sebastian got news from Chicago, the two spent all their time at the bow. With Sebastian holding tight, Shauna climbed up the bow rail to search the horizon for home. When she got down, Sebastian stood forward to block the wind and recite a story he had prepared.

"I've never met anyone like you," he began. "You don't just fill in the blanks to complete a sorority recipe or the garden club dress code. You're your own person. You have ideals, ambitions, and an unswerving moral compass.

"And then there's what totally blows me away. I can't honestly say that I know myself, but you had me pegged right off the bat. And you're beautiful, and luscious, and endlessly kissable. Three weeks ago, I woke up smiling. I thought I had everything I wanted and that it was love. I wasn't even close.

"This week, when I'm with you, I finally feel what I've heard about, read about, and dreamed about. I am totally head over heels, upside down and right side up, inside out in love with you."

Shauna smiled and said nothing, but she took Sebastian by the hand for the walk back to her warm cabin. Sebastian never wanted to let go.

"Shauna, you're right about us rich people being spoiled, but you would be just like me if money fell in your lap. Let's make the best of it. Come tour Europe with me. We won't miss a trick, will be introduced to heads of states, dance in the streets of Paris, and laugh ourselves to sleep every night."

There was still no response from Shauna, though she did lean closer.

"Okay, Shauna, it's settled. And anything you want you will have—the best restaurants, diamonds bracelets, the latest fashions, and someday our own Mediterranean villa or Wisconsin estate, or both if you prefer."

Shauna pushed away to cross her arms over her chest. "Oh, so it is me with whom you want to spend the rest of your days, perhaps feeding cows?"

"Married, yes! And children, yes! And you and I together always, yes. You're the smartest, most independent woman I've ever known."

"I see. Am I not also sexy?"

"I prefer to answer that question with my lips."

As they were about to leave the foredeck, the two heard excited voices. The faint lights of England were sighted. The next morning, solid land would be under their feet.

Shauna said nothing as she leaned on Sebastian's shoulder like every woman is capable. Sebastian rode the moment to her cabin.

"So, Shauna, it's settled then. You and me, tomorrow, Paris by sunset."

"Perhaps someday. For now, every month I will check the *European Economic Gazette* to find out what you're up to. I have two issues that require my attention."

"Which are?"

"Running the largest cooperative business in Ireland and meeting my fiancé for dinner, who happens to be a socialist, just like me."

"And what am I?"

"The fact that you don't know the answer to that question proves to me that you have not as yet asked yourself enough questions. My opinion is that you are spoiled by money and privilege, but worst of all, you think you have the right to both, and I think you have earned neither. We live in different worlds, except here in bed." She smiled. "Now turn off the lights."

"For the last time?"

"For the last time."

6

The line at customs was long and the room dark and damp, and it smelled like stale sweat. At the end of each line was an officer who was obviously annoyed to be there. The passengers had interrupted his teatime and taken his fresh air.

Sebastian paid no heed. He was busy looking sideways two lines over at Shauna, who occasionally graced his stare with a pleasant smile that lit up the room for him, if only for a moment. Never in his life had he wanted someone so much. Never in his life had he had his heart set on doing whatever it took to make it happen. Never in his life had money let him down. He detested his helplessness.

Sebastian's morning shave had been troublesome. Shauna wanted no part of the face looking back. He was defective merchandise, a rogue bet, a spoiled hinderance. His self-image imploded. Smiling Jimmy was the lucky one.

The only thing it takes to break a heart is to have one, and Sebastian's ached more and more the farther Shauna got in line, then crumbled to agony when one smile let her through and on her way. When Jimmy smiled without pausing, the guards pushed him back three feet. At first, he thought it was a game. Jimmy pushed back. It did not go well, or quickly.

Sebastian sprinted to the cab station, with Jimmy barely keeping up, as everyone on the dock gave them disapproving grimaces, but no one was knocked down and only one suitcase slightly tipped. Sebastian was counting on one more dinner invitation to save the day. He planned to recite socialist party slogans, defend the people, and denounce bureaucracy. He knew Shauna wouldn't believe him but was hoping the effort would win the day.

The day was lost. By the time he made the curb, her cab was driving away. She looked back from the rear window. Jimmy didn't understand why two people were getting further apart who were happier and happier the closer they were. When Shauna's car disappeared around the corner, Sebastian slumped to the ground. He had lost the energy and desire to say anything or do anything, so he just sat.

"You… you… miss home?" Jimmy asked, squatting down beside him, making a curious spectacle of the pair beside proper English manners. "No cry… we go home… okay, Seb?"

Sebastian hugged Jimmy for the feeling of not being alone. Jimmy was fine with that; he hugged everyone and never felt alone.

"Jimmy," Sebastian said, sniffing between emotional interruptions, "one second, you hold life in your hands and it's soft, cuddly, and warm. Everything makes sense. Then a second later, your arms are empty, the wind blows cold, and there is nothing left to smile about. I can deal with the pain. It's the emptiness and worthless void that has me down, and there is no place I can go and nothing I can do to escape."

"Seb, at home… we want fun… we go for ride… where Mercedes?"

"That's right. Thank you, Jimmy."

There's nothing like a shiny new automobile to get a guy thinking. For Sebastian, it was the looks the hometown girls gave him when he drove by in the most expensive roadster in the state. "There will be other girls," he said to himself, not actually believing it but liking the words. "And I don't have to apologize to anyone for parents who worked hard to help me out.

Okay then," Sebastian continued to himself, confusing Jimmy by contorting his face through a labyrinth of expressions dramatizing justification. "You spend your life trying to be nice and help people, and then when you fall on your face and need help yourself, the world is not there for you. Everyone has problems. I'm fixing mine and moving on. The world, and Shauna, can just take care of themselves and go jump in a lake."

The last sentence Sebastian spoke out loud with a timbre that Jimmy suspected would bring back his happy-go-lucky, get-lucky best friend. It didn't, but the show got Sebastian to his feet. For the rest of the morning, Jimmy would look over at Sebastian every few minutes. Not once did Seb look back or say a word. It was best to keep Jimmy out of his thoughts. He also knew that his thoughts were not doing him any good either and were in fact dead wrong, but that didn't stop his imploding brain from running on and on and on.

Sebastian, in a civil tone, informed the driver that tourist information would not be necessary, that, in fact, he would appreciate silence, and then offered the driver a bonus to forget the train station and take them straight to London. No one spoke all the way to Eastleigh, through Winchester, around Alton, and then by Guildford.

Green countryside did what magic it could: almost nothing for Sebastian and too much for Jimmy, who jumped up and down. When life is irritating, everything in it follows suit, and Jimmy's questions didn't help. He didn't understand why the farmers built their barns so close to the house. Back in Wisconsin, if you were downwind of manure, even one hundred yards away was less than ideal. The driver said that the oldest farms have living quarters above the animals. It helped them stay warm in the winter. Then he made a joke about people not having deodorant back then. The cows complained. Sebastian didn't laugh and even gave the driver a dirty look before pulling his jacket over his head. He wanted the world, or at least that day, to go away.

Big Ben, Tower of London, Buckingham Palace, Tower Bridge—"Blah blah blah blah" was all the driver got out of Sebastian. Jimmy, on the other hand, was so enthusiastic it took the driver five minutes to wipe nose prints off the backseat windows.

Mommy Elizabeth had made the room reservations. She picked a hotel that had been built using over one thousand tons of imported marble from Italy, Turkey, and North Africa. The only things not made of rock were the beds.

And, of course, there was a line at the front desk. It was that kind of day.

"Oh, Mr. Williamson," the front desk clerk said, with a mousy voice weary from complaints he needed to smooth over, "It's an honor, and might I say, if we'd known the time of your arrival, we would have expedited check-in for you. And, of course, if there is anything we can do to make your stay special. . ."

Sebastian turned around to introduce the manager to special Jimmy, who wasn't there. On the way in, Jimmy had seen an older couple struggling to get luggage out of their cab, so, naturally, he helped them all the way to their room and was then surprised to be handed money—funny-looking money, at that. Jimmy was thrilled and went straight to the gift shop for candy, officially making that afternoon one of the best days of his life.

Sebastian saw no need to share his depression with Jimmy, a risk for anyone within ten yards of his moping, so he worked a deal with the chief bellhop: Jimmy got a bellhop's hat and could keep every tip he made. Sebastian paid the chief bellhop just as much. It worked out best for everyone. The guests stopped complaining about slow service.

There were only two things Sebastian wanted: a hot bath and a cold bottle of vermouth. He got both, and neither did him any good.

7

Sebastian had no interest in the next day. It showed up anyway. Days tend to do that. The morning began with three deep breaths. Sebastian then avoided reality by not opening his eyes. But eyes don't like to stay shut when the rest of the brain is online; it's a breach of contract that Sebastian reluctantly acknowledged, only to be confronted by a ceiling of naked cherubs holding harps, a surprisingly heavy instrument to take airborne.

"Go away," is actually what he said to the entire regiment of flying angels. No one was on Sebastian's good side, not even Jimmy, who just woke him up, repeating, "Cook key... cook... key," phonetic pronunciation that had actually worked when he handed his morning room order to the cook the night before. A dozen were stacked like an Egyptian pyramid outside their door. Jimmy removed one after another from the bottom until they toppled over. "Cook key, Sebastian?"

Sebastian preferred silence to sharing feelings with Jimmy, who wouldn't understand and had his own way inside Sebastian's head, mostly from expressions and body movement. The news was not good. Sebastian had read himself to sleep reviewing the financial specs and budget flow sheets of the family's European investments. "Jimmy, we have to get downtown to the bank. Something funny is going on."

"Fun. . . funny. . . fun today?"

"Of course. Every day, just more for you than me. Take the cookies with you if you want."

"I want to stay. . . suitcases. . . clean up trays. . . be with friends. . . we have funny hats."

"I'll let the manager know. Tell Rigby, the bellhop captain, to give you jobs."

"Jobs! Jobs! Money. . . I help you out."

London's morning fog kept a cap of mist over the city all the way to their Royal Crown Hotel. Fancy rocks aside, the windows dripped condensation, the rugs were moldy, and the hallway creepy. The elevator attendant, a youngster with blond hair, put special effort into opening both eyes wide for guests, then dozed off against the wall between trips, which is just what Sebastian and Jimmy saw when the doors opened.

"Good morning, gentlemen, is there anything I can do for you?"

Sebastian detested scripted patronizing, having lived his whole life surrounded by it, and liked to screw with brains by repeating whatever he heard. "Good morning yourself, is there anything I can do for you?"

"Why, yes there is, sir. You can do for me whatever I can do for you. That way, the boss will be happy and someday I can save enough money to finish school and get the hell out of this blooming stuffy closet on ropes."

At home, Sebastian would have mentioned a scholarship program, perhaps one that his dad had set up for factory families. An hour earlier, inspecting family finances over room service breakfast, Sebastian learned that the scholarship fund had gone belly-up, the first of a long line of surprises kept from him.

The lobby was bustling but hushed and was permeated by an inappropriate sense of regret over last night's fun, combined with confused dread at having to leave the pampered world of status for the streets. Sebastian lowered his head prepared to charge brick walls, or worse, bankers. Jimmy skipped to the bellhop stand to be with friends.

On the other side of town, the office of Continental Investments happened to be next door to the bank that took their deposits. They claimed there was no conflict of interest, and by that they meant the bank looked after the investment firm and the investment firm did everything they could to put money in the bank and keep it there.

It was only a thirty-minute walk to the bank. Sebastian decided to "have a go at it."

Pale, pasty, and altogether limp of spirit was the impression passing strollers left. "Perhaps it's the weather," Sebastian said to himself. "Back home, everyone smiles back." No one did all the way down Hoborn Street to Chancery Lane that crossed Cary Street before passing the Freemason Hall, the Royal Courts, the Royal Opera House, and a newspaper stand attendant who was a royal pain.

"Like I said, sir," he began, with the same look a teacher fires at tenth graders who fail math, "A shilling is a bob and a bob is a shilling. What's so difficult about that? And a quid is a pound, and one bob is worth two hundred and forty pennies, and you owe me five for the newspaper and magazine, so pay up."

A few extra pennies turned the conversation around. Rigby, standing beneath the sign that said "Rigby News," then helped Sebastian out by explaining that, in London, a flat was an apartment, crisps were chips, a cot was a crib, a nappy a diaper, and a dummy a pacifier, which to Sebastian made the most sense since, in America, most politicians were called dummies.

"One final word of advice, young man. Do you see that guy over there with the blue uniform without a gun? He's not a policeman, he's a bobby. If he tells you to walk on the pavement, then get out of the bloody street, because over here pavement is the sidewalk. And at dinner, if the waitress asks you if you want a starter, don't say whiskey, it's appetizers that she's asking about."

Sebastian thanked Rigby for the extra effort, and came to the conclusion that the British were not dull and lifeless, just bored.

The First National Bank of London was a drab brown brick edifice with marble trimmings and four half columns bolted to the front for effect, which made the building look like something a child had decorated by gluing fancy stuff on the outside of a shoebox. Inside, the presence of stacks of money, unlocked vaults, and redundant guards created a boding air of tension.

Sebastian presented himself to the clerk at the front of the lobby. She smiled and asked him to take a seat and wait. Back home, George Greiger, the president of the Fond du Lac Cooperative, would greet him personally before escorting Sebastian to the board room for brunch and a Havana cigar. Sebastian wasn't accustomed to being asked to sit for an unspecified length of time, and the table with tea and crackers said "for employees only" and was on the other side of a three-foot-high wall separating a dozen vice presidents crammed together in the back of the main lobby. As far as Sebastian was concerned, there was no reason for the fence to be there in the first place.

One hour later, Sebastian was led to the president's office on the second floor, where he discovered why the vice presidents were elbow to elbow. The president's office sprawled across the entire second level and had double main doors that looked like the entrance to Nottingham Castle.

Sebastian walked across the room to meet Lord Kensington, who looked well beyond retirement age, and sat beside a tediously sniveling assistant. When Kensington opened his mouth, his lips moved but the rest of his face was as frozen as the expression on his grandfather's portrait behind him.

"Top of the day to you, my son. It's a pleasure to meet one of the Williamsons. Your mother and I have been jolly well making a slam of business together. I trust your stay has been a pleasant one. If there's anything I can do to help, just ring me up. The bank will do everything we can to make your trip special."

"Well, yes, Mr. Kensington—"

"The customary greeting for his lordship," Snively interrupted, "would be Lord Kensington. His family dates back further than the Magna Carta."

"That I believe, and yes of course, pardon me," said Sebastian, as he pulled a stack of reports from his briefcase. "Back home, people don't come with titles. Anyway, I'm confused—"

"That is totally understandable," Lord Kensington abruptly cut in. "European finances are far more complicated than your dairy-state business dealings, but don't worry, we have everything under control, you can trust us."

"That's good to know. But just a few questions—"

Snively took the next shot. "Young man, Lord Kensington is the most respected financial advisor in all of Europe and a very busy man. Collect any thoughts you might have, put them on paper, and submit them to my office. Everything of merit, I move along."

Sebastian knew that the best way to deal with some people was to ignore them and hope they went away. "Nevertheless," he said, smiling, "question number one, if you would grace me an explanation, is about one of our holdings, Ostkirchen Metallfabrik. Until last March," he reported with an insistent tone while looking through numbers, "the plant was generating profit. Then orders dropped, and keeping the doors open has cost my family thousands of dollars."

Snively would not be deterred. He stepped a foot closer to fortify his opinion. "Again, young man, let me remind you that Lord Kensington is the expert here. He does not owe you an explanation. Be thankful that we have accepted your investments."

Sebastian said nothing and sat back with arms folded, looking directly at Kensington, who answered directly.

"Now, now Alcot,"—that turned out to be Snively's name— "the young man has a lot to learn. We must be patient."

Kensington magnified his presence by walking around the desk to stand in front of Sebastian, who remained seated like a student in the front row of kindergarten.

"Here's how is it. Yes, the metal factory was filling orders from Artykuly Gospodarstwa Domowego in Warsaw, but then we learned that the president, Aleksy Nowak, has communist sympathies."

"I fail to see what that and business have—"

"We need to catch you up on modern times," Kensington said with bitter impatience. "Communists are a God-hating group of anarchists with no respect for private property and free enterprise. Capitalism made England what it is today. For the sake of the free world, for laissez-faire economics, for the love of God, we must, absolutely must, do everything in our power to thwart the spread of the devil. It is our duty."

Sebastian let two seconds pass. "And all this time, I thought your duty was to maximize the investments of your clients. How could I have been so wrong?"

"Your sarcasm, child," Snively snapped, "is not excused. If you are to survive in Europe, you must know your place."

Kensington returned to his seat with an armored expression ready for combat. "Will there be anything else? All the information you want is listed in our monthly report."

Sebastian stood, stance wide, with his right arm extended. "What do you think I have in my hand, old man? Nowhere does it say you cancelled orders to play European politics with American money. And where did the money come from to keep that metal factory in business?"

"Allow me, sir," said Snively, hesitantly stepping back. "The contract we have with your family grants us complete management control."

"For a steep fee."

"Yes, lad, for a fee. You don't get brilliance for nothing."

"No, not for nothing, your advice has been costing my family millions for years. And two of the seven factories on my list aren't even covered in your last report. What happened to them?"

In slow, ponderous words, Snively explained what Sebastian had learned the first day of economics class in Madison, and he already knew, that Mommy Elizabeth had floated stocks that were then sold completely to leverage multinational industrialization, all of which was paid for by a gigantic bank loan from the First National Bank of London, which Kensington also ran. The contract Sebastian's mother signed clearly stated that if mortgage payments were not made on time the bank had the right to take over and do what they wanted, including foreclosing on everything owned in the States.

"You see, we did you a favor by liquidating those two companies. The money paid the mortgage. You got a month off."

"And two less factories to contribute to the enormous monthly payment you sold my mother, while you collected a commission from the sale and a million dollar management fee."

"We have offices all over Europe. A dozen lawyers are required to make sure the paperwork is in order."

"Oh, yes, the paperwork. Something that you've convinced yourself makes the world go around."

Kensington stood to make a point. "Now you listen here, you insipid little mommy's boy. The glory of England defeated the German army, brought peace to the continent, and once again rules the world. We are in charge. You need to learn respect."

"George Washington disagreed with you, and so did James Madison, whose house you bombarded to get your greedy little hands back on America that you stole from the world so you could puff yourself up on a bigger throne!"

"This meeting is over. Security will see you to the door," Snively barked.

Sebastian stood to his full height to walk toward Snively, who backed up.

"Hold on, meathead. There are two are more items on which I must insist. First, I need you to put my family's one hundred thousand dollars of cash reserves in a special account accessible to me only, and second, I need a letter of recommendation to the hotel manager at Lujo Vista Al

Mar Seaside resort in Spain introducing me as the owner, with total control of the hotel and its financing. From this day forth, you are forbidden to communicate with them."

Kensington and Snively looked at each other. When Kensington said nothing, Snively realized the ball was in his lap.

"In addition to selling off plant equipment—" Snively started to say.

"And putting thousands of employees out of work as you feed like a vulture."

"Pipe down. Our decision. Not your call. Anyway, we needed more cash—"

"To pay yourself and the bank for doing nothing."

Kensington got off his chair and started for the door, a signal to Snively that he couldn't be bothered. Snively took his place behind the desk in an attempt to place Kensington out of sight. Sebastian was a step ahead. He walked beside Kensington as he attempted to leave, demonstrating to the old man that he had no problem moving the discussion anywhere in the building as loud as he deemed necessary.

"Just let me guess this one," Sebastian proclaimed. "You sold the best profit-making business we owned and absconded with the cash reserves to the last penny, knowing that bankruptcy is imminent, to throw my parents out in the streets. How could you! They trusted you."

Kensington decided to take over. "It's not our fault that your mother made bad investments. It happens every single day of the week."

"She invested in what *you recommended*, after your team wined and dined her in Chicago, something that apparently makes money for your *every single day of the week*."

"I've wasted too much time with you already," said Kensington, making for the door. "Out of generosity, I will have the bank pay for your two-night hotel stay. If you wish any more money from us, you will need to fill out a requisition form downstairs and wait for the next committee meeting."

"And let me guess, it meets once a month."

"No, it meets every *other* month," said Snively with a sneer.

"Well, I'm broke now. I need money now, and from now on, I am part of every committee that deals with our holdings."

"I'm afraid that will not be possible," said Snively, even more smug.

"Oh, I can't wait to hear this one. Now what's your excuse?"

Snively's world order was shaken. With unkind intent, he lost control and stood in front of Sebastian, pounding a stiff finger into Sebastian's chest as he spoke. "You disrespectful American trash. You have no idea who you are dealing with. How dare you talk to Lord Kensington that way."

"I'll talk to crooks anyway I damned please," said Sebastian, as he shoved Snively back to land sprawling on top of Kensington's desk.

The physical world was for plumbers, carpenters, and soldiers. Kensington and Snively backed away in mortal fear, but not before a hidden alarm drew three security guards to their rescue.

Suddenly the room went quiet. Kensington said, "Well, we have covered every issue. In the future, we will keep you up-to-date with a monthly newsletter. Any further interaction between us will be by appointment only. Have a nice day."

"Just one more thing, Lord Kensington," said Sebastian, as he also lowered his voice, "as of immediately, I am taking over control of all my family's assets."

A satisfied smirk betrayed Kensington's real self when he steadfastly declared, "The bank loan is a done deal. And one way or another, we will foreclose within the year. There is nothing you can do about it. But I do have a proposition for you. Let us take care of the details and, for the next twelve months, I will move a thousand dollars a week into your private account. You can tour all of Europe. It will be one long vacation."

"Followed by the breadline and my parents living in a tent," replied Sebastian. "I understand now why there was some question years ago in America about which side to help in the war, and the president was right:

the Germans are murderers, the English are thieves. I congratulate you on being able to ignore every tenet of Christianity to bully the world at the same time you force-feed Christianity to convince those you colonize that their suffering will be rewarded someplace else. My impression is that Germany and Britain, both Aryan cultures, are hypocrites from sunrise to sunset."

"Guards," Kensington ordered, "make note of this man. He is a communist. Do not let him in the building again. And," he added, facing Sebastian, "management will continue as I see fit, and my thousand dollars a week offer is permanently off the table. My assistant, however, will have a one-way boat ticket available for you on the way out. I suggest you return to the States and grow corn."

"Your hearing is going, old man. I told you that I'm taking over management of the company."

"That is not possible. Our signed paperwork lists your mother as the chief executive officer, and she has designated all responsibility to me. End of story."

"Beginning of story. I had a lawyer look at that contract," Sebastian said, pulling out a folder of papers. "And here is signed and notarized legal documentation transferring management to me, which if you do not do at once, will have you in court tomorrow paying every solicitor's fee and my next two months at the hotel."

"You goddamn Americans! We should never have let you keep the country we staked out for you."

8

Sebastian's brain, like all brains, was a marvelous piece of God-made machinery that pouted, wept, and sometimes preferred dismay, the feeling that followed him to sleep, the mental alignment that glorifies, magnifies, or disintegrates reality to kick back, write off, and, most importantly, give a damn or not give a damn. It was a long night.

Brains don't come with steering wheels, but a good night's sleep often does the job. Sebastian realized that, like everyone, when it came to living, he liked to straighten up, clear messes, and organize days into neat little stacks. It was no fun when life came along and knocked them all over. Sebastian's dominoes did not look good. A month earlier he looked into buying a second car, a convertible for warm sunny days. When he got out of bed, he went through his wallet to put aside enough cash to buy two bicycles.

Then he laughed. "I'm not stressed by life; I'm challenged by it. And life will not win! Sebastian will succeed!"

From that morning on, inside his head, he referred to himself as Sebastian, and marveled how strange the human animal is to talk to itself all day. Referring to himself as Sebastian reminded him of when Mom would call him down for dinner. He felt closer to home.

Throwing the covers off, at full attention, lying in bed looking up, Sebastian saluted the cherubs. "Ready for duty. Mission accepted. I can do this. Europe get ready—Sebastian is here!"

Jimmy was lucky. He always slept well. Perhaps it was because parts of his brain were missing. The doctor said other parts of his brain might learn to make up the difference and that male brains don't mature until age thirty, so there was hope. Meanwhile, Jimmy's nights were never haunted by desire, flawed plans, or reckless abandon. He never burned neurons chasing dollars or slinky objects of affection. Sebastian envied Jimmy for having so few crossed wires.

Which isn't to say that Jimmy didn't have his problems, and wasn't also a problem, and a blessing, like the time he walked into the car dealer and ordered the prettiest car in town to give Sebastian for his birthday. Jimmy knew the rumble seat fit him perfectly before he told the dealer Mommy Elizabeth was giving it to Sebastian, which turned out to be true since she did in the end.

Jimmy knew numbers. All he had to do was say "one," "two," or "three" on the phone before any food he wanted, and room service had it outside the door, which Sebastian opened to find a bellhop pushing a breakfast table with two plates and four cookies.

"Say, young man," Sebastian asked, "does the gift shop have boxes and wrapping paper? And can I get two boxes of your finest cookies?"

During the night, Sebastian's brain decided to smoke the peace pipe, and his mom did tell him never to pick someone up and throw them across the room. "You know, Sebastian," he said to himself, closing the door when the bellhop left, "back home, Mom saw dollar bills and grabbed every one within reach. Over here, Kensington sees vaults of gold and can't resist. There is no end to it. So what. Someday we'll learn."

Sebastian dressed, stood tall, and faced the door like the leader of a parade. Jimmy knew the look, "You have... have plan... Seb... I go too... we have fun."

"Do you remember our favorite book that Mom read us when we were young? Well, that's just what we're going to do: follow the yellow brick road, the solid-gold brick road. Jimmy, I've decided not to give a damn. This screwed-up, mixed-up world of ours can go to hell as far as I'm concerned. They can squeeze themselves into prunes for all I care. From now on, we're looking after ourselves, you and me and nobody else, and we're going to make lots and lots of money and have lots and lots of fun."

Sebastian needed to organize accounts, establish lines of communication, and clear the air at the bank. Troy, the elevator blond, delivered gift wrapping and more than enough cookies. Sebastian, with Jimmy at his side, walked to the bank and right past the guards to the back of the lobby, to the only person who smiled back. The name on her desk read "Julie Smithers, Vice President." She was not wearing a ring and was really, really cute. Sebastian suddenly realized what he wanted to do and where he wanted to go. It was easy. She was looking back.

Blue-eyed Julie was petite, sparkling, and retained joyful as her prime default. Sebastian spoke first.

"Good morning, Miss Vice President."

"And a good morning to you, sir. You came back. Usually they don't."

"It takes more than one fathead to ruin my week."

"Oh, does it now?" Julie tipped her head back, raised both eyebrows, and then with a coquettish head tilt added, "Oh, I see. And what, may I ask, does it take to make a week for yee?"

"Candlelight dinner with a beautiful, intelligent woman, who preferably knows someplace in this giant sponge you call London where a man can get food that doesn't taste like milk toast. I miss flavor."

"My mom makes an Irish stew fierce enough to take a bite out of a dinosaur."

"My dad makes an onion soufflé that makes the man in the moon's eyes water. Can you beat that?"

"If ye be wanting, you can come over and share dinner with us tonight and find out for yourself. And bring along the man in the moon. My mom's a widow."

"The man in the moon is up to something. Does the invitation still stand?"

"Why, rightly it sure does, and you can bring your brother with you."

"Oh, he's not my brother. He's my best friend, and he likes to help clean up."

Jimmy nodded enthusiastically. Sebastian looked around to see if anyone was listening. Everyone was pretending they weren't.

"Won't old fathead object to you fraternizing with customers?"

"Now you just hold on there, lad. You've been invited for eatin', not fraternizing, and it's Uncle Fathead, who has been invited over for stew every Friday night for the last ten years and has yet to show up."

"If I can get Uncle You-Know-Who to come over, how would that bode for fraternizing?" asked Sebastian.

"If you mind your manners, anything is possible. And just so you know. . . someday I'm going to run this bank."

"You know, she just might do that," said Lord Kensington, making a special trip to greet Sebastian. During the night, Kensington's brain realized Sebastian could remortgage his property a block away. If any bank was going to foreclose on the Williamson estate, Kensington wanted to make sure it was *his bank*.

Sebastian had turned himself into a prized customer. He was escorted to the second floor, where smiling Snively poured champagne, served French pastries, and then handed out cigars to ruin the flavor. Sebastian had a plan. He explained his plan. Kensington listened to Sebastian's plan. "It might just work, young man, and I'll keep making money off the loan interest anyway. Perhaps your family will stay put." It was the beginning of what might be a happy ending, so you might say it was a happy ending day, something every day deserves.

On the way out, Sebastian told Julie to expect three for dinner.

"You know, deep down," she said, almost believing it, "he's not such a bad guy. He's just living in the wrong century."

"And has himself confused with the king of Siam," said Sebastian.

"There's a lot of that going around."

"I've noticed."

Jimmy's eyes bobbled back and forth faster by the second. He shared all of Sebastian's excitement. With a smile wider than ever, he looked Julie in the eye and said, "Oh... pretty... pretty... Seb wants to kiss you."

Sebastian and Julie shared a blush and a look.

"Isn't... isn't life... isn't life great, Sebastian!"

9

The dinner was satisfying, the company charming, the conversation stimulating, and the figgy pudding disappointing, which Sebastian nevertheless complimented and Jimmy stuffed down. After dinner, Sebastian discovered that England lay below just as many stars and just as bright a moon as the rest of the planet. It was a fine night for a stroll.

Alas, Julie kept her distance.

Sebastian accepted Lord Kensington's invitation to move into the rear living quarters of his castle. Twice, Jimmy took down a full medieval armored suit and wore it to dinner. The castle was only five miles from Kensington's private polo club, where galloping steeds were forced to stop and go all afternoon. The star of the show was Jimmy. At halftime, he refused to return to the sidelines until every hoof-beat divot was properly replaced, after which he chased a squirrel the length of the field, which included two ninety-degree turns, only one of which landed Jimmy flat on his face with the squirrel standing on hind legs not six feet away, daring him to try again.

It didn't take long for Sebastian to feel right at home. One night, it was explained to him that he would be doing the family a favor by taking Julie to the ballet, since the family supported the arts and made a poor showing by not making an appearance. Sebastian obliged and was rewarded by

Julie with a kiss, a cup of cappuccino, and the driest almond toast on earth. After Julie told her friends that Sebastian had taken dance lessons, a gang of ten did the town the next night. The evening ended with six kisses and a hint of heaven on the horizon.

Julie had two sides: one, like Shauna, was hardworking and compassionate; the other, like Pricilla, came with a boyfriend cutout that Sebastian was expected to look like, behave like, and speak like—in other words, who he was supposed to be for the rest of his life and which sounded just like Pricilla's unpublished manual of elitist posturing.

One month later, there he was, wearing the latest suit, talking to only the right people, and swinging an umbrella down the street. He actually said, "Pip, pip, my boy," to a fellow stroller at the same time he saw his reflection in a storefront window. "Holy Jesus!" he said to Jimmy, walking behind him and being less noticed by the day, "Who the hell is that? Could that be me? What am I doing? England has turned me into a fancy boy living in a dollhouse, pretending the world doesn't matter and only we do."

In truth, Sebastian knew Lord Kensington was not to be trusted. If Kensington succeeded in seducing Sebastian into apathy, using his own niece as bait, the Williamson empire would evaporate and the Kensington fortune benefit. He also knew that no one in the family would approve of a marriage between a common American farm boy—no matter how wealthy he used to be—and royal blood. The couple was doomed from the start. Sebastian was looking at menial labor or a subsistence-wage clerk job for the rest of his life.

"Jimmy, we're in trouble," he announced. "We've got to get out of here. Turn around, we're going back to pack. We're leaving for the machine factory in Germany."

Jimmy packed his suitcase every morning. The longer they stayed, the weirder Sebastian got. And Jimmy loved trains. Both stood outside on the rear platform of the lounge car as it left London. Each reminisced in their own way.

"Jolly old England turned out more chuckles than we expected," said Sebastian, nonchalant.

The trip took them through Colchester on the way to Harwich, where an economy class steam puffer was to take them across the English Channel, the world's largest moat. In ancient days, it was known as Vikings Main Street, where they did their shopping—actually chopping and shopping, specifically stabbing, bludgeoning, incinerating, pillaging, and raping, an endless list of bad examples, but only because it gave their lives meaning, and, they were told, was the only way to get to Valhalla. Since no one was attacking them, the only way to die in battle was to attack everyone else. Many theories have attempted to explain Viking behavior and their outlook on life and death. Some cite bad leaders, others bad meat, or perhaps they crossbred with a visiting troop of Klingon aliens.

The boat Sebastian and Jimmy boarded was a rust bucket—a converted cargo transport. It banged against the floating dock and, at low tide, had a ramp so steep it was unfit for anyone not qualified for the Olympics. Jimmy stood at the top offering a helping hand and suitcase service. He handed Sebastian each piece of luggage over the rail, assisted a dozen down the gangplank, and then boarded with pennies jiggling in his pocket.

The sea was rough, the air damp, and the entire boat smelled like burning coal, but it did the job at half the cost of boats that passed inspection. Jimmy was confused—no sooner did the coast of England disappear on the stern than the continent showed up at the bow, where Jimmy spent the remainder of the passage telling Sebastian that the Channel was his favorite ocean.

Boat morning was followed by back-of-the-line afternoon. First, they waited to go ashore, then to get their passports checked, and finally to walk five blocks in a crowd massive enough to fill a football stadium. They all had tickets for the same train.

Just like the boat, coal-dusty cushions and coal-smoky air were everywhere, aided and abetted by cigarettes and pipes that collected tar by the hour. Sebastian and Jimmy were the only two among the six in their compartment who weren't motivated to burn something, which Sebastian expected when he sat next to the open window across from Jimmy, who stuck his head outside, looking both ways. Every time the train stopped, Jimmy got out and waved to the engineer from the boarding platform. The only thing more fun that getting on a train was doing it again and again.

Next to Jimmy was a full-hooded nun whose eyes were never seen and whose hands rolled beads the entire trip. Next to her, a businessman negotiated elbow space to review papers and look important in his black three-piece suit. Beside Sebastian was a young German couple returning from Amsterdam fun. They were so hungover neither spoke as they took turns dozing off while leaning on each other.

The countdown to insolvency had begun the day Sebastian left Fond du Lac. He knew every penny counted, which is why they headed straight for the youth hostel when they stepped off the train in Dusseldorf. Bunk beds, barracks living, and bad air were nothing new to Boy Scouts, along with noisy, late stragglers and at least one in the corner who wouldn't stop talking.

"Come on, Jimmy, let's take a walk and come back when the room settles down."

The youth hostel was across the street from the winding Rhine River, which flooded every spring to make the two hundred yards between the youth center and the river impossible to build on but ideal grazing land for sheep. With a bottle of Liebfraumilch, Sebastian and Jimmy sat down on the grass at river's edge at sunset.

"Sheep… sheep just like home. Just like Fox River," said Jimmy, looking at Sebastian with a smile that turned curious when Sebastian filled and handed a cup of wine to him. "I no drink."

"I know, buddy, but I'm tired of stepping in every time someone offers you a snort, and you've never tried it. Here are the rules. First, look around at everyone before you start; perhaps a toast is planned. Second, sip, do not gulp. And third, try your best to be the first human being in history who doesn't drink too much."

An hour later, out there by themselves in the dark, both realized that what they missed most was the silent company of friends back home. They learned that being together was all that was needed to feel complete, and that if nature surrounded every day, then no day went unfulfilled. Jimmy played tag with the sheep. The sheep weren't interested, but one did hold still long enough for Jimmy to pull the sheep's wool ears to both sides of his chin to imitate Santa Claus.

The first drink got Jimmy dancing. The second put his head in Sebastian's lap, where it stayed for thirty minutes as Sebastian thought about life from every direction and the eternal value of wonderful feelings and of love. Then he carried his best friend to bed.

10

Something happened to Jimmy. He woke up with a headache and words in his head that were lifted from a book of quotations that was lifted from the ship's library: "No race, creed, or sex has a monopoly on vice... or virtue."

He also wasn't his usual happy self, but also not grumpy, morose, or sour—nor bitter, confronting, or sorrowful—more just "don't give a damn, let the world hit me in the head, who cares."

It occurred to Sebastian that introducing Jimmy to alcohol may not have been a good idea. It then occurred to Sebastian that in his entire life, there hadn't been a single person who ever suggested that it was a good idea.

There was a line at the kitchen door for the bowl of oatmeal and cup of coffee that came with one night's bed. In the dining room, Sebastian found two spots on the bench next to the wall on the third table over that fed men only. The ladies ate in a private, more tidy space.

The portions were small and the faces long. Post–World War One Germany was not a happy place. Unemployment was up and productivity down. Reparation payments, referred to as blood money, had crippled the economy. Not one reichsmark was left for social services or the infrastructure. The entire population was demoralized, and seeped rancor both appropriate and exaggerated. One sentence in English at the table brought looks that, of all people, Jimmy returned. Sebastian always knew what a danger Europe was to the world. Only that minute did he realize how much of a danger it was to itself.

Rejuvenating the machine factory in Ostkirchen, Nordrhein-Westfalen, was the first step toward turning red ink to black numbers and force high-horse Kensington to eat his words. Jimmy used his few rentenpfennigs to buy lapel carnations from a sickly street vendor on the way to the train that took them as far as Warendorf. Ostkirchen was a farm-country local village that just happened to have impressive iron works dead center. Only one bus drove through a day. They missed it.

Sebastian consulted his budget and decided to splurge for transportation in the form of two used bicycles with sturdy racks for their suitcases, which allowed them to take the farm path all the way to Ostkirchen. The path, not wide enough for a truck but just wide enough for farmers to pull a horse-drawn wagon to town with their harvest, wound through farmland manicured for thousands of years. Every tree knew its place, every stick was collected, and along the way rest stops appeared, most complete with a bench and a statue of Mother Mary or a crucifix, which caused Jimmy to stop, dismount, genuflect, and cross himself in traditional fashion, something he picked up at home, not from Sebastian, who confessed to nothing and suspected everything, thanks to Fritz, his favorite philosophy professor in Madison.

Halfway to Ostkirchen, they enjoyed a ten-minute U-turn. Between fields, woods, and a stream, the trail was bisected by a stone road no wider than the path. It was perfectly straight in both directions. It was in excellent condition.

"Oh my God," Sebastian said. "This is one of them! Jimmy, this road was laid down two thousand years ago by the Roman Empire. Not only does every one lead to Rome, but they are all, like this one, perfectly straight. Let's head down it for a few minutes and pretend we're traveling to the city that changed the world, for the worse."

Once back on the path, they saw barns, farmhouses, waving farmers, and crops waiting harvest. Then a tall steeple appeared that Sebastian concluded must be Ostkirchen. The cow path approached the town from behind the church, where generations of locals were buried, and then ended up in the middle of town. In truth, what they called a town was a single road with one right-angle road heading out of town. Traffic, the five cars that drove through a day, didn't like either, since they had to slow down until they left town. Main Street boasted two pubs, a general store, and the shooting club.

Sebastian and Jimmy left their bikes leaning against the fence behind the church to explore the town by foot. The streets, all two of them, were empty. It was Sunday, which explained the wide-open church doors and stragglers making their way. Seb and Jim sat in the last pew, an obligation that still required them to stand, sit, kneel, and mumble on cue. The ceremony confused Jimmy. First, a group of peaceful citizens filed in, sat down, and then one of them got up and yelled, scolded, and screamed hell and damnation. Jimmy didn't understand why that guy, the one in the worst mood, was allowed to ruin the meeting. Sebastian's grandmother spoke German for the first ten years of her life in Green Bay, a city with a European pub on every corner. He caught the gist of the goings on. The priest began condemning the defeatist attitude of Deutschland. He then declared that the pope had designated atheist communism to be the world's greatest threat to peace. It was every German's duty to defend the homeland and Jesus Christ by opposing godlessness. The Vatican must remain powerful at all costs.

What the country needed, the priest went on, was a strong leader to make Germany great again. The legally elected president of the country, Hindenburg, in the minister's opinion, was not up to the job. In the priest's back pocket, under his robe, father Beck had volume one of *Mein Kampf*, personally endorsed by Dr. Joseph Goebbels. Beck encouraged all young men to join the *Hitlerjugend,* the youth organization identical to the *Ballilla* that Mussolini established in Italy. "Wir warden Erlog haben! Deutschland, Deutshland uber alles in dem Welt!"

Jimmy frowned at all the noise. It didn't seem right to him for one person to make all the others mad. He and Sebastian left the harangue to mellow outside. The factory wasn't hard to find; it was right across the street, separated from church bells by a house and tiny barn that Sebastian recognized as the home of the manager and still one-quarter owner of the machine factory.

Sebastian and Jimmy retrieved their bikes to wait across the street for church to end. The family residence was a white stucco structure that had been in the family for over two hundred and fifty years. One side bordered the factory. Out back was a field and a barn with a cow, a pig, and chickens. A year earlier, the manager, Karl Loeman, had hoped to buy an automobile. That year, he prayed not to be evicted.

When mass ended, Karl led his wife, Greta, his sons, Hans and Gerhard, and his daughters, Roswitha and Marlene, across the street to their front door, where they found Sebastian and Jimmy sprawled on the steps next to their bikes.

"Herr Loeman," Sebastian said getting up, "*Schone Sie zu treffen.*"

"Nice to meet you too. We speak not good but some English."

"Great. I'm Sebastian, and this is Jimmy. We just stopped by to introduce ourselves, but there's no hurry, no reason to work on Sunday. Jimmy and I will get settled and be back tomorrow."

"*Unsinn,* youngster. The nearest Hutte is thirty minutes on those bikes of yours. *Du musst bei uns bleiben.* You must stay with us."

Zaftig Marlene had smiling Jimmy by the hand halfway through the front door before Sebastian accepted their hospitality. He was inwardly relieved and his limited finances grateful.

Sebastian entered the world his German grandmother had talked about. The Loeman family lived close to nature. Out back was a cow, fed daily and milked at sunrise by mother Greta, who boiled the milk *a la*

Pasteur to serve with cream floating for breakfast. Feeding the chickens grain and the pig leftovers was her afternoon job, after cleaning the house and dusting. Every six months, a butcher would show up, make a racket, and then leave meat and gallons of bright red pig's blood. Sebastian's first breakfast was a fried blood-flour mixture that looked like a rat died on his plate after being smashed to pieces with a sledgehammer. The taste was surprising greasy and did take a while to get used to, which turned out to be one month longer than Sebastian and Jimmy stayed.

Breakfasts were quiet and dinners cordial. Greta explained that the family was lucky. Half of the town was out of work and half-starved. Those for whom her husband could find work were lucky to afford meat on the table once a week. The Loemans had meat every night; each morning, every member of the family got one egg from the barn out back.

Sunday dinner was the highlight. Sebastian and Jimmy looked forward to it every week. It began with bath time. Since heating water was expensive, the luxury was only permitted once a week. Karl got to bathe just before dinner. Mother was one half hour earlier, and before that, Hans the oldest, Gerhard, Roswitha home from the university, and baby Marlene, just twenty-one and ready to start a family. Since Sebastian and Jimmy were the last to sign up, their bath time was two in the afternoon.

"Come," said Gerhard, as he grabbed Sebastian's and Jimmy's hands. "We go across *strassa*, drink beer in pub." He was a tall German, with a forehead that looked like an oversized brain had pushed it out. His teachers agreed. At age twelve, he tested higher than other students and so therefore, as hundreds of years of tradition abided, was switched to pre-university schooling and the rest of his life determined. Gerhard's older brother, Hans, on the other hand, did not have such a good day when he was tested. His teacher shook her head and pointed to the door that signed him up for trades school, where he spent the next four months filing down the same piece of metal to learn discipline.

The town was cold and windy, but not the pub. After Sunday dinner, the entire younger generation, all ten guys who lived in town, were at the bar. They huddled around Gerhard after ordering beers and shots of schnapps for their American visitors. From the tap, each glass foamed to the top. Jimmy reached out to cool his throat.

"*Nein—nicht jetzt*," three Germans repeated. Proper etiquette, Gerhard explained, was to sit and look at the foamy glass until it settled, a long two minutes to be sure, and then and only then, after the bartender topped it off, begin with a shot of schnapps. Most importantly, one does not sip beer, one *drinks* beer. Unless at least one-third of it disappears before the glass leaves one's mouth, one is not a true German. Sebastian and Jimmy played it safe. They went fifty-fifty. Sebastian volunteered to dispense with Jimmy's schnapps, something everyone in the pub understood when one beer took Jimmy off his chair and to the corner, where he grabbed a broom and had the best of times sweeping up, including under everyone's feet when they lifted them at the bar. The bartender gave him a penny that he gave right back to pay for a boiled egg trapped in a bottle of diluted vinegar.

Karl and Greta Loeman were Germans, but they were also people, which made a huge difference. Karl didn't even look German, more roly-poly Italian perhaps, short and sociable, never abrupt, demanding, or mean, and not what the government was looking for in a soldier, so in the Great War, he'd stayed home and made bombs.

Greta was a bomb, a muscular *hausfrau* with arms that could tackle the pig or take out the eldest. She stood a foot taller than her husband but never pushed him around. And it was no fooling around and obedience above all else. One night, after Sebastian respectfully asked why Germany's political leaders and Rome's religion business were more important than the happiness of her own family, Greta came to an instant conclusion: "As a child, you were not beaten enough."

Apparently, there was a correct amount of beatings that a child should suffer if they were going to except dogma without thinking, which apparently was the goal because it was also apparent to Sebastian that Greta was convinced that the national government and a group of confused bachelors in Rome were indeed more important than the safety of her own family. It's an argument that Sebastian did not concede, and he had no hesitation quoting Thomas Jefferson for backup. Jimmy added three sentences himself, one of which fit the debate.

Everyone had opinions chiseled in stone. Greta's favorite was, "*Ordnung ist die Halfte des Lebens.*" Order is half of life.

Sebastian scratched his head for dramatic pause and then said slowly, with complete confidence, "Then disorder is the other half." That got him a laugh, a hug, and a kiss on the cheek.

Karl was a good man. He wanted to do right by the people who worked for him, but he had to lay half of them off. He wanted to do the right thing for his family, but then watched the country he loved turn his sons into soldiers. He wanted to be a good husband, but Greta blamed him for the state of the world and not being strict enough. He also wanted to do right by God, but disagreed with sermon after sermon and said nothing.

Before drifting off to sleep, Jimmy got in the last word: "For evil to succeed, good men need only do nothing."

11

Riding into town on a bicycle made Sebastian one of the guys. He liked the feeling and asked Karl and Greta, the only two who knew he was the new owner, to keep that fact to themselves.

"I would like to start with a tour of the plant," said Sebastian, cracking the head off his boiled egg perched on its tiny pedestal after his stomach disqualified vampire stew. Karl and Hans were busy in the office all day scheduling projects and billing customers. Gerhard had one more year of school in Warendorf before leaving for Heidelberg University to be trained as an architect. Every morning, he caught the bus at seven, finished at one, drank beer with schoolmates until three, and then returned. Roswitha was only home one weekend a month from Humboltd University in Berlin, and Greta had her hands full keeping house and tending livestock.

"I can show Sebastian around," offered Marlene, keeping her eyes on him.

"*Sehr gut,* my daughter. Bring him to the office when you're done."

Marlene's youthful blue eyes were almost covered by blond bangs between straight cords and pigtails to each side. Marlene had grown up in the machine shop, learned to operate every piece of equipment, and had the oil stains to prove it. A toothpick model she wasn't. Sebastian smiled. He had had his fill of dainty debutants afraid to chip a nail.

Sebastian and Marlene passed the loading dock on their way to the back entrance. Marlene stopped to help bent-over Dieter Muller unload sheet metal. He was the oldest worker employed, and amused the family with stories about working with Otto von Bismarck. The way Dieter told the tales, it was he, not Otto, who dominated European affairs for decades.

The machine factory was separated from the house by a wide, brick-paved truck port. It had rained overnight. The morning sun reflected in pools of water. The factory was a giant, red-brick building that had turned black over the years. At shoulder height were push-out windows that were almost as black as the bricks. Marlene and Sebastian entered without Jimmy, who stayed home to help Greta. Together they finished every chore by noon, with Jimmy asking for more.

Out front, on the street, a clean white door led to the business office on the second floor. Employees and their dirty boots all entered from the back next to the loading dock, like Sebastian and Marlene did. Sunlight barely made it through the fume-stained ceiling windows, which could be opened to let out foul air by pulling ropes on each wall. The first step introduced Sebastian to "*Grune Tante*," or "green aunt," the water-oil mixture used by every machine to reduce friction when one metal worked on another. It was piped around the building before being dripped or sprayed on parts being machined. Only half made it to the catch buckets, the rest soaked floor and shoes.

"You will need boots, young man," Marlene said, looking down at Seb's loafers.

"And a thick wool sweater," he replied. "It's freezing in here."

"Only eight months a year," said Marlene, with a smile exercising her sense of humor.

Emil Stein, the head machinist, was known not to have a sense of humor, but he worked hard and was the last to leave. That day he was the first one to walk over to greet Sebastian.

"*Morgen* Marlene, what do we have here? Another worker, one who will work for nothing?"

In German, Marlene explained that Sebastian was visiting to learn about the factory and try to improve sales. Emil shook Sebastian's hand, which is when he learned the best way not to be bothered by oily fingers was not to look at them.

"*Wunderbar*," Emil said. He then continued in slow German that Sebastian understood, "Half our machines are empty, and half of my friends are home praying for work."

Emil interrupted his lathe job to walk beside Marlene and Sebastian. Emil, but mostly Marlene, pointed out the latest boring mills, shapers, planers, drilling machines, grinders, presses, saws, and welding stations. From blueprints, the shop could construct anything from crop harvesters to a submarine.

"And cannons, land mines, and machine guns?" Sebastian asked.

"We used to. Politics are a problem, young man."

"So is losing money. I have a plan."

"Good luck with that. I must return to work. Always a pleasure, Marlene."

Halfway through the tour, Hartmut Wolf, even younger than Marlene, asked her to help him calibrate his leadscrew bracket. Before they finished, two other workers snuck over, looking for recommendations. They were having trouble with threading dials and carriage alignments.

"They ask me," Marlene said, turning to Sebastian, "because shop master Emil is old-fashioned. He adds after-hours classes when someone is uncertain and records his disappointment in the company log."

The last worker to approach Marlene pleaded with her to step aside. Werner, a tall, nervous, middle-aged fellow losing his hair, had a predicament.

"Marlene, *Entshuldigung*, but there is a problem. I have two thousand frame bolts to thread manually because of a casting fault, and I'm to blame. Please don't tell Emil. I must not lose this job. My wife is expecting our second."

"So clamp them in a vice and thread manually. If Emil hasn't seen the plans, he won't figure it out."

"Yes, yes, but that will take days. There is no way to hide it."

"I'll help. Pull the dust curtain over and bring in the first pallet. I haven't dripped *Grune Tante* in weeks. Sebastian, you must excuse me. We'll catch up later."

Sebastian looked around to see heads in every direction snap back down to their machines. Everyone knew what the problem was. No one wanted to be blamed.

"How many threaders do you have?" asked Sebastian.

"Plenty."

"Which one is mine?"

"Really?"

"I wouldn't be a gentleman if I left a beautiful lady like yourself unescorted."

"Who are you? You are not like the others London management sent."

"I'll take that as a compliment. Let's get to work."

The three pulled it off. Marlene even sent Werner home on time for dinner with his wife while she and Sebastian finished the job, each grunting as they manually levered a foot-long, one-inch-wide steel rod into a threader that spilled grease-water from the waist down.

"You're smart, you're pretty, you work hard," Sebastian said between grunts. "Why aren't you at the university?"

"Or I could say, you're young, handsome, and intelligent, so what are you doing with more grease on your hands than mine?"

"You first."

"Okay. I could have gone to the university, but I'm the only one in the family who likes working with their hands, and someday I'll run this factory."

"What about Hans?"

"Don't tell Papa, it would break his heart, but Hans doesn't like this kind of work and wants to move away. His dream, believe it or not, is to drive a train. He has had a thing for trains since my dad bought him a toy one as a kid."

"I can understand that."

"Now your turn, Englishman."

"Englishman! How dare you. I'm no stuffy blowhard. I'm from America."

"And you came all the way from America to do menial labor for pennies?"

"Oh, no. I came all the way from America to meet you."

"Something tells me you have done this before."

"Are you referring to metallurgy?"

"I'm thinking you know less about the properties of metals than you do about flirting."

"So how am I doing?"

"On the machine there, B-minus. As far as the rest is concerned, I'm not experienced enough to know, but I like it."

12

Gunter Wolf was Ostkirchen's first National Socialist, and the second one in town to walk around with a copy of *Mein Kampf.* He despised Bolsheviks, hated England for starting the Great War, and resented America for sticking its nose in when Germany was about to win. He blamed Washington for forcing the fatherland to its knees begging for crumbs, while England maintained colonial exploitations that had already stolen two-fifths of the planet's dry land.

Gunter was one of twenty-seven thousand members of the National Socialist Party. Every other political organization outnumbered them and refused to take the National Socialists seriously. Like Sebastian, they were in Gunter's way. Gunter Wolf was waiting outside the factory's back door, leaning on the black brick wall and smoking a cigarette.

"Long shift, Marlene?" he said, ignoring Sebastian.

"Gunter," Marlene said with polite restraint, "I told you that I would meet you in the pub after work if I was thirsty. Why aren't you there now?"

"Because I thought you might want to walk over with me, and I'm curious about the Englishman who is learning our secrets."

Sebastian stepped back to let Marlene play out the situation. Gunter sensed retreat and took one stride sideways and two forward, placing himself directly in Sebastian's face, a standard National Socialist greeting.

Marlene placed both hands on her hips and spoke loud enough to turn Gunter's head.

"Sebastian is not English. He's from America."

Gunter's height equaled Sebastian's, who had a muscular upper body, but lifting steel since he was fourteen gave Gunter a clear twenty-pound advantage, and he knew it, and he knew, or thought he knew, that he could coldcock the American with one blow, so he didn't hesitate to move six inches nearer.

"So, you're an American, are you? England's lapdog. First London attacks George Washington and kills colonists, and then you help them murder us. *Du bist verruckt!* So why didn't you help us defeat the English bastards?"

Sebastian stepped even closer. Both men knew they were within punching range. Only Gunter had his fists clenched. Sebastian remained baritone, but projected ten decibels louder than Gunter.

"Because you sank the *Lusitania*. Only cowards attack unarmed civilians. Murder comes too easily to you."

"Now listen closely, you two-bit Boy Scout, those who help the enemies of Deutschland *are* the enemy of Deutschland. Stay out of Europe!"

"I will go anywhere I damn please, sauerkraut breath, and I suggest you improve your manners; there's a lady present."

"A lady," Gunter sneered with a laugh, "Marlene is one of us, a *heftig* German *hausfrau*, not one of your helpless American women."

"I have flattened bigger men than you for saying less," Sebastian bellowed, "but today is your lucky day. I can't be bothered. Run along, and I suggest you try harder to be a human being next time."

Sebastian took another step closer to Gunter. Both men could feel each other breathing. Gunter stared rivets and meant business but then noticed that Marlene had moved beside Sebastian, not to his side. Gunter slid over to confront her.

"Marlene, I heard today that we are going to make weapons again. I assume that they will be sold to Berlin to make Germany great once more. Only a traitor would arm our enemies."

Sebastian pivoted perpendicular to Gunter's right shoulder, which meant Sebastian had him flanked and could wallop him with ease. Gunter understood the military tactic but decided not to kick out Sebastian's kneecap, a possibility that Sebastian was prepared to prevent with a side step and an occipital lobe slam. Gunter watched Sebastian raise both arms to shoulder height in preparation. Gunter blinked. He knew there would be another day, and preferably a dark alley and five against one.

Gunter stepped back and leaned against the wall. He kept his eyes on Sebastian to let him know it wasn't over. Marlene took advantage of the distance to place herself between them.

"Gunter, you work for us. Who we sell to is our business, at least it used to be. This is a new world. Papa told me that a single individual now coordinates our factory with many others spread throughout Europe. That person calls the shots and has decided to make and sell the world's best artillery to the highest bidder."

"And," Sebastian added sarcastically, "if that upsets your game of toy soldiers, Gunter, then I suggest you build your own factory."

"Or take over this one," Gunter grunted.

"Feel free to get in line and take your turn," Sebastian fired back, unfazed.

"We are Nazis. We do neither," yelled Gunter, standing at attention before spitting on the ground and walking away.

Marlene approached Sebastian and touched his forearm, a gesture noticed and appreciated.

"I'm so sorry. There is much bitterness in Germany. Gunter lost his dad and uncle in the Battle of Verdun. Without the British counteroffensive, we would have taken Paris and the war would have ended in our favor. Without America, Britain could never have mounted that offensive.

And just so you know, I am also German. Last year, I joined the Women's League of the National Socialist Party, but I stopped going to meetings."

"Why?"

"Because Gunter broke the jaw of my boyfriend."

"Oh, I see. And does your boyfriend work here?"

"No. He's not Jewish, but his parents worked on the Russian border and named him after a relative, David, a name guaranteed to cause trouble these days. Right after his jaw was wired, he moved to South America."

"Do you miss him?"

"Yes. He was kind and considerate, but not a fighter like you."

"Don't get me wrong. I fight for myself and those I care for. This country stuff is for the birds, fool's gold for the blind."

"You may underestimate yourself. You just risked a beating that was not your fight."

"When he challenged me, Gunter made it my fight."

"You should know that Gunter tells everyone I'm his girlfriend."

"Are you?"

"I kissed him at a dance or two, but that's all. The only man I've ever made love to was David, and he's gone forever."

"Why are you telling me all this?"

"I don't know. I just feel safe with you, for the first time since David left. And what about you? Did the love of your life also ride off into the sunset without you?"

"No, I was the one who had to leave, and then I learned she changed her mind, and I've been drifting with the tide ever since."

"Does that make today a high tide or a low tide?"

"A rising tide."

"I see," said Marlene in a whisper, "and just when does the boat sail, with me on the dock waving goodbye to you forever?"

"Now it is you who underestimates yourself. Look in the mirror, Marlene. You will find power, beauty, and intelligence. One minute ago, my plans changed. I was leaving for Spain to retool factories there and make Spain my residence, but now I've decided to stay here. You know what they say—who has Berlin has Germany, and who has Germany has Marlene."

"I think you've got that one wrong, but thanks for thinking of me as a woman—it's been a long time. But also know that I'm a German citizen dedicated to my family and the soil of my birth. It is a matter of duty."

"One's first duty is to truth, followed by love. No one knows the future."

"I do. In the future, there is no you and me because you will leave and I will stay. But thanks for helping today. Whoever your boss is in London, he made a wise choice sending you to do his errands. I'm going to wash up for dinner. I'll see you then."

Sebastian started across the truck port with her. Marlene turned and stopped him in his tracks.

"Please, I would rather be by myself right now. Macho male behavior doesn't puzzle me, it just makes me sad."

13

Marlene crossed the cobblestone pavement to the back door of the house. She entered but left the back door open for Sebastian, who didn't follow but did watch her remove her boots in the foyer and place them on the drying rack. Marlene turned to face Sebastian. Her face was not sad, her face was not happy, it was just a face.

Sebastian whispered to himself, "What a pretty face."

The town of Ostkirchen was one monstrous factory surrounded by dozens of disappointing square houses in the middle of miles of farmland. Instead of heading to the back door, Sebastian turned to the fields out back, where he admired rows of cabbage, potatoes, and carrot tuffs. It was mid-July. Last night's storm had cleared the air and left not a cloud in the sky, that glowed light until nine every night. It was dinnertime.

Sebastian needed a moment. He stopped at the chicken coop to empty his pockets of breadcrumbs, which were a big hit, mostly for the rooster standing guard. Sebastian next stopped to pat the cow, who turned her head, appreciating the company. He then pulled the apple out that he'd snuck off the snack tray as he leaned against the fence. He held it out for the pig. "Hello Mr. Hog, how's life treating you? And how simple your life must be. I just learned that women in Europe are just as confusing as they are at home."

Sebastian shifted his weight to one leg and streched over the fence on his forearms. "Did I do something wrong? Why does Marlene not want to be with me?" The boar crushed the apple with one bite, peed where it stood, and then turned around to crap at Sebastian's feet. Sebastian appreciated the honest feedback.

With shoes off and hands scrubbed, Sebastian joined the family in the dining room at the front corner of the house that was built right to the sidewalk. There were windows on two sides covered by white mesh cloth that allowed the family to see out while no one could see in. It was a quiet night, with not one car or pedestrian in sight. Papa was waiting to say grace. Sebastian scurried to his seat.

"Dear Lord, we thank you for all that we have when so many have little and we know that with your help and the hands of friends, soon no one will go to bed cold or hungry."

A choir of amens circled the table as every head looked up, except Jimmy's. He never looked down. He was extra happy; in front of him, spread the length of the table, were plates of pork chops, green beans, potatoes, salad, and pancakes. No one moved; they were waiting for Papa, who got first pick of every plate before he handed it over to Mutter on his left, who then passed each course to Hans, Gerhard, and Marlene, before the food ended up in front of Sebastian and Jimmy.

Flapjacks ended the procession. They were a special order. Jimmy had been such a help all day that Mutter allowed him to make a request, something otherwise reserved for birthdays. Jimmy picked pancakes but didn't see syrup. He pointed to the stack on his plate.

"*Naturlish junger,*" said Mutter Greta as she reached over to what looked like a gravy boat. Jimmy smiled right up to the point where gravy, not maple syrup, drenched his griddle cakes. He said nothing but knew that Sebastian, looking over, missed home as much as he did.

The meal began with a wine toast. After that, no one interrupted Mother or Father. Everyone took part in the conversation and later passed a small plate around. The meat was well cooked but came with a layer of fat at the edges. Each child, and Mutter, carefully cut off the undesirable fat and added it to a plate before the plate ended up in front of Papa.

"You children are spoiled," he said, repeating an opinion for the two hundred and thirty-seventh time. "During the war, fat kept us alive."

"What kept us alive," Mutter added, "was hiding food from the German soldiers the winter they searched our barn. And the rumors that some of our neighbors were forced to make blood soup out of the dead has never been substantiated."

"Perhaps not," said Papa, "but they made it through the winter and no one knows how."

The oldest son, Hans, who took after his dad, short, wide, dull, and sullen, never asked questions, and was obedient to the letter of the law. Nothing in his life tumbled melodrama. Gerda Voigt, the daughter of a close family friend, was the only girl he'd dated, and so therefore it was assumed that someday they would marry. She did keep his secret about wanting to leave town, and looked forward to it as much as Hans did.

The second son, Gerhard, was part of the new generation. He wasn't selfish per se, but both his parents sensed stubborn arrogance, which in Germany meant that you didn't accept every single idea parents and ministers dished out. Gerhard's best friend was Weiland Engel, whose oldest brother, Eberhard, had just graduated from the University of Freiburg, and returned to teach upper school in Munster. Both the young men, with Gunter Wolf at their side, were seen crossing the street to pay a visit.

"Herr Loeman," Wieland said after the three were invited in. "Please excuse the interruption. My brother, Professor Engel, is visiting from Munster. We are having a meeting of the Ostkirchen Philosophic Society this evening and would like to invite Gerhard and your two guests to join us."

Papa's permission was required for everything except going to the bathroom. It was considered a matter of respect or, in other families, fear of reprisal. Karl never said no unless he got a signal from Greta, who acquiesced that night as long as the boys finished their salads, served last by custom as they believed the fiber helped clean teeth, which made sense except for the scattered leaf bits that lodged between teeth, resisting the plan.

Every night, after dessert, the family went for a walk down the cow path by the church, past two farms, and then back. The northwest field behind the last farm was the location picked for the evening's philosophy seminar. Marlene lagged beside Sebastian.

"Okay," said Sebastian, aroused from the lassitude of overeating, "I'm confused. An hour ago, you didn't want to be with me, and now you are here. So, you do like me?"

"We'll get to that later. For now, make up some excuse, like you have a headache or are still tired from traveling. Don't go with the boys."

"Why not? I took philosophy in college. I can hold my own. What gives?"

"To begin with, there is no Ostkirchen Philosophic Society. Yes, they start off trying to outdo one another remembering quotations, but it's a cover for a drinking party."

"I'm over twenty-one and have experienced the witch's brew. Again, what's with the hype?"

"Gunter can barely read; he's no philosopher. I'm sure he put the others up to it. He plans to drink you under that table and then drag you back on top of a cow that he will leave tied outside to humiliate you."

"My dad's hard cider is 50 percent ethanol."

"Gunter's homemade rum is 70 percent alcohol, which he will hand you as he dilutes 20 percent schnapps for himself."

"Again, been there, done that. I don't run from anyone. I'll be careful."

"There's more. After a few drinks, he will insult you and pick a fight. He's clever when it comes to that, and he'll make sure you sound like someone who hates Germany. No one will help you. You'll end up in the hospital just like my boyfriend David. Please don't go—for your own good and mine."

"So, you *do* care about me. You like me."

"I never said I didn't like you. I just said that we are from two different worlds and that we will never be a couple so there is no reason to go down that road. . . or this path. Turn around, we will walk back together."

14

The setting sun lit up farmhouses like a giant flashlight. The rays also highlighted barn details and brightened white pansies, yellow wildflowers, and purple thistle spears. The sky was clear, the air dry, and what little breeze there was called it a day.

The family strolled as one until Hans detoured down Bergan's path to visit his sweetheart, Gerda Voigt. He planned to present Sebastian as their savior, someone who could put the factory back on its feet so they could set a date, which would come after Hans had finished conductor training and secured a full-time position anywhere in Germany except Ostkirchen.

Gerhard walked beside his mother and father, explaining his dream of designing cities that included retail shopping, parks, and bike trails connecting every residential neighborhood. The gleam that lit up his eyes did not compromise the ache both his parents felt at the thought of Gerhard moving out, like their oldest daughter, Roswitha, had already done. In private, Karl and Greta referred to Gerhard as the smart son, the good son, the one who always stayed with them for after-dinner walks.

Marlene also obliged convention by keeping her mom and dad company. She was the good daughter, the hardworking daughter, the mechanic, dishwasher, and all-around peacemaker who never mentioned her own dream, and never expected it to come true. She had a strength that never lost sight of compassion. The entire town expected as much. Marlene's improvements to the assembly line gave everyone in Ostkirchen hope.

Sebastian sensed as much from the way the staff treated her in the plant. After dinner, when she cleared the table, cleaned up, and dedicated the night to her parents, her qualities were even more obvious. What he couldn't figure out was who she really was. He knew everyone had a dream.

Right after they passed the Bergmann homestead, Karl and Greta sat down on the bench Trudi Bergmann had placed there beside "blessed" Mary, a presumed historical figure celebrated for presumably withholding affection, an assumption accepted with remarkable simplicity, and also the only birth control in town.

Marlene kept looking back at Sebastian and Jimmy, hoping they would turn back. They did not. Jimmy reached for Sebastian's hand, something they did for years after the accident, much to the chagrin of the old folks who said it wasn't proper for two men to carry on so disgracefully, even though girls could get away with it.

In Germany a boy holding a girl's hand was totally acceptable as long as they kept their distance and didn't piss off Mary, although no one understood the logic of that either, except for the thing about obeying orders, what the Germans were too good at.

Jimmy stopped to pick wildflowers short of the rest stop.

"Jimmy," Sebastian asked out of earshot of the group, "what do you think of Marlene?"

Sebastian long suspected that Jimmy's inner voice and logical thinking were less damaged from the fall than his ability to express himself, and Jimmy found other ways, like handing over flowers, making a face, or throwing a rock on the ground, which was something Sebastian had almost cured him of.

"Marlene... Marlene," Jimmy said with sweet softness as he hugged Sebastian, sensing that was what Sebastian wanted to do with Marlene.

"I quite agree, my friend," said Sebastian with a dreamy smile. "She has more elegance and finesse than those smarty-pants gals we met flaunting English aristocracy. She is a daughter of the people. Instead of complaining, she rolls up her sleeves and does something about it. Grace, beauty, and charm lift her above class snobbery. She's a lady." Then he paused.

Jimmy knew Sebastian well. Most all his pauses were followed by "but," so Jimmy beat him to it. "But. . ." he said, looking up to Sebastian.

"Yes, buddy, that's it. But what is she going to do? No one in this town appreciates her, and she has nowhere to go. She also has no idea that the family is about to lose everything they own. She'll probably end up marrying the postman and spending the best years of her life washing diapers."

Life is a trip that takes you for a ride when you least expect it, like that night, when Karl and Greta watched Sebastian and Jimmy catch up with them holding hands, which reminded the couple of the first time Karl had reached over to hold Greta's hand, which she pulled back three times before giving in to what she'd been hoping for all week.

It was on that very bench many years earlier that Karl and Greta had discussed a dream they shared but never mentioned again. As far as they were concerned Arnold, Karl's older brother, was welcome to the factory, every cent of profit, and the soot-stained windows. Karl and Greta had a plan of their own, which included a farm, clear air, and the smell of spring planting.

Life got in the way. Arnold expected Germany to emerge victorious within six months of August, 1914, the beginning of the Great War. He was raised marveling at the boasts the old-timers repeated describing their victory in the Franco-Prussian War, that ended in one year, leaving Germany on its way to becoming a more dominant world power than England. The Great War was to make it so. On August 6, 1914, Arnold, already an officer, led his battalion out of the trenches across a field of fire. The exchange was to be a total victory, like every prior engagement.

Arnold almost made it to the enemy line when an artillery fragment splintered his lower vertebra. There was no pain, but the mortal injury left Arnold panicked. He was able to pull and half swim through mud using only his arms. He almost made it back to the German line when a counterattack caught up with him and a nearsighted schoolteacher from Liverpool skewered his neck with a bayonet. Arnold's carotids were missed, but the hole in his left jugular vein never clotted. Six hours later, his last drop of blood flowed downhill.

Karl's younger brother, Walderman, was also out there defending Germany, or attacking the world, or making rich people richer, or serving the chancellor, or obeying the king, or taking orders from the church, or whatever else was said to convince a man that he was supposed to die for no good reason at all.

Walderman died for being a good person. In the middle of the Gallipoli campaign, he was separated from his unit after a failed attempt to push forward Germany's front line. He wandered for hours on his way back and came across a crawling solder, whom he helped in the direction the stricken soldier recommended. The soldier had deserted the battle when he became the last man in his troop still alive. The sergeant who came across Walderman assumed both were deserters. There was no discussion, just one bullet through the temporal lobe for each man, followed by a letter shaming the family for having a son who deserted the fatherland. Arnold's brave death was the only reason Berlin didn't deny both military stipends, if you count one year of paltry cash worth mentioning. It was not until after the war that several fellow soldiers went on record defending Walderman, and Berlin sent a letter of apology, along with enough money to buy a horse.

Karl never asked by what right a piece of land labeled Deutschland had to demand the deaths of his two brothers. Greta never challenged the right of Karl's father to insist that Karl take over the plant and chain her lover to a desk, breathing soot for the rest of his life.

Neither Karl nor Greta asked what right an old man wearing a black robe living in the past had to dictate when they should kiss, how they dare hug, or if they were allowed to make love, which he claimed was authority handed him from God himself, after passing through two thousand middlemen, all taking their cut. In short, no one in all of Europe ever asked why those who claimed to be right had the right to say so while all the time they were wrong.

Marlene got close, like that night, when Sebastian stopped walking to stand in front of her, and Marlene looked over his shoulder to shudder at the sight of Gunter, Wieland, and Eberhard coming their way, carrying two cases of beer, three bottles of schnapps, and a gallon of home-made rum. Marlene asked why men were allowed to carouse the world as power-hungry, drunken fools while women had to stay home, act proper, and of course take on airs to snub as many other women as possible. Marlene also asked why all the principles that were discussed in theory on Sunday disappeared every Monday morning and why keeping men alive, children safe, and everyone well-fed were not priorities, along with the real meaning of Christianity. As far as she was concerned, all wars were civil wars, and every war the expression of hatred obsessed, the most foul of all mental disease.

Marlene was a good girl, who liked everyone and wanted everyone to be happy. She never bought into Europe's number one rule: make sure you despise the right people.

Marlene watched the boys drag Sebastian and Jimmy away to their drinking party. Then she kept her parents company all the way home, cleaned up the living room, and sat down to read, but mostly to worry about Sebastian, and the world.

15

The Ostkirchen Philosophy Society met in the middle of a square mile of sprouting soybeans. The meeting hall was a twelve-foot-square tool shed halfway between the Bergmans' farm and their neighbors, the Bauers. The inside was decorated with the latest in rakes, hoes, shovels, hand plows, pitchforks, scythes, and sickles. In the middle of the room was a handmade pinewood table that accommodated six chairs if two were placed at either end. The podium was an overturned bread box.

The guest speaker, standing behind the podium, was none other than the nowhere-renowned Professor Eberhard Engel. At his side were brother Wieland Engel and Gerhard Loeman. Opposite them were Gunter Wolf, the too-German German, and smiling Jimmy, who spent half the night seated next to Sebastian and half wandering with the cows grazing nearby.

Professor Engel did not rise to speak until preparations were complete, which included twelve shot glasses of schnapps surrounded by two dozen bottles of beer and six glasses of a rum fruit drink the boys called "rocket fuel"

"The twenty-third meeting of the Ostkirchen Philosophy Society is now called to order," said Professor Eberhard, using a wet pickle as a gavel.

The night began with a toast. Every participant rose, raised a shot glass, and then sang the German national anthem, which proclaimed

Germany above all else and everyone on earth. Sebastian wasn't sold on the fatherland thing, but he went along with the ritual enthusiastically, as Gunter listened to every word and kept lifting Jimmy's schnapps glass every time Sebastian reached over to put it back on the table.

For the benefit of the new students, Professor Eberhard reviewed the rules. He would begin by reciting a quote that might be real or invented for the occasion. The first person to raise his hand got a chance to name the author, which if right would make him the next speaker and require all others to down one drink of their choice. Sipping was not allowed and there was half a bottle and half a glass minimum for beer and rocket fuel, the drink Gunter challenged Sebastian to taste every time.

"Alrighty, then, gentlemen and invisible ladies," said the professor, trying hard not to smile and doing a lousy job feigning aloofness. "The first tidbit of philosophy this evening shall define the field: 'The discovery of what is true and the practice of that which is good are the two most important objects of philosophy.'"

Sebastian's and Gerhard's hands both went up simultaneously. The professor deferentially offered opportunity to their guest.

"That would be Voltaire, thank you very much," answered Sebastian, rising to the podium. "Drinks are on me, guys. Jimmy and I will hold off."

The group lifted four shots of schnapps, one of which Gunter used to hide a snarl.

"Are approximations acceptable, Professor?" asked Sebastian, with heels tapped together and a soldier's salute.

"Of course, my son, as long as there is no hesitation in your presentation, which would forfeit your turn and require a penalty drink."

"In that case, I have a paraphrased paragraph: 'Man is without doubt the most interesting fool there is. Take the Bible for example. It is full of interest, with noble poetry, clever fables, good morals alongside execrable ones, blood-drenched history, a wealth of obscenity, and upward of a thousand lies.'"

Sebastian looked around. No one budged.

"You got us," said Gerhard. "Good job. We drink, you remain standing."

"Hold on," said Gunter, aggravated. "How do we know those words aren't made up?"

"Gunter, you know the rules," said the professor. "Fakes are allowed and only penalized if you challenge the speaker. But as you recall, if Sebastian has a source, you will be required to drink two bottles of beer while the rest of us sit this one out. What will it be?"

"I challenge," roared Gunter. "That's the dumbest thing I ever heard."

"Bookstores all over the world disagree with you, Gunter. Everyone loves Mark Twain."

Gunter stood, angry-eyed, to lodge a complaint. "Foul play! This Twain person was not on our parochial school reading list."

"Perhaps you should talk to your teacher about that," Sebastian said quietly.

"Do you have a problem with German education, skinny?"

"Not at all, Gunter," Sebastian said in a most friendly tone. "Germany has advanced chemistry, physics, and math further than any country on earth. Hell, in China this very second, students are studying German to read your papers. It's just too bad you don't know how to enjoy yourselves."

Sebastian's light tone and gracious grin kept the group in his favor.

"Fair is fair, Gunter," Professor Eberhard added. "Now drink twice. And Sebastian, you're still champ. Do you have another string of thoughts for us tonight?"

"Yes, I do, including words from my college philosophy professor Fritz Kohn and ending with several authors you should recognize. Guess just one, and I will drink a bottle of beer."

"Or a glass of rum punch!" Gunter insisted.

"Or rum punch, and sit down."

"Agreed," said moderator Eberhard.

"Okay then," began Sebastian, looking up to search his memory. "Here it is: 'History is indeed little more than the register of crimes, follies, and the misfortunes of mankind. No one who is correctly informed of the past will be disposed to take a morose or desponding view of the future.

"'We therefore conclude that life is the art of drawing sufficient conclusions from insufficient premises, which means none of us are who we think we are as all of us swear it isn't so because that is what we were raised to repeat. Custom is the despot of mankind.'" And then, raising a fist, Sebastian finished with, "'We must resist the tyrant of tradition.'"

Sebastian looked over to Gunter without malice. Gunter looked back, confused. "What's that? What tyrant? What dictator?"

Sebastian, tipsy on the verge of goofy, bent over with hands wide open, stretched out to Gunter, who pulled back at the strangeness of it all. "Gunter, listen to me. Search for truth, and when you hold it in your hands, don't let it go. Follow it, because then and only then do we obey the will of God."

The good professor smiled, enjoying every word, before he asked, "Sebastian, is that it? Where's the quote? You do remember the game, don't you?"

"Yes, yes. I was just hoping Gunter and I could see eye to eye instead of gun barrel to gun barrel. You see," he said, turning to Gunter again, "You and I are not who we think we are. I could be you, born in Germany, and you could be me born in the American Midwest. Fate is 99 percent momentum."

Sebastian stood quiet when the professor raised his hand. "Gunter," said the professor, "I think what Sebastian is trying to say is that we are all cultural phenomenon, with biologic needs that are nonnegotiable, and that real truth requires self-revelation and questioning authority. That, I might point out, was advice handed to us by Sigmund Freud, the German-speaking neurologist from Freiberg. And Sebastian," Eberhard said, lowering his voice, "your specific quote is?"

"My friend Fritz's favorite."

"That is?" prompted Eberhard again.

"'Believe not because some old manuscripts are produced, believe not because it is your national belief, believe not because you have been made to believe from childhood, but reason truth out, and after you have analyzed it, then if you find it will do good to one and all, believe it, live up to it, and help others to live up to it.' Gunter," Sebastian emphasized, "we are all, everyone at this table, born into a cage of cultural confinement, tradition if you will, and will never be free unless we break out and look back from someplace else."

"And where is this 'somewhere else' that you talk about, Sebastian?" Eberhard asked.

"Ourselves. Our real selves."

"That, young man," Eberhard said, "is the title of one of my six-month electives. But for now," he said, looking around for takers on Sebastian challenge and seeing everyone at the table holding up a hand, "the author! Yes, Gunter."

"Siddhartha Gautama, otherwise known as Buddha. Sebastian, this entire glass of punch has your name on it. Make it disappear."

Sebastian raised his glass and then repeated before downing it, "In conclusion, honor is the reward of virtue, and resistance to tyrants, individual and cultural, is obedience to God."

Sebastian returned to his seat just in time to prevent Jimmy, who was far past his one-drink limit, from downing the punch Gunter handed him. It was the last thing Sebastian remembered, although much to his chagrin, holes of recollection surfaced for days.

Gunter followed with words of a Deutschland hero who would have done more good ignored, "'The great questions of the day are not decided by speeches and majority votes but by blood and iron. It is better to point bullets than point speeches.'"

Weiland Engel tagged Bismarck as the author and then rose to add fuel to the fire by quoting German chancellor Bethmann-Hollweg on the eve of the Great War: "'Great Britain is going to make war on a kindred nation who desires nothing better than to be friends with her.'"

The professor was familiar with the quote but waited until no one raised their hand before jumping in, and then he upped the stakes with words from Bernhardi's *Germany and the Next War*: "'The inevitableness, the idealism, and the blessing of war, as an indispensable and stimulating law of development, must be repeatedly emphasized.'"

Inebriation left Sebastian with double vision. He thought he saw Viking horns sticking out of every German at the table and a halo around Jimmy, who had made it back to the shed just in time to pass out in the corner, hugging a bag of corn seed.

Sebastian was out of it, but still standing, and couldn't resist contradicting the Stormtroopers surrounding him. Without winning the round, or being invited, he wobbled back and forth where he was and proclaimed, "'There is no such thing as an inevitable war. If war comes it will be from the failure of human wisdom.'" Then, switching from Bonar Law to Martin Luther: "'War is the greatest plague that can afflict humanity; it destroys religion, it destroys states, it destroys families. Any scourge is preferable to it.'"

Sebastian attempted a firm face but needed to stare at the door to steady himself.

Gunter knew the saying and snatched the opportunity to introduce Adolf Hitler: "'Any philosophy, whether of a religious or political nature, fights less for the negative destruction of the opposing ideology than the positive promotion of its own. By the living God, to learn history means to seek and find the forces which are the causes leading to those affects which we subsequently perceive as historical events.'"

"*Absolut*" and "*Sieg Heil*" were heard around the table as everyone stood to sing the German national anthem one more time, which Sebastian joined because it was so much damn fun.

"He who would live must fight," continued Gunter at fever pitch. "He who doesn't wish to fight in this world, where permanent struggle is the law of life, has no right to exist."

Sebastian offered no resistance, as gravity alone was giving him more than enough trouble.

"To hell with England," Gunter screamed, looking directly at Sebastian. "And to hell with Sebastian's boss and all the other money-pinchers enslaving Germany and denying us our rightful place in the world. We will destroy them!"

Gunter's challenge breached etiquette, which every German at the table realized. The shed went silent. Sebastian stepped around to face Gunter head-on, who was nowhere near as unstable as Sebastian, who then raised one arm and with spit spray exclaimed, "To hell with Kensington, lying bankers, and the goddamn British Empire. It's an aristocracy of money-bags. They're not going to take my factories away!"

Gunter was speechless. The boys were confused. Sebastian remained unstable until he managed, hand over hand supported by the table, to return to his seat.

Gerhard Loeman, the least deranged mind at the table, stared quietly for three seconds before asking, "Sebastian, what do you mean by 'your factories' and the part about the English taking your family's factory away?"

"Oh, oh," slurred Sebastian. "I did it. I wasn't—wasn't supposed to say that. Jimmy, where are you? Oh, there. Let's go home."

It was time to head home anyway. Eberhard carried Jimmy out of the shed. Gerhard and Gunter placed one arm around Sebastian's waist as his arms dangled. Both Americans were dragged outside and lifted to ride face down, bent over cows.

Sebastian wasn't down for the count, just out of it. Not ten yards later, he slid off the heifer to walk a crooked mile. "Listen guys. . . you. . . you yest can't tell anyones. . . okay. . . okay, okay, okay. . . not the workers. . . and no Marlene. . . no. . . no. Promise?"

Sebastian remained conscious all the way to town, long enough to tell the sad story of Mommy Elizabeth, sexy Pricilla, and numb-to-the-world Zeek. "But I have a plan, my young comrades. . . I do, I do. . . now listen up. No son of a bitch snotty English cheat is going to make fools out of us. We'll show them."

"You're damn right we will," chimed in Gunter with genuine wrath. "What are we going to do, Sebastian?"

They were getting close to town. The group stopped and faced back so as not to be heard. "Well. . . think, think of it, fellas. What is the one thing this shit-ass, goddamn, screwed-up selfish world keeps doing to itself and keeps trying to do better?"

In a somber drone, Eberhard, who knew better but was also young enough to flare, said, "Kill each other."

"Exactly. So we are going to help the world do just that, and get rich. I'm tired of getting soaked riding a bicycle. I'm tired of checking my wallet to see what I can afford to eat for lunch. I want to dine at the best restaurants. I want a new car, a big house, a boat, servants, and to do whatever I damn please, and if that means arming the world with weapons, then so be it. From now on," Sebastian said, hesitating for a second, looking like he was about to rum spray the side of the cow Jimmy was on, but then didn't, "I'm looking after myself and taking what I want."

"I see," said Eberhard, enough of a professor to know bad vibes when he heard them. "And what about the rest of us, and the rest of the world?"

"The world is screwing me over. I should be rich, and the world is screwing you guys over too. So I say. . . I say. . . fuck 'em!"

Eberhard said, "I don't think 'fuck 'em' qualifies as a plan. What else do you have?"

"Gunter," Sebastian said, "you make rifles, right?"

"Yes, but we're not supposed to."

"That's my plan. Fuck 'em. And I have some ideas that will revolution-ize warfare."

"Be more specific," Gunter insisted.

"Smaller, faster bullets that turn every rifle into a machine gun. Back home, my buddy and I could take out twenty rats a minute in the dump, and people are bigger. We can do this. I can buy back the factory. The Loemans will stay in business, and I'll get a Mercedes."

Gunter was a serious operator. He looked Gerhard, Wieland, and Eberhard in the eye. That's all it took. All three zip-mouthed them-selves silent.

"Sebastian," Gunter finished, "I'll meet you in the storage room tomor-row. You give me plans. I'll make a prototype and get in touch with poten-tial buyers, but all on the hush, understand. Not one person must know."

"How long will it take?" asked Gerhard.

"One week, tops," said Gunter.

"Okay," said Gerhard, taking over. "We'll meet again for a private shooting party in the club in two weeks. If we are going to pull this off, we must all be brothers."

Gerhard extended a hand, palm down, in the middle of the group. All four men added theirs before Gunter said, "For God and country."

"And for me," added Sebastian. "But for now, we speak no more of this."

Marlene had left the living room to stand outside, where she saw four men on their feet and one on a cow, which she assumed was Sebastian in damaged condition. She was across the street before she got a good look at what followed, and then she squeezed her eyes closed, not believing what she saw. Sebastian and Gunter had one arm around each other, and the other over the shoulders of Wieland and his brother, Eberhard, both with one free hand to raise in salute. On cue, all four goose-stepped their way into town. Two windows opened for a look.

The next morning, Sebastian was the last one out of bed. The sun was shining bright. There was not a cloud in the sky. That made it worse, but he managed to get dressed and tiptoe to the dining room, where everyone had been and left except Marlene, who was looking forward to his entrance.

His egg was cold and the rest of his breakfast had clotted to the plate. Marlene slid a warm glass of milk and a shot of schnapps in his direction. "Drink these, they will help."

Sebastian looked up with a sheepish smile of gratitude but didn't have the fortitude to maintain fixation.

"So," Marlene began, "how is lover boy this morning?"

"Lover boy?"

"You don't remember kissing me last night?" Marlene said, with hands on her hips.

"I kissed you?"

"You tell me. And would you like to know what else you did, young man?"

"Do I have a choice?"

"No, and you're lucky Papa and Mutti didn't wake up or you would have woken up in the barn."

"So, do I start by saying I'm sorry?"

"Are you sorry?"

"For what?"

"I'm enjoying this game, Sebastian," said Marlene, as she moved over to sit next to him.

"I got to tell you I'm not. And I am sorry, unless I told you that I love you, because, and I know it sounds crazy, but I think I do."

"You did say you loved me, and then you asked me to marry you. Young man, you are some piece of crazy cake, that's for sure. Do you have any idea how confused you are? According to you, we are going to live out our lives together here in Ostkirchen raising children."

"How many?"

"Six."

"Do I get a Mercedes?"

"And a boat, although God knows what you're going to do with it."

"And what am I going to do with you?"

"Last night, you suggested several positions."

"Did you pick a favorite?"

"We'll get to that later. What the hell's wrong with you? You haven't been honest with me for one second."

"Why do you say that?"

"You kept referring to my factory as yours."

"Well, then, if we get married, it will be both of ours, right?"

"I don't buy that. You're on thin ice. Get it together, cowboy."

16

Two weeks later, every cloud was good news. The crops needed rain. At the end of the after-dinner walk, Gerhard and Marlene excused themselves to pick flowers, or so they said. As soon as Papa and Mutti were out of sight, the argument began.

"Killing is a man's game. You're not going!" exclaimed Gerhard, rigid and unyielding.

"I helped Gunter bore the barrel, and I machined the trigger release all by myself! I'm going!" said Marlene, lightly punching her brother in the stomach, who'd learned as a child that she packed a wallop to be feared.

"I'm the boss and I say you're not."

"You're not my boss, and I'm tired of being trotted around like a poodle! I'm going."

"Hans and I are the elder males of the family, and your contemptuousness is pissing me off. You're not going."

"You're a schoolboy who won't get his hands dirty, and Hans can't wait to get out of town."

"Papa will back me up."

"No, he won't. He'll ask Sebastian," said Marlene with comfortable tact.

Gerhard broke posture and quavered his response. "What do you mean? What do you know?"

"Really? Gunter won't take orders from anyone, but since the boys' club marched back to town, he jumps whenever Sebastian snaps his fingers. How could you possibly think I wouldn't notice?"

"How long have you known?"

"Since yesterday."

"How did you get it out of him?"

"Blackmail."

"What do you have against him?"

"Wouldn't you like to know. And I'm going."

"Sebastian won't put the project at risk. You're not going."

Marlene declined to respond and walked on, ignoring her brother, which she continued to do when they reached town and he said, "We're going home, follow me."

Marlene turned left, passed Schulz's tavern, and headed directly to the shooting club, a thick-walled brick building one story high set back sixty feet from the road. There were no windows, neither noise nor stray bullets ever escaped. The spring on the solid wood door was damaged. When Marlene threw it open, it swung all the way to the wall, getting the attention of everyone inside, Sebastian, Hans, and Gunter.

The rear of the club was a bar, complete with beer on tap, hard liquor, and a grill to fry blood pudding to prove that men were men and their stomachs could handle anything, or when they didn't, make a grand show of blood-spewed vomit. Tables and chairs were placed between the thin bar and a glass window partition separating the firing range from those who were waiting until they were drunk enough to fire weapons.

Sebastian, Hans, and Gunter stopped talking when Marlene walked in. Through the glass, she noticed several rifles laid out for comparison—a Beretta, a Carl-Gustav, and two British Vickers-Berthiers. At the end of the gun table was Sebastian's prototype.

Germany had millions of Karabianer 98k's, slow to reload and expensive to replace. There were other problems. Germany lacked the industrial capacity to upgrade weapons, and the rest of Europe was watching. Gunter was expecting a visitor from Nuremberg who had his own agenda, and a secret society.

The object of war is death, and all the gas-operated and recoil-system killing machines did the trick, but were heavy, slow to rearm, and had a wound-to-kill ratio that needed improvement, and by improvement, the military meant as close to hell as breathing souls dare.

The object of a bullet is not to put a hole in the intended. The object of impact is to eliminate all hope of surviving the minute. A bullet penetrating a human body is like clobbering a water balloon with a sledgehammer: you want enough force to explode the entire balloon in every direction. Likewise, hitting a man anywhere from neck to groin is intended to send a fluid shock wave that rips spleens, macerates lungs, dissects aortas, and macerates bacteria-spewing shredded bowels to deplete a body's blood supply in seconds.

A clean shot to the head also suffices, which is why several pumpkins were placed in front of targets at the end of the range. One bullet is all that's needed to scramble the brain. Next to the pumpkins were several rubber water bags with skins thick enough to resemble living abdomens. The object of the demonstration was to prove that just as much force could be delivered from Sebastian's lighter, smaller-caliber, higher-speed weapon as the old clunkers. Sebastian, with the help of his Spanish factories, could sneak in materials and partially constructed firing mechanisms.

Sebastian was preparing to put death on sale.

His German had improved to the point where few could tell him from an original, and he had named his line of murder "*Sturmgewehr*" or "assault rifle." If you wanted long-range, sniper-scope death, it was a rifle; if you wanted a machine gun to turn back an assault, *Sturmgewehr* was the answer. And that was just the top of his bag of tricks: land mines, hand grenades, and neuroleptic paralyzers, which could poison water supplies and yet not be considered illegal gas warfare, were also on the table. All Sebastian was asking for was money, and lots of it.

Gunter made his way directly to Marlene and, with impersonal arrogance, informed her, "You're a woman, you have no right being here, you must leave immediately."

"I'm here, and I'm staying."

"I've had enough of your insolence. We have a guest who wishes not to be seen by outsiders. You are leaving," continued Gunter, unrelenting.

Sebastian was standing next to the bar, sipping a beer. He put it down when Marlene walked over.

"Well, Sebastian, what do you say?"

Sebastian tilted his upper body backward, opened his eyes wide, and raised his eyebrows. "What? You're talking to me? Does this mean two weeks of the silent treatment are over?"

"That depends on what you say next."

Sebastian turned nonchalant to the fellows with a smile that said all was well with the world—his world, of course. "My good buddies, there is one thing you should know. . ."

Marlene moved over in front of Sebastian, tilted her head, and hoped he would not say what she thought he would say.

He didn't. "Anything Marlene wants, Marlene gets. I, that is *we*, would be glad to have you join us, Marlene."

"Nuremberg won't be happy," said Hans.

"Then Nuremberg can go jump in the lake. I already have orders from Mussolini, and Stalin said he'll get back to me. It's a seller's market. I'll be a multimillionaire by the time I'm thirty. Is there anything special you would like for Christmas, Marlene?"

"Yes, I want what belongs to my family."

"Which is just what I'm trying to do for my mom and dad. If my plan succeeds, none of our parents will ever have to worry about money again. Well, look at that, aren't we getting along fabulously?"

It took a weary trip to Cologne and Sebastian's last penny to stock the room with ammo. There was no need to waste a single bullet until the mystery buyer arrived.

Two long black Mercedes pulled up. Armed men stepped out. Then the front passenger door of the second car opened and a single visitor approached. He was fat and wore the quasi-military uniform of the National Socialist Party. Sebastian thought the uniform was pompous and silly, but he kept his mouth shut. The man checked the room. He was not happy. "Good evening. You brought us all the way out here for this dinky little shooting gallery?"

He raised one arm, bent an elbow, and prepared to slap Gunter in the face.

"Herr Goering," said Sebastian, "this is my shooting gallery, and when you're here you will be polite or you will leave. But there is also one thing you should know. There is a weapon over there that, if I so chose, no matter how many armed thugs you have outside, I could use to take out you, your gang, and anyone else you're hiding before you back out of the parking lot."

Goering's face did not react, but he did look at the line of guns, including the open box with the prototype, and then walked over to Sebastian.

"I like you. Are you German?"

"Part German, and so far, I don't like you."

"That is exactly my intention."

"Then you have succeeded."

"So, the only question left," Goering said with a threatening look, "is will we work together, or will I kill you?"

"Two months ago, I told Lord Kensington to go to hell. I have no problem delivering you to the same destination. Do you want a demonstration or not?"

"Kensington? That man has closed more factories in Germany than I can open."

"He's not closing mine, and I have others on the continent."

"I'll be right back."

Marlene moved to the back of the room, at that moment wishing she's stayed home. Hans joined her. Sebastian looked to Gunter for support. It did not come. "I'm not sure that was a wise move, Sebastian. These guys mean business."

"I am sick and tired of businessmen pushing me around. You don't scare a bear by running away. You scare a bear by grabbing a stick and charging full speed ahead."

"A black bear, yes," Gerhard pointed out, "but a grizzly, no."

"And you charged that bear real good," said Gunter as he moved to the rear, hoping Sebastian would be the only one shot.

Six Brownshirts entered with pistols drawn, two aimed at Sebastian, and two held by men facing the guys hiding in the corner behind the bar. Then the door opened slowly. Behind Goering came a moderately short man with a not unattractive face, a small square mustache, a well-tailored National Socialist uniform, and an air of timidity behind glaring eyes. It was obvious that he called the shots. No one spoke, including Sebastian, who was nevertheless loathe to grovel conciliation.

The leader put on a stiff make-believe smile, looked over at the guns, and then noticed Marlene in the corner, where he walked. "Good evening, my beautiful German *hausfrau.* Are you the bartender?"

"No, Herr Hitler," Marlene said with a curtsy, instantly regretting the childish fawn. "I helped manufacture the weapon. My family owns, or used to own, the plant across the street."

"Yes, I know all about it," said Hilter, leaning over the bar as he casually supported his head with his elbows. He had positioned himself directly in front of Marlene.

Sebastian took two steps closer to Hitler, who got the message with mixed respect. "Yes, that Kensington," Hitler went on, "a troublemaker to be sure, and all I want to do is put food on the table, protect hardworking families from being exploited by foreigners and immigrants, and make sure the fatherland can defend itself when the Russians attack. The Godless Bolsheviks are on the way, that much I'm sure of. All right, let's see what you have."

The demonstration followed. Sebastian was only allowed to offer advice. Each Brownshirt got a rifle. One held Sebastian's prototype. Every gun punctured the rubber targets, but only the prototype exploded water all the way to the ceiling.

"I also have the capability," Sebastian said, sitting on a barstool, leaning back, "of copying any weapon in the gallery at a fraction of the price you would pay anywhere else."

Hitler smiled with an aloof dignity that was as frightening as it was reassuring.

"Herr Goering will be in touch with you, and it will be weapons first, money later."

"I wouldn't have it any other way," said Sebastian, "and every weapon comes with a one-hundred-percent money back guarantee."

"Of course it does," said Hitler, smiling more sinisterly, "and I guarantee we will find you if there is a problem."

Again silence, and a room of statues happy to be breathing. On the way out, Hitler passed Marlene and stopped to give her a pinch on the cheek that she reflexively pulled back from as he said, "Perhaps we will meet again, my dear. *Auf Wiedershein.*"

Sebastian saw his guest to the door, shook hands with the man, and watched them drive away before turning around to see Hans, Marlene, Gerhard, and Gunter pouring two shots of schnapps and one glass of beer each, which disappeared before Sebastian returned to sip his beer. It was late. The boys left. Marlene asked Sebastian to join her at the bar.

"Do you have any idea what you just did? Who are you?" said Marlene, trembling.

"I'm me, and my mom could rip apart that little Hitler guy any day."

"You were mean, and fearless."

"Yes, I get this way when I haven't had sex for a long time. Come to think of it, maybe that's Adolf's problem too, and I don't like the way he looked at you."

"I don't like the way he looks at the world. And there is one thing you left out. You just had sex."

"What!"

"You don't remember, do you?"

"I don't believe you," said Sebastian.

"Who said you had to?"

"Okay, if we did have sex, and I'm not saying we did, how was it?"

"The best sex I ever had," smiled Marlene.

"How many times have you had sex?"

"Counting that night, let's see, twice—and the first time was painful."

Marlene moved within kissing range. "My turn. How many times have you had sex, Sebastian? Or should I say Seby darling?"

"Seby darling? Where did you get that?"

"Answer my question, young man."

"I've never had sex. You were the first."

"Oh, really," Marlene said, getting closer, "then who are Pricilla, Shauna, and Julie?"

"What!" Sebastian yelped, jumping back. "How...what...you know?"

"After you threw up the first time, you passed out and mumbled a lot of information, and not once did you mention my name."

What Herman Goering, Adolf Hitler, and six Brownshirts with pistols couldn't pull off, Marlene accomplished in ten seconds. Sebastian backed up to the wall, then, with broken tone and attempted sincerity, said, "First of all, I'm never going to drink again."

Marlene handed Sebastian her beer. "Here, you need this more than I do."

"Thanks. Does beer count as drinking?"

"Not in Germany. For us, it's the same as white bread."

"And secondly, will you marry me?"

"Perhaps. But first, I want to make love with a man who doesn't throw up or finger paint on my sheets. Know any candidates?"

"Like I said, I'll never drink again," said Sebastian, as he emptied the bottle into his glass.

17

An hour after the National Socialist representatives had left town, Marlene got her wish, and Sebastian's life finally made sense. A grand summer followed. Orders poured in from every corner of the continent; the entire town was back to work. By September, raw materials were beginning to run short, but no worry, Sebastian had a plan, and it was the fall, when warm days and still nights had better things to do than work.

Sebastian traded badly needed farm equipment for twenty acres of semi-wooded land and a cabin on a shallow stream off the farm path halfway to Warendorf. He offered to make it a honeymoon cottage, but Marlene insisted on a minimum of a year's stability before signing up for life. The entire town, Karl and Greta included, looked the other way when Marlene moved in. There was nothing the town wouldn't do to make Marlene happy, and there was nothing the town wouldn't do to keep Sebastian's paychecks coming.

Even Jimmy was on the payroll, portioning time between plant stockboy and Mutti's helper, which earned him a kiss on the cheek every morning. Every afternoon, he treated his factory friends to one beer and two hard-boiled eggs, but abstained himself on account of his having to drive his new vehicle, a brand-new eight-speed bicycle that took him to

Sebastian's every night before he returned to sleep in town and get one more kiss from Mutti as she tucked him in.

Every morning, Marlene loved pulling the bedroom curtains open and not seeing a soul; trees, blowing wheat, and a meandering stream allowed the couple to forget the troubles of the world.

"Darling."

"Yes, Marlene."

"Have you ever woken up, looked out at blue sky, and found life so perfect that it couldn't possibly be true? Are we dreaming?"

"Life is what you make it, and love is a miracle."

"A miracle, is it? Does that mean that God is back in your life, Sebastian?"

"He never left. I'm just working out the details. At the moment, I've got my hands full."

"Of me! Let go, Sebastian, we'll be late for work," said Marlene, as she put both arms around him for a long kiss.

"We've been late every day this month. It's important to be consistent."

A stream flowed through the property. It flooded every spring. The watershed it drained was vast, the water pure, and hundreds of fish managed a life of ease. Jimmy and Sebastian would catch and return or, on occasion, fry up a dozen for fish sandwiches.

Sebastian and Jimmy built an arched bridge over the stream. Sebastian described it as a miniature of what Marlene could expect at Sebastian's lake compound when she agreed to move to Fond du Lac. Her calm smile let Sebastian know that he would never get his way. He wasn't disturbed, but also knew that Zeek and Elizabeth were expecting him any day. Sebastian's idea was to invite them to live in Germany. Elizabeth could visit Paris once a month. Marlene pointed out that her folks wanted to retire up north with their farming cousins, which meant the family house of generations would be theirs for life. Zeek and Elizabeth could live in their cabin. To sweeten the pie, Marlene suggested that they pave the road, buy them two brand-new Mercedes, and decorate one of the cabin bedrooms for visiting grandchildren.

Sebastian never gave up on Fond du Lac. He brought it up at least once a week. After two months of debate, the score was Sebastian zero and Marlene everything. Sebastian feigned regret at every defeat, but in his mind, he knew Spain would need hands-on attention, and he loved the peaceful northern German countryside.

One discussion did end in a draw. On top of the bridge, Sebastian added a landing, able to support a bench that could either face sunrise or sunset. Marlene wanted sunrise and Sebastian preferred sunset, pointing out that the last thing he needed most mornings was bright light. Jimmy settled it, "Why. . . why. . . not both build. . . one for kissing and one for fishing?"

"Okay, five more minutes on the bridge and we'll bike to town," said Sebastian when Marlene approached with two packed lunches. A meadow breeze outlined her body through a half-buttoned blouse, where Sebastian glanced before saying, "The finest beauty the world has to boast is right here in front of me."

Marlene's frisky laughter, complete with subtle hip contact, was so graceful that Sebastian's only wish was that time would never take her away, a spell broken when Marlene pointed to her watch and took Sebastian's hand.

"So, tell me, the love of my life," asked Marlene, packing her bike's saddlebags, "just when did you realize that you love me as much as I love you?"

"Remember the day that you and I worked together in the plant and Gunter and I had that little disagreement?"

"The one that almost ended in a fistfight?"

"That's the one, all right. Do you remember what happened next?"

"I said we live in different worlds, don't try to kiss me, we will never be a couple, and then I walked away. Hardly an endearment."

"That's for sure, but it did make me consider what life would be like without you. I discussed the situation with a friend."

"And he said?"

"That life without you would be crappy, and please don't have bacon for breakfast."

Marlene had one foot on a pedal ready to push off. "Give me a five-minute head start to town. If I win, I order a dress from Paris and you never mention the price."

"And if I win?"

"After Jimmy goes home tonight, you pick the room and any position you want."

Sebastian looked down at his watch, "On your mark. . . get set. . . GO!"

Sebastian caught up with Marlene at the town line, but the effort left him with barely enough energy to complete the final sprint that had both side by side. When they crossed Church Strasse, both kind of thought that they were ahead, but neither wanted to move the relationship to the all too familiar "I won," "No, I won."

One-upmanship aside, they decided to call it a draw, which actually ended in mutual victory at the family breakfast table when Marlene got up, ignored by the group, and whispered her compromise in Sebastian's ear: She would pick out an on-sale, low-price Paris gown, and in return would wear nothing at all that night when she would walk to the top of the bridge, lean over on pillows, and wait for him to "join" her.

Sebastian smiled, and passed on the bacon.

Breakfast was followed by office work, that was followed by more of-fice work, which was more often the norm than not—so many orders to fill, so many blueprints to review, and more and more trips downstairs for quality control. Marlene and Sebastian didn't want to lose the feel of what they were doing, so they also devoted one afternoon a week to working presses and wielding.

It was a firm rule to get out while the getting was good, early enough to make family dinner, complete the family walk, and bike home by sunset.

Exquisite delight ended the day. The climax to the climax, you might say, was returning to the bedroom to lie down and look out the window at shooting stars.

"I have a confession to make," said Sebastian softly. "I misquote Shakespeare."

"I see," said Marline. "What have you got?"

Sebastian rolled over to face her. "The summer hath it joys, and the winter its delights, but love is the blessing that makes it all right."

18

September was a fine month. October broke even with as many frosty nights as hot days. The morning sun had just cracked the horizon to erase all but two constellations on the western horizon.

The company truck, a black Ford Model T, made in a Berlin-Westfalen factory, was packed and ready to go. Marlene and Sebastian stood on cold bricks next to the dark family factory beside an empty family house.

"Tell me again why we aren't still sleeping?" said Sebastian, scratching his head.

"Because we want to get a head start."

"It feels more like a head flattening, and getting up early doesn't make the day any longer, just less fun."

"Everyone else has already left. The farmer's day begins with the sun."

"I'm not a farmer, I'm a lover," said Sebastian, sneaking around back for a few kisses on Marlene's neck with ambition to move on to her lips.

"You are also the person the entire family has heard about for three months and wants to meet today. I want to make a good impression."

"By showing up tired?" he asked.

"No, by showing up only two hours late. And don't worry, you're off the hook."

"What? I'm on a hook? What hook?"

Marlene hugged Sebastian before leaning over to say, "The get-married hook."

"I'm confused. How many hooks are there?"

"Sebastian, you know as well as I do that there are many who say we are living in sin and should get married. They don't approve."

"Tough tiddlywinks, I don't approve of them."

"Don't worry, no one will put you on the spot. They will be too busy feeling sorry for you."

Sebastian swayed back and forth, looking as perplexed as he felt. "Feeling sorry for me? I think I should go back to bed and start the morning all over again. Nothing makes sense. No wonder I avoid this time of day."

"Very funny. However, to bring you up-to-date, remember when you got down on your hands and knees on the bridge and proposed to me, and then had a bee sting your eyelid, which left you with a puffy, watery eye?"

"Why are we talking about this, Marlene?"

"Because a certain story has circulated about you."

"I see. And you wouldn't have anything to do with that would you?"

"It was half my mom's idea and half mine, so I'm only half-guilty."

"Of?"

"That you were devastated and cried when I rejected your proposal of marriage and that you still want to marry me."

"Which is basically true. So I guess my question is, why did you make that a headline?"

"I didn't publish anything. Mom just happened to mention it in a letter to her sister."

"Who just happened to mention it to everyone within a five-kilometer radius."

"Actually ten," Marlene said sheepishly. "The family farms are ten kilometers apart."

"I'm still looking for the good news."

"You're off the hook for not marrying me. You get to be the good guy."

"And what does that make you?"

"Too liberated for the likes of northern Germany, but they won't bring it up because if they do, I'll just say I want to wait until I'm pregnant and then look around to see who's blushing."

"And the guys who are smiling."

"They're always smiling."

"Oh, pardon me, I forget the power of beauty."

"However," Marlene continued, more pleading, "go along with it, and you'll get sympathy instead of being called a playboy."

"Does that make you a playgirl?"

"Absolutely. Do you have a problem with that?"

"Only one—I don't get enough of it."

"I'll meet you on the haystack behind the last barn at ten o'clock."

"Tonight? You and me? That's not scheduled time. I have a clock in my head ticking by the days, one second at a time. If we 'frolic' in the hay, as they say, we could… Oh my God! Yes!"

"Maybe just this once…"

"Or two or three days…"

"Maybe."

"And does a haystack mean we are more or less likely to have a son?"

"It depends on who is on top, and I'm not telling, and I'm in charge."

"Well then," said Sebastian, opening the front door of the truck cab that had square walls and looked like a carnival ticket booth stuck behind an engine on wheels, "your carriage awaits you, Cinderella, sex goddess of the north."

No one got anywhere fast in the company truck. Forty-five kilometers an hour was pushing it, and that was after Sebastian added a third gear and Gunter overdrive to the axle; but if you weren't in a hurry, its upgraded suspension moved tons of cargo without complaining. Without cargo, the bed lifted three inches off the frame every time Sebastian hit a bump, which worried him enough to look around.

"Marlene," he said, trying to cover up morning crankiness, "tell me again why the back of this truck doesn't have one of our new harvesters that does the work of four men."

"Because then we wouldn't need thirty people with pitchforks to clear the fields and bail the hay. Five families and three generations would have no reason to spend a week together."

"Working."

"Not just working; there are family dinners, a music festival, a town dance, and the opportunity for the kids to get to know their cousins. And everyone bunks in with someone other than their own brother or sister. It's been like this forever."

Sebastian looked over, surprised but not smiling.

"Now hold on there. I'm not bunking with Uncle Rudolph or Cousin Spit Foot. Farmer socks are bad enough in an open field. Count me out."

"Certainly, my spoiled American lover. You and I will make a bed out of the back of the truck and drive to the end of the dirt road to the woods, totally private, and not one gossipy relative in sight."

As they approached Warendorf, Marlene directed Sebastian down Zur Hauptshule Strasse just as morning recess let loose hundreds of kids running, jumping, and skinning their knees. Sebastian was glad they stopped. The break left his hand free to hold Marlene's as both looked over and imagined several of their own playing, a reality just years away.

The best evolutionary explanation for tears is that they have a mind of their own and they communicate better than words. Sebastian teared up beside Marlene doing the same as both appreciated what they had together, that Marlene thanked God for, and Sebastian, first time realizing, thanked his mom.

The next turn took the couple down Stiftshof Strasse to Freckenhourst, officially part of Warendorf, to Stiftskirche St. Bonifatius, a rock and brick church that was built in 1129 and looked more like a tent-topped Islamic mosque than a crucifixion murder auditorium.

Six-inch wood doors on giant hinges were wide open and morning prayers were in progress as stragglers made their way up the stairs. Marlene had her first "wow" of the day when Sebastian pulled over to park, got out, and started for the door.

Sebastian didn't go in. He stopped short to examine the side of the monstrous rock structure that had sat perfectly still for one thousand years, but not without wear, which fascinated Sebastian.

"Look at the side of this building, Marlene," said Sebastian, eager to share. "It's like someone blasted it with sand but barely scratched the surface. This meeting hall could last another ten thousand years."

Marlene had grown up in a house that felt that old, and she had walked on two-thousand-year-old Roman tiles since she was five. "And," Marlene said, sharing positive feelings, "look at how well the hand-carved stone statues of angels and saints have held up."

"And I like the way they peaked the arches, the weight is much better supported," said Sebastian, again having to feel the past by rubbing his hand along it.

"You're headed for the door, Sebastian; would you like to do what so far you have refused to encourage?"

"Oh, the organized religion business. No, that's not what I had in mind, but something else just occurred to me."

"Which is?"

"That the priests who built this meeting hall and those who worked the building got married and had sex, or didn't get married and had sex; apparently it came both ways."

Marlene was good at retreating within rationality to lay bare what was still in contention. She acknowledged that, in the past, church people could get married and that Aquinas approved of terminating pregnancy for nuns and laymen before "the quickening" fourth month. She also knew that records clearly showed that even after they decided to not let priests get married, they could still have a wife or mistress if they paid the Vatican extra tax.

Sebastian remembered the opinion of Professor Kohn, who didn't believe that God sat on a cloud with a mouth full of souls and a peashooter to spit souls into microscopic chemical bags. Professor Fritz even brought up Aquinas to point out that the reason Aquinas and his contemporaries were convinced that God added souls later, or, said differently, that when a neurologic human support network reached sufficient complexity to reconnect to one's eternal identity, it was not just to justify their own parenthood planning, but also because they felt sorry for the parents of their generation. The mortality rate for children was astronomical. After ten years, eight pregnancies and seven deliveries might leave a family with only three living children. They were convinced that God did not relocate an eternal soul in a living body until age six or seven, the age of reasoning.

Sebastian tried and then failed to hold back a laugh from the joke he was about to lay on Marlene. Then he went right to it and laughed again. "Think of it, Marlene. If fetuses had souls, and most don't even hold on tight enough to last a month, then fluffy-cloud heaven would be overpopulated with baby souls crawling around. Doing what? Peeing and pooping for eternity? Hell, two-year-olds are dumber than dogs! And," he said, raising a finger, making a professor-like conclusion, "there would be more babies than people who have grown up. Everybody says how bad slavery is and then has no problem enslaving themselves to antiquated dogma."

"Sebastian," Marlene said, lowering her head and speaking softly at the same time her gaze was dark and serious, "our eternal connection is a nurturing. Each one of us is an eternal echo."

Sebastian looked over, unfazed. He was both impressed how deeply Marlene understood life and amused she had misunderstood him.

"Marlene, I agree with you. Children are saints, and one of us, just like we are one of them."

Marlene reached over, first for Sebastian's hand and then for the side of his leg, a sign he knew meant the coast was clear and the beach ready for landing.

"And," Marlene continued, flirtatious, "kids are also great to make. Do you have any more sex stories, Sebastian?"

"You ain't heard nothing yet, my dear," said Sebastian, playfully placing his arm around Marlene to walk back to the truck, the ugliest vehicle on the street. "The sex business got better. Pope Leo woke up one day and decided to tear down Celestine's Basilica in Rome, which had been standing longer than this guy beside us, over twelve hundred years."

Marlene, hinting doubt, asked, "Now why would he want to do that?"

"To build a brand-new one that served his needs. He registered seven thousand prostitutes, and that's in a town of less than fifty thousand residents, which means that when you subtract all the women, kids, and old people, you end up with an impressive guy-to-hooker ratio. The sex business made more money for the Vatican than selling tickets to heaven. To this day, the pope holds the record for constructing the largest brothel in history."

"That was a different time, Sebastian. We shouldn't judge."

"Shouldn't judge? You mean like they judge us now?"

"You know what I mean."

"Oh yes, my dear Marlene, love of my life, the most beautiful woman I have ever known, smart, able, and intelligent! Yes, I do know what you mean; the question is, do *you*?"

"I know people change, Sebastian."

"And they can change back. And don't believe for a second that the congregation wasn't in on it. Throughout the Middle Ages, 'proper' churchgoers were fearful that rambunctious gangs of horny young men would cause trouble, so they built and manned cathouses out of town. The rules Europeans made up for themselves turned the clergy into the only profession a young man could aspire to if he craved wealth, power, good food, a grand bedroom, and naked women—or naked men."

After a few seconds of silence and one noisy pothole, Sebastian looked over to Marlene for a comeback. She had none and was neither bright-eyed nor smiling.

BOOK TWO

19

Life is always on the move, unless you count death, which Sebastian didn't, since it's just a layover. But there are pauses, like the week Marlene and Sebastian spent farming the harvest, which included sunset banquets and sing-along breakfasts. The highlight for Jimmy was meeting Olga, Marlene's buxom distant cousin, who, like Jimmy, shared limited awareness, but unlike Jimmy, had no explanation for it. She never spoke but was always willing to help, and she followed Jimmy with her eyes whenever he was in sight.

The last night they spent on the farm, Jimmy surprised Sebastian by walking up to Olga and holding out his hand just like Sebastian had just done for Marlene. Olga surprised Marlene by accepting the invitation, and the four strolled off.

The trip had gone otherwise as expected; Uncle Muller gave Marlene the required hug and invited the two to stay for free at his inn in Stuttgart. Aunt Gretchen and Uncle Gustav made sure everyone knew they ran the most successful clothing store in Berlin and that every member of the family would get 30 percent off. There was also talk about a trip to the nearby North Sea. Twice Marlene promised to go, and twice squall forecasts beached the fishing yawl Uncle Manfred had offered the couple for an evening's sail, accompanied by limitless Halibut and tender red lobsters hot off the muffler.

Erdmann Schneider was there. Cousin Dorothea Loeman had married the Jewish tailor before letting the family know and against the wishes of both sets of parents, who hadn't spoken to them since, which of course meant that Marlene insisted that she and Sebastian visit Munich and invite both families to the beer garden, which they did three months later when it had become even less fashionable to mix religions, an obsession, strangely enough, that no one was embarrassed to admit before God.

Happiness comes in six-month intervals. Not a problem for Sebastian and Marlene; they recharged every morning. It was the world that kept going bad, like the end of the April Berlin trip that was half-business and half-pleasure. The ballet, the symphony, and the streets of fancy stores that charged more for their reputation than materials all went well; the business dealings not so much. Sebastian learned that being an arms manufacturer carried risks, like everyone he met carrying concealed weapons that of course they had to show Sebastian as they mentioned that if anyone started shooting, all hell would break loose.

Everyone who bought guns from Sebastian had the idea of aiming the weapons at somebody else, which of course meant that the person about to be shot wanted to kill Sebastian first, a problem Sebastian tried to solve by selling to both sides. It was complicated: one side always had more money, and both sides were crammed with lunatics on a mission.

Like the night the two left the Hotel Am Steinplatz for the Brandenburg Gate. The rain had stopped but drizzle remained to warrant Sebastian's English umbrella, and staying as far from street splash as possible, which they did by hugging corner after corner as they turned down Frasanstrasse. Suddenly a balding, middle-aged man wearing a black raincoat opened it just far enough to show Sebastian the revolver aimed at him.

"Are you Sebastian Williamson?"

"I am, and if you want another word out of me, you will put that gun away before I lose my temper and fire mine."

The intruder then aimed his pistol at Marlene. "If I were you, I wouldn't do anything to risk Marlene's life."

"The best way to protect her is to kill you immediately. Once again, for the last time, take three steps backward and put the gun away. My miniature is pointed at your skull."

Sebastian never bluffed, and he knew that he could legally defend himself by ending the life that threatened his, but that wasn't his way, and trouble just made more trouble. Marlene slowly slid sideways, knowing that two targets are harder to hit than one, and she wasn't bluffing either. "Sebastian," she said, trying to defuse deterrence, "perhaps we should listen to what the man has to say."

Sebastian never took his eyes off his target. "I talk to people who talk to me. I kill people who threaten me. Which way do you want it, my friend?"

"Okay, okay, don't shoot. My name is Alejandro. We must talk, and there, see, I put my gun away, and I never took the safety off. No problems, señor. Please don't hurt me. I'm a simple man. And so was my brother, who they killed because he tried to help someone. Bad things are happening. You must help us. The only reason I brought the gun is because I had to be sure."

"Sure of what?"

"That you were not working for them."

"Who are 'them'?"

"The ones who plan to kill you and take over your factories. You must get to Spain at once. The people need you."

"You're from Almeria?"

"Yes, that's where we intercepted the message."

"That said?"

"'Sebastian Williamson will not leave Berlin alive.' I beg you, do not go back to your hotel. Disappear before it's too late. If you die before you establish ownership in Spain, the government will give your factories to the fascists."

Sebastian grabbed the first taxi to drive Marlene to the nearest rail station, where he insisted she immediately board the first train for home. She refused. He refused her refusal, then carried her on board with a big smile to look like they just got married as he asked the conductor the way to the honeymoon suite. Marlene finally agreed, but only because they didn't know yet about their second try for a baby, and the shots that missed them as they'd jumped into the taxi and sped off were meant for the whole family.

After Sebastian stepped off the train, he noticed two swarms of travelers: those with baggage waiting to board, and those with baggage leaving. At the end of the boarding platform were two men carrying nothing, who stopped short as soon as he came into view, then quickly turned to look down at the latest headlines at the newsstand. Sebastian resisted turning around to search for Marlene.

Sebastian ached to watch Marlene leave. Her train pulled away with Sebastian's back to it. It was comforting enough to know she was on it. A second train was also scheduled to depart. Its passengers crowded around Sebastian. No one moved; the order to board had not been given. The two suspicious gentlemen, one tall and the other average, both wearing black homburg hats and spring raincoats, didn't take a step but did periodically look over.

"So," said Sebastian to himself, "am I paranoid or almost dead? When in doubt, always take the safest course of action."

Seven conductors made their way through the crowd to the passenger cars to open the doors. Black smoke filled the air above the locomotive as it built a head of steam. With an urgent rush that was not appreciated by fellow passengers, Sebastian boarded and walked toward the front of the train. The two men at the newsstand slowly made their way beside the last passenger car.

"Okay, maybe I'm not crazy. At least Marlene got away. What to do now?"

Sebastian headed for the coal tender behind the locomotive. Almost there, a matronly woman guarding two youngsters asked his help stowing luggage. "My, isn't Berlin a fine city, young man. Nowhere in all the world can one find better museums and art galleries." Behind her back, both boys stuck out their tongues and pretended to vomit, then laughed, together dividing up the candy that bribed their cooperation.

The door between the baggage car and the coal tender was open. Sebastian snuck out to have a smoke, or so it looked. He watched the last passenger climb on board, who turned out not to be the last passenger. The moment the train began to move, the two men jumped into the last car. They were definitely up to something, and Sebastian wasn't about to trust his life on a dinky derringer and two-to-one odds.

The train was barely moving when it left the station. Wetland surrounded the terminal. An elevated mound of gravel covered with coal chips supported wood ties and steel tracks across a marshy grassland still half-underwater from spring rain, which made a perfect landing for Sebastian's jump, except for the frog and giant grass snake that didn't expect his arrival.

Unbruised, unbitten, and knee-deep in water was well and good but not good enough. Sebastian lunged to hide behind an island of tall swamp grass. When he peeked through a slit, he saw neither the shapes nor faces of the two men following him. He nevertheless crawled away.

Sebastian didn't stand up until he got to the freight yard, where his saturated mud suit fit the hobo dress code, a perfect disguise to jump an empty boxcar heading east. Five hours later, his free ride backed into a sewing machine plant in Magdeburg that also distilled schnapps, a bottle of which completed Sebastian's disguise as an unshaven, traveling drunk. He was on his way to Spain's Costa del Sol, the warmest, driest, most beautiful Mediterranean beach in all of Europe.

It could be imagined that the first "out of Africa" immigrant fell asleep on a floating tree during a southerly breeze to end up at the Riviera, but it was an Arab clan that officially founded the city of Almeria in 955, only to have a half-assed crusade take it away from them and transform the

Alcazaba Moorish fortress overlooking the city into a Christian cathedral, which kept the towers, drawbridge, and protected paths in case pirates returned. Sebastian noticed none of this when he rode in at midnight on a senile mule that he'd traded his derringer for.

20

Sebastian crossed the city limits seconds before midnight on one of only twenty-six days that year that it rained in Almeria. His poncho leaked water down his chest and his legs were drenched. When he got off his donkey to read a sign, his shoes squeaked and squeezed out water. There was no one in sight, and he wasn't about to ask for directions to the best place to hide from assassins. Besides, he already knew.

"Tortoise" was the name Sebastian gave his donkey. Tortoise refused to budge until it finished off a gone-to-seed grass patch in the park. When the beast next eyed gardenias, Sebastian left on foot. One hour, ten coughing spells, and an attack of the chills later, he stumbled on La Cathedral de la Salvacion, the church his relative Javier ministered.

Javier believed that his Catholic church, like God himself, must never close its doors to the poor. Sebastian qualified. He wheezed febrile as he made his way up the steps and through the front door that took all his strength to open. He was not alone; a dozen homeless men and two ragged moms with small children were sleeping in the last four pews. No one woke up. Sebastian tiptoed by, dripping.

It felt good to be out of the rain. The walk up the transverse aisle was slow. Three lit candles wiggled on the side altar in front of the door to the vestibule, a perfect hiding place. The door was locked. Sebastian decided to fit in at the back of the church. He fell asleep shivering.

Sebastian's original plan was to slip out at dawn to sneak around back to the monastery. As far as he knew, Javier was the only priest in residence in the oldest, most dilapidated house of worship in the city, which was why the bishop let Javier get away with his open-door policy. Exhaustion extended Sebastian's slumber halfway through the eight o'clock mass. When he woke and sat up, the front half of the church was filled, and his uncle had just cleared his throat to begin the day's sermon.

"I am a humble servant of the Lord," said Javier, a thin, gray-haired man wearing a clerical white shirt, black cassock, and red stole. He spoke without haste as he made eye contact, one by one, including Sebastian, whom he did not recognize when he sat up four pews from the door.

After required readings, Javier added a medley of his favorites:

"My fellow Catholics, he who works for sweetness and love helps make reason and the will of God prevail. Why stay we on earth except to grow, and if we do not lay ourselves in the service of mankind whom shall we serve?

"My fellow citizens, we have come to difficult times in Spain. We find injustice and are impatient, we see hunger and ask why. Many suffer who are not carried for. During times like this, we must remember that God has a plan for humanity and that we must look beyond nation and race to the future of the human race. No man can put a chain about the ankle of his fellow man without at last finding the other end fastened about his own neck."

Then with raised hands, he added, "We poor mortals pray to God for guidance. He knows how often we make this earth a bitter place for one another. God wants us to love our neighbors as we care for ourselves."

Javier next turned to look behind him at the savior on the cross. "I have sworn service upon the alter of the God who loves us all, who reminds us that conventionality is not morality and that self-righteousness is not religion. The cause of freedom is the cause of God."

Father Javier Martin paused for a second after having a long look at Sebastian, who was perspiring and flushed. "So in conclusion, my friends, always remember that faith is a living thing, it must grow. He preaches well who lives well."

Halfway down from the pulpit, Javier gazed back to Sebastian just in time to see him slump over.

When Sebastian came to, he was lying on a straw mattress, looking up at ceiling beams in the basement of the church. Water dripped in from a crack in the wall next to the bed. It was only a problem twenty-six days a year and couldn't be repaired without money. The only light was a prayer candle on a small wooden table next to the bed. From the other side of the light, he heard a young woman's voice.

"How are you feeling?"

"Like I died and went to hell."

"That's close. You're in the basement of the church. We couldn't take you to the rectory. People are looking for you. Are you Sebastian the industrialist?"

"No, I'm Sebastian the broke son of an honest, hardworking American. Who are you?"

"I'm Carlotta Suarez. When my mother died of pneumonia, the authorities would have sent my two brothers and myself to separate orphanages. Father Martin let us live down here for six months, which is how long it took for him to find a family willing to take us all. I have helped him out ever since."

When Carlotta moved beside the candle in full view, Sebastian had a Lake Winnebago flashback. At home, at dusk beneath blue sky, the lake, trees, and cottages all took on a reflected crimson tint. Carlotta's black hair shone with the same beauty below mysterious dark eyes, a petite nose, and a perfectly vertical profile. Sebastian's first impression was that she must be years younger than himself. He was wrong; as it turned out, she had a year on him and two years of grad school he never got to.

"Wow, you're beautiful," he said.

"My God, you men never cease to amaze me! You're soaking wet, unable to stand up, gasping for breath, and with all that, sex is the first thing that comes to your mind!"

"I'm sorry, you're right, and thanks for helping me. It's just that, for a second, you looked just like a French Canadian I once knew. It was a reflex. I'm actually in love with a woman in Germany."

"And yet, you're here."

"Beats dying. And if all goes well, I will return and ask her to marry me again."

"Again? How many times have you asked so far?"

"Seven. Apparently not my lucky number."

"Has it ever occurred to you that she may not want to marry you?"

"Not once. It's a political problem."

Sebastian tried to sit up but got his head less than six inches off the pillow before he broke out in a sweat and fell back. He did, however, manage to turn his head sideways as Carlotta moved to the foot of the bed in full view, which is when he noticed her dark skin, bare shoulders, thin waist, and wide hips, which brought on a smile that he was not embarrassed to share. "You see," he said, weak of voice, "my only companion for the last three days has been a mule, although, on multiple occasions, its stubbornness did remind me of a woman."

"Wow, what a coincidence," Carlotta said with a soothing voice. "Donkeys remind me of men."

Sebastian's dripping shoes were on the floor next to his mud-soaked socks, which allowed Carlotta to tickle his feet, saying, "When my brothers got out of hand, this is what I did to them. Are you always impenetrably brash?"

"Are you always the smartest person in the room?"

"Yes."

"I believe that. What happens next?" asked Sebastian.

"First, I remind you that I don't like moneygrubbing businessmen making the world a battle ground to fatten their wallets."

"And I don't like what Spanish Catholics have done to the world for the last thousand years," Sebastian replied.

"On that we agree. What else do you know, money man?"

Without compromising, Sebastian pointed out that of all the horrors that have besieged humanity, the Spanish Inquisition ranked most putrid, not just because the innocent were persecuted, tortured, and put to death in vile pain, not just because an entire continent struggling for subsistence was denied economic growth, and not just because healing the sick was made a capital offense; no, his take pointed out that those who littered history with abuse did so in the name of God, and then dragged the corpse of totalitarianism generation to generation, century by century. He blamed the selfishness of kings and queens, with Vatican hypocrites at their side enjoying the luxuries serfs, no better off than slaves, were ordered to provide.

Sebastian's voice strengthened for his final remarks. "And all the king's horses and all the king's men couldn't put Humpty back together again, because they were doing whatever they damned pleased to anyone they damned pleased, like Spain genociding the entire continent of South America for gold and slaves as they handed each a cross and said, 'Obey, or you're going to hell.'"

Carlotta's smile vanished, her lids dropped, and with watery eyes, she sat down on a stool and said nothing.

"I'm sorry, Carlotta. Did I go too far? The wrong of the past won't prevent you and I doing better."

Carlotta looked up attentively. "You and me?"

"Yes, our generation. You know better. Hell, *we* know better. And wow, how is it that I keep running into so many intelligent women over here? This never happened to me at home, and I love it."

"Perhaps you were just too busy French-kissing to notice."

"Don't knock it until you try it."

"What makes you think I haven't?"

Sebastian admitted that the American colonists got lucky. Their king was three thousand miles away hunting fox, and the Protestants, agnostics, and deists in America had no problem telling the pope to shove his tyranny up his chalice. In Spain, on the other hand, the nearby pope enforced local servitude with whips, chains, bonfires, and a hanging noose, which made it very difficult to finish a sentence and impossible to write a declaration of independence.

Carlotta pointed out that she also detested the political power the church had over the people and that she hated King Alfonso XIII even more. She and thousands like her were working to change Spain. Their goal was to separate church and state, offer secular education to every child, complete women suffrage, and legislate land reform that would give citizens a chance to run their own lives.

"And those dumbass lords, dukes, and all the other made-up stupid names," said Sebastian, feeling the power of simpatico, "must give the land back to the people they stole it from."

"Yes, absolutely," said Carlotta, limply raising a clenched fist in agreement. "Power to the people. And," she added, with a sly, hesitant look for Sebastian, "all the rich industrialists who do nothing but cash checks will get their due."

"That, my dear, is not me. Yes, I have, or had, much in my life, but my family always shared with others. I'm with you one-hundred-percent. What do you need?"

"You can start by taking care of yourself and not dying. After that, we can use some money."

"Money. I'm good at that—and if you need rifles."

"Let's not go there. Father Martin will be down as soon as the coast is clear. Meanwhile, drink this soup and take off those wet cloths. There's a spare priest's robe in the corner. Get some sleep. I've got to get to work."

"So, are you going to help me take off my clothes?" Sebastian said in a soft and playful tone.

"I'm getting the feeling that you're going to be just fine," she replied.

"Yes, but you would have more pity on me if you had to spend three days riding on the back of a jackass."

"All the more reason not to let a jackass ride me."

"Touché—and thanks again, Carlotta."

21

Carlotta walked up the aisle, out the church, and down the stairs. The rain left the worn steps damp and slippery. Green moss grew at the base of the stone handrail that Carlotta kept one hand on as she stepped down cautiously. The sky had cleared and the temperature was on its way to tropical level—just what the morning brunch crowd was hoping for across the street at Manjares Gourmet.

Out front, there were three rows of tables under Cinzano umbrellas and another two rows around the side. Not everyone sat before generous helpings. Carlotta saw two men, one tall and one normal size, sitting at the farthest table, eyeing the church. She recognized them. They were the generalissimo's aides, half yes-men and half hit men. Naldo Ruiz, a union organizer who challenged the system, hadn't been heard from in weeks. Of course, everyone denied everything, and an investigation was in progress that would most likely never be closed.

"Don't look, don't speed up, do nothing suspicious," Carlotta said to herself, turning down Calle Acuario. "Those apes can smell fear a mile away. If the army planted big shots across the street, dozens of peons must also be on the job. Sebastian bought himself a heap of trouble. Spain is going crazy. Some days, I wish I could just dig a hole and curl up inside."

Sebastian knew that death and taxes weren't the only things you could count on. Deceit and thievery were just as common, but his instincts told him to trust Carlotta, and Javier was family.

Sebastian didn't make a run for it, but the morning was lonely. Father Javier Martin knew he was being watched and that the government, or a bishop used by them as an informant, could show up asking questions any second, so he stuck to his daily routine to avoid suspicion: Confessions after morning mass followed by sick visits at the hospital before opening the soup kitchen for lunch—what there was of it. It wasn't until late afternoon that his itinerary returned him to the church, where he snuck down with saved snacks for Sebastian.

Javier entered the dark recess with a vertical finger over his lips. "We must whisper, Sebastian. The walls don't have ears, but on the other side of that crack, there might be a pair." Then, sitting down to pour gazpacho, he said, "So you're little Sebastian, who grew up taller than the last three generations. The American Midwest must suite you. How is my cousin Elizabeth?"

"As strong-willed as a lion and as powerful as a dump truck, and happy. She runs her own life and is feared by all, except Dad, who laughs off her eccentricities."

"When we were six," Javier said with a dreamy look, "she took my favorite toy truck and told me that she would set it on fire if I turned her in."

"Did you?"

"No, I prayed instead, and two days later, she brought it back with a dent."

The soup hit the spot; between bites of salt bread, Sebastian dispensed with the spoon to lift the bowl to his lips. Javier, true to his profession, took the opportunity to add words from his sermons that were borrowed from the Bible or other men's writings.

"I worry about you, my son. I hear that you have turned our family holdings into cannon factories to supply those who would take away the liberty that God our father has given to all men. I fear desire for wealth has corrupted your soul. Sebastian, I beg you to reconsider the path you have taken."

Sebastian sat back, satiated, and politely suppressed a burp. "Well, Uncle Martin, or Uncle Father Martin..."

"Please, call me Javier."

"Okay then, Javier, I won't disagree with you. Any path that looks down the barrel of a gun has problems, but I also don't care to be bullied or robbed. If the family business doesn't turn a profit, my parents will lose their house and go hungry."

"A man's wealth is the good he does in this world," Javier said. "And a good conscience is a continual feast, my son," he added in a soothing and decisive tone.

"Which begins by defining the word 'good,'" said Sebastian, just as confident. "To you, good means following what others have told you to do. The problem with that is that we owe God truth, and you don't find it taking orders, which is how kings and popes have led sheep to war for two thousand years. If I don't sell them guns, someone else will."

Javier dragged a short, crooked chair closer to Sebastian and then sat down to collect his thoughts. "The laws of God—"

"Laws? Whose laws? Who wrote these laws?" interrupted Sebastian. "I believe every human being must be their own doctor of divinity. Javier, I know you are a fine man. I respect your dedication and compassion for others. What I don't understand is why you take orders from foreigners."

"I don't take orders. I follow the will of God."

"Again, as defined by whom?"

"Sebastian," Javier said with a hint of impatience, "there is wisdom that we conclude in our heads and wisdom that we feel in our hearts."

"One's heart can be misled by appearances and lies. There is no better rule than to consider the evidence. Every personal conviction must be subject to reason."

Javier closed his hands in prayer as he looked to heaven. "Patience and gentleness are power. The final analysis proves that there is only one great happiness in life: to love and be loved. We must live moral lives."

"What you call morality, Nietzsche called the best of all devices for leading mankind around by the nose. Thoreau witnessed the repressed moral behavior of his time cheat many out of the best life has to offer."

"Jesus said—"

"Oh no you don't," Sebastian said, raising his voice, "you're not going to pull that one on me! Jesus said! Jesus wants! God will! God won't! Face the truth, Uncle, you don't even know if a guy named Jesus even existed or said any of those things, which are more likely a collection of fine thoughts by numerous caring human beings and not a bolt of lightning from above. So, see? You're just obeying orders like everyone else, just like the people who want to kill me. If you want me to take you seriously, everything you say must be compatible with objective reality, which doesn't go away just because you ignore it."

"As defined by whom? You?" Javier said, just as mocking.

"No, as defined by us, and rationality, and unprejudiced analysis, all of which must promote equality and freedom for all. Thomas Jefferson pointed out that rebellion to tyrants is obedience to God. Are you certain the God you know is the God you *should* know?"

"Yes, I do know that in my heart, and I will do all I can to serve the Lord."

"You might want to look at the menu first—and who printed it."

"Man does not live by bread alone," said Javier, after he got up to slowly pace, with his hands behind his back, twice looking out the crack for signs of eavesdroppers.

Sebastian leaned against the opposite wall as he spoke. "Javier, you're right, man doesn't live by bread alone. Man lives by slogans and catchwords. Apparently, thinking takes more time and is frowned upon."

Javier matched Sebastian's confidence with polite sternness. "Nothing corrupts a soul more than burning resentment. Bring love to your heart, Sebastian."

"I do, and a question just as important asks why you don't bring love to your bedroom."

"I serve the Lord by sacrificing the pleasures of the flesh."

"Now that's a strange thought, which falsely assumes that God does not treat us all as equals and enjoys the suffering of others. One does not buy heaven with pain; one promotes heaven with love. Omitting the highest form of love on earth cannot possibly be the will of a loving God. So therefore, in my mind, the only question remaining is why and when did the church go wrong? I think it has something to do with old farts getting too decrepit to set a bad example, so they provided worse advice instead. Are you going to fix it? We need to determine what is true from made-up malarkey."

"Truth!" Javier said, aiming aggressive eyes at Sebastian. "God Almighty has ordained the pope his vicar on earth. The pope speaks God's truth and we must obey!"

Sebastian walked over to look out the crack, then turned to Javier, who was standing his ground, firmly gazing back. Sebastian took on the childish look of a troublemaker who had just gotten his way. "So, there it is again. Every time I discuss life with one of you religious guys, I get someone who doesn't think for themselves and ends up saying 'so-and-so says,' or 'the pope commands,' or 'the book reveals' this or that. Prepackaged, unfounded conclusions men like you refuse to challenge, which I do admit does make it easier to live in a holy water cave. The problem is that outside your cave, the world is in deep trouble."

"Sebastian, that's not true," exclaimed Javier with gusto. "I think for myself."

"Feel free to prove that to me any time, Javier. Meanwhile, call it anything you want, but for my money, whatever crushes individuality is despotism. If you look in the mirror, you will see a guy who looks just like thousands around the world, all saying 'no' to 'I love you, dear' when the lights go out."

Shuffling feet were heard at the front of the basement. Both men went silent and stood in the darkest corner.

"Hello, hello! Father Martin—Sebastian—are you here?"

"Yes, Carlotta, Sebastian and I just finished discussing the state of the world."

"Which Javier thinks should be handed over to a senior citizen with loose bowels, and I think must follow humanitarian principles."

"And," Carlotta added, enthusiastic about politics, "did you add that tribalism remains the predominant and most evil force manipulating the world today?"

"I did not, Carlotta," said Sebastian with a casual air, "and thanks for being on my side."

"Hold on, cowboy, I never said that," Carlotta pointed out, adding a playful shoulder punch that brought a smile to Sebastian's face as he thought, *She touched me.*

"We also left out," Sebastian added, "that human beings can be considered molecular robots programmed to preserve self-serving molecules called genes, which we accommodate or pay the price."

"If you're talking about that Gregor Mendel fellow," Javier insisted sternly, "you have crossed the line. God made the world. I will not have heresy in my church!"

"Your church is it?" said Sebastian. "I thought the house of God belonged to everyone."

"You know what I mean."

"Yes, I do, Uncle, and I love you just the same, but don't ask me to have sex with you. I don't want to spoil your perfect record."

Carlotta hid a giggle and then looked over, expecting more entertainment. She did not have to wait long for Father Martin to comply, most unpleasantly.

"Sex with you! Now you listen to me, young man, God made Adam and Eve; God did not make—"

"Lonely priests, horny nuns, and grouchy virgins," Sebastian stuck in, playing to Carlotta, who had more and more trouble holding back a laugh. "And for the record, God made all of us and loves all of us equally, even men who deny women their physical company to waste nights masturbating."

"Now you listen to me," Javier said, losing his temper, "sex is a dirty—"

Carlotta stepped forward to place herself between two penises and four testicles, all on standby. "Father Martin, Sebastian is ribbing you to get just the reaction you're providing. Love is love; one should not deny others love, and Sebastian is in love with a girl in Germany. I'm certain they get naked on a regular basis. If you disagree with him, you attack her. Take my advice, stay out of it."

Sebastian put an arm around Carlotta. "And, old man, if you notice, neither one of us are ordering you to keep your hands out of your pants. Do what you want to do. But just one more question. Tell us the truth. Isn't there a nun, or a housekeeper, or a cleaning lady, an old friend, or perhaps another priest, who you would rather have on your dick than your right hand?"

"That's enough, Sebastian," Carlotta insisted, "you've made your point."

"Made my point," said Sebastian, who interrupted himself with an unstable giggle. "My point—you know, I think you're right about guys and the sex thing. All you had to do is speak the words 'my point' and I was there."

Carlotta blushed and smiled, then looked over to Javier, who was adjusting his robe, which he that moment realized brushed against his own missile system, which felt really good.

22

The great escape was next. Javier and Sebastian were the same height, neither overweight, and both walked a long stride. Javier was most often seen in public with his hood up, meditating. Step one was to use Carlotta's eyeliner to add facial wrinkles to add thirty years to Sebastian, who didn't appreciate having his sideburns bleached. The dress rehearsal was a success.

It took an hour for Carlotta to get Sebastian's makeup just right. She kept staring at the lines she drew to balance each wrinkle perfectly. Sebastian kept staring at Carlotta, thinking, and even saying once out loud, "My, you're beautiful."

Then there was the time and date. Once a week, after morning mass, Carlotta would accompany Javier to the Hermanas de la Misericordia, a nunnery that, in addition to their other work, sorted, cleaned, and distributed donated clothing to the poor. It was always Thursday morning.

"I don't want to wait another six days," Sebastian said, resolute, hands on his hips. "Every day we do nothing increases the risk of detection, and there's a deadline."

"That's not until the end of the month," Carlotta said, placing her hands on her hips directly in front of Sebastian.

Sebastian retained the face of determination, went silent, and then slowly smiled a quiet joy.

"Okay, I guess that make's sense. So, what do I do now? Go crazy down here in the dark?"

Carlotta froze her confronting posture, kept her voice strong, and then said, "Well, do you know how to play backgammon?" She let her arms slide down at the same time a sneaky smile took over.

"Yes," said Sebastian, moving the table in front of the bed, where he sat, as Carlotta slid the only chair in the room to the other side and said, "I'll be right back with something to eat."

"I like my backgammon with white wine and potato chips, but corn chips will do."

"Certainly," said Carlotta with an accusing glare. "Will there be anything else, your highness?"

"No, my queen, I am most satisfied."

"Fine," said Carlotta. "We're playing a penny a game, with no limit on double-downs."

Javier joined in. It was a happy time. Each played a different strategy. Javier sat back and took not one risk that might have won the game. Sebastian went for it all, always going for the move that might either win the game or lose it. Sometimes he won and sometimes he wished he had. Carlotta played it both ways: when she was out front, she would not add risk, but when she was behind and the situation didn't "feel right," as she said, she would risk all. Sebastian got drunk, Carlotta ended up with all the pennies, and Javier laughed and told stories about Wisconsin when he was young, which kept Sebastian at the edge of his seat and Carlotta curious enough to want to go there.

"It's your move," said Carlotta. "And pay attention, we're not out on one of your dates, you know. This is serious business."

"I'm always serious," said Sebastian, as risky with love as he was with backgammon. "Do you realize," he went on, in the middle of his own happy hour, "that I'm about set a lifetime record?"

"Okay, I'll bite," said Carlotta, playfully sarcastic. "What record?"

"Six days—almost one hundred and fifty hours—in a church. I'll be good for life."

"Oh really? Does that mean you've changed your mind about standing at the altar with your grease mechanic?"

"She runs the machine shop and helps out, and I have a plan. If they open a window, I can stand outside and yell, 'I do!'"

"I see," said Carlotta, nodding her head and appearing satisfied with the explanation. "And I'm sure that's just the wedding your sweetheart always dreamed of."

Sebastian, as he was wont to do, rode the passion and allowed whirling thoughts to spin his mind. He looked at Carlotta, who enjoyed the moment just as much. Sebastian interrupted the silence. "Perfect wedding… What is your perfect wedding, my dear?"

"Oh, you wouldn't be interested," she said, looking down, exposing a shyness Sebastian hadn't expected.

"I am, and please."

"Well, all right. You see, I believe that all of us—you, me, Javier, and all human life—share a common existence as an eternal family, and when you climb to the top of a mountain and look down at everyone living on earth, and then look up to God, that family feels closer, and feeling closer is followed by *being* closer, and more loving. I want to get married on the top of a mountain. My marriage will begin a family above the family of mankind."

Sebastian bowed respectfully, then stalled two seconds for fear of appearing emotional. "That makes perfect sense."

"And are *you* going to share? What is your perfect wedding going to be?" Carlotta asked.

Sebastian tightened his lower lip and raised his chin. "Well, to be perfectly honest, I don't have one."

"Don't have one? What about you being in love and all that can't-wait-to-get-back-to-get-married stuff? Have you lost your taste for warm beer and old sauerkraut?"

"Hold on there, let me finish. Yes, it is true that I don't have a perfect wedding in mind; it could be St. Peter's Cathedral or in nature under blue skies like yours. But I do have a perfect wedding night."

"Wait just one minute," Carlotta said, moving so close Sebastian felt the temptation, "you led me to believe you and your blonde did the trick every night."

"No, only ten days a month, except last month. When was the last time you had company over, and in?"

"None of your business."

"Ah—you're a virgin, aren't you?"

"None of your business."

"Oh, I get it, you claim you're a liberated woman who won't be forced into a stereotype or crammed into a straitjacket but then refuse to take off the one you were raised in."

"It's not that," said Carlotta.

"Oh," said Sebastian, bringing his face even closer to Carlotta's lips, who did not retreat, just looked back.

"It's just that most of the guys I know are dim-witted, old-fashioned jerks."

"Most? Not all?"

"None of your business. You changed the subject. We were talking about your perfect wedding night. Are you going to add two new positions or more lubrication?"

Sebastian leaned over to rest his head on his hand as he slowly shook his head back and forth, smiling, "My, aren't you the wild one. What do you know about lubrication? Is that also part of your perfect wedding?"

"We were talking about *your* night," said Carlotta, direct and serious.

Sebastian closed his eyes to focus the image in his mind, then, in praying position with his fingers on his chin, opened both eyes and reached out to hold Carlotta's hand.

"What I see is a bedroom, a varnished pinewood bed, white sheets, and tall bedposts. It's adjacent a living room with a porch and a perfect sunset, where I look over to see the love of my life, who is the most beautiful sight on earth and also has a mind that plays, and laughs, and loves. Then comes the best part, when I say to myself, 'I will share my life with this woman.'"

"That's very sweet," Carlotta said, holding Sebastian's other hand, which prompted a final revelation from him.

"And then I surprise myself. At the end of my little melodrama, I hear myself saying, 'Thank you, God.'"

23

For the next week, Sebastian got closer to God—exactly eighty-seven steps closer, up the back stairwell to the bell tower, where through hardwood slats, he observed the goings-on below.

At eight every morning, two men standing on the corner seated themselves across the street and ordered a light breakfast. Exactly four hours later, they left and a second pair of strangers occupied the same table. An army of underworld demons had dedicated their lives to the death of Sebastian.

Carlotta resisted a single peek across the street that might betray awareness, but she grew skittish by the day and slept poorly. It was the darkness she feared most, which was when the powers corrupting Spain would kidnap political opponents, tie them to a tree in the woods, and then add bullets. It was all the rage in Italy thanks to Benito Mussolini, the founder of modern fascism. Carlotta considered him the most dangerous man on earth. In 1922, he led a small army of thugs on Rome to intimidate King Victor Emmanuel III into appointing him prime minister, and not one person asked why adding the four letters k-i-n-g before his name entitled him to ignore the wishes of the entire country, even though that was just what every k-i-n-g did, like George, the k-i-n-g of England, who paid the k-i-n-gs of several German states to send thirty thousand young men to kill George Washington, Thomas Jefferson, and Benjamin Franklin. When Washington dug in on the other side of a bridge near Trenton, George's generals volunteered the German boys to march across first. The Hessians fell like ducks in a shooting gallery, except for the blood, despair, and screams of pain. How not comforting it must have been for those German mothers to learn that the children they reared and loved so tenderly died useless, miserable deaths so their k-i-n-g could afford a new sofa.

Mussolini faced a big problem—the people knew better. Il Duce found a solution. After forcing laws making Italy a one-party dictatorship with himself in charge, he used the taxpayers' money to pay the salaries of his secret police to kill taxpayers. Those working for him would break into a home before sunrise, drag the victim to the street, and complete execution before dawn. Anyone who talked about it or made a stink would get the same treatment.

More visual terrorism was reserved for public officials who opposed Mussolini's crimes. They were dragged from their beds and slaughtered while their wives and children were forced to look on. Mussolini's most outspoken opponent was Giacomo Matteotti, a young criminal law teacher who selflessly helped the poor in his province and sacrificed his own assets to support social work. On June 10, 1924, Giacomo was abducted by Mussolini's fascists and gruesomely murdered. The church tried to blame the murder on the Freemasons. Documents were discovered that proved the murder was personally ordered by Mussolini. The outrage was extraordinary. Mussolini's career was over. Jeering crowds demanded the king depose Mussolini.

It was going to happen. It should have happened. It would have happened. It *didn't* happen, because Pope Pius XI ordered every priest to resign from the prodemocratic Catholic party that was demanding Mussolini's resignation. Without the priests, the people's party disappeared.

On Dec 20, 1926, several months before Sebastian left for Spain, Pius XI went public to announce that "Mussolini has been sent to us by Providence." Cardinal Mistrangelo, the archbishop of Florence, was one of many who thanked Mussolini, embraced him, and then kissed him on both cheeks.

Carlotta knew that similar horrors were befalling Spain. Those watching Sebastian were just the first step. Mussolini had outlawed labor unions. In Spain, till then, Carlotta and concerned citizens could still speak to gatherings of workers, which was why no one would sell her life insurance. Her most agonizing frustration was failing to get the Catholic church to protect the people they said God told them to protect. The bishop, citing Vatican orders, ordered Javier not to attend Carlotta's meetings. The Vatican also insisted that Javier do nothing when Mussolini had thousands of dedicated clergies executed, which raised the number he murdered to over two hundred thousand.

And the rumors were true. Benito Mussolini was a known atheist, at least he was before the afternoon he visited the pope, after which he praised the world's leader of spirituality, who in turn publicly supported Il Duce and ordered every diocese to do the same. The equivalent of forty million dollars was next transferred into bank accounts of the pope's relatives. Paperwork was also completed to make the Vatican its own city.

Javier told Carlotta that she was overreacting. She wasn't—she was reacting. Carlotta kept asking Javier to remember God's ultimate concern, the spiritual and material welfare of the people. Stealing food from children and killing Mom and Dad didn't fit the picture. Without apology, Carlotta pointed out that evil bred evil and that the rifles used by the secret police ended lives on one end at the same time they condemned the eternal souls behind the trigger.

Javier labored under the assumption that his cassock was bulletproof, which was true as long as he saluted the bad guys and looked the other way. "It's what the pope, my boss, ordered me to do." To Javier's credit, the concept of crucifying the good guys was puzzling. He prayed that God would show him the way. God never did; the bishop beat him to it, with the threat of excommunication.

The night before Sebastian's planned escape, Carlotta trembled for hours as she fell asleep, and not just because sunrise could be Sebastian's last, but also because she might not see another day herself if one of the general's spies got a whiff of their plans.

The next day's sun was a welcome sight. All Carlotta had to do was attend morning mass, wait for Sebastian to come out disguised as Javier, and then walk across town to the mission. The Federal Bureau of Registrations was on the way. Sebastian would identify himself, present stock and ownership credentials, and then officially register in person, which he planned to do by also listing each one of his forty relatives in Wisconsin who were in line to take over if anything should happen to him. The names brought a smile to Sebastian's face. By right of the US Constitution, every one of his relatives owned at least three hunting rifles, knew every stranger walking through town, and were real good shots.

"Oh my God," said Sebastian, looking in the mirror. "I am so glad I'm not a woman; painting your face with these pencils every day is a pain in the ass."

And he did a bad job.

"Pull your hood down over your face," Carlotta said when Sebastian, disguised as Javier, stepped out of the church. "Your wrinkles are running."

"Oh, sorry," whispered Sebastian. "They got messy wrestling with Javier."

"Explain," said Carlotta quietly between her teeth, not contracting a single facial muscle.

Looking down and moving from one rosary bead to another, Sebastian mumbled, barely heard by Carlotta, "I insisted that I tie him up to make it look like it was all my idea in case we are caught or they figure out the whole thing later, and I assured him that you would be back to set him free."

"He refused?"

"He did."

"What did you do?"

"Knocked him out and tied him up anyway. And you, my dear, listen closely. As far as you're concerned, I am Javier, who suddenly will surprise you by running into the government building. My robes will be off at the front door. I hope no one notices, but if anyone does put two and two together, your life is in danger, so no hero stuff—that's my job."

"Along with dying?"

"If need be."

"Oh crap!"

"Quiet down, Carlotta, and look down. What is it?"

"I am looking down! Get back inside. You're wearing shoes. Javier always has sandals on. What were you thinking?"

"I'll be right back."

"And bring a handful of clothes so it looks like you forgot something, other than your head of course."

"Very funny, and did I mention how sexy you are when you worry about me?"

When Sebastian returned, Carlotta was waiting at the bottom of the stairs. Halfway down, he waved his hand forward just like he had seen Javier do to concentrate on praying. Carlotta complied and kept three paces ahead. Neither looked over to the two stationed across the street. They did not follow.

"Can I whisper now?" said Carlotta when no one was in sight. "What took you so long? Is there a problem?"

"Not really. Javier had awakened by the time I got back. I refused to untie him. Then he said he had to pee, so I grabbed a bucket and took out his penis."

"Oh my," Carlotta said, suppressing a smile. "I'm sure he didn't like that."

"Not one bit, but he has a nice big dick, at least after I got my hands on it."

The unobstructed sun made it feel like the two of them were walking beneath a giant iron, but the air was dry and moving just enough to offer a breeze. Sebastian kept his eyes on the rosary, Carlotta looked over to anyone walking by and smiled, adding an occasional, "Bless you," her customary greeting.

"Sebastian, quick," Carlotta spoke twice as loud as necessary. "Drop a piece of clothing and bend over! Do it right now!"

"Okay, done. Now what's going on? And try to filter out the hysteria I detect."

"There's a hooded priest coming our way."

"So, I'll keep my head down and mumble."

"Those aren't Spanish robes, and I think I see the outline of a gun. You go ahead! Turn right, and as soon as you are out of sight, run down the alley between Calle el Almendro and Calle Mosto. The farmers market crowd will hide you. I'll stay here and try to slow him down."

"You will do no such thing. Disappear. I'll take it from here."

"This is my country and my problem," said Carlotta, voice stern. "You have one second to run, or I stand in front of you to catch bullets."

The stranger approached, his eyes following Sebastian. The gunman changed direction in pursuit. Carlotta blocked the way, holding up a handful of used clothes. "Pardon me, Father, do you have anything to donate to the orphans of Almeria?"

The man said nothing, but he used his rifle, held tightly in both hands, to butt Carlotta to the ground, fracturing a hip, which left her immobilized and moaning in pain. Sebastian made it down the alley, across market square, into a restaurant, and then out the back door. The rest of his trip cut a jigsaw path through more back alleys than open streets.

The last stretch connected La Imperia Lola Flores to Calle Sierra Morena. It was only twenty yards from the Federal Registry. Lunch break had begun, the street was crowed, a wall of walkers were in the way. Sebastian sped up his pace around them and kept his eyes open. "Almost there," he said to himself. "I hope Carlotta is all right."

She wasn't, and neither was he. At the base of the government building stood the robed man Carlotta had pointed out. Ten feet farther were two of the familiar restaurant sitters, and halfway up the stairs were their afternoon replacements, each determined to make sure Sebastian was not to have a good day.

"Shot in the back, shot in the face?" said Sebastian to himself. "If I am to die, I prefer to know whom to haunt for eternity."

Sebastian maintained his slow pace, hoping to get close enough to the first gunman to jump for his rifle as soon as he lifted it up. The robed gunman surprised Sebastian by turning around to look first at the two assassins on the pavement, and then the other two standing guard halfway up the stairs. Sebastian assumed this was the signal they were looking for.

The gunman in his way took six steps closer before both hands disappeared inside his robe. The four backup gunman slipped their hands inside their suit jackets for a firm grip on their shoulder holsters. Their robed leader was directly in Sebastian's path.

"If I can get within three feet of the little monk guy," he said to himself, "I might be able to lunge far enough to grab the barrel of that long gun before he aims it at me and then wrestle it away to take on four more guns. Damn—that has to be the worst plan I have ever heard."

Death is always the last door, and no one gets to turn around. There were no options. Sebastian's only regret was that he never had a chance to complain about noisy grandchildren.

At three feet, Sebastian stopped to look up from his overhanging hood. The robed gunman was no fool; he moved farther away. Sebastian instantly sensed checkmate, game over.

It was either be dead or take a long shot and then die. Sebastian went for the lunge. He fell on his face. The robed gunman turned like a matador. Then, from the ground, Sebastian heard the cocking of four pistols preparing to fire. They went off as scheduled, but not as expected by

Sebastian, since to his amazement, the man beneath the robe opened fire with his automatic weapon and made Swiss cheese out of the four hit men.

Sebastian ran into the building.

It was a good day to have a friend—who disappeared into the crowd, bleeding down his right leg. Sebastian signed the papers, which also listed Jimmy in line for ownership.

24

Sebastian was bewildered, shaken, and confused. The doorstep deaths lingered ugly discomfort. He nevertheless maintained a tough-guy stare and don't-mess-with-me posture.

What he didn't know was that when Marlene returned from Berlin, she was perfectly honest with Jimmy. Jimmy was then perfectly honest with Marlene when he told her that if she wouldn't help him, he would ride his bike to Spain by himself. Gunter was at his side with a suitcase crammed with advanced weaponry, and Mutti had sewed Jimmy a monk's robe. Gerhard forged papers that identified Jimmy as a monk sworn to silence on his way to the Monastery of Rocio to honor Virgen Del Rocio. Gerhard supplied a stack of cards for Jimmy, with pictures on one side and sentences on the other in several languages asking for help finding food, housing, or how to get to the next waypoint, an easy task for Jimmy since his sense of direction was impressive.

As Sebastian hit the ground, two bullets had found Jimmy, one creasing his skull and the other a direct shot to his right leg, which passed through, missing his femoral artery. A block from the shoot-out, he fell between bushes, removed his robe, ripped bandages, and limped away with a bottle of rum sticking out of his pocket to fit in with the alcoholics begging for change, which netted him a handful from the few who didn't avoid him.

Inside the registry, Sebastian said nothing, but shot worrisome looks. Some expected, everyone had heard, the gunfire outside. When Sebastian reached the administrator's office, all the papers he needed to sign were laid out on the desk. Two officials backed up to the wall in mortal fear. When the deed was done, Sebastian was tensely escorted to the back door, where he turned and looked everyone in the face. They got the message—if there was a problem, he would be back—in a worse mood.

Jimmy, or a disguised facsimile, was nowhere in sight, but blood was. Sebastian walked an expanding search from where the trail ended, which extended beyond the spot Carlotta was last seen. He stopped short of entering Complejo Hospitalario when he saw three uniformed *policia* looking for the wounded gunman.

When he reached La Catheral de la Salvacion, Sebastian looked up to where he had spent a week watching the world walk by. He was glad he wasn't still there, or worse, six feet under.

"Stay where you are," Javier said, opening the door, jittery. "It will look better."

"Better to whom?" said Sebastian, sitting down and facing the street as he leaned over on one elbow.

"That I can't tell you," said Javier, sitting beside Sebastian, attempting to mimic a casual posture but looking more like a mouse searching for cats. "All I can tell you is that the powers of evil find you a threat to deal with. There's a rumor circulating the halls of corruption that you have infiltrated the city with gunmen like Jimmy."

"Jimmy!" Sebastian exclaimed, standing, fully energized. "Where is he? Is he all right?"

Javier ignored Sebastian and walked to the south corner of the cathedral to trim flowering ivy. Sebastian was right behind.

"You must not look frazzled," Javier said, shaking. "They may still be watching."

The restaurant across the street was between meals, a lonely waiter the only person in sight. Facing the cathedral, Javier informed Sebastian that both Jimmy and Carlotta were doing fine downstairs but couldn't be moved and should not be disturbed. An hour of yard work was suggested to defer suspicion. Sebastian held a bucket while Javier made his way around the church. No one was in view when they reached shade behind the southern edifice.

"Sebastian," Javier said, quietly calming down. "How did you manage to silence the four most menacing executioners in Spain?"

Sebastian hesitated, wondering how Javier had learned so much so fast, then answered not honestly, "Murder is my business. I'm good at it. Anyone going after me, I get first."

"Well, my son," Javier said, with a look of fear directed at Sebastian, "you have the authorities—what is it you Americans say?—oh yes, scared shitless. Instead of killing you, now they want to be friends, and put in an order."

"And you know this how?"

"The cardinal paid me a visit, but don't ask me more. I shouldn't have said anything."

"Whose side are you on, Javier?"

"God's side, Sebastian. What's your answer?"

"To God or the fascists?"

"Both, Sebastian."

"My answer to God is to stop making creatures difficult, selfish, and violent."

"Who are also compassionate and loving," Javier added.

"Not on my watch."

"Well? What about the guns? I'm supposed to ask."

"Oh, yes. The killing sticks. Money talks. Show me the green, and I'll put in an order."

Javier threw his scissors point down into the ground, faced Sebastian, and then put both his hands on Sebastian's shoulders. "No Sebastian! You must not! It is written: Bend your swords into plowshares, raise not your hand against the enemy, and forgive those who trespass against us."

Sebastian spit on the ground beside the scissors. "Listen, Uncle, if anyone on this goddamn continent of yours actually behaved that way, I would, but they don't, and I won't. Today, the bad guys tried to murder me to get rich. Now I take advantage of them to make *me* rich. Fair is fair. And besides, thou shalt not *be* killed supersedes thy shalt not kill."

Javier managed to hide behind a calm, professional tone. "May the Lord come to your aid, Sebastian. Consider the responsibility we have to the next generation."

"We *are* the next generation, Javier, and no one is coming to rescue us."

"Consider your children, Sebastian. Jesus said, 'Let the children come to me.'"

When they reached the crack in the foundation Sebastian looked in and saw Jimmy and Carlotta sleeping comfortably beside a Mother of Mercy nun. Javier stood watch. "The doctor will be back in the morning. He's convinced both will walk again."

Sebastian was relieved but remained wilted of spirit. "I'm sorry, Uncle. A second ago, I looked over and thought you were the enemy."

"And I looked at you and saw the devil. May God help us both."

Behind the rectory a grapevine lattice kept a wood bench in the shade. It was Javier's favorite place, which he shared with his nephew, whose mind was elsewhere until Javier moved beside him on the bench and put his arm around the young man in a most unusual way. Both needed human contact, but for different reasons.

Enemies or not, during the week, Sebastian had gotten to know the men staking out the church across the street. The tall one ordered expresso and a plain croissant and played with his omelet like a boy digging a tunnel. The short one couldn't keep his eyes off beautiful women and jabbed his buddy every time a winner walked by. Both laughed when the waiter tripped over the dog brought to breakfast by an old man, who slipped his pet bacon under the table.

From the ground, Sebastian had seen both men fall wounded as they looked him in the eye with disbelief and horror. The tall man was hit in the neck and managed to stay alive for almost a minute before he went unconscious, which is when he let go of the ruptured artery. The short fellow got it in the pericardium. As he lay facedown looking over, spurts of blood filled his nose and mouth, then stopped flowing and clotted as his eyes remained fixed on Sebastian as his pupils dilated.

"Those men were human beings, just like you and me," Sebastian said, drooped and depressed, his voice weak and hollow. "And they had mothers, friends, maybe even children who will never see them again."

Javier attempted tender conviction. "They followed the devil."

"That's it? The devil? That's what you got?"

"What more is there?"

"Only the whole world and life. We live on a planet of worms, Javier. Those men didn't die because of the devil. They died because they accepted inherited ideas, like everyone must grovel before kings and popes, who slave and starve them as royalty sees fit. Those men were degraded with words and poisoned with ideas, which were, in reality, clever lies designed by history to augment injustice."

"Ideas?" said Javier meekly.

"Yes! Ideas!" Sebastian said, raising his voice in anger. "Mere strings of words, an order of images that link pictures in brains desperate for consistency, so desperate that they accept hogwash as long as it comes in tidy packages and everyone agrees. There is no reason to echo the stupidity of the past, like you and your silly pope thing. Why would anyone choose to follow the successor of Julius Caesar? Hell, Mussolini wants to be the next Caesar! My God, man, Caesar was the selfish maniac who nailed your alleged Jesus guy to death, and all of 'Christian Europe,' like those dead, dumb schmucks, now wants to be just like Caesar. From where I sit, no one gives a damn about your Jesus."

"Who died for our sins," insisted Javier without a hint of compromise.

"Sins! There's another idea that has flowed through ruts in time so deep we've actually come to believe God is an accountant who runs a billing service. Those men didn't die because of their sins; they died because they accepted ideas based on false premises and disinformation. Free minds rebel against dogma!"

25

Two months – and eight Marlene letters later, Jimmy was able to walk with a limp. Carlotta got her sexy hip swing back. There was more good news: competing retainers and predelivered deposits left Sebastian rolling in dough, which he knew what to do with. Mommy Elizabeth's stock fiasco taught him never to trust shifty-eyed, get-rich-quick, Wall Street hustlers. Sebastian preferred the real thing—equity you could put your arms around and know it belonged to you and not a list of coconspirators slithering in unison.

Enter gold, land, and farms making food, whose price went up the hungrier the world got, which was pretty much all the time. Every spare penny was invested, with one exception: Sebastian figured that if he was close enough to smell the ocean, he should be on it, and it wasn't Lake Winnebago's runoff algae bloom; it was the mother of all seas, the blue Mediterranean, which Sebastian and Jimmy viewed from the deck of their townhouse overlooking the harbor.

They began their morning in fresh air, picking fruit from a plate of oranges, bananas, peaches, grapefruit, and mangos. For protein, there was the catch of yesterday fresh from their fancy electric icebox, that was stocked with grouper, halibut, haddock, and sunfish, which the Spanish called moonfish.

"More, Jimmy?" said Sebastian as he got up from the table. "I'm also heating up a bowl of soup."

"Me go, me go," Jimmy vocalized as he beat Sebastian to the kitchen.

"Jimmy," Sebastian said, "let me wait on you for a change. Enjoy the view."

"No... no... Okay... okay... I help... I like to help."

And he did every day, on occasion stringing full sentences together: "Sebastian, we fish today... we fish today? Sicily, Sebastian? Sicily? Always fish in Sicily?"

"Yes, good fishing and fun harbors, but not today, we don't have a week off."

"Rivi... Riviera?"

"No Saint-Tropez either, that's at least an overnight."

"But you can spin wheel... roll marbles."

"I gave up gambling the last time I lost my shirt."

Jimmy reached over and pinched Sebastian's polo shirt. "Here, you have shirt... you find shirt."

"Today, we sail out and back on a light southwesterly wind after we bring the boat in from deep water. You fish off the back. Carlotta and I talk politics with her friends."

"Trouble... trouble? Wear guns?"

"Just our pistols, the usual, but bring the box of long guns and a dozen missile launchers just in case."

"Grenades? Mortars?"

"You know... what the heck... But keep them locked up out of sight below deck, and we shouldn't need them. Everyone coming aboard is on Carlotta's side. They're working to make Spain a democracy. It's just safer to discuss it at sea, at least for now."

On their way in from the outdoor patio, Jimmy, with wide-open eyes, turned and looked at Sebastian, who knew what was on Jimmy's mind. Jimmy said nothing as he waited for Sebastian's reply.

"Yes, Jimmy, it won't be long, maybe a few weeks, or perhaps a few months, and then we'll go back to Germany. For now, we must do our duty, and by definition, a duty is something you don't want to do but must."

Jimmy's answer contained a melancholy tone. "Okay, Seb, I wait."

Sebastian attempted a wise, fatherly nod, and almost got off scot-free.

"And Sebastian," Jimmy said, looking him straight in the eye without blinking, "Carlotta. . . is she. . . is she duty, too?"

Both grinned at the same time. Both looked down to the walkway for Carlotta.

"Is it my fault," Sebastian said, laughing through the sentence, "that I love the love of a beautiful woman?"

"Me too! Me too!"

"Yes, you too, Jimmy, and soon I'm sure."

"You. . . now. . . you and Carlotta. . . but me. . . me?"

It was Sebastian's turn to play let's-talk-without-saying-a-word as he lifted his head and opened his mouth as if asking, "What?"

Jimmy looked up and down before repeating, "Olga. . . We see Olga? Right, Sebastian? Olga?"

"The first day we're back. I promise."

More of a breeze would have been nice, but just enough will always do for sailors. Sebastian and Jimmy were ocean explorers who referred to noisy motorboats as "stinkpots." They lived to feel wind fill the sails and water crest at the bow. Everywhere they went, dolphins surfed the bow wave of *Jubilation*, Sebastian's seventy-eight-foot sloop.

It was a quick trip down to the stone walkway that abutted salt water. At high tide, the ocean lapped the top of the walkway. At low tide, a six-foot drop made boarding a challenge, but nothing a ten-foot gangplank over the stern rail couldn't manage.

In the States, Sebastian always moored to a mooring. In Europe, he learned to tie the stern to hard ground after backing in from a secured anchor. The secret was to back in from twice as far out as one would expect necessary. Tide and wind direction would throw boats off every time. Jimmy got it right his first try by ignoring prop walk, gunning the engine in reverse, and using three times the distance Sebastian tried to get away.

Sebastian's little buddy never failed to impress him, which is why Sebastian saluted Jimmy from the bow when Jimmy, and not Sebastian, gave the order to drop the anchor that day, followed by digging it into the harbor bottom using two gentle tugs before Jimmy brought the stern six inches from the stone wall and Sebastian stepped out to attach lines from the stern cleats to walkway rings. Sebastian then jumped back on board to adjust tension as Jimmy snubbed the anchor line to pull the boat away from the walkway. It was a perfect Mediterranean docking, which everyone at the yacht club called a Mediterranean mooring.

Sailors breathe easy when their baby is tucked in safe and tidy; sometimes, they even notice the rest of the world, like the petite brunette who walked by. The morning of the meeting was a lucky day for Jimmy. The Spanish beauty came back for a second look. Jimmy was wearing his yacht club outfit. She sent over a wink.

And my, was she yar—the boat, not the girl, that is. Sebastian couldn't keep his eyes off her. Again, the boat, not the girl. Jimmy, on the other hand, stood at the stern winking in case the brunette looked back. She did. Jimmy then took a piece of white chalk to draw an arrow on the stone next to the plank leading aboard. He wrote, "Paradise this way."

The sloop was ready for Carlotta's committee, who paused to admire *Jubilation* before boarding. Her smooth water line and high-chin spoon bow were as irresistible as her tapered stern that was designed by Neptune himself. She hugged deep, sat boldly, and supported a powerful eighty-foot rig to speed those on board over twelves knots as she barely disturbed the ocean while adding not one atom of carbon to the environment. A miracle on earth she was, ready to take Sebastian and Jimmy anywhere on the planet they wished to go, and just as many places they didn't.

Sebastian had had enough of the continent and those who crawled its dust. The sea was freedom. He walked to the bow, inspected the anchor rode, and then gazed out. The call of the ocean was irresistible, and nowhere on earth did he feel closer to God, the universe, and eternity, the first name he came up with for his toy. In his mind, eternity was a ship of souls sailing above time, just like a sailboat is a ship of mortal vessels sailing over water.

All lines led to the cockpit, where Jimmy gripped the running backstay as he stood ready to extend a helping hand to those on shore he wished would step lively. He couldn't wait to sit on the wind without spending a cent or making a sound. Jimmy had completed daily inspection, every wooded-through hull fitting was lubricated and tagged, safety lines were doubled, and jack lines were in place if a blow or white squall advised tethering.

As he waited, Jimmy centered the rudder midship with one of the two wheels; no matter which way she heeled, the helmsman always had the best view in town and was within reach of lines to adjust the mainsail, genoa, fractionated jib, boom vang, outhaul, uphaul, and running backstays. She was user-friendly and begged to be tickled. It was love at first sight.

Imagine a table set for eight, with back cushions so soothing you never wanted to get up and a midship view in every direction, including astern to the working cockpit, where Jimmy kept an eye on things. Forward of the deck table was a companionway for going below, where woodwork fit for the Louvre was crafted into a generous dining room, rounded lounge seats, a navigation station, two iceboxes, a full kitchen, five staterooms, and three heads—the nautical word for bathrooms ever since the crew of square-riggers crawled out onto the rope netting at the head of the boat next to the bowsprit to do their business. The wake splash would clean the hull, but to be safe, the figureheads below the bowsprit never looked down.

A sailboat is slow for transportation but fast for a house. Neither Sebastian nor Jimmy expected that they would feel as much at home at sea as they did in Fond du Lac, but it happened. After their guests arrived, Sebastian and Jimmy waited for them to finish coffee and Danish. Both stood at the bow. Sebastian had one thought in mind as he looked out the harbor entrance: "That's where I want to be, far away from land and all the problems men make for themselves." Jimmy put his arm around Sebastian. The longer they ignored the world behind them, the happier they were.

26

The first time Sebastian and Jimmy walked into the Virutas de Embalaje Yacht Club, prestigiously located between two lavish oceanfront royal mansions, Jimmy went straight to the bar and got in line behind three waiters dressed in navy-blue, pleated dress pants with matching blue bow ties. Their white shirts were pressed perfectly beneath short serving coats that had a single waist button and the club's anchor logo on both sleeves. When Jimmy got to the front of the line, he grabbed a tray of appetizers and asked for a waiter's uniform. Sebastian bought him three.

To the astonishment of the overpaid aristocracy, and to toy with the stereotype, Sebastian then stood in line behind Jimmy and ordered a beer American style: "Slide me a tall one, partner. Thanks a heap." Both were packing a new look, pearl-handled six-shooters straight from Dodge City.

Jimmy was wearing his yacht club garb the morning Carlotta approached with her friends. He offered to help their guests aboard. The communist was the only one who refused the hand of someone who should be considered an equal and not a servant of the pampered elite.

Carlotta sat down at the head of the table in front of the companionway. She called herself a free woman's feminist but held no position or allegiance to Mujeres Libres, the formal party. To her left, on the starboard side, was Leonid Vozenilek, the local representative of the Communist Party of Spain, who did not sit until both Carlotta and the woman beside him, Conchita Ortiz, were seated. Conchita was Estat Catala all the way—a separatist who embraced a variety of anarchist sentiments.

Two men filled the port seats: Estovan Garcia, the Basque nationalist who cared less about Spain than his own passion for local independence, and Gilberto Alverez, representing the Workers' Party, who shook Estovan's hand. They were both confirmed socialists, both middle-aged, and both overweight. Each wore green factory-workers uniforms and combed their brown hair straight back. They were men of the people and made sure they looked the part.

Sangria, chitchat, and guacamole dominated the table until land disappeared off the stern and Sebastian joined the group by invitation. The first order of business was to come up with a name for themselves. The twenty homespun parties that were attempting to combine votes spent more time arguing among themselves than they did opposing the fascists. The only thing the first thirty minutes accomplished was agreeing that they all leaned to the left and most, with the exception of Leonid, favored democracy. Leonid was outvoted but acquiesced reluctantly. The name of their group would be the Democratic Republican Front, most always referred to as the Republicans.

The goal, Carlotta pointed out, was to establish political harmony providing justice and equality for all so that future generations could enjoy freedom and be protected from those who would take advantage of the poor.

"Why, yes, of course," said Comrade Vozeniliek, standing up briskly and then grasping the table to steady himself, counterbalancing the boat's tilt, "and we in Spain have no obligation to those who have exploited us for centuries. As long as industrialists control our country's purse strings, they can hire and fire whom they wish and keep the working class half-starved and desperate."

Estovan, Gilberto, Carlotta, and petite, wavy-haired Conchita all knocked gently on the table, approving the pronouncement.

"And what's more," Vozeniliek continued, "we will need a strong leader to enforce the will of the people, someone who can level castles to plant potatoes. No one need starve. The best fortune one can be born to is a pursuit that finds happiness in employment, which could be making baskets, digging ditches, or growing food. Honor lies in honest toil. We must share the fields, our food, and our fortunes."

Carlotta noticed Sebastian leaning back, trying to avoid involvement. "Well Sebastian, what do you think?"

Sebastian looked her in the eye as the middle of his lower lip raised to a frown and then moved his gaze to Vozeniliek. "Your revolution left millions dead and even more starving to death. In Spain, just whom do you have in mind to run this perfect country of yours?"

"A powerful leader will be necessary."

"Throughout history," Sebastian said directly, "necessity has been the excuse for *every* infringement of human freedom. It is the argument of tyrants, the creed of slaves. Your system will be overtaken by totalitarians before the horse leaves the gate. And there is one more thing that I know for sure: the best government is the least government, and the fewer laws the better."

"Hogwash," Vozeniliek countered with disgust. "Someone must stand up to pigheaded kings and deluded religious fanatics. The people deserve freedom."

Carlotta interrupted Sebastian's reply. "Leonid my dear friend, what guarantee do we have that when rising from the chains of oppression, the communist czar we get will not be worse than the church state that holds our heads under water now?"

"All communists are brothers."

"So were Cain and Abel," added Sebastian. "I expect your system will result in identical tragedy."

"You," said Leonid Vozeniliek with fire in his eyes, "are a fool!"

Sebastian sat back and looked at Carlotta, who had her hands to-gether, begging him to cool down. He did before adding, "Your obstinacy of opinion is certain proof that you have not thought the matter through. Everyone else at this table prefers democracy. If that is not your wish, per-haps you would like to fish off the stern with Jimmy and leave us alone. Only the foolish and the dead never change their opinion."

Leonid looked around before waving a hand sideways. "If you insist, then certainly, for now, continue."

Sebastian slid back and crossed his arms for less than a minute be-fore he leaned forward to listen attentively to Carlotta, who he thought at first had changed the subject by pointing out that the human race almost went extinct. "Recent digs have documented that our ancestors dwindled to fewer than a thousand. The animal world that we now protect nearly did us in. The only reason we didn't vanish from the face of the earth is because men can be bastards and women just as tough. There is meanness and opportunism among us."

Not what the table expected, but they were curious enough to silence the air, waiting for Carlotta's conclusion.

"That's why," Carlotta said, looking directly at Vozeniliek, "we can't hand any man or woman absolute power; they will morph back into clubbing apes and dig graves for everyone who opposes them. And rule number two," she said, as Sebastian grinned, lightly tapping the table in approval, "is that we vanquish the audacity that suggests violence of any kind is a legitimate means to an end. Sebastian is right: every one of us is Cain, everyone one of us could be Abel."

"Yes, yes, yes. . ." repeated Sebastian, as he continued to tap the table with his left forefinger as his right hand drew and spun his six-shooter, "this is what Abel needed."

Estovan the socialist and Gilberto the socialist were up next, taking turns sharing the platform like good socialists should. They began by pointing out that socialism began the first day two primates shared the same path and then evolved paved streets, planed cities, and organized healthcare. "It has never been a question about the wisdom of socialism," Estovan pointed out calmly, "it is only a matter of degree."

"And," Gilberto added, "if we are to live in harmony, with everyone's expectations met, socialism must be extended to ensure that every man and every woman is offered meaningful employment and every child is guaranteed the highest quality education."

"Yes, yes. . ." howled Vozeniliek, "but how you are going to keep out the rats? Socialists are infamous for hegemony and embezzlement. I tell you, I tell you right now, socialism is a weak substitute for real progress."

"Leonid," Carlotta said, gently placing her hand on his forearm, "let them finish. They know as much about exploitation as you do."

Sebastian left the midship soiree to help Jimmy finish his noon sextant sighting, but didn't miss a word. Carlotta moved the discussion along with less emotion and more reasoning. The subject was financial debt and the stress it chains to every day.

"So," Gilberto responded, "on this, we agree with the Russians: every castle, every title, every crown head, and all class structure must disappear from the face of the earth."

"To be replaced by what?" Sebastian asked politely.

"A life free of debt," Estovan said, subdued and joyful.

Sebastian was in total agreement when the two went on to chastise the church for belittling mankind with made-up original sin and then further diminished confidence by saying, "You're a bad person. . . you're a bad person. . . you're a bad person."

"That's not how the *Little Engine that Could* made it up the hill," said Sebastian.

"And what came next? 'You're poor. . . you're poor. . . you're poor,'" said Gilberto, who pointed out that civilization was already capable of providing a comfortable living for every human being on the planet from what was produced. The problem was distribution, waste, wars, and the nobility.

"And also," Estovan said, "there is no reason we must fear poverty and the trepidation it shatters. The earth is here. Everything we need is here. If we share and care for one another, no one will want or worry."

"Okay," Sebastian said, half taking the bait. "How are people to be paid?"

"In proportion to work hours," answered Gilberto.

"I'm not buying this," Sebastian said, turning his head to the side, looking to Carlotta for a comment and getting none. "Human beings are lazy, like me. I once thought I would never have to go to work. Why bother getting out of bed in the morning if your house and a job will be there one way or another?"

Estovan laughed, remembering his own pampered upbringing. "Have you ever tried staying in bed in all morning? It is *really* boring. We human beings need and want something to do. Challenge makes life."

"And if one does get lazy," Gilberto interrupted, "they don't earn extra income, they eat beans, and they walk to the park. But if you work hard, invent something special, or develop artistic talents, you order steak and weekend in one resort after another. Socialism doesn't mean doing nothing and going nowhere, it just sets the stage for everything else."

Gilberto stood up to watch a dozen flying fish leap from the sea, one of which bounced off the foredeck and back into the water.

"Extra work can always result in luxuries, just not the ridiculous disparity that the world now insults God with. The slate will wipe clean at the end of each life for the next generation to enjoy equal opportunity."

"That pay thing sounds a lot like capitalism to me," said Sebastian.

"Perhaps," Carlotta chimed in, "but only to reward extra achievement with things like this boat. Personally, I would prefer a stable of horses."

"Then go for it, my dear," said Estovan, shaking her hand.

"*Reichsmarine! Reichsmarine!*" yelled Jimmy from the stern, pointing north.

Sebastian grabbed his binoculars and steadied himself at the bow. "SMS *Arcona*. . . Gazelle-class cruiser. . . three thousand tons. . .ten, one-hundred-five millimeter guns. We are definitely outgunned. Jimmy, hoist our German flag alongside the yacht club burgee pennant. We'll be fine."

And they were. The ship, however, did slow down for inspection as it passed, when all six on board, including Jimmy at the helm, raised champagne glasses to toast the officers on deck, who were so close that Jimmy counted the medals on their dress uniforms. To add a playful touch to their guise, cute little Conchita put her arms around Leonid's waist as Sebastian and Carlotta held hands.

"It is important," said Sebastian in mock seriousness, "that we are as convincing as possible."

"By doing what?" Carlotta asked, as she looked over to the monstrous steel structure steaming by at twenty knots.

"Oh," Sebastian said, "I know just the thing."

With that, he swung Carlotta around, placed his left arm behind her back, wrapped his right arm even lower, and lifted her off the ground for a big kiss felt around their worlds, which Carlotta clung to longer than the tall guy.

27

When the wind shifted, Sebastian took the helm. Waves sideswiped the bow and swells lifted the beam every thirty seconds. A flock of seagulls followed astern, waiting for Jimmy to toss over more leftover bait. Sebastian was a fine helmsman; their wake ran true. No autopilot on earth can forecast course adjustments as accurately as a sailor standing watch. The greatest adventure on earth is the domain of the human mind, a grand disappointment that day, thanks to the German gunship.

As Jimmy looked back, he was as pensive as Sebastian.

"Do you remember when we played in my mom's big tub, Jimmy?"

Jimmy nodded and smiled through sad feelings. Back in the tub, he and Sebastian would float boats, play battleship, and then play checkers. The head injury ended all that, but the memories remained.

"It was so simple," Sebastian said, no longer the man with every answer. "We had toy guns, toy boats, bikes, and our BB guns to chase snakes away. We would even play soldier, remember?"

Jimmy nodded, no happier as he watched the destroyer disappear.

"All that metal," Sebastian went on in a dirge, "all those young men taken from their homes, thousands of pounds of explosives ready to kill or, just as likely, detonate to blow up everyone on board. And the expense! Each one of those ships is a hospital that was never built.

One-tenth of the European fleet is worth more than it would take to end world hunger."

Jimmy communicated as often with his hands as with broken words, that moment moving his eyes around and spinning his right index finger next to his temple, signaling, "Crazy. . . yes, crazy."

"No one wants to hear the truth if it contradicts the make-believe they have settled for, but what we were told doesn't make sense, and we don't want to face facts, like building ships and bombs to kill people because men are required to be honorable soldiers. All us boys are told that it is our duty is to kill and be killed for a piece of land on a map that someone drew a line around with a pencil hundreds of years ago. And of course, it's better to be dead than question why."

Jimmy bowed respect for the opinion and then pretended to hold a baby in his arms, rocking back and forth as he smiled, looking down.

"Yes, Jimmy, having a family, falling in love, living life, and, yes, going fishing are worth so much more than that tin can of death out there."

Carlotta, still glowing from the rush of affection, made her way aft to stand at the end of the elevated dining deck.

"I heard what you said, Sebastian," she said with a shiver of fear. "Peace on earth is a pathetic fallacy. Plato saw the public as a bewildered herd of beasts floundering in the chaos of public opinion, which, for the most part, is governed by the entitled to dominate public consensus."

"And every historical period," Sebastian added, turning to face her, "contains its own idea of Utopia, which today, in England, Germany, France, Russia, and Spain, includes their flag flying over every front door on the planet. Jimmy is right. People are crazy."

Carlotta sat down on the first of five steps leading back to the working helm station. "So what are you going to do about it, Sebastian?"

"The plan is simple. It begins by refusing to encourage made-up religions and trumped-up patriotism at the same time you do what you can to kick royalty in the ass. As for me, I fully intend to beat them at their own game. I will be rich, secure, and safe on the ranch of my dreams, thousands of miles from here."

"You can do better than that, Sebastian."

"No, I can't, and I don't want to."

"Yes, you do."

"Do what?"

"Help me and the Republican front harness capitalist machinery to work for the people as we establish egalitarian justice. We will redistribute wealth to help the underprivileged of the planet and, in so doing, eliminate the need for young men to die generation after generation on ships like the one that could have just sunk us."

Sebastian had no reply. Carlotta returned to the table, but not before Conchita, who had some kind of enzyme deficiency that made her susceptible to drinking alcohol, had polished off her second glass.

"Jimmy," Sebastian said, suddenly sensing a brick wall between himself and Carlotta, "let those blundering fools on land ruin their lives. A beautiful woman is a joy forever, and all we have to do is share love with our special someone and we have saved our world. We'll work and play with pride. We don't need to do anything else."

Jimmy glanced the saddest, most serious look Sebastian had ever seen.

"So you think I'm wrong too?" asked Sebastian.

Jimmy shrugged his shoulders, but his mood did not change.

"Why the hell should I give a damn about Carlotta anyway? Who cares what she thinks? I'm my own man, but wow, this is a day of days." Sebastian added, cooling down, "When I got the Dear John letter from Pricilla, I was hurt, but I knew it was all for the best. When Shauna would have nothing to do with me, I felt shallow but mostly missed her in bed. Marlene made me happier than I had ever been, but now she's not here and it seems like forever since I've held her in my arms. I suppose the last few months have proved that I can live without her.

"Then Carlotta comes along and nurses me, a complete stranger, back to health in the middle of the battle of her life, and not for one minute did she put herself first. And listen to this, Jimmy, when she just walked away, I felt like we did as kids when it was getting dark and we hadn't found our way out of the woods, you remember, with coyotes and wolves howling. And yet, nothing else here scares me—not the bad guys, not their weapons; but there it is, almost like being nauseous. I have everything I want. There is no reason for me to feel empty inside. I'm beginning to think I haven't the slightest idea what I'm doing."

Jimmy held both hands out in front of him, shaking nervously, and then put them together and they quieted down.

"I think you're right," continued Sebastian, "but how could this be happening to me? What did I do wrong? Why without Carlotta do I suddenly feel lonely?"

From midship, Carlotta yelled, "Sebastian, we're finishing our meeting. Would you like to join us?"

"One second! Ready about," he said, manning the port and starboard genoa lines. "Hard alee!"

As *Jubilation* turned around, Leonid insisted he man the helm to free up Jimmy, whom he perceived was overworked by Sebastian. Jimmy handed Leonid the wheel and joined Conchita, who was standing on the top bar of the bow pulpit, facing forward. Jimmy grabbed a life jacket and secured it around tipsy Conchita, who, unknown to Carlotta, had snuck forward a bottle of schapps, which, unknown to Sebastian, Jimmy was offered.

Carlotta returned to the table to establish eye contact with the two socialists beside her. Sebastian stood at the opposite end of the table to keep his eye on Jimmy and Conchita on the foredeck. They were walking over hatches that Sebastian wisely secured before putting to sea.

Happy Conchita was in the mood for a parade, which on board went around the mast, with Jimmy right behind her holding up an American flag.

"Uh-oh," said Sebastian, "Jimmy doesn't drink."

"Uh-oh also," said Carlotta when she turned around to see two drunks marching in a circle for their own Fourth of July parade, "neither does Conchita."

"Yeah… Yeah… July… four," sang Jimmy, wobbling less than Conchita.

"I guess that's as good a place to start as any," Carlotta said, turning back to the group. "Spain needs a Fourth of July. I admire the example the American colonies set the day they told kings, popes, mullahs, and rabbis to go to hell."

Jimmy and swaying Conchita heard every word. Before beginning another rotation, she stopped, faced the stern, and proclaimed, "Europe, the hell with you! The ruling class are idiots, the continent is in decay, no one uses good sense, and the whole bunch of crapheads deserve the solitude and despair they get from the stupid organized insanity of warfare. They fight, they lose, God cries… Give power to the people instead!"

When the parade resumed, Carlotta got back to business. "We shouldn't have given her that glass of champagne, but don't worry, she'll be fine."

Carlotta followed America's Fourth of July reference with Thomas Jefferson, who pointed out that the God who gave mankind life also gifted liberty at the same time. "Ralph Waldo Emerson," she then said proudly, "sized up a civilization by the extent it to which it allowed smart women to participate. We live surrounded by those who pray to Rome and Mecca and claim God told them to, yet neither group allows women to participate or hold a single position of leadership in their scheme of worship. Individual insanity is rare, but apparently national insanity is the rule."

Carlotta also pointed out that five hundred years before Catholicism cut and pasted the Golden Rule, and over a thousand years before Muhammed repeated the same thought backward, Confucius recommended that what you do not want others to do to you, do not do to others.

Jimmy held Conchita's hand when she walked by the mast and then stopped just a foot short of the open companionway. Conchita raised the hand Jimmy was holding, who had the American flag straight up in his other, and proclaimed in high-pitched, squeaky tones:

"We are not reformists! We are revolutionaries! To hell with authoritarian regimes! To hell with the supercilious hypocrisy of phlegmatic preachers! To hell with Stalinist sophistry! To hell with fundamentalists who believe they are better than everyone else! And go to hell anyone who gets in our way! Nationalism is an infantile disease! Get ready world, class struggle is alive and dangerous. The cause of freedom is the cause of God!"

Sebastian made his way down the port rail to stand next to Carlotta. "Now who is she quoting?"

"I haven't the slightest idea," Carlotta said, amused. "I think everyone at once."

Sebastian felt better standing there but resisted putting his arm around Carlotta as he nodded agreement. She mentioned that human history had always been a race between education and catastrophe and that if the teachings derived, or blamed on the "unholy" Bible, as she called it, flatly violated reason, then the texts themselves amounted to a crime against reason and also God himself. "It is better to know nothing than to swear by what is not so."

Sebastian thought of himself as somewhat of a wild-ass rebel, but as he listened to Carlotta, he felt more like a first grader. "Your Twain," she said, "criticized Europe and the American population it bred for forcing its way by making sure everyone inherited the idea that all men without title and a long pedigree, whether they had great natural gifts and acquirements or hadn't, were creatures of no more consideration than so many animals, bugs, and insects."

Sebastian was mesmerized by Carlotta. She took advantage of the opportunity to read from *A Connecticut Yankee in King Arthur's Court.*

Before the day of the Church's supremacy in the world, men were men, and held their heads up, and had a man's pride and spirit and independence; and what of greatness and position a person got, he got mainly by achievement, not by birth. But then the Church came to the front, with an ax to grind; and she was wise, subtle, and knew more than one way to skin a cat—or a nation; she invented "divine right of kings," and propped it all around, brick by brick, with the Beatitudes—wrenching them from their good purpose to make them fortify an evil one; she preached (to the commoner) humility, obedience to superiors, the beauty of self-sacrifice; she preached (to the commoner) meekness under insult; preached (still to the commoner, always to the commoner) patience, and nonresistance under oppression; and she introduced heritable ranks and aristocracies, and taught all the Christian population of the earth to bow down to them and worship them. In short, they insisted that commoners love and honor the lash that makes them slaves. Dogs know better—they bite strangers who kick them.

"I also recall," Sebastian added, "that Mark Twain blamed the church for the death of human liberty and the paralysis of human thought."

Carlotta's voice resonated with aggression when she added her own opinion: "Exodus, Numbers, Deuteronomy, Joshua, and Samuel all report that God commanded Moses, and others, to slay 'man and woman, infant and suckling with the edge of the sword.' Any manual that recommends stabbing eleven-year-old girls, cutting the throats of five-year-old boys, and smashing infant skulls on boulders is an affront to God, which makes the book and those who promote it the enemy of God himself.

"The irony of Amalekite genocide is that, throughout history, the ancient reader's digest named 'the Bible' was used to justify barbarism, not to mention opportunism, like the massacre of the Midianites, when Moses protested against leaving survivors as he said, 'Now kill all the boys. And kill every woman who has slept with a man, but save for yourselves every girl who has never slept with a man.'"

Sebastian loved hearing fire and brimstone turned on those who spewed it.

"Carlotta, I couldn't agree more. We must stop fooling ourselves and apologizing to each other. It is time for the truth—THE EMPEROR HAS NO CLOTHES!"

"From now on," Carlotta added, holding up Sebastian's arm like a prize fighter who'd just won the title, "we support God, not self-serving, man-made organizations!"

Carlotta and Sebastian both looked around to see Jimmy and Conchita listening quietly.

"God's divine plan for the universe," Carlotta continued calmly, "provides us with a means to understand the universe, ourselves, and his will. It's called science. Facts matter. Reality counts. Our children deserve to hear the truth in public schools and not be brainwashed by a mandatory system."

"Yeah, hurray! That a girl," cheered Conchita, as Jimmy swung the flag back and forth.

Sebastian was asked to make a closing remark. He chose Abraham Lincoln: "No man is good enough to govern another without the continual consent of all others. Governments exist to protect the rights of minorities, and in the end, we are all a minority of one."

"We shall therefore," said Estovan, standing beside Gilberto, who was already on his feet with fist held high,, "no longer be controlled by spoiled aristocrats, ruthless tyrants, selfish bosses, or misled preachers."

"What we will do," Gilberto asserted even louder, "is reconceptualize social justice to enlarge the full range of human potential. We will be masters of our own fate and slaves to none."

Conchita went back to marching circles and singing songs in Spanish. Jimmy was right behind her, making noises like a drum beating cadence. Last in line was Sebastian, who reached over to pull what was left of the schnapps from Jimmy's back pocket. Carlotta and Sebastian finished the bottle off.

28

Love is a gift of no equal, but it can also be a disappointment of no comparison for those who allow it to pass unheeded. Boaters are lovers. They share a mistress who never sleeps and is rarely silent. When she breaths the power of creation sings, only to howl like a banshee when she rips loose a gale, or worse, a typhoon to bury the iron men who go down to the sea in ships. Her most enchanting melody rocks keels below twinkling stars to sleep sounder than in a baby's crib.

Sebastian and Jimmy embraced the Sirens every chance they got. Carlotta kept the big guy company at the helm. Conchita sobered slowly, sitting over the anchor locker at the bow with Jimmy, who kept smiling, and smiling, and smiling.

Gilberto moved to the starboard side of the table to face Estovan, who attempted to ignore Vozeniliek, who stuck his two cents in every three seconds to recommend communism. The three drew up a list of supporters they hoped to rally. The outcome appeared obvious: over 80 percent of the population of Spain favored democracy, a fair day's wage, and release from the bondage of kings and bishops, who presented lists of obligations they insisted were owed them for doing nothing, unless you counted sabotaging the economy, corrupting reason, and ignoring the Golden Rule.

Leonid Vozeniliek did make one point that chilled the crew. Five years earlier, just as many Italians, including the national Catholic Party, also favored free elections and absolute democracy. "And now look at them," he pointed out, "no one dare speak their mind. The people must revolt."

"Violence," Estovan insisted, "will not be necessary in our country. There are good people in Spain. They will listen."

Sebastian was eavesdropping from the stern. "It's impossible to hear anything when gunpowder is going off. I like the 'more tanks the better' idea, just keep the keys to yourself, don't give them to Stalin. Would you like me to put in an order?"

Sebastian noticed Jimmy and Conchita using hand signals at the bow. Conchita's brother was born deaf, and she had communicated with him using sign language since they were kids. During the three hours it took to languidly sail back to port, Jimmy learned half of the alphabet and 70 percent of conversational phrases, including, "Your place or mine?"

It was rare that Jimmy pressed Sebastian to do anything. That afternoon, he made four requests. The first was to let him take the helm when they backed into the dock. He would use the customary signals to instruct Sebastian what to do and when to release the kedge anchor, and impress Conchita by being the boss. Request number two was to leave Estovan, Gilberto, and Leonid on the dock. Request number three was take-out dinner for four. The last item was a bottle of chilled champagne served at a candlelight dinner on deck, anchored miles away.

Sebastian was always happy to leave land behind, especially that night, with a noisy party in full swing up in the yacht club. Their friends snuck them out five plates of appetizers, three dozen shrimp, four two-inch beefsteaks, and a pound of the wedding cake.

The apparent wind was no longer apparent. They motored to the Golfo de America, where they hugged the coast to Cabo de Gata-Nijar. The boat was as flat and solid as dry ground. Jimmy had a favorite bay. Digging in anywhere you see open sea is, technically speaking, against the rules. But the summer doldrums were upon them and a stationary high was in charge. Besides, any wind that might come their way would be off the land, and an onshore breeze wasn't expected until noon the next day, which would make for a pleasant sail home.

It was a quick trip. Four hundred feet of chain made it possible for Sebastian to anchor in fifty feet of water. Jimmy freed their two-hundred-pound fisherman's anchor, and Sebastian backed her down, dug in, and then killed the diesel for the moment of joy. *Jubilation* sat motionless on a mirror of water that reflected blue sky and wispy white clouds.

"Are you sure you know what you're doing?" asked Carlotta, leaning against the port safety lines, pointing her finger at Sebastian.

"Now that you mention it," Sebastian said, smiling, satisfied, as he made his way over to Carlotta, "I haven't been sure about anything since I left Fond du Lac... until you."

"You know what I mean," she said with her hands on hips. "They're not in their right minds."

"I'll leave that for you to decide, and don't bid no trump."

"What are you talking about?"

"I agreed to Jimmy's requests if he agreed to play ten hands of bridge with us after dinner."

"Does he play bridge?"

"Knows the rules but has never been able to bid. The words get him fouled up."

"So you asked him to play a game he can't. Now I know you're crazy."

"You're just figuring that out now? Where have you been?"

Dinning at sea was memorable, followed by Carlotta taking Sebastian by the hand to the other side of the table to face her for bridge. The way Sebastian figured it, if Jimmy played his first game ever, then Conchita had accomplished what no doctor west of the Hudson had ever managed, and if Conchita was sober enough to count trump, then the rest of the night was on her. Jimmy and Conchita won. Sebastian and Carlotta lost.

An hour later, Conchita and Jimmy returned to their favorite spot at the bow. After wiping the table down, Carlotta slumped back against the cushion and looked at Sebastian.

"You," Sebastian said joyfully, "are the worst bridge player I have ever known. Why did you jump to clubs after I opened with spades and you came back with diamonds?"

"Because they had a string of diamonds and your opening bid meant the points were covered. And we took the hand, smarty-pants."

"Yes, we did, and Conchita played the best defense possible, and Jimmy was the sharpest I have ever seen him. Are you happy now, mommy? Is it okay for the children to play by themselves? I have a theory," Sebastian continued as he made his way to the bow with one bottle of champagne and four glasses. "Maybe you have diamonds on your mind. Is it possible that you might want one on a ring someday? Would you like to go shopping when we get back?"

"The last thing I need is a man bossing me around."

"Come to America. On the other side of the Atlantic, women boss men around. I think it has something to do with the humidity."

"Ask me again in ten years. Right now, I have a family to protect and a country to save."

"In an hour, it will be dark and your country will disappear. You, me, and the universe will be all there is."

Carlotta sidled up to Sebastian and to give him a kiss he savored with another. Then she wrapped both arms around him and buried her head in his chest, which was a most wonderful feeling for Sebastian until it occurred to him that her hug felt like a child holding on to her daddy in the dark.

"Hypothetical scenario," Sebastian said, watching Jimmy and Conchita finish their one, and only, glass of champagne. "A boy and a girl both decide to walk into a bar and order a drink. Each then decides to pick up the drink and consume the drink. Each, on their own, then decides to have two more. At the end of three drinks, why is the boy responsible for his behavior but the girl is not?"

"You know the answer to that," she said whimsically. "It's because everything is your fault."

"Like this," he said, placing a long, wholesome smack on lips he hadn't been able to get his mind off all day.

"I'm not sure," she said, in soft tones only love finds. "Perhaps you should try again."

The next kiss released more than enough passion to take over the night. Carlotta led Sebastian to the companionway on the way to the captain's quarters.

"So do you agree," said Sebastian, instantly regretting the comment, "that if a man has the right to get drunk and have sex, then a woman also has a right to get drunk and have sex?"

Carlotta didn't bother to bother, just kept walking until she closed the door of Sebastian's cabin, where he was told to lie down.

"Do you agree," Carlotta said, "to lie down and do as I say?"

"And everything else possible in this universe to make you happy."

"That's more like it, Sebastian."

"But there is one thing you should know Carlotta."

"And that is?"

"I didn't plan it... I didn't want it... but I am in love with you."

BOOK THREE

29

On the morning of October 24, 1929, Sebastian remembered what he had said years earlier as if it were yesterday.

"Marlene, can we talk? Thank you. The world is going crazy. Bankers make up their own rules, politicians agree with anyone who will line their pockets, and the church continues to put its own future above the needs of the people. I must be perfectly honest: the trip to Spain has left me confused about everything, like living here in Europe with you, which still sounds wonderful, of course, but the continent is heating up. The stories you heard are true. I almost died. My breathing would have been silenced if Jimmy didn't put his own life on the line. Both of us almost disappeared from the face of the earth.

"A thing like that makes a guy wonder about everything, like why live here surrounded by maniacs when we could be living in America surrounded by family, lake cottages, and western pines? And I know you've said that you couldn't possibly desert your country, your family, and the factory the town depends on. I also know how you feel about your German heritage, and I admire your confidence that life in the fatherland will improve, but I sense a dark shadow. In the years to come, I may not get along with your Germany.

"So, and it pains me to say this, I'm thinking maybe, after one more trip to Spain, I should go back to Wisconsin for a while. And of course, I'll return. We can wait to see what history has in store for us before making the next move. I really need a break. And of course, I still love you. I just don't know what to do next. What would you suggest?"

It was a fine speech. Sebastian delivered it perfectly, with an added tear that he did not expect. The speech also garnered the result he was hoping for: a long, two-armed hug. But not from Marlene; it was from Jimmy, whom he was practicing on, and who turned out to be the only person ever to hear it. When Sebastian got off the train in Warendorf, Marlene ran up and gave him a big, two-armed hug that didn't make it all the way around because she was eight months pregnant. She knew Sebastian needed to stay focused if he was ever to return to her, and no one snitched.

Sebastian never forgot the first words out of Marlene's mouth: "My darling, I missed you so much. *We* are glad you've come home."

There were more surprises. Half the town helped finish their dream house, with a new well, a baby room, and three more needing only wallpaper to match the sex. There was also a barn, a garage for tinkering, and a guest cabin one hundred yards downstream for Jimmy, or Marlene's parents, or Sebastian's parents.

Marlene attributed Sebastian's lack of euphoria to battle fatigue. It looked like he was in shock, which was true, but he recovered seamlessly minutes later, when Marlene agreed to call their child Zeek if a boy or Elizabeth if a girl.

Instead of heading for Ostkirchen that day, Sebastian detoured to the church. By the time he got to the cathedral, images of a little tyke jumping up and down on his bed in the morning started Sebastian giggling and caused him to pull over to give Marlene a hug, which freed her from thoughts that had refused to vacate her mind.

Sebastian never forgot how good that hug felt, and also what happened next. When he pulled up to the front of the rectory to ask the priest to schedule a ceremony, the necessity for which would be obvious as soon as Marlene walked in the door, she refused to budge.

Sebastian pointed out that the second they said "I do," she would be an American citizen who could leave Germany at any time without Berlin's permission and that little Zeek, or little Elizabeth, would be legal heirs to his mounting fortune, which would make him happy knowing so.

"We must think of our children, Marlene," did not change her mind.

Sebastian got out of bed, opened the double doors on their bedroom, and walked out onto their second-floor private deck overlooking the stream and garden on the other side of the bridge. He was alone. Marlene had tiptoed out earlier to help Gunter inspect tank turrets before the machinists arrived.

Sebastian didn't always bike to work. Sometimes he took Stalwart, his jet-black mustang. "It's been years and I still don't understand," he said to himself as he was getting ready to go to work, referring to Marlene's answer at the church doorsteps that day, when she gave him a kiss and said, "Let's go home."

She declined, citing something about German pride and, believe it or not, the legal right she had over her, that is to say their child, if she remained a German citizen in Germany as opposed to an American who might be required to leave with her husband or lose custody in court, a strategy than made Sebastian feel more like a pawn and less like a loved father.

There was more. Marlene got on a lady high horse about running her own life, which again confused Sebastian, since it was Marlene who built the house, planned each day, and made the next decision, "Let's have another baby."

She was enthusiastic until the morning of February 23, 1929, when twenty-four hours after little Zeek came down with the sniffles, he was discovered lifeless. Marlene grieved, "One year, you're in paradise beginning a family, the next, life tips the scales all the way to hell."

Neither Sebastian nor Marlene ever imagined anything in life could hurt so much or cut so deep and last so long. For the entire six months since they had lowered little Zeek into his little grave, the sun had not shone once for them.

But that morning, the September of new beginnings, as he sang "Jingle Bells" and didn't know why, Sebastian was certain the best day of his life had just begun. The previous night, Marlene not only warmed up to him after months of withdrawal, she also left a note on his pillow before she went to take a bath before heading back to the bedroom. The note said: "I love you—forgive me these last few months, I haven't been myself. It was like part of me was ripped out and thrown away—but I'm back now—and oh so lucky to have you in my life. Let's have another baby, and then another baby, and then another baby until you want to stop. And Williamson sounds like a great name to me, and you're half German anyway. Talk my mom and dad into a month's visit every year, and we'll catch the next boat to New York."

The tide had turned. The sails were set. Sebastian couldn't imagine a day with better news, until the end of the day, when he couldn't imagine a day with a worse ending.

30

Faces are good at telling lies but bad at keeping secrets; Marlene was no exception. For months after little Zeek died—through the brittle winter, a spring that never thawed, and an entire summer wasted of joy—Marlene nevertheless remained the angel that she was, like stopping by the bakery every morning to pick up breakfast biscuits and dessert strudel for the family.

The bakery, Aufgehendes Brot, was only an eighty-two-step detour down Ostkirchen Strasa. Marlene's old schoolmate, Ada Mayer, often left the front door open to cool down the store after morning baking. That day, she left it open all day since a late summer heat wave was passing through. Dry fallen leaves followed Marlene to the desk.

"Good morning, Marlene," said Ada, leaning forward, hinting for news at Marlene's smart step. "Aren't you the cheery one this morning. What's going on? I could hear you singing half a block away, and what's with the Christmas carol?"

Marlene spun a pirouette, the way the two had done years before in dancing school. "Ada, have you ever fallen out of love and then back in love again?"

Ada tightened her lips, concerned. "You don't love Sebastian any-more. . . or did. . . or. . . what are you talking about?"

"No, no, Sebastian is Sebastian. It's impossible not to love a man so genuine and kind. I'm talking about life! When little Zeek died, life lost all meaning. It had no flavor, no promises, no future I cared about; I was obsessed with the uselessness of it all."

"Let me guess: the stock market turned around, and you stopped locking Sebastian out of your bedroom?"

"I don't care about the market or flimsy banks, but as of ten o'clock last night, I am again open for deposits. And it was great, and Sebastian was wonderful, and it was better than I remembered. Before I open the strudel for lunch, I might just put myself on the menu again. Say the words or draw a picture, and Sebastian is always hungry for love, and thank God, once again, so am I."

Ada followed Marlene to the door for one last hug. "I'm so glad, Marlene. I didn't want to tell you, you being down-and-out and all, but every Wednesday when my dad goes home early, Gunter sneaks in between my legs. Then I bend over. I guess it's love. For sure it's great sex."

Sebastian's trip to the office was not a straight line either. The first half of his gallop stuck to the trail, curving by trees, rocks, and property lines, each one anticipated by Stalwart, who leaned over in midair to throw all four hoofs to the side as Sebastian leaned like he did on his motorcycle around corners. The last half of the sprint was a racetrack straightaway Sebastian had blazed through family fields to the back of Papa Karl's barn, where the foaming mustang lost her saddle and was released to graze until Sebastian's ride home, which was usually casual, but that night, with Marlene back, was at full speed.

Papa Karl had a bad habit of bragging about how much money Sebastian was making. Secret orders from Japan were even showing up. Sebastian asked him to settle down; the less the world knew about them, the better. To keep the old man happy, Sebastian made him the head of a committee to improve the company image, beginning with washing down the entire soot-tattooed factory before painting it white. Karl loved the job, worked outdoors, and added old friends to the payroll, for whom he bought drinks every night.

When Sebastian got to the just-painted front door of the just-paneled and just-expanded office, there was a sign that read, "Sebastian, please come over to the house before you begin work. Marlene."

"Oh great," he said. "Another leaking pipe. Two hundred paid mechanics, and I end up handyman and house plumber. Oh well."

It was a silly gripe that only lasted ten steps, just long enough for it to dawn on Sebastian that it may not be a pipe that Marlene wanted him to plunge, a theory that he did not discard but put on hold when Mutti met him at the door with a hug and a kiss and then another hug that smelled like potatoes. Marlene had told her everything.

"Oh, my special almost son-in-law!" she said, pulling her apron down and fluffing her frizzed hair. "More babies, a wedding, grandchildren on my lap, and don't you worry, you work hard, I watch babies. Oh, so happy! Marlene, she loves you, I love you, Papa's king of the town again... *wunderbar... wunderbar!*"

Marlene was standing in the doorway to the dining room. Her eyes beamed joy. Sebastian waited patiently for Mutti's embrace to let up before following Marlene into the dining room, where he discovered the ladies had prepared his two favorite breakfast dishes—French toast and a Spanish omelet. Mutti made a giggly remark about Sebastian needing all the strength he could muster, then laughed after a grateful look to Marlene for making her life complete.

Thirty minutes of cheesy eggs, lip-smacking syrup, and erotic butt pats later, Sebastian pulled his chair back far enough to allow Marlene to sit full saddle on his lap facing him. "It's been a long time since we did it this way," she said, purring in his ear.

"Until last night," Sebastian said, "it had been a long time since we did it any way, so long that I wondered if I would remember what to do."

The day warmed. Before she left, Mutti opened windows on both corners of the dining room, which left the sheer cloth curtains blowing back and forth. Marlene saw no one and heard Mutti out back before disappearing beneath the table to reacquaint herself with her favorite visitor.

When smiling Sebastian finally made it to the second-floor office, he was silently greeted by a grinning staff that had tripled in size, and knew all. The morning would have been perfect if it weren't for the numbers appearing on the ticker tape.

One month earlier, on September 20, Sebastian had poured champagne at every desk when he learned that his nemesis, Lord Kensington, along with Clarence Hatry and associates, had been jailed for fraud and forgery. For six months prior to the debacle that crashed the London Stock Exchange, Kensington kept offering Sebastian deal after deal, all of which Sebastian refused to consider. Hundreds went broke trusting the skunk. Sebastian saw it as a sign to bring all his wagons into a circle.

There are times when the person who gives you the worst advice is actually the best guide, because you head in the opposite direction. The more Kensington pressured Sebastian to invest in get-rich-quick schemes, the further Sebastian distanced himself from the money jugglers. He moved all he owned into gold, treasury bonds, cash, booze, and utilities. It drove Kensington crazy, an added bonus as far as Sebastian was concerned.

Then there was the buying-on-margin thing. Kensington told Sebastian that his bank could invest a million dollars for Sebastian without Sebastian handing over a dime. All Sebastian had to do was sign papers to borrow the money from Kensington, which Kensington guaranteed would be paid back from profit in only six months, with stocks going up so fast and all. "Unless," Sebastian reminded himself every time Kensington pestered, "the old fogy is lying or has forged a scheme to fail so everything the Williamsons own will belong to him after all, as industries collapse and thousands lose their jobs. Been there. . . done that. . . go to hell, Lord Asshole."

It had been a month since Sebastian heard the good news about Kensington getting what he deserved. The problem was that the entire world was about to get what only Kensington, stock big shots, and government baboons deserved. After the London Stock Exchange crashed, Sebastian wrote down little notes every time bad news came across the ticker tape, which ran constantly trying to catch up. He taped each note to the top of his desk. Sebastian called them his army of stupidity and wondered how long it would take for Kensington, and others just as greedy, to burst the bubble of paper money.

Before he sat down at his desk, Sebastian looked at his collection of ill wind: industry overproduction, low wages, weak agriculture, choking tariffs, dept proliferation, oversupplied warehouses, zero sideline cash reserves, excess bank loans that couldn't be liquidated, and, worst of all, faltering share prices at the same time margin selling was growing, while governments took no action and America's Federal Reserve looked the other way.

News from America convinced Sebastian that the media had adopted a new motto: "When all else fails, make things worse." The ticker tape read, *Washington Post*: "Huge Selling Wave Creates Near Panic as Stocks Collapse." And *The New York Times*: "Prices of Stocks Crash in Heavy Liquidation."

Shock news is never good news. The deluge of foolishness that plastered Sebastian's desk was overwhelming. At the end of the day, Sebastian graciously declined the beer Pappi offered him across the street. He then thanked Mutti on behalf of himself and Marlene before passing on dinner as well. Mutti smiled knowingly, added a wink, and gave him a hug that proved that at no time in a woman's life is she asexual.

That night, Sebastian and Marlene redefined sexuality. After she fell asleep in his arms, Sebastian quivered as he whispered, "Marlene, please don't ever leave me like that again. I was lost. I can't do life by myself. I know I try to be tough, but I was afraid of losing you and what we have.

I fear about the future. . . I love you. . . Help me stay solid. . . You give my life meaning. With you at my side, I have purpose. Without you, nothing that I propose makes sense to me, and I just stop caring."

He couldn't sleep. Fear had taken its toll. Sebastian kept thinking about his desk. He biked back to town, not making a sound. When he got to the office, Jimmy was already there. Letters from his dad about Fond du Lac were just as worrisome as the megatrends that kept Sebastian up.

Both read the ticker tape letter by letter. It said, "The New York Stock Exchange has totally crashed. The economy has bed-rocked, not one industry will survive, fortunes lost, jobs will be no more, and most will go hungry, or worse."

"And all this," Sebastian said, "because business junkies are so hyped on themselves that no one wants to sell an apple for a fair price. All they care about is themselves, and no one cares about anyone else. And all this in a world that claims to be Christian. If someone named Jesus did once live on earth, he just rolled over in his grave."

Sebastian and Jimmy went up on the roof to look west to imagine what their folks, America, and the world must then go through.

"Not one pebble of this avalanche of catastrophe had to happen Jimmy."

31

Two years later, in the late fall of 1931, Sebastian remembered the conversation as if it were yesterday—because it was.

"Marlene, do you know that you are still beautiful even when you don't make sense, and that I still love you?"

"Sebastian, do you know that just because you're tall and handsome doesn't mean you see things clearer than the rest of us, and I love you too?"

"Marlene, it's because I love you so much that I must insist we avoid the rally in Warendorf."

"Sebastian, it's because I love you even more that I am willing to overlook your lack of commitment to half your ancestors."

"All of whom, I am certain, would insist that we avoid deranged Adolf. The man is not what Germany needs. Marlene, we are not going to Warendorf."

"Sebastian, we are going to Warendorf!"

"No, we are not going to Warendorf!"

"Yes, we are going to Warendorf."

"Marlene, how about we compromise? I will drive and sit next to you at the meeting if we can start having kids again."

"Sebastian, my mind hasn't changed since the stock market crash. This is not a good time. Germany is starving. The world doesn't need more mouths to feed. I refuse to bring a child into this madness."

"The world has always been screwed up, and we're not starving. My investments are holding value, my factories are picking up, and I'm making a fortune selling short. Everyone in Ostkirchen has a job."

"Yeah, three days a week."

"For now, and they still get full pay. We're doing great."

"And what about the rest of the human race, Sebastian? Should we forget about them? Attending the rally is the least we can do. And besides, it's all your fault."

"My fault?"

"Yes, it's your America that handed Britain the Great War. It's your America that agreed to cripple Germany with reparation payments, and it's your America that withdrew investments and destroyed the German economy two years ago."

"Oh, here we go, the patriotism thing again. Marlene, we, I mean us, I mean every one of us, are all citizens of the of the same planet. This disturbed world of ours will never find peace until patriotism is put in its proper place—on a shelf in a museum. As for me, I live in the land of Williamson. You might want to stop by someday."

"We are going to Warendorf, Sebastian."

"No, we are not going to Warendorf, Marlene."

That was indeed, word for word, what Sebastian remembered the next morning when he secured a love seat to the bed of the delivery truck where Gunter and Ada would sit facing backward behind the cab as Sebastian drove beside Marlene and Jimmy, who shared the suicide seat.

"Tell me again," Sebastian asked as they pulled out and Gunter and Ada bundled up outside, "why we are taking this rickety old heap when my brand-new Mercedes has a full tank of gas?"

"Because we are one of the people," said Marlene, sweet and appreciative.

"I don't want to be one of the people. I want to be me."

Panic and deflation were up to no good. When the money world messed up, nine thousand American banks went bankrupt, unemployment in Germany rose 232 percent, construction halted, deflation spiraled, crop prices dropped, industrial production whimpered, farmers lost their land, mining and logging shut down, and foreign trade sunk to half of what barely kept Germany alive before the crash. The only good news was that the dehydrated cash flow dropped wholesale prices 29 percent, but to no avail, as few could afford food, and most went to bed hungry.

But not to worry; Hitler knew whom to blame and how to fix the country. The only thing one needs on planet earth to fill a stadium with wild-ass cheering people is, sadly enough, a stadium. The roar of the crowd was heard for miles. The assembly had just sung, "*Deutschland, Deutschland über alles.*"

Following anticipated grumbling from the peanut gallery, except for Jimmy, Sebastian parked fifty meters from the farthest parked car that was itself a kilometer from the field.

"And if you notice," Sebastian said, hopping out of the cab sprightly, "I turned around so we are facing Ostkirchen. We're free to make a clean getaway anytime we like."

Alone, we fear the dark. Together, the dark fears us. In a mob, nothing on earth is safe. Organizing a meeting is just the beginning of a wrong turn. Somewhat more difficult, but recurrently doable, occurs when the people aren't happy but are unhappy about one thing or another, real or perceived. In that case, all one need do is draw a line between what people are unhappy about and those who will be blamed, justified or not. The next step is to yell loudly over and over again. No one knows just why that helps, but the most consistent theory suggests that the noise makes people think less.

It is also recommended, by those who should not be recommended, that when you describe the present way of life, which just happens to be better than anything in the past, make it a horrible tragedy that must be dealt with aggressively. That way, the people will ignore morbidity and mortality.

To be fair, there was some sanity in the crowd; there were many Germans who politely pointed out that rationality worked better, and was peaceful, and was safe. No one heard them because everyone else was screaming.

Warendorf was a madhouse, and it didn't happen overnight. A decade earlier, a sour little man, named Adolf by his loving, Christian mom, announced his twenty-five-point program at Hofbrauhaus Munich. The next year, reparation payments played right into his hands, making it even easier for Stormtroopers to terrorize political opponents.

In 1924, the little Austrian corporal was sentenced to five years in prison for a minute fraction of the criminal behavior that he got away with. Had he remained behind bars, the world would have escaped an apocalypse. He was out in eight months, and the vacation did nothing for his mood, so naturally he came up with the idea of starting a new party, with him as absolute leader, of course. The National Socialist Party he reorganized in 1925 had only twenty-seven thousand fellow fanatics; every other German knew better. That same year, the people of Germany voted to elect Hindenburg president.

Prison gave Hitler plenty of free time to begin his manifesto, *Mein Kampf*, published by the party in 1925. He wrote that books don't change the world, speeches do. A year later, there was enough momentum to organize *Hitlerjugend*. It's never too early to spoil a perfectly good childhood, and a decade of propaganda can go a long way. Dr. Joseph Goebbels took care of the details. Just as harmful was Reichsfuhrer S.S. Himmler. A flourish of meetings began after the last Allied troops left Germany. The Nazi party gained one hundred seven seats in the election that followed, all from more reasonable incumbents.

The other side of unguided history is *Gemutliche Kammaraderie*— German people together, completing the warmth that comes from belonging and believing in a national family. From toasting friends entering a pub to town dances and country fairs, it was natural for everyone to wrap an arm over the shoulder of whoever was standing to either side and sing and smile, and then hiccup before having another glass of beer.

Much to Sebastian's surprise, he and Gunter had moments. The two would figure out a solution to a difficult plant problem or win a shooting contest, and the first thing they knew, they were walking off the field arm in arm, but not like with Ada, who made Gunter happier putting an arm around him all the way to the six-thousand-seat stadium.

The stone structure rose four stories, looked surprisingly similar to Rome's Colosseum, and was pierced by entrances that looked like perfectly arched mouseholes, each one guarded by *Sturmabteilung*—Stormtroopers and Brownshirts—who looked like boys at various levels of puberty, all but a few barely filling their oversized shirts below baggy pants that dragged the ground as a rule. The excitement of the moment ignited Gunter, who grabbed Ada's hand and quickened his pace, leaving Sebastian, Marlene, and Jimmy behind. Sebastian slowed down to enjoy a look from Marlene, who accused him of being a nonconformist, his favorite modus operandi.

A giant swastika flag was draped over each entrance. Gunter and Ada waited impatiently where the crowd condensed to a funnel. When the three caught up with them, Gunter got back in line and stiff-arm saluted the flag, which was surrounded by a gauntlet of Brownshirt boys holding nightsticks and not smiling.

"Now Sebastian," Marlene said with a scolding mother's tone, "do not cause trouble."

Sebastian smirked politely, enjoyed the morning's drama, and was disturbed that Marlene's first concern was the impression they made on others. "My dear Marlene, I don't cause trouble, I respond to trouble. And," he added under his breath to placate Marlene, "don't you think these brown babies would be better off playing in a sandbox or, even better, standing on a corner waiting for the wind to blow a girl's skirt up?"

The five shuffled their way to the entrance. Gunter added a second salute on his way through ahead of Sebastian. The two Brownshirt boys lining the entrance had made it to man size and hadn't shaved to let their facial fuzz prove it. Both had their eye on Sebastian, who neither saluted the swastika nor closed-fist agreed with them. Both blocked the way by stepping in front of Sebastian, Marlene, and Jimmy.

"Perhaps," said the youth in Sebastian's face, who was brown-eyed and darker skinned than the rest of the Hitler Youth, "you would like to take the oath of allegiance to our leader before sitting down."

"The truth is," said the second youth in a mocking tone, inches from Marlene, "we insist."

A dozen Brownshirts then collected beside them, holding clubs and grimacing. From the back, one was heard to say, "Perhaps the old man would like to take a walk with us." Then, after a round of evil laughter, "There is a breathtaking view from the top of that six-story building over there. We should all head over and have a look."

Sebastian took a short step forward to put his face next to thug number one before sliding to his right to split the distance between Marlene and the other child brat and then, slowly, with confidence and conviction said, "Now why would I want to take in the sights from the height of that building when right here I have the height of idiocy from the mouths of adolescents who know less about life than cockroaches?"

"Now hold off, stop this right now," pleaded Marlene, as Sebastian enjoyed the heat of reality settling in. "Sebastian and I are loyal German supporters. He just doesn't like to be pushed around."

The two brown bullies looked at each other, then to the crowd waiting, which dared not peep. Again the tallest, the obvious leader, took charge. "I see. Then you will have no problem repeating the loyalty pledge. Stand at attention!" he yelled.

Sebastian did not.

"Raise your right hand."

Sebastian did not.

"Repeat this: I promise obedience to my country and my leader, Adolf Hitler."

Sebastian did not.

In high-tone, shrieking words, the Brownshirt then yelled, "You will promise, and you will promise right now—or else."

Or else were a dozen Brownshirts with clubs in their hands and a target standing next to Marlene.

Sebastian remained calm, spoke directly, and didn't blink an eye. "Listen very closely, Mr. Boy Scout Droopy Drawers, my life is none of your business, and your indifference to cruelty is disturbing. The only thing I will promise you is that I will put my foot up your ass in three seconds if you don't get out of my way."

Jimmy stepped in front of Marlene, ready to take on the right flank, knowing that Sebastian would have no trouble dropping all four rotten peanuts on his side. With arms crossed over his chest, Jimmy reached inside both sides of his coat. He and Sebastian looked forward to testing their stun guns.

Marlene, as desperate as the situation deserved, panicked and pushed her way between Sebastian and Jimmy with her arms out sideways in front of them. The taller boy, by far the bigger asshole of the gang, slapped her in the face, only to discover that the moment his hand left her face, Sebastian, with an instant lunge, had his windpipe in a death grip with his left hand at the same time his gun met the boy's right temple. Jimmy held two wired pistols loaded to spray neuroleptic comas at will.

It's not every day that screaming turns the tide. It was Gunter's turn, who ran back yelling, "Halt in the name of Adolf Hitler!"

The distraction stalled the standoff long enough for Gunter to show Brownshirt number two, the one still breathing, a letter that read: "To the people of Germany and the world. This letter is to introduce my good friends and loyal supporters, Sebastian Williamson and Gunter Wolf.

Please extend to them every courtesy and box seating at the Warendorf meeting to which I have personally invited them. Adolf Hitler."

The boys gathered round to touch the paper and their hero's signature. Sebastian let their almost but not yet dead, leader drop to the ground.

"Oh," said second-in-command Brownshirt, stumbling for words. "We are terribly sorry, sir. Please don't say anything about this to Der Fuehrer. It was a misunderstanding."

Marlene's color returned. Sebastian looked over to her as he said to the kids, "Young man, this country is a misunderstanding."

"Yes sir, of course sir, this way please. . . It will be an honor to escort you to the front row. Der Fuehrer is expected in ten minutes. I'm sure he'll be glad to see you. And again. . . we are so sorry. . . we thought you were someone else."

Neither talking about violence nor witnessing violence comes close to *feeling* violence. Marlene's slap in the face and Sebastian's death grip left her confused. After that not once did she look at Sebastian like she always had. The man she loved had transformed into a murderer. And worse, those who she thought might be helping Germany wanted to murder him. Gunter did not cheer her up when he said, "In this life, we must fight for what we deserve. With Sebastian's help, Germany will win the next war. We need him, Marlene."

Sebastian, on the other hand, saw Marlene as he always had—a brilliant, caring, loving, and of course beautiful woman who desired only the best for everyone; but then, that's what everyone says.

On the way home, Sebastian and Jimmy laughed every time Sebastian mimicked Hitler making a speech and pounding the podium. Jimmy grunted noises that were a dead ringer for Hitler's rudeness. Neither Marlene nor Gunter made a peep. Ada laughed because Sebastian and Jimmy were funny, and politicians aren't required for yeast to rise.

That night, little was said at dinner, and what was said made no reference to the day or the plight of the world. Sebastian and Marlene joined the family for the customary after-dinner walk but kept on going for a slow return to their private lives.

That night, they made up—kind of. Then they made love—kind of. Then Marlene fell asleep—for sure. Then Sebastian did not—for sure.

Once again, he found himself on the back deck looking for shooting stars, but for the first time he was alone, physically and emotionally. He went to his desk and pulled out a letter he was waiting to open. It was from Carlotta, and read: "Years of hard work and sacrifice have paid off. We have the votes! In days, perhaps by the time you get this letter, Spain will be a free democratic nation just like your United States of America. We did it, Sebastian! Our congress can use your guidance, and my arms miss you. Please come back to Spain."

The request was added to the list. Sebastian received ten letters a week from subsidiaries begging him to visit Spain to resolve in-house disagreements. The new government also had be dealt with. Just two days prior to Hitler day, Marlene fielded the most recent of over a dozen calls from home offices across Europe, every one insisting Sebastian pay them a visit.

The time had come. To help him sleep, Sebastian packed. His world did not sit well. Sebastian did not sleep well.

32

Marlene tripped over Sebastian's suitcase outside their bedroom door. The breakfast was warm, the conversation chilly. Marlene was wearing the see-through negligee that kept Sebastian coming back for more. It didn't. Both knew last night was off schedule and may have started the baby clock.

"Don't worry, Sebastian," she said, standing beside him with both arms around him as she rested her head on his shoulder. "This time, I will write if last night did the trick, and I do love you, and I do want to raise a family with you... someday... I'm sure of it."

At the door, Sebastian faced Marlene for a final hug that felt suspiciously sentimental and almost mournful. The past was what it was—the future not a clear view for either of them.

"Sometimes I wonder," he said, resisting a tear as he faced Marlene, who was already soggy, "is life confusing, or is life just life?"

"Sebastian," Marlene said, already missing his presence, "all I know is that the day you walked into my life, my life stopped being my life. Every second since has been *our* life."

Sebastian grinned with the twinkle Marlene knew was still there. "Marlene, when I first saw you, all greased up and sweaty, it was like a glowing angel from heaven came down to point the way."

"And now, Sebastian?"

Between sniffs, Sebastian pulled back, held both of Marlene's hands, stood up straight, and then, after a glimpse of windblown trees outside, said, "Marlene, my love, more than anything else, I wish I knew the answer to that question, and so many more."

"Sebastian, there is no rule that says every day in paradise has to *be* paradise. We'll get through this, I'm sure."

"Yes, of course, Marlene," said Sebastian, standing at the door, holding his suitcase. "And I'll write you."

"Sure, just like you did last time."

"No, I mean it. I really will this time."

Sebastian had reserved a private compartment for the ride across Europe. He flopped down, head bent and spine wilted like an eighty-year-old man. He sat next to the window and looked back at Warendorf. It disappeared behind rustling leaves and locomotive smoke.

Jimmy signed, "Bad day, Sebastian?"

"Bad day. . . or bad life," Sebastian answered out loud. "I don't know which, and I don't know why."

Jimmy raised his eyebrows along with his hands in a gesture of disbelief. "Don't know?" He then signed, "Beautiful Marlene, gorgeous Carlotta, new Mercedes, and money, money, money. What's your problem?"

Sebastian sat back, looked to the sky, and then drifted thoughts like the clouds floating by. "Jimmy, it's just that I'm now convinced that alongside reasoning, nature also evolved irrationality. If I don't know who anyone else really is, how am I supposed to know who I am?"

"What?" was all Jimmy had to add, with limited understanding.

"You see, Jimmy, Marlene believes in her country and the god of Rome, but neither bears the scrutiny of logical analysis, which means she has surrendered both her freedom and her free will to stupidity and refuses to consider even a single suggestion to the contrary. It's like she's on a runaway train that dead people set in motion centuries ago. Does anyone on this planet live their own lives?"

"I do!" signed Jimmy.

"Yes, you do, my fine friend, and I've never told you this, but the truth is that I need you more than you need me. So, my good buddy, what do we do now?"

"We get. . . new train. . . the Carlotta and Conchita train."

"You know," said Sebastian in a droll tone, "maybe you're right. It's possible that I'm overthinking this fragile mortality of ours. Maybe we overvalue youth. Maybe youth is something that just happens, and then it's gone."

Many hours later, following overeating and sequential napping, life looked better, and there was no confusion at the train station in Almeria, just a lot of noise from a brass band and thirty well-wishers welcoming Sebastian back. They were representatives from each of Sebastian's four Spanish factories, grateful that he let them off to vote for democracy after months of leaving early to campaign. The two men standing next to Carlotta were paid by Sebastian to protect her during the final tumultuous weeks. Beside them were Estovan Garcia, Gilberto Alverez, and Leonid Vozeniliek, who was wearing a brand-new suit and handing out Cuban cigars, which Sebastian wondered might have been paid for with some of the thousands of dollars he diverted to the Republic.

King Alfonso XIII had just been handed walking papers. His exile was permanent. The last of a horrific family of barbarians no longer exploited the country. The rest of Europe was not so lucky. The Austrian Credit-Anstalt had just collapsed. The financial crisis that followed in Central Europe bankrupted Germany's Danatbank and many more.

Those of wealth could have helped but did not. Millionaire Hugenberg abandoned democracy and fair play to support the National Socialist Party. Kirdorf, Thyssen, and Schroder next added their wealth to the demagogue. The only good news was that the American president, Herbert

Hoover, suggested a one-year moratorium for reparation payments and war debts. Hitler had his own plan; he called it, "Go to hell."

Spain was never a bed of roses. In the nineteenth century, when England bombarded the White House to kill as many Americans as possible, liberals in Spain drew up the Spanish Constitution of 1812, which sought to limit the power of the monarchy. King Ferdinand VII was not happy. He dissolved the constitution with a flip of the wrist, then did such a bad job running the country that twelve separate coups murdered their way to power.

At the beginning of the twentieth century, Spain was besieged by so many problems that it remained neutral throughout the Great War. After the war, the liberal populous joined the armed forces in an attempt to evict the corrupt central government. When they failed, Miguel Primo de Rivera pulled off a military coup, followed by General Damasco Berenguer, and then Admiral Juan Bautista Anzar-Cabanas, each one continuing a policy of "rule by decree," which translated "do as I say or die."

Even more confusion resulted when the people tried to decide whom they hated the most, Cabanas or King Alfonso. To avert further bloodshed, a decision comparable to looking for lifeboats after the *Titanic* hit the bottom, Alfonso called for municipal elections and ran for his life. On April 12, 1931, Carlotta's Republicans won every provincial capital. Conchita danced in the streets. Carlotta sent a letter to Sebastian.

Everyone supported the new Republic, especially the rural workers who endured the worst poverty in all of Europe. Carlotta's government instituted an eight-hour day at the same time wages went up. Land tenure was redistributed. And as always with politics, there were losers, like the landowners who couldn't hire cheap labor. Unions also refused to follow recommendations; many, against Carlotta's insistence, limited women's employment to preserve their labor monopoly.

Jimmy's girlfriend, Conchita, helped pass laws replacing Catholic schools with religious free education, which removed the Vatican's most powerful and most lucrative stranglehold on the peasants. After two thousand years of not playing fair, the Vatican pointed the finger at Spain. Pope XI, mislabeled "pious," blamed Carlotta's democracy for ruining the country.

After Carlotta's constituent assembly approved the new constitution, it should have arranged regular elections and adjourned; the people needed to speak up and fight back inch by inch to shake out snakes and weed the gutters. The assembly did not schedule yearly elections. It decided to run the country themselves for two years, which turned out to be more than enough time for troublemakers to come up with an alternate agenda.

Carlotta wasn't worried. Everything had gone off as planned, including Sebastian back in her arms as soon as he jumped off the train. And he felt something glow inside of him alongside a rush of enthusiasm that he never felt in Hitler's Germany. It was a grand afternoon, and Sebastian had the coin to take *Jubilation* off the hard and back in the water.

33

The Catholic church always had a reputation as a bully. Just ask any-one hanging from a rope or tortured in prison. Apparently, among other things, the Rome-based organization had a problem with forgive-ness. But to be fair, Spain did have more of its share of Jews and Muslims to deal with, most of whom refused to convert even with their feet on fire.

And the church didn't fool anyone. It consistently sided with the aristocracy and, of course, the monarchy, who lived in mansions by the sea or perhaps in Paris, while their serf-slaves worked themselves to death on "their" land for low wages and high taxes.

In Spain one of the casualties was God. The people figured out what was going on. It didn't make sense for them to support an institution that was stealing bread and freedom at the same time—so they didn't. By 1930, only 3 percent of the population of Madrid attended services. Overall, two-thirds of the country refused to sleep with the enemy.

The church did what it could to maintain the status quo and hold on to the best seats at the dinner table. In addition to landowners, kings, and rich folk, the Vatican needed at least some popular support to feign legitimacy. The problem was that the more the people knew, the less likely they were to support Catholicism. The solution was obvious.

Every school was a church school that mostly taught discipline, if anything. The results served as evidence: 80 percent of the people of Spain remained illiterate, which made the Latin voodoo show all the more impressive.

"I can't wait to see the smiling faces on the first graders on their first day of school," said Carlotta, standing beside Sebastian at the helm while Jimmy cast off, "and they won't waste hours repeating penance, or mouthing rosary words, or getting rapped on the knuckles. We'll have math, and science, and writing classes, and a full-sized football field next to a gymnasium. Who knows, maybe we'll end up with an Olympic gold medalist."

"It's a fine thing you've done, Carlotta," Sebastian said, as he bent over to give her a quick kiss on the top of her head, with one eye scouting the bow. "How many schools do you have on the drawing board?"

"Within the year, the minister of education, Marcelino Domingo, has promised me seven thousand. Every youngster will finally get the chance they deserve. And again, who knows, perhaps right here in town, we might educate a youngster who grows up to be president."

"Spain sounds more like the Statue of Liberty every second."

"And during the second year of our stewardship, another twenty-five hundred schools will be added. By the end of 1932, we plan to have enrolled over seventy thousand students, four times the number now in school."

"And there's more," Conchita added, stepping over the boom line. "The new constitution guarantees freedom of speech and freedom of the press, declares all citizens equal, and abolishes the titles of the nobility. We did it! We opened free political discourse, secularized marriage, and took education out of the hands of self-serving clergy. Thank God above! We finally have separation of church and state!"

The offshore breeze was barely a knot, just enough to ease *Jubilation* from the dock while Jimmy ran to the bow to take in anchor rode.

"Are we right on her?" Sebastian yelled forward.

Jimmy raised an arm with bent elbow that pumped up and down like a conductor blowing the whistle, his signal for "Roger that."

"Okay then, Jimmy, snub her down. I'll run her forward to pull out the hook."

"And the election," Carlotta gushed on, "was the freest and most proper in Spanish history. Our coalition of bourgeois republicans and general socialists won three hundred seventy-seven seats, while the right-wing guys—you know, the high clergy, grandees, officers' corps, and upper classes—won only sixty seats. We are the people!"

Jimmy and Sebastian stowed what they had before they left the dock. They thought they were going for an afternoon's sail but had planned to live on the boat anyway. Carlotta and Conchita took an hour to fill hanging lockers and cabinets with enough outfits for a month. "Surprise! Surprise! We're moving in," exclaimed Carlotta, a young man's dream, along with clear skies, fair winds, and an astounding yacht.

Carlotta's congress had adjourned, Conchita's school didn't officially open for another thirty days, and Sebastian's companies were on vacation slowdown. There are times when it's best to mellow. That morning Sebastian, Jimmy, Carlotta, and Conchita had the Mediterranean playground all to themselves.

At the wheel, both boys stood watch for nets dragged by fishing boats. The girls joined them with a plate of fresh fruit, and there was more to come. Conchita had four crates of food brought on board before Sebastian boarded. Carlotta handed Sebastian a slice of cantaloupe with the request for a quiet anchorage lee of a wooded island and then added that it wouldn't be quiet for long.

Jimmy hand signaled Sebastian, "Do I pinch you to see if you're dreaming, or do you pinch me to see if I'm dreaming?"

"We're both dreaming, Jimmy, and it just goes to show you how much we love the love of a woman."

"And," out loud Jimmy got out, "Special. . . special. . . so special. . . and smart."

"Of course they're smart, Jimmy, they picked us, didn't they?"

Jimmy nodded and stood straight, attempting to look sophisticated. "Yes indeed, yes indeed."

"Take over, Jimmy. I'm going to talk to Carlotta."

She was standing outside the door of the captain's quarters. Sebastian leaned against the wall two feet away. "So, what happened to 'must work, no time, big deals, don't bother me' Carlotta?"

"Oh, I left her on the dock."

"Will she be waiting for us when we get back?"

"Perhaps, who knows? What else did you have in mind?"

"Plenty. Just everything, actually."

"Let's take it one day at time," she said, leaning against the bulkhead next to him, which brought Sebastian over for a kiss.

Sebastian backed up to look through the companionway to Jimmy at the helm, who had his attention instantly.

"Jimmy, Greece is our destination. We need a watch schedule for the passage. Let's do couples in eight-hour shifts."

Jimmy saluted formally, while Conchita at his side scanned the horizon.

"Fatigue at sea is a real problem," Sebastian announced to all aboard. "Sleep is essential. We must take advantage of every opportunity. When not on deck, I suggest the off-watch team hit the hay." And then, more slowly, while looking over to Carlotta, he added, "The more time spent in bed, the better."

Sebastian ended with a wink for Jimmy, who raised both arms and jumped up and down with glee, until Conchita looked over.

"Yes, yes... our duty... our duty... and our heaven."

34

Automobiles take trips. Sloops make passages from one world to another. Beneath a moonless sky packed with stars so intimate Carlotta couldn't tell them apart, *Jubilation* glided silently.

They were heading to one of the five destinations that sailors list as the world's most special, along with the Caribbean, the South Pacific, the Hawaiian Islands, and the coast of Maine. The wind would get them there. It would just take a few days, which was the best part—having nothing to do with civilization while nature served joy in a perfect world beneath heaven above.

The sail plan was to leave Cagliari and Palermo to port and Malta to starboard on the way to the Sea of Crete, where they would drop a hook inside Milos Bay. It was steady as she goes on a perfect beam reach.

Sebastian and Carlotta took the second watch, which began with hot chicken soup and cold white wine. Jimmy and Conchita nodded goodnight as they backed down the companionway, both looked like kids who just snatched the entire cookie jar. That pretty much sums it up.

"It's a nice thing Conchita is doing for Jimmy," Sebastian said, with his right hand on the wheel and left arm around Carlotta, who snuggled in tight. "It's not often he gets to feel like a man."

"The gratitude is mutual," said Carlotta in playful tone. "Years ago, Jimmy was her first, and though since then there have been others with various levels of affection, she told me Jimmy was the only man she ever met who was with her all the time, attentive, caring, and forever spirited to please. She likes Jimmy. In a way, and don't repeat this, she's also not complete, but together they make magic, like you and me."

"My, aren't you the wild one this evening," said Sebastian, smiling at her beauty. "It's not often a woman admits that she enjoys lying naked between the sheets as much we men do."

"Oh no," Carlotta said, holding her hand in front of her mouth. "I wasn't supposed to tell you. It's a secret. Once a year, all us women have a meeting to figure out how best to drive you men crazy and then pretend we had nothing to do with it."

"I always suspected that," said Sebastian in a deep, serious voice as he pulled Carlotta in closer. "And I must hand it to you, you're doing a great job. Our side is completely devastated."

"I see," said Carlotta, making a slow, calculated reply. "Does that mean you surrender?"

"Body and soul."

Sebastian lashed the wheel with the rudder midship, then moved the traveler to the rail to reduce windward force at the same time he adjusted the jib just enough to balance leeward influence. A few turns on the winch was all it took to balance the sails and keep *Jubilation* on course without touching the wheel. Neither land nor a single vessel was anywhere in sight, nor would be until dawn.

Jubilation kissed one ocean swell after another as she made love to the Mediterranean, as naked as everyone else on board.

"Sebastian," Carlotta said, lying flat on soft deck cushions, looking up, "I've never done it under the entire universe."

"And I've never imagined the universe could be so beautiful."

Later that night, Sebastian was amazed at how much love he felt for Carlotta, and he wasn't even thinking about sex, which they had just finished for the second time. Both sat bundled up midship, keeping an eye out. It was time for hot chocolate and truth.

"Sebastian?"

"Yes, my love."

"I know I'm the one who jumped into our relationship again, and I do love you. . ."

"My radar tells me the ship in running true but I'm about to run aground."

"Perhaps."

"That is?" he asked.

"Well, you know, it's very important for two people who spend their lives together to know each other well and kind of agree on most things."

"I agree with that. Does that count?"

Carlotta pulled herself away, took one of the blankets to wrap around herself, and faced Sebastian by sliding forward and turning. "I know your politics. I know you're a generous person, and I do love you."

"Okay, I'll say it, but what is it?"

"Well, there's more than one reason why I keep going to church to help Javier. You see, God is very important in my life. I'm one of those old-fashion believers who wants to do what God wants me to do."

"And I respect your convictions," said Sebastian, growing suspicious. "I haven't heard the 'but' word yet."

"But the problem is," she said more forcefully, "you don't believe in God."

Sebastian hesitated to attempt straight-faced serious but couldn't hold the pose for longer than ten seconds before comfortably explaining, "I don't believe in the God of the churches around here, that's true. But that doesn't mean I don't believe in a divine being looking over us and out for us."

"I don't understand. What do you mean?"

Sebastian took a deep breath, looked up, and raised a finger, requesting a minute to organize his thoughts.

"Okay, here it is. If life is for the living, and the living make life, then those living should make the best life possible, like God is doing making the best universe he can, for now, and we all evolve.

"People get all messed up about the pain and suffering part of being alive and then having to die, unfortunately sometimes in agony. My conviction is that we don't die, in a sense; we just move on, and we must accept and embrace mortality for what it is, and what comes after, which I am personally convinced includes sequential mortality. When the time comes for me to go, I plan to say, 'Thank you, God, that was great. It's going to be hard to beat, but I'm ready to go on to the next life. So what's up? Give it your best shot, and thanks again.'"

Sebastian looked for but got no response from Carlotta. He continued, "Well, you see, Carlotta, my final opinion is that we must fully accept that God loves us and that if the option were available or optimal, and that's where existence gets cloudy, there would be no pain or suffering or, perhaps, I don't know, the challenges that we face every day being alive. So, there is only one possible consistent conclusion. It is what it is. He has no choice. Eternity, this universe, is a work in progress, and we're here to help."

"Wow!" Carlotta said, reaching over to touch Sebastian's hand, "I didn't expect that. When did you start thinking about something other than boats, cars, and naked women?"

"Hey," Sebastian said, pulling his head back, "I'll have you know I took three years of philosophy in college."

"Oh, was the classroom across from the girls' gym?"

"Well, yes, and also the only class where you got a chance to prove you were right and get the professor to change your grade. Philosophy is relative."

"I feel better," Carlotta said, slowly at ease. "You do believe in God."

"I'm not finished. Please don't misunderstand me. I have unkind opinions about the God thing here in Europe."

"Let me guess," said Carlotta, taking a teacher's tone. "You're about to quote your American friend Mark Twain, who said that every established church is an established crime and an established slave pen that we must assault any way we can with every weapon promised to hurt."

A smiling Sebastian gave Carlotta a pat on the back, which he retracted after getting a strange look. "So we agree, then," he continued, with hesitation, "that all of Europe is in bondage to past history?"

"What do you take me for?" said Carlotta abruptly. "Your relative Javier, for example. I know full well there's a wall of words between what's going on in his consciousness and his real self, but he's a good man; he just needs to be guided. Javier has been misled to believe that the pope is an ally of God. There is nothing more dangerous than an idea when it's the only one you've got and you refuse to consider others."

Sebastian bowed respectfully. "I congratulate you again, my dear. You have proven the cost of liberty is less than the price of repression. You pulled off a miracle. Spain will be forever in your debt."

"Thank you, Sebastian. That means a lot to me."

"However, if you don't mind, I would like to add a pinch of realism. Your Cardinal Sáenz ordered every Catholic in the country to vote against you. And you left generals in charge who now miss the perks tyrants handed them. It might be best for you to lower your overall opinion of mankind."

Carlotta walked to the rail with a fancy Queen-of-England attitude, then flipped her wrist like royalty at court waving a handkerchief to the common people. "Yes, of course, my man, we have it all worked out. We will redesign Christianity. I shall order a second Reformation."

"Oh, that's all?" blurted Sebastian in disbelief. "My dear, you can't call a meeting and take a vote. Catholicism is a closed system that lives by a single impulse and a codified set of laws that assume ascendency over everyone, including you. If you're not careful, you'll get clobbered before you open your mouth. And don't expect reality, rationality, or common sense to come to the rescue. Religion's best trick is burying the truth."

Carlotta's sour expression let Sebastian know that she was not happy about him taking the wind out of her sails. "Okay, smart guy, what's your idea? How do you plan to fix the planet?"

"The way I see it," Sebastian said, pulling Carlotta over closer, speaking quietly, and kissing her on the neck, which changed both their moods, "it's the pain and suffering thing again that has Europe messed up. You… we… us… the whole planet… are not being punished. We are just dealing with matter, like God does. The entire sin-debt thing is made-up stuff to blame for bad news and cover up ignorance, which places organized religion in the driver's seat. Really, get a grip! Who does that? The only question is why is the continent still going along with the scam?"

Carlotta leaned back with both hands behind her head. Sebastian beamed at the view as she said, "I agree, the church needs to rethink itself. But go on, your point is?"

"Here's the bottom line. Every one of us has been sucked into the Jesus story, which makes us sign up for church-state stupidity, which ironically ends up *causing* the pain and suffering that the philosophy of Jesus begs to *prevent*. I believe the appropriate assessment of European Judeo-Christianity is—fucked-up. Levelheaded thinking is more profitable. It makes a difference if you do the right thing instead of the wrong thing."

Every time Sebastian mentioned God, Carlotta looked up, thanked Him, and then held her handsome partner tighter.

"Final answer, Carlotta…"

"You mean final, final answer, Sebastian?"

"Yes, and also final, final, final answer. What I believe is that God loves us, cares for us, and shares eternity with us. So therefore, we have been gifted eternal identity. Yes, I am certain that we are immortal, if you want to use that word. However—not a but, just a however—the nature of all that is blurry and beyond us at this time. But—the most important but of all—we must deal with and accept another dimension. All one needs to do to organize and sustain life is support a system of consistency storage accessible to individual identities at the same time the matrix maintains individual identity in wave forms. We always are. . . we always will be."

Sebastian took a long, deep breath before finishing.

"And, I suspect, it's not just a dimensional transfer from us here and now to there and always. Eternity gifts us time to explore all reflections of existence. And then Fritz, my philosophy teacher, would add that there was going to be a quiz on Monday, and try not to fail life."

35

Carlotta and Sebastian's first watch at sea was spectacular. At two o'clock, a waning moon made an entrance that reflected off a resting sea calmed without wind. Sebastian winched the sails taut before letting the motionless sloop change heading to go nowhere. The water was so flat the moon's details were as sharp off the water as in the sky. For two hours, Sebastian, in a robe, and Carlotta, sporting her sexiest see-through white negligee, lay side by side on cushions on the foredeck, waiting for something to happen, which turned out to be three knots of wind off the port beam at quarter to four.

Sebastian jumped up to trim sails. Once again, *Jubilation* was on her way. He and Carlotta then returned to their stateroom to put on the previous evening's outfits. When Jimmy and Conchita stuck their heads out an hour later, it appeared that Sebastian and Carlotta had stood watch all night as they were.

Sebastian recommended that the night watch tuck in before the sun rose. Jimmy and Conchita prepared cheese omelets and hotcakes on a tray with two cups of coffee and two glasses of warm milk. The wind picked up and veered north, not always a good sign, but still manageable without an active helmsman. The four ate midship, watching the sun glow on the eastern horizon.

"Tell me something, Conchita," Sebastian asked, with a sly look for Carlotta, who returned a more serious challenge. "If I went into my garage to build a toy wagon and then came out pulling one that only had three wheels and fell over, would it be reasonable for me to turn around and blame the wagon for falling over?"

"Of course not," said Conchita, half-asleep, leaning on Jimmy, holding his arm.

"Hold off," said Carlotta, looking at Sebastian impatiently, "you must consider question number two as well."

"That is?" Conchita asked, without emotional response.

"What if you are the wagon, and you notice one wheel is missing? Is it then therefore your—that is, the wagon's—fault for not adding the fourth wheel?"

Jimmy quick signed Sebastian, "I hope this is not how you spent your night."

"No," Sebastian signed back, "just the last twenty minutes, after Carlotta tried to talk me into going to church to pay off original sin."

Conchita looked back and forth, puzzled. "And why is this important?"

"Wait a minute, Carlotta," said Sebastian, looking at her as seriously as she looked back. "Since you stole my metaphor, I get to adjust it. Conchita,"—who was even less awake than when she sat down—"before you answer, I must point out that you, the wagon, have had blinders secured to both eyes since childhood, so you can't see the missing wheel, and you also have been told that your brand of wagon is the only one ever blessed by God. So therefore, you don't know you're wearing blinders or missing a wheel."

"In that case," Conchita said, shrugging her shoulders, trying to close the discussion, "I guess you wouldn't be able to do anything."

"See," said Sebastian, a bit pushy, "Conchita agrees that it's not the wagon's fault."

"She didn't say that, Sebastian."

"I think she did."

"No, she didn't."

Jimmy ended the conversation: "Tired... tired... people... should not argue... only... only kiss."

"Get to bed, you two," insisted Conchita. "We'll see you this afternoon."

As the sun rose, *Jubilation's* perfect port breeze backed astern. An intruding low-pressure system was tracking north from the Azores; its center missed London, but moisture did make it ashore. No one in Buckingham Palace had to water the flowers.

Dry Spain missed it again, but dense clouds did arrive, and the wind picked up, coming from where they came, going to where they wanted to be, which sounds like a good idea, unless of course one's sails were hoisted bow to stern, which they were, but not a problem for Jimmy, who ran out the boom ninety degrees to starboard and attached a preventer to the bow chock. The genoa was trickier, but with Conchita's help, Jimmy attached the spinnaker pole to the mast using the topping lift. He then ran the jib out to the pole placed at a right angle to the port rail. The wing and wing, as they say, looked like the barks of old getting blown downwind before the Bermuda rig was invented.

Jubilation was a princess at holding a steady heeling angle but not so good without lateral forces opposing one another. The boat's motion was erratic. Jimmy tightened the lines to hush noise as the mammoth hulk rocked back and forth starboard to port, downright soothing. Sebastian and Carlotta fell asleep in each other's arms.

Jimmy and Conchita mostly signed, which made communicating from the other side of the boat like whispering in each other's ears, and aboard *Jubilation,* Conchita knew just how to get Jimmy's attention: all she had to do was stand at the bow. That morning, as always, the two had nothing to argue about, and disagreed on a single subject only: the fishing line Jimmy was trolling behind the boat. Conchita had a craving for grilled swordfish spice-blackened on the grill hanging over the stern rail. Jimmy was obsessed with tuna steak, Texas-barbequed on the outside, sushi-rare in the middle, with nothing more than butter and lemon to complete the presentation.

Jimmy's luck held two days in a row. The sixty-pounder that he reeled in turned into lunch and feasts for the freezer, minus ten pounds that Jimmy left on ice for Sebastian and Carlotta, who grilled it to top a gigantic salad bowl, which all had for dinner alongside four pieces of deep-fried, powdered French toast that Carlotta threw together for Sebastian.

After eight hours sleep Sebastian and Carlotta emerged from the stairwell. They were all smiles, some giggles, and kissy, kissy, kissy. Not one thought was surrendered to dogmas, bills, or political demigods. They had blue skies, fair winds, and each other. The schedule was play, more playing, and a lot of fooling around.

There are three kinds of wind at sea: too much, too little, and "we don't care." It was a "we don't care" day. Less wind turned into nothing at all. With sails stowed, the gang spent what was left of the afternoon jumping off the beam to swim around the boat before boarding from the stern ladder. Jimmy went in with mask and snorkel to spear fish. He also armed three shotgun sticks. Neither the sound of struggling bass nor the smell of blood attracted sharks, something that disappointed Jimmy, since he wanted to grill one buttered in lemon juice.

Jimmy's afternoon was Sebastian's morning and the only eight-hour stretch all four shared together. One at a time, each took turns at the wheel. All joined group fun, like a game of bridge on the pop-up table in front of the starboard wheel and spinnaker dunking when the wind turned wimpy.

There were also rough days—two of them, in fact—when a meandering low gusted winds to over thirty-five knots and the rails went awash, which was Jimmy's favorite time to sit on the deck, harness secured and stanchion lines at head level, to dangle his feet in the water. He kept promising to kick a fish on board if one got close enough to the surface. That never happened.

Truth is beauty, and beauty is truth, and all despair imagined. Sebastian and Jimmy would let nothing and no one rob their ladies of peace, like the Sunday morning Conchita and Carlotta mentioned church requirements and a scorecard that no one wins. Jimmy polished off his best reading, quoting Dickinson:

Some keep the Sabbath going to Church –
I keep it, staying at Home –
With a Bobolink for a Chorister –
And an Orchard, for a Dome.

Some keep the Sabbath in Surplice –
I, just wear my Wings –
And instead of tolling the Bell, for Church,
Our little Sexton – sings.

God preaches, a noted Clergyman –
And the sermon is never long,
So instead of going to Heaven, at last –
I'm going, all along.

36

Every night, Carlotta and Sebastian shared ecstasy that echoed joy till sunrise. Every morning, Carlotta gave Sebastian a piece of her mind, like how, before the election, the city council met behind her back to kiss the generalissimo's ass, who was on the take from King Phillip, who wined and dined the military beside elite landowners who threatened unemployment and starvation if their workers voted for Carlotta's party, which they did anyway since they trusted her and reviled those tugging their chains.

Sebastian was good at back rubs, and an even better listener, both of which he did morning after morning when Carlotta lambasted those who forced their agenda without concern for others. At the end of every sentence, Sebastian tightened his cheeks into a frown and wrinkled his forehead in consternation. When Carlotta listed the government's abuse of power, Sebastian's standard reply was, "They had no right to do that."

It wouldn't take long, perhaps a bagel or two, with or without lox and cream cheese, for Carlotta to get to the good part, how she and her team whipped them good at the polls, after which Sebastian would wall-to-wall smile and repeat for the umpteenth time, "You did it, Carlotta! The future of Spain is assured!" even though he didn't mean the second part. What was important was moving the discussion along as he mostly kept his eyes, and mind, on the mainsail telltales.

By the end of the sixth day at sea, Sebastian estimated that they were nearing the Greek island of Lefkada, but he also knew the limits of jostled sextant sightings, and a week of dead reckoning is always dead wrong. At five in the morning, he waved to Jimmy at the helm as he followed Carlotta to bed, then fast fell fast asleep in the middle of Carlotta's follow-up head massage.

Jimmy smelled flowering shrubs the moment Sebastian disappeared. His suspicion was confirmed when he spotted gliding gulls and diving cormorants. He shushed Conchita with finger to lips. He then left her at the helm to tiptoe forward to douse the jib, which ten minutes later was lashed to the deck. Their progress slowed as Sebastian snored on. There was more than enough wind to mainsail into Milos Bay, turn upwind, and then come to a stop before the bow anchor was lowered one link at a time, also not making a sound.

Jimmy's goal was not to wake those below deck. The tricky part was freeing the boom line to backwind the mainsail, which, with Conchita's help, he pulled off without a decibel. The boat reversed to run out anchor rode that wiggled itself secure. What followed was a sailor's joy— "we're here, we did it"—relaxation that finds not a single atom in the universe out of place.

Jimmy was right to hide landfall until Sebastian and Carlotta had eight hours of shut-eye. Ten minutes after they woke up and looked out of their aft cabin porthole, they were on deck, dressed and ready to explore a volcanic island unrivaled for its geological wealth and hot spring baths.

They docked their skiff beside a seaside restaurant in Agios Nikitas and went for a walk, then later returned for dinner to watch the greatest show on earth—the march of civilization. Before baklava finished their feast, teacher Conchita had their week organized chronologically, beginning with Phylakopi to marvel at the rock walls still standing three thousand years after the Bronze Age city was constructed and a half a century before they knew Egypt, already a civilization ten thousand years old, was right next door.

Tripoli village and its amphitheater began day two. Conchita stood onstage and closed her eyes to imagine ten thousand Roman citizens attending a play, or town meeting, or music festival. Right next door were the catacombs, where four hundred years later, Christians persecuted by Rome, hid and buried their dead, a major mind shift for mankind since those entering Rome at the time were greeted outside the gates by growling dogs waiting for dinner, delivered daily in the form of dead bodies discarded in the field. Christians who buried the dead were convinced that their relatives, like themselves, would someday rise and walk the earth once more, a no-brainer selling point compared to the roar of Roman brutality; and not completely in error, Sebastian pointed out before adding, "One more dimension and they would have nailed it, without the distraction of two thousand years looking at the nailed-up guy."

On the third day, Sebastian put his foot down to insist they snorkel Sarakiniko's beach, crystal clear water surrounded by white volcanic rock slabs as smooth as polished ivory. Sebastian suggested the moon might look just like it, without water, of course. Twenty-four hours later, the boys' beach day was traded for a day touring Plaka Castle, the Venetian masterpiece dating back to the thirteenth century when Venice rose to glory and kicked out prior squatters. The next day's surprise was Sebastian's request to visit a church, the Byzantine Church of the Trinity, celebrating the "now you see them, now you don't" three gods in one package. Devised in 842 CE, it was a relatively recent invention, as Carlotta pointed out, which helped the pope establish Caesar-like status. The three-nave basilica with vaulted domes was identical to a Roman court of law, which made perfect sense to Sebastian, since one system of oppression was no different than another.

No one was dancing in the white-washed beach bar when they made their way back at sunset. Everyone was on their feet by midnight, waving arms, and singing to beat the band, which was still playing. An hour later, with sore feet, they rowed out to *Jubilation* under the influence of alcohol, majestic beauty, and the love of humankind.

Sebastian insisted on their next port of call in a manner that confused Carlotta. He wanted to visit the site where Greece went wrong, and civilization had yet to rectify the tragedy. The destination was Katakolo, a small peninsula with a temple built for the god of all gods, he who rules all and justifies all, the nonmortal whom every European totalitarian kept in his back pocket—Zeus, the god of war, murder, and pillaging.

Mount Olympia, a javelin's throw away, was the island's main attraction. Sebastian suggested they run there, just like in ancient times.

"What? Don't you think you can do it?" he asked, teasing Carlotta.

"Of course I can. I have no doubt. It's just. . ."

"Just what?"

"Well, Sebastian, if you must know, it would be fun, but I'll get all hot and sticky."

"Like last night. I love you like that."

"Naked, straddling you next to a shower on the boat, yes. After a twenty-five-mile hike to Olympia, no."

"We can be just like those who competed in the first Olympics, and I'm certain they all sweated it out."

"With hairy legs and BO No, thank you. That's not my image."

It was a swift compromise. Sebastian handed Carlotta a stack of bills for shopping and reserved two fast mules—if there were such a thing—to carry the gals to the site Jimmy and he would run to, provided that when they got there, Carlotta and Conchita had fig leaf garlands to crown their fellas champions and bring a second pair to be worn in bed that night by the ladies.

Sebastian had two fathers: Zeek, of sound body; and philosopher professor Fritz, for thinking, and who required Sebastian to memorize *Prometheus Bound*, Aeschylus's play written in 450 BCE, which was performed in Athens, the birthplace of Western civilization and democracy. The city was named after Athena, the goddess of wisdom.

Prometheus was the Titan who defied Zeus and stole fire from the gods for the benefit of mankind. But it wasn't fire that he stole, explained

Fritz, but rather what it symbolized, namely reason and intellect, which made Prometheus the hero who opened the eyes of humanity to knowledge. Every week, Fritz had drilled Sebastian, who would rather have been drunk chasing women undergrads, on the message of the most famous play in antiquity—that we must, every day of our lives, resist tyranny and the frustrations of reason falling on deaf ears at the feet of sheer power.

Zeus was not a nice guy. Like all those who clutch power, he would do anything to keep it. When he was told that his wife, Metis, was about to give birth to a child more powerful than himself, he ate her on the spot. To no avail. Hephaestus snuck up behind him cleaved Zeus's head wide open, and pulled out the goddess of war, gowned and armed.

With lightning and thunder available on demand, Zeus held his own but didn't hesitate to punish Prometheus by chaining him to a rock, where every day an eagle would rip him open and eat his liver, only to have it regenerate at night to be painfully shredded the next day, and every day that followed.

In college, Sebastian imagined what it would be like to act out the play on the actual steps of the Parthenon, so they sailed to the island and checked in at the local yacht club, Yiot Haven. An hour later, in a rented Ford, the four sailors were looking down on the city as Conchita volunteered to add a line or two while standing next to Sebastian in front of the south porch of the Erechtheion in front of the maidens of Athens. The sky was clear. A cool breeze was blessed by all. Sebastian threw his jacket over his arm like a toga and faced the crowd, numbering three, if you counted the pigeon Jimmy was feeding behind his back.

"Are you ready?" Sebastian asked.

Instead of answering, Carlotta and Jimmy applauded, which attracted a handful of tourists walking by.

Sebastian began by throwing his right arm straight out as he talked into the air above the crowd, by then numbering half a dozen:

My name is Prometheus,
I am the foe of Zeus, and one at feud with all the deities
that find submissive entry to the tyrant's hall.
And my fault? Too great a love of humankind.
Yea, to my friends, a woeful sight am I.

With a smile and a wink to Carlotta, schoolteacher Conchita stepped in front of Sebastian to make it a two-person show. "Hast not bore boldly in aught else transgressed?" she said in her lowest possible voice.

"I took from man expectancy of death," replied Sebastian, facing her.

"What medicine found thou for this malady?"

"I planted blind hope in the head of him," Sebastian said, looking skyward.

"A might boon thou gavest man," said Conchita.

"Moreover, I, Prometheus, have conferred the gift of fire."

"And have frail mortals now the flame—bright flame?"

"Yes, and shall master many wants thereby," proclaimed Sebastian. He walked to the edge of the stone wall supporting the virgin statues behind him, looked to the city, and then faced an audience that had grown to three dozen.

Go thou and worship if you must, I will not fold my hand in prayer
to be the dog that licks the foot of power.
I care nothing for Zeus, yea, less than naught!
So let him do whatever he wants to sway the word
in his little hour of power.

Carlotta and Jimmy then jumped up on the rock shelf to face three rows of curious spectators. Just as Sebastian was about to begin his finale, Carlotta stepped forward and boldly said, "To short-lived men, purveyors of prerogatives and titles, I've a word for thee, and the word is freedom!"

With force and volume in excess, Sebastian won back the audience:

I hate all the gods, because having received good at my hands,
they have rewarded me with evil,
and there is not wrong however shameful, or no shift
of malice whereby Zeus shall persuade me to lock my lips.

Carlotta continued with arms held high amateur acting that worked:
Therefore, let lightening leap with smoke and flame,
and all that is beat and tossed together, with
whirl of featherily snowflakes
and loud crack of subterranean thunder,
none of these shall bend my will or force me hither.

Sebastian finished quietly, with a bow that brought applause and a few drachmas for their effort, "And he that do so shall fall from power. This I have long ago thought and long ago determined."

+++

A heap of happy days later, after six weeks away, *Jubilation* was provisioned for the passage home. They slept late, had breakfast on the shore, and bought a bucket of goat stew for the evening's meal at sea. Jimmy was at the wheel. After securing the anchor to the deck, Sebastian joined Carlotta standing midship to look back at the acropolis.

"My mind is totally blown," said Sebastian, more dumbstruck than Carlotta imagined he could ever be.

"Explain, Sebastian," she said, holding his hand tenderly and looking at him as he kept his eyes on the shoreline.

"I can't decide if it's incomprehensible or just tragic."

"Now you've lost me. Are you all right?"

Sebastian wasn't. He couldn't free his mind from the goings on in Berlin and Italy. The thought of Christian soldiers murdering Jews and each other had him petrified. "The horror of murder pervades every second of life with fear," he said. "The impact of what humanity might have been and might be this very day is devastating. It's Zeus. . . it's like he's the devil."

"You mean warfare, Sebastian? Yes, our course, it's awful, but it's all right now. Things are getting better. You don't have to be upset. What's happening? I've never seen you like this. . . here. . . look at me. . . please!"

Sebastian turned and gave Carlotta a hug to hide his face before a sniff and two long breaths. "Okay, here's the thing. Those guys who lived back then. . . they put two sticks in the ground hundreds of miles apart and measured the angle of the sun's shadow at high noon, from which they not only determined that the earth was round but actually calculated its size."

"Yes—Euclidean geometry, of course."

"Not only that, they came up with the idea that all matter is made up of atoms and discussed equality and equal opportunity and dozens of things we haven't even got to yet."

"Okay. . . sure," Carlotta said, leaning her head on Sebastian's shoulder. "Now tell me what's *really* bothering you."

"You know me too well, my love. The problem is that all those great minds and brilliant discovers lost out to Zeus."

"Meaning?"

"Long before they were corralled by Alexander and then conquered by Roman legions, Greek minds made the ultimate discovery, one that, if allowed to flourish, would have saved civilization and have us, I don't know, perhaps walking on the moon or touring Mars by now."

"And what is that great epiphany?"

Sebastian straightened up and found the strength to return with certainty, "They looked at their history, examined the documents of the past, and then effortlessly concluded that all the stories about Zeus, and Venus, and gods in the sky, were total nonsense." He then turned to Carlotta, held both of her forearms, and faced her. "Carlotta, they knew! They knew!"

"What?" said Carlotta, noticing Sebastian's hands gently shaking.

"That every one of their god stories, and all the stories, and our stories, were all fables and fairy tales! They have nothing to do with God and everything to do with fear and exploitation. Look at the world today! It's a mess and getting worse! Why won't anyone on this planet listen to reason? Why doesn't anyone read Prometheus? Why won't anyone do something about it?"

Conchita left Jimmy at the helm to face Sebastian.

"You're too hard on yourself, and on civilization, Sebastian. The 'fables' of which you speak have done us good. It is true that Prometheus reminded the Greeks of the value of rationality, but don't forget that the Bible added stories that foster love and forgiveness. I agree with Ella Wilcox, who said, 'So many gods, so many creeds, so many paths that wind and wind while just the art of being kind is all the sad world needs.'"

"Her final advice I like even better," added Carlotta. "'Laugh, and the world laughs with you; weep, and you weep alone.'"

Sebastian did neither. He just looked down, turned around, and went below to be alone.

37

The sea isn't always easy to get along with. She has her moods and refuses to accept excuses. Her best trick is making the world disappear, magic more successful than hiding bills or avoiding scowling faces. The ocean, like life itself, presents adversity every day of living, which fortunately, on *Jubilation,* was no more than one lost stanchion, a stiff mast chum, and decks that needed a good scrubbing.

The second half of the return trip was a slap in the face: sustained twenty knots with gusts over thirty-five, and drizzle that froze noses and soaked socks to the toes, which made snuggling below deck after a warm meal and a hot shower all the more luxurious. The schedule was to love and be loved, kiss and kiss again.

Carlotta and Conchita took shelter under the dodger that tented over the companionway. From there, they toasted their men standing watch at the stern, kept dry in oil suits beneath a canvas bimini top stretching from one running backstay to the other. The wind was fierce. Jimmy documented a new record for the number of miles left behind in twenty-four hours, which was a good thing and a bad thing.

Then the wind dropped, the sun shone, and shivering ceased. Carlotta was the first to sight land at the bow. She followed Sebastian forward. He brought binoculars to look for landmarks to adjust their course. Speed was a memory, they barely moved, but the sky turned blue, the sea green, and birds were added to the scenery. Thirty minutes later, the wind died completely. The boat stood still. No one cared.

After making his way to the bow, Sebastian steadied himself by holding the forestay. He leaned, looking forward, holding binoculars to his eyes. He studied the horizon for five minutes without moving or saying a word. Carlotta downed her last bite of granola as she rose from the cushion over the forward cabin, where she thought Sebastian would join her. He didn't, so she then grabbed the same forestay opposite Sebastian, who still didn't budge or look over at her.

"And just what do you see out there, honey?" she said, sweet as sugar.

"Wonders to behold."

"Those are kissing words, partner," said Carlotta, mimicking a cowboy from a Zane Grey novel.

Sebastian took her up on the smack and added a few more before he returned to look out.

"Can you be more specific?" she asked, toying with conversation.

"Oh. . . wait a minute. . . it's getting clearer. . . yes. . . my. . . my. . . isn't that something?"

"Well now," said Carlotta, wetting her lips with suspicion. "Go on."

"I see a farmhouse. . . yes, that's it. . . and it's painted white with a porch the length of the building. It has a wide front door and another off to the side, where a two-sided windowed hallway connects to a brand-new garage. And that's just the beginning. Right next to a Mercedes in the first barn are two more barns, one for cows and the other double lofted for winter storage. And around that farm—wait until you see this!" he said with growing enthusiasm. "There's an orchard ripening apples, pears, and peaches beside horse-high wheat and golden corn making a living in the sun."

"That sounds like a lot of work to me," said Carlotta, monotone.

"Not at all, my dear. Half of one of the barns is filled with automated tracker equipment, with canopies. It will be like going for a ride in the country, except that food grows behind you. And the nights on that front porch watching Grampa and Gramma play with Felippe and Gilberto and Raquel and Sophia. . ."

"And little Sebastian?" Carlotta interrupted, smiling.

"Perhaps, but just one of them."

"I think one of them might already be too much."

"Yes, I am just toooooo much, aren't I?"

"That you are, indeed," she said, beginning another kissing spree.

Sebastian secured the binoculars to the bowsprit before walking back to the cushion with Carlotta, but instead of joining her sitting, he knelt down in front of her to hold her hand. "Carlotta, in one week, I can stock *Jubilation* with provisions to last a month. Three weeks after we cast off, we'll make Nova Scotia, and two weeks after that, you and I will dock in Green Bay, Wisconsin. I have a cottage, and I will build that farmhouse for you and our kids. Europe is a volcano ready to erupt. We can have the life of our dreams. Will you marry me?"

Carlotta slowly let go of Sebastian's hand to walk forward and then turned to face him. Sebastian sat back with legs straight and face blank.

"Sebastian," Carlotta said without emotion, "that's a beautiful picture, but don't think for a moment that it will get me all teary-eyed to jump into your lap. And no offense, I know you love me, but you're being just like a man."

"I am a man, Carlotta," Sebastian said resolutely.

"Oh, you know what I mean."

"No, I don't, Carlotta. What I do know is that good things are better than bad thing. I don't see anything complicated here."

"I do. You're a man, and like every other man, you expect a woman to drop everything in her life to live your life. It's not fair. I have a life too."

"Of course you do," said Sebastian, getting closer and breathing easier, "and you can have any life you want—doctor, lawyer, Indian chief, business leader, or bakery chef. You know we do have those things in America?"

"But mostly farmhands and cowpokes."

"No. . . Fond du Lac has a symphony, Appleton a theater group, and Chicago the latest ballet alongside boring opera."

"I have my work, Sebastian," said Carlotta with hands on her hips.

"Carlotta, we'll work to achieve the good life. Let's start there and work back. You know we'll be happy, and knowing you, our life will end up just the way you want it. Let me make your dreams come true. . . in America."

Carlotta moved not one inch closer. "I'm a very important person, Sebastian. I head the Committee on Domestic Affairs. Don't you realize that I have a country to build?"

"And you've done marvelously, but you're one piece of a giant jigsaw puzzle. The world will do what the world will do. Let's make our own world. Just think of it! Plenty of money, tons of friends, a brood of kids—and nobody shooting at us. We owe it to our children."

"And when I explain to them their Spanish heritage," she said louder, "do I mention the part about how their mother deserted Spain in its time of need?"

"You do not belong to Spain. You belong to yourself," Sebastian said, softer and slower, navigating troubled waters.

"Times are changing, Sebastian. In the past, when you men were out there living it up, making a fortune, and chasing sex as you please, we women were forced to stay home without the right to own property, get an education, or say our piece."

From the stern, Jimmy heard the conversation. If Sebastian had turned around, Jimmy would have signed the suggestion to shelve the discussion. Sebastian did not turn around.

"And all this," Carlotta said in low tone suggesting anger, "from the gender that screwed up the world."

"Again," Sebastian said, suddenly matching Carlotta's combative tone, "men aren't the enemy, women aren't the enemy; history is the enemy, and we are all victims."

"Victims!" Carlotta said, with high tone and rising volume. "If you want victims, just look in any house on the street and you will find a woman mending socks and changing diapers in a Victorian girdle that was forced on her."

"Yeah! By her mother! Who also stood right next to her dad, enforcing rules that required sons to prove they were courageous by running into bullets. And, to make matters worse, those ladies swooned over the power-hungry males that pushed other men around. Also, I would like to point out, while those ladies were home, heaven forbid surrounded by children in a warm house and well-fed, their men were stabbed through the neck with bayonets and left to die in the mud, or perhaps shot in the gut to crawl under a bush to die of peritonitis, or captured and tortured to death. If you ask me, your sex got the better deal."

"Some men died, some didn't. All of we ladies were chained to the kitchen."

"Where their moms and dads told men you wanted to be. In the past, a man was told that he was a failure if he couldn't make enough money for his wife to stay home while he coughed his lungs out in a coal mine."

Sebastian, already unsteady, animated more aggressive and didn't notice Jimmy signing him to shut up before matters got worse.

"And again," Sebastian said, looking directly at Carlotta, "it's about history. It's not *we* ladies Carlotta, it's *those* ladies… you weren't there. And it's not *you* men, it's *those* men… I wasn't there either. All the more reason to wipe the board clean and start over… in America."

Carlotta pointed at the diesel. Sebastian fired her up. When the dock was in sight, she said, "Sebastian, you know I love you, and you also know how passionate I am about saving Spain."

"I do. It's one of the reasons I love you. You're the most impressive woman I have ever met. Our kids will be as special as you are."

"Okay. . . Okay. . . Sebastian. . . why don't we just put our instincts on hold for now? We'll play the game out. Give me two years to set Spain in the right direction. I owe my countrymen as much."

"If I know human beings, there are a dozen people under you who would love to step up and be top dog. You are assuming, like we all do, that no one can take your place, that you are absolutely essential for success. Think about it. Do you really believe that's true?"

"Two years, and I will give you my answer."

"Which means you don't have an answer. . . which means you don't have a yes."

"Or a no," Carlotta said, holding on to Sebastian. "I must end what I started before beginning how I want my life to end."

"So," Sebastian said, breathing out, exhausted, "it's take it or leave it?"

"Oh, you silly boy," Carlotta said, moving her finger around Sebastian's belly before teasing lower. "It's take it tonight, and tomorrow night, and this weekend, and on and on. Yes, we're in love. This is the way to keep it that way, the only way, for now."

"Roger that. . . two years it is," said Sebastian, deflated.

Jubilation's entrance to the harbor was announced from the deck of the yacht club, which called city hall, which had a reception committee waiting with a car at the dock.

Sebastian and Jimmy were at the bow adjusting anchor tension when the yacht club boys extended a ramp to the stern. Carlotta and Conchita had their bags packed at the rail. The first visitor to board *Jubilation* in months was Leandro Vasquez, also the deputy chief of financial affairs. He carried the girls' luggage to the car. Galeno Ortego, the tallest blue-eyed Spaniard Sebastian had ever seen, waited on the shore with open arms and a hug for Carlotta that neither cut short.

By the time Sebastian and Jimmy reached the stern, Carlotta and Conchita had been herded to the waiting car. Sebastian watched Carlotta through the back window as the car drove off. She looked up from the stack of papers she was reviewing to throw Sebastian a kiss as she mouthed "tomorrow," and then pointed to herself, Sebastian, and the sailboat.

"Sebastian," Jimmy said, "will. . . will. . . will she. . . she. . . bring Conchita?"

"Jimmy, I don't even know if she'll be back. All I do know is that we'll be here."

BOOK FOUR

38

Two years later, Sebastian had no choice, according to what Gunter said, who had joined the Nazi party to lobby for contracts but would get nowhere unless Sebastian returned to play the game with the new regime. Once again, the jobs of the entire town depended on Sebastian waving the right flag at the wrong people.

Marlene wrote two letters in a row. She talked about the plant and her family and had an optimistic outlook, and then she appealed to Sebastian's business sense by pointing out how much he also had to lose. She didn't mention her marriage to Gunter, or what Sebastian heard was on the way.

If he had a chance of refusing, the excuse vanished when Carlotta insisted that he do what he could to help the German people. "Sebastian, the world comes first, we come second, and I do expect that to happen, but for now, Hitler's National Socialist Party is unstable, it could go either way. Rally the Germany people behind democracy and fair play. Help them do what we did for Spain. Who knows, maybe Italy will be next. It's the will of the people."

Adolf Hitler has been described as the greatest criminal of all time. They say that because he *is* the greatest criminal of all time. Of course, he wouldn't have gotten anywhere without his gang, Benito Mussolini, and a certain Eugenio Maria Giuseppe, who, as Pope Pius XII, supported Hitler up to and through the war. And yes, he knew about Auschwitz—and yes, he knew about Adolf Hitler's "successful" genocide plan—for the race that bore Jesus Christ. No one of sufficient intellect took Hitler seriously until the Vatican blessed Adolf's leadership and instructed parishioners to vote accordingly.

The Sebastian who left Germany was not the Sebastian who returned to Germany from Spain. Neither was his transportation, which was a magnificent Mercedes-Benz 770, also known as the *Großer Mercedes* ("Big Mercedes"), with a back seat wide enough to sleep on. When it was Jimmy's turn to drive, Sebastian preferred sitting in the back seat. He brought a pillow and a blanket to pull up around him as he slumped over in the corner, overdramatizing remorse.

Jimmy liked to drive. The two took turns all the way. Sebastian leaned over to look out at the Mediterranean as they drove north by the ocean before heading to the German border. When the sea disappeared, Sebastian shrunk four inches and sighed.

"You know, Jimmy," he said, not looking over, "all life finds sorrow and, at some point, hopelessness despite the bravest of resolutions. Worse than that, all life finds defeat, which begets surrender that extinguishes the will to fight for life itself. One simply gives up."

Jimmy dutifully kept his eyes on the road and said nothing, but right after he tightened both lips in resolution, he reached down to the seat next to him, picked up a discarded bottle cap, and with a quick turn and fast right hand, bounced it off Sebastian's head, who emerged from his blanket hideout with a peculiar smile.

"Okay, I get the message. I'm an idiot. So what's new? Of course we don't give up. And I suppose you could say that when we lose it, it's not exactly us losing, it's us contaminated by problems, like poor sleep, rotten food, bad advice, and diseases. Deep down I really do know that the old us will be back. We will be back, won't we, Jimmy?"

Jimmy nodded yes. For the rest of the trip, no more bottle caps flew.

The driveway through the woods to his cabin in Ostkirchen was more beautiful than Sebastian remembered, and he thanked himself for meandering the entrance to add wilderness effect, which relaxed both Jimmy and Sebastian at the sight.

The four poplar trees planted in the middle of the grand entrance turnaround had grown, their clustered leaves stretched above the second-floor bedroom balcony, where Sebastian used to sight Marlene waiting when he got back from work.

Marlene was not there. Gunter was not there. Both had said that they would be.

"Perhaps the bridge?" Jimmy said, stepping out of the car. He then pretended to race Sebastian around the house to their old fishing hole. Sebastian pretended to chase him; both had one thing on their mind, picking a lure, kicking back, and enjoying fresh air.

Marlene and Gunter weren't on the bridge.

"We wait… what we do… we fish?" Jimmy got out staccato, knowing Sebastian was an easy sell. Both knew the rules, number one being that if you found a pole and a pond, and the day wouldn't miss an hour's break, then fishing was mandatory; that way, with or without dinner, they catch the day. They had no need for fish that day since they were expecting the customary Loeman family feast in town. Six frightened but then happy fish were returned to the brook.

Jimmy and Sebastian both looked to the road when they heard gravel-sliding turns from a car moving faster than caution recommended. It was Gerhard, who immediately ran to the back.

"Oh, thank God I found you before you go to town," said Gerhard, breathing hard. "Don't go to town. Stay here. You know nothing."

"You are absolutely right," said Sebastian, offering Gerhard a fishing pole. "Join us, have a seat. When do Marlene and Gunter show up?"

"That's just it," said Gerhard with a grimace, "there's been a problem, and there is a problem. But this very important! Marlene made me promise that you will promise to absolutely stay out of it. Go to work to-morrow like everything is fine. You know nothing about Marlene, where she went, or what she is doing."

Gerhard collapsed onto the bench, leaned over to hold up his head with both hands, and then half mumbled into the ground, "I told them get out of town. I told them, I told them. And cousin Dorothea, it's all her fault. She knew better but still let Erdmann publish the editorial. In Munich, it's like confessing to be an anarchist and asking to be shot."

Sebastian and Jimmy reeled in and stowed their poles as Gerhard settled down, repeating over and over, "I promised her that you will promise me. Do nothing. What will be, is."

Sebastian and Jimmy nodded before looking back at each other. Gerhard explained that Munich was a hotbed for beer-garden rally Brownshirt fascism. Being Jewish and resisting Hitler had made them the enemy. An order was issued to arrest Dorothea, Erdmann, and their two daughters. They were to be transported by freight car to the closest concentration camp, where they would disappear like all the rest.

Gunter insisted that they do nothing, but Marlene demanded that they drive to Munich to sneak the family out of town and across the Swiss border. Gunter caved in, but there was a problem. The SS got there first. When Marlene and Gunter reached the second-floor landing, they looked into the apartment and saw two soldiers with pistols drawn, who had just broken the door down. Dorothea's oldest daughter, Sarah, panicked, grabbed her doll, and started running to her bedroom. The soldier yelled halt. She did not. He fired at the girl, exploding the doll three inches from Sarah's face. Both soldiers then aimed, prepared to fire again. Both shots were deflected as the soldiers slumped to the floor. The steel hall lamp base, when swung like a bat, was more than fearsome enough to knock them out.

Marlene didn't even remember making the decision. She saw children at risk and couldn't stand by the injustice. Gunter stood shocked, at once petrified that they had just broken a law punishable by summary execution.

"When the soldiers came to, they barricaded the neighborhood and called for reinforcements," said Gerhard, weeping. "Marlene had twenty seconds to talk. Now, you and Jimmy promise to do nothing, Sebastian. It's what Marlene wants. Do nothing. It's too late."

39

Adolf Hitler began his debauchery in the beer gardens of Munich, where the loud and rowdy were easy to please, and everyone was already drinking down their IQ. *It's a shame the city has bad breath*, Sebastian thought to himself as they entered, *Munich is every inch as gorgeous as Paris, and the mountains add to it.*

Sebastian sat in the back seat of their customized Mercedes that flew two swastika flags from each bumper and had a badge on the door identifying themselves as Berlin government authorities. Jimmy was the corporal at the wheel. Sebastian, with mustache and goatee, wore a black secret police officer's uniform that reminded him not to smile. In a folder next to Jimmy were enough real and counterfeit documents to take them anywhere, which did work at the outskirts of the neighborhood in which Marlene, Gunter, and the family were trapped.

"We have been sent from Berlin to report and also to help," barked Sebastian out the side window to the guards when they were stopped. "The fatherland has no room for anarchists, communists, or lawbreaking Jews. We must bring law and order to Germany!"

Sebastian demanded to see the captain in charge. Sebastian then listened to a five-minute report. He next told the commanding officer that he would do his own investigating and that when they searched a house, it was important to leave everyone in the street until the entire block had been cleared. *"Ja-voll, herr commandant,"* were the last words Sebastian hoped to have with Nazis, but there was the matter of finding Marlene.

When Gerhard realized that Sebastian was on his way, one way or another, he totally came clean. In private, Dorothea and Erdmann Schneider talked about their neighbors, who opposed Hitler and were worried enough to begin digging a tunnel from their basement under the park fence. It wasn't finished but would make a good hideout, and it was also the only thing Sebastian had to go on.

Jimmy drove Denningerstrassse to Cosimastrasse, and then up the dead end where Sebastian wanted to start. The street was filled with families as the soldiers searched and ransacked floor by floor, beginning in the basement, where Sebastian and Jimmy stayed longer to snoop. It was the neighbor's house all right, and tile basement floors can slide sideways, that one corner did. Before the soldiers missed them, Sebastian and Jimmy were below ground, and not alone.

At first, all they heard in the dark was breathing. Then, in a quiet whisper, Sebastian said, "When we're together, have you noticed how often we get shot at?"

"It is you!" gushed Marlene, crawling over to hug Sebastian.

"And me," Sebastian heard Gunter say from the distant mud-dripping tunnel. "And the family is here, safe so far as well."

Sebastian welcomed Marlene's mud hug because it came with Marlene, who pulled right back to give Sebastian a sock on the shoulder. "What are you doing here? You were supposed to stay home, not come here and risk your life with us."

"Well, you see, that's just it. I'm not down here to get into trouble. I'm down here to save you and be the hero. So there."

Marlene held on to Sebastian until Gunter crawled over, who hugged Sebastian before asking what the plan was. The plan was to arrest them all, at four in the morning when things settled down, and then drive right out the gate.

"And if that doesn't work, do we fight?" asked Gunter, who, before Sebastian could answer added, "I don't think it's right to kill German soldiers."

"It is right to kill in self-defense, Gunter," Sebastian insisted. "And those guys with funny shirts and evil plans will kill you, and us, and Marlene, and the ideas this country needs to survive. So the plan will work. Don't panic. But if you want to sit there and let one of those morons shoot you to death, help yourself. I plan to fire back."

Jimmy brought sandwiches, apple juice, and candy bars. Three hours in the dark would do it. As they waited, Sebastian and Marlene explored the far end of the tunnel. They discovered that it was barely half the distance needed, but there was a nice wood bench at the end for both to share.

"So," said Sebastian, resting his head on his hand like the thinker statue, "is this your new lifestyle Marlene? Fast, furious, and dangerous?"

Marlene did smile but was just as swiftly serious. "I don't know why I reacted like that, Sebastian. I saw something, and even though violence is against my moral imperative, my instincts as a mother took over. I shouldn't have snapped. I should have known better."

Sebastian put one of his hands on Marlene's as he used the other to gently lift her chin as he got closer. "I'm not disappointed in you, Marlene. I'm proud of you. You saved the lives of two children, and now their whole family."

"Not yet. We. . . and you. . . and Jimmy, could all die, and it would be my fault."

Sebastian faced Marlene to hold both her shoulders. "Marlene, I have a plan with excellent odds of success. I have reduced risk but also dangerously upped the game, and it is a game we don't want to play. . . but—"

"But," said Marlene, interrupting Sebastian.

"There are smarter ways to do the same thing. Like stun guns with memory wipeout."

"Neither guard saw me."

"Wonderful."

By three thirty, the street was clear, and rustling and occasional gunshots were heard only from the other side of the neighborhood. Sebastian had uniforms for Gunter and Erdmann, complete with sidearms to add firepower if the need arose. They sat up front with Jimmy. If questioned, they would repeat that they were assigned special forces with instructions to take orders only from their commanding officer.

Gunter and Erdmann, with seriously menacing faces, stood guard, looking in both directions when the women and children were led out handcuffed and thrown into the back seat. Eyes were seen in windows from half the houses in sight. Not one Nazi was in sight.

Leaving through the same gate they'd entered was a good thought, but the officer on duty had changed, and his replacement a bit slovenly, not to mention grumpy. He took the papers from Jimmy and turned to call for verification inside. The gate remained down, but not Sebastian's window, through which he yelled that any delay in his mission would be reported and that if the station was not respecting orders from the office of Adolf Hitler, then an investigation would proceed.

The slow-paced guard turned to check the resolve on Sebastian's face. What the captain didn't know was that just below the open window was a revolver ready to fire, and no wood gate could stop a big Mercedes 770. Sebastian stuck his hand out for the papers. The guard handed them over with a slight bow. The gate opened.

40

The family was dropped off at a farm owned by a friend who had plans to get them over the border by dark. When Sebastian's car pulled out of the barn, its conservative look was back. They were no longer soldiers, one of the best feelings there is.

As soon as the space opened up, Gunter and Jimmy lay down and went right to sleep. Marlene kept Sebastian company up front as they pulled away. Marlene turned all the way around to wave through the back window as they left. As she slid around to face forward, she noticed Sebastian looking lovingly through the rearview mirror, and his right eye was beginning to tear up.

"Why, you old softy," Marlene said, quietly getting closer. "You really care about that family."

Sebastian swallowed, pinned his eyes to the road, and said, "Well, of course. They are very nice. It's just. . ."

"Just what, Sebastian?"

"Well, like you say, one of those brick-brained Nazis almost murdered those defenseless little girls." Then, turning for a look over to Marlene, he added, "What the hell is wrong with them? The muck Europe is stuck in is unacceptable."

"Yes, yes, Sebastian. And we will change it. I have political contacts. Everyone wants to bring democracy back to Germany."

"You're getting nowhere."

"Organizing is somewhere, and we have plans. Spain is doing fine. We will too."

The sun rose to silence. Marlene described the day's first light as beatific. Sebastian grunted agreement and then commented on the last glimpse of the morning star. Then there was more silence. With an occasional glance, Marlene waited for Sebastian.

"Marlene. . . you see. . . it's just. . ."

"Yes, Sebastian. What is it?"

"Well, when I was young, life was a playground of slides, teeter-totters, and merry-go-rounds. Then I left for Europe and mayhem showed up. Instead of wide-eyed appreciation and enthusiastic adventure, it's avarice, greed, prejudice, and concentration camps. So yes, of course I keep asking myself why I'm here—or for that matter, why are you here too?"

Marlene took a deep breath and then put her hand on Sebastian's leg. "We are here to help. We are helping. And you and I also share wonderful feelings together."

"There are other feelings. Ones that we don't want."

"Now what, Sebastian?"

It had been a long twenty-four hours, but Sebastian kept his head up and eyes on the road, addressing the bleakness of the day.

"Marlene," Sebastian said, depleted of energy, "these bodies of ours get old, sick, fall apart, and then kill us. Every step of the way brings disease and suffering, which we make worse by breathing bad air and eating unhealthy food."

"You and I stay in shape. Most people do."

"Helps, but no matter what we do, our body parts fall apart," said Sebastian mournfully.

Marlene interrupted with a schoolteacher's tone. "What does all that have to do with the sunrise?"

"Concentration camps."

"Okay, now you've lost me."

"Here me out. I have the day's philosophic special. So, we all have an aging body-part problem, pain and misery included. So what do we do about it? Do we invest time, energy, and resources to correct physical ailments, eliminating pain, and extending a full life? No, of course not. That would make sense. Instead, we bankrupt ourselves making weapons and march around with guns to blast to smithereens as many body parts as possible, with tortuous death the goal. Marlene, we're looking the wrong way. We're doing the wrong thing. Human beings have ruined life. Thanks to our stupidity, life has become the victim of itself!"

With one hand lifted off the wheel to gesture, Sebastian then proclaimed loudly, "Just in case disease, suffering, and death don't come soon enough, planet Earth remains obsessed with warfare." Sebastian mimicked childish brattiness: "My country is better than your county. I am better than you. I get what I want, and everyone else must agree with me."

Marlene reached over to rub Sebastian's shoulder. "You're tired. When we get home, you're going straight to bed."

"When *we* get home?" Sebastian said, looking over, suddenly forgetting the world's problems.

"You know what I mean," Marlene said with a flirty side-look. "When you get to your place with Jimmy and my husband and I get to our place."

"Why yes, of course, my dear."

Sleep was not an option. Nonstop and wide open, the Mercedes barely made it back before the Wehrmacht deputy was scheduled to inspect and negotiate. From the back door, Gunter was the first up the stairs to run to his desk, immediately followed by Marlene and Sebastian, sitting peacefully reviewing papers when the deputy and four armed guards barged through the front door without knocking.

The officer in charge was a greasy-haired little guy, basically an accountant with an attitude. The four Aryans behind him never spoke but cast shadows taller than Sebastian and Gunter. The first duty was to repeat the loyalty oath to Adolf Hitler and the Third Reich. The fatherland always came first. Marlene almost giggled when Sebastian agreed and then added enthusiasm that the soldiers bought.

The tour and "inspection" followed. Deputy Baumann asked questions about the grade of steel and brittleness of parts that let Sebastian know that he hadn't the slightest idea how to make weapons. What the deputy was good at was repeating, "More weapons, less money. That's what is going to happen. More weapons, less money. And don't worry. To help everyone in Germany get a job, Der Feuhrer has decided that every citizen will work for less money. You won't have to pay them as much. But don't you worry, there will still be enough for you. We keep our friends happy. I expect that we understand each other?"

For a second, Sebastian thought Baumann was actually asking a question; then, comparable to saluting, Sebastian said, "Yes, sir! Of course, sir."

After the agreements were signed, Sebastian invited Deputy Bauman and his men to join them for one of Mutti's famous ham dinners. They declined but did share toasts with the office staff at the pub across the street before they left.

Four weary travelers said nothing over dinner. Munich was not mentioned and never would be. Marlene talked about gaining political support for an improved agenda. Sebastian was certain she believed she would make a difference. Pappi brought out papers documenting the best farm harvest ever. Mutti kept looking over to Marlene, who was indeed beginning to show. Gunter was polite and agreeable but remained stunned. Jimmy looked straight ahead, trying to stay awake. When his eyelids closed, he would shake his head back and forth. Jimmy and Gunter excused themselves early, long day and all that.

Marlene and Gunter's house was on the other side of the path home. Marlene walked in the opposite direction for ten minutes to keep Sebastian company. The moon was so bright, moths cast shadows. The air was so clear, every breath brought happiness.

"Sebastian," Marlene said, holding one of his hands to bring both face-to-face. "Today, you saved the plant, the town, and my life."

"And my own self-respect," he replied. "Until today, I wasn't sure just who I was or what I was turning into. I mean, look at the people I deal with to make money. Every buyer causes nothing but trouble."

"Don't get me wrong," Marlene said, flat and serious, "I'm still not sure who you really are, but you have a good heart and a brave soul. Thank you again. And now you are free to go. You can return to Spain and go sailing."

Sebastian stopped to sit on a bench nearby. Marlene sat at the other end of the bench and then turned to face him.

"Well, Marlene, that's a funny thing," Sebastian said, scratching his head. "Spain thinks Germany is in trouble and that I should stay here to help for a while."

Marlene jolted back six inches. "Wait a minute. You have a woman who says she loves you and then tells you to disappear for six months? Why didn't she come along? Why doesn't she want you with her?"

"She does, but…"

"But?"

"She has all these meetings, and she's Spanish, and she's in control. But just temporary. Soon there will be time."

"I see," said Marlene suspiciously. Then, pointing to her stomach, she said, "For this?"

"Why, of course. You know me. I still want that basketball team."

41

In Almeria, Sebastian had become a dinner party adornment for Carlotta's political agenda. Their trips to Madrid didn't help, with too many weekends wasted in hotel bars. And there was a limit to how many hours one was willing to spend varnishing sailboat brightwork.

So Sebastian stayed in Ostkirchen to design and test products as he expanded the business and his income. He was needed, and he handed Marlene money to support democratic candidates. The world left them alone, and alone they did just fine, although the news never stopped coming, or stinging, like the April report from Berlin, where the high Catholic clergy held a conference with Adolf Hitler. He told the group that he was a devout Catholic who respected the pope, saying, "I have been attacked for approaching the Jewish question. The Catholic church has viewed the Jews as parasites for fifteen hundred years… I'm going back to the times… I am doing Christianity the greatest service."

The clamor that should have been was never heard. Rolling boxcars were.

Berlin was good at bad news. The Weimar constitution was "suspended indefinitely." There was no longer freedom of speech, rights of assembly, or postal privacy. Anyone could be forced into the army, sentenced without a judge, or just shot for being in the way.

Ostkirchen was out of the way, so no one bothered. The mood there was triumphant. Everyone was back to work, and Sebastian, against government policy, slipped cash to those who volunteered to work overtime to achieve production goals. A department store opened up on Main Street that sold everything from pots and pans to honeymoon negligee. And the pub had its first-ever line outside after they hired a chef for special Friday and Saturday night meals.

Best of all, the yearly town festival was back. It began at one o'clock sharp in the park at the east end of Main Street. The entire town was joined by farming friends from miles around. Games, kids rides, and fresh-powdered fritters were just the start. A shooting contest followed. A papier-mâché turkey was hoisted to the top of the highest tree. The three richest men in town—Sebastian; Marlene's dad, Karl; and bank president Dietrich Sauer—took turns trying not to win. He who exploded the bird paid for drinks, dinner, and the band that night in the municipal auditorium.

The three fellows shared one rifle. Karl went first. He aimed for a cloud. Dietrich didn't put his glasses on to have an excuse for missing, which he did admirably. Sebastian was tempted to tease one more round but instead put the others at ease by hitting the target and raining candy from the sky. The crown cheered. The children ran to clean up.

At four that afternoon, every male between the ages of ten and one hundred lined up in military formation, knee-high boots first to last, veterans in uniform up front. The march down Main Street was accompanied by a brass band. The entire parade goose-stepped in perfect unison. The ground shook like it had for hundreds of generations. Sebastian loved it. He felt like a giant wizard taking possession of reality.

At six, dinner was served; at eight, the beer kegs opened; and at ten, a bottle of champagne showed up at every table. The band started with a funky polka before easing into full orchestral dancing between group sings of the national anthem and others from the fatherland songbook. The evening was cozy, safe, and loving.

Gunter and Marlene spent most of their time with his relatives, who took turns telling Marlene how excited and willing to help they were when the baby came along. Marlene was well cared for, and she saved two dances for Sebastian. Most of the night, Sebastian roamed the room, repeating, "No, it is I who thank you. It's *your* hard work that keeps the plant busy."

At midnight, a final bottle of champagne was ordered. Sebastian preferred peace and quiet. It was enough that all had gone well and everyone was happy. He maneuvered to the back door, then outside for a casual walk home. Jimmy was sleeping out at Mutti's, who also put up Olga for the weekend.

The Loeman family house was dark. Mutti refused to head home until the last drop had been tasted and the last dance ended. Past the chilly church, the city lights dimmed to invite stars to join the evening, which is when Sebastian heard a noise and noticed a shadow approaching from town.

At the next turn, he jumped behind a bush and drew his revolver.

He quickly recognized the stalker: No one else in town was that thin but also packed with curves in every feminine way. It was Ada Mayer, who, like Sebastian, had enough of watching Gunter and Marlene live out "happy ever after" while she and Sebastian pretended not to care.

Sebastian stepped out, blocked the path, and waited for Ada to approach, who looked up at him through boggy eyes and said, "Hello, Sebastian."

"Hello, Ada, are you looking for the big bad wolf?"

"Nope, I'm not," said Ada, slightly confronting. "I'm looking for the big good wolf."

"Well, he's not here. Turn around, I'll walk you home," said Sebastian, as authoritarian as he could muster considering the time of night.

"Perhaps, but let's talk first. Do you respect me, Sebastian?"

"Yes, of course."

"And am I intelligent?" Ada asked directly.

"Your mind is quick, but you play dumb when all the time, you're one of the smartest in town."

"Do you therefore trust my judgement?"

"Absolutely."

"Then I, Ada Mayer, do indeed know what's in my own best interest, and I believe yours as well."

"Neither logic nor sentiment betrays you, Ada."

"Then get this. Gunter and Marlene aren't the only ones in town who deserve a hot night and warm sheets all the way to breakfast. Let's not walk me home. Let's go to your cabin instead."

Sebastian stepped back and said timidly, "Ada, I'm not worthy of such joy. But more than anything else, I do not want to harm or pain you in any way. I'm leaving town. I don't know when and I don't know where I'll go, although so far America is winning and Spain is losing. I need to get back to who I was to figure out who I want to be. Until then, I'm not ready to settle down."

"Is it another woman, Sebastian? Do you have a commitment?"

"Commitment?" Sebastian repeated, slightly sour. "Oh no, no commitment. That was made perfectly clear to me, on several occasions."

Ada didn't wait for additional information. Instead, she held Sebastian's hand and slowly led him toward his cabin.

"You know," he said, relieved of resistance, "all this week, when I stopped by and you brought out my special warm Danish with fresh frosting, I kept having this strange thought of what it would be like to put a little frosting on your lips for a kiss."

"Sebastian, I'm not exactly sure what to make of that image, but I like the kiss at the end. If you want, I can open the shop and find some frosting for any place you desire."

"Oh, yes—I mean no—I think," Sebastian got out, sounding like a nervous schoolboy who just sighted Santa Claus. "Frosting? Of course not, silly—but your lips—"

"Miss kissing as much as you do. And we're lucky. We *want* to kiss."

"Will there be anything else?" Sebastian asked, placing an arm behind Ada's back.

"Well now, let's see," said Ada, taking her time. "How about we swim in the pond naked, dry off on the bridge, and then visit the hammock before going inside."

"And then fall asleep in my bed?"

"No. . . and then fall asleep in *our* bed."

42

Fun makes a difference. There was plenty of it in Ostkirchen. Marlene gained twenty pounds, then gave birth to twin girls. Gunter added a barn behind their house and then added a pair of ponies to the steeds he and Marlene rode.

Sebastian gained ten pounds, most of it from frosting, some from Sunday dinners. Even though he wasn't family, he was honored with the title "Uncle Sebastian" and invited over as often as not. He always accepted on Sunday and was grateful that Ada, still Marlene's best friend, was also always welcome.

The after-dinner strolls were everyone's favorite. As they drifted along, Sebastian and Marlene would end up side by side, with Gunter and Ada behind them. It seemed like every week something would happen or occur to Sebastian or Marlene that they just had to share with each other. They were never not, in some way, together.

Gunter became a problem, which prompted dinner rule number one: no politics until after dessert and then only with those not walking away. Gunter changed the day the German army doubled its size and gained five times the firepower of the combined armed forces of Britain and France. Out of the clear blue sky, Gunter would sound off about how Germany would finally take its rightful place in the world, whatever that meant, and that no other country on earth dared mess with them, thanks to Hitler, who kicked and poked constantly, only to have the rest of the world make excuses, look the other way, and then leave for ice cream.

Meanwhile, life remained good in Ostkirchen, and every day a little better. But there was a problem—the damned world kept changing. The news was never good. Marlene's efforts proved useless, and dangerous. Then there was the Jewish boycott and the suppression of all political parties not affiliated with the National Socialists. In 1934, after 90 percent of the electorate voted for Hitler, a plebiscite voted Hitler to be named *der Führer*. His first official act was to assassinate everyone who looked at him cross-eyed. His next project appointed himself war minister to march into Austria before meeting with Mussolini to engineer his master plan, which offered arms to every dictator willing to add land and soldiers to his satanic empire. Fat Franco raised his hand.

Then the big news arrived. From Morocco, Franco marched thirty thousand troops across the border to invade Republican Spain. He announced that his little army was about to overthrow the legitimate democratic government and install himself absolute dictator. Adolf and Benito smiled. They had weapons they wanted to test on breathing people before they turned them on the world.

Sebastian was furious. His last and only hope for Europe grew from Spain's example. "Carlotta and her Republican idealists must not fail! It would be the end of everything. Not even Fond du Lac would be safe."

"No, no, no!" yelled Marlene at Sebastian. "You don't want to be anyone's soldier. Spain's war is Spain's war. You'll be killed. You just can't, Sebastian."

The discussion began calmly in the driveway. The thought of crazy Sebastian running off to get shot drove Marlene nuts. After her outburst, she approached Sebastian, hugged him tightly without letting go, and then pitifully added, "You help us all put life together. Don't waste yours. Stay here. Your blood is as easy to spill as the rest."

It was the end of the day. Sebastian and Marlene had worked late to adjust an order, which barely kept the account, since Mussolini's national weapons factories were turning out superior weapons with extra discounts for homicidal maniacs. Mutti promised two dinners on the table when they got out. She was standing in the pantry, heating sauerkraut and sausage when the weary pair walked by, obviously not getting along.

Instead of sitting, Marlene calmly faced Sebastian and said, "Every war is a game of Russian roulette, Sebastian. You and I need to realize that the world is bigger than we are. We do what we can and hold on tight to the love we have for each other."

"That is about to be invaded, just like Spain," Sebastian said, as he plopped a giant spoonful of mashed potatoes on his plate, so loudly that Karl, sitting in the living room, put down the paper to add one more eavesdropper.

"We can also trust and pray to God," Marlene added.

"God didn't give us life to spend it apologizing for our presence. Right has more right to be than wrong. Europe has it all wrong. We must make it right. To me, it's simple."

"You've been steaming around like a locomotive all afternoon. I'm not convinced your brain has had a chance to think this through."

After loading his plate and adding mustard for the sausage, Sebastian didn't take a bite. Instead, he swung sideways, and softly and slowly stuttered his reasoning: "Marlene, you and I did all we could. The momentum in Germany overwhelmed us. Germany is lost. Italy has been gone for years. Spain is officially a free democratic state until proven otherwise. Franco only has thirty thousand Nationalist soldiers. There are eight hundred thousand loyal Republican Spaniards ready to fight for their freedom. Volunteers from all over the world are on the way. Everyone knows what's at stake. How can I sit back and do nothing?"

Mutti and Karl felt better when the volume of the conversation lowered. Sebastian and Marlene felt better well-fed and then decided to walk the path together.

"If you want to keep my nightmares down," she said, "you will make me two promises."

"I owe you much more. What's on your mind?"

"Number one: you will wait at least two weeks before making a final decision."

"Agreed."

"And if you are foolish enough to risk losing what need not be risked, you must absolutely, with no compromises, promise me that you will not volunteer or sign up for any military unit. You'll end up a bolt on an assembly line, as someone's else's stupidity sacrifices the rest of your years."

"Okay, observer and consultant only," said Sebastian, who knew he wouldn't take orders from anyone anyway.

Quiet returned. The crickets chirped. Marlene mentioned Hitler's pledge of neutrality and how he insisted he had no intention of invading Belgium or Poland.

All the way back, Sebastian and Marlene agreed that they lived on a continent where the inhabitants were exploited by a crippling minority and that governments that should be elevating the conditions of life seduced and bludgeoned the populace into slavery so deep no one bothered to look up anymore.

They both also agreed that the cause of freedom was the cause of God and that the only success eternity recognizes is living your own life as a loving spirit.

Sebastian disagreed with Marlene's military assessment. "Marlene, look at the numbers. Franco only has thirty thousand dupes. The volunteers from around the world will add one hundred thousand soldiers to almost a million loyal Spaniards who are ready to die to save democracy. The odds suggest victory. The love of liberty is the love of others. All the dictators have is the love of power."

"And big cannons and every prejudice of their breeding."

Then again there was silence as Sebastian reached over to hold Marlene's hand.

"You know," he said when they got back to town, "the way I see it is that a nation that values anything more than freedom has a problem, and therefore might lose its freedom."

"Like," Marlene wisely added, "thinking your fatherland, or business, or pushing others around, or saying the right thing, or heaven forbid saying the wrong word is more important than freedom."

"That when gone is a loss for all and a gain for none."

"Perhaps what this planet needs," Marlene said, with a fake laugh and a final hug for Sebastian, "is more words for stupidity."

"Yes, that's it. And less stupidity itself. Then we'll be all set."

BOOK FIVE

43

The Spain Sebastian had left was not the Spain to which Sebastian returned. Trust was in short supply and hope a variable commodity. From the sound of Carlotta's last letter, Sebastian concluded that she was out of hope, for words anyway, and had taken up the sword. Carlotta didn't ask Sebastian for a gun. He would have refused—he knew what a bad shot she was. Her neighbor showed her how to load an assault weapon. She joined a Republican brigade and marched off.

"Every war is a high-noon, six-gun shoot-out," said Sebastian to Jimmy as they approached the Spanish border. "If you're not ready to die, you're not prepared to kill. Carlotta won't last a week."

"And Conchita?" Jimmy asked.

"So far, I know nothing. They may be together."

"How. . . do we. . . find them?"

"We can start with Javier."

Mistake number one. Under penalty of excommunication and eternal damnation, the bishop, obeying Vatican orders, informed Javier that he was fighting for the survival of Christianity, which somehow translated into spying on Carlotta, reporting Sebastian, and helping a dictator enslave a country by ignoring the common good.

Javier was standing outside his church when Sebastian and Jimmy drove up. Since the war had broken out, the few parishioners Javier had left were never seen. The facade's mortar was crumbling, and weeds grew everywhere. Even Javier's robe had seen better days, and not just from the tomato stains left by the crowd; three patches barely held it together.

Sebastian pulled up passenger side to curb, which didn't do Jimmy any good, since a hydroplaning milk truck had sideswiped them in the middle of a thunderstorm ten miles from Paris. Every speck of chrome, including both door handles, was smashed to bits below a dent that ran from front to rear fender. Jimmy crawled out the window.

"Hello, Javier," said Sebastian, jogging around the car for a hug. "It's great to see you again, and the worse condition your church gets, the younger you look. Is that your strategy?"

Javier enjoyed a chuckle before pushing Sebastian back to arm's length for a good look. "Yes, it is. We can't all be like you and get more handsome by the year."

Jimmy followed with a handshake and a box of Mutti's anise cookies.

Javier brought Sebastian in for one more family embrace, during which, in his ear, he whispered, "Don't turn around or look around. We talk out here first and then, after a little show, disappear inside."

"I get it," whispered Sebastian, who released Javier and then spoke loud enough for anyone to hear, "So have you heard anything from Carlotta? I'm in town closing a weapons deal with Germany. Perhaps we can all go out to dinner some night."

Small talk followed down the aisle of the empty church to the basement, where Sebastian noticed an improvement: the crack in the wall had been sealed. Javier's first comment betrayed weakness of logic. "Sebastian, the church has Eugenio Maria Giuseppe to guide us along the path to heaven. Spain needs Francisco Franco Bahamonde to steer us clear of godless anarchy. God remains our first and last loyalty."

Sebastian stalled a second while he looked to the floor, then over to Jimmy, who Sebastian knew shared his opinion.

"Javier," Sebastian gently intoned, "examine every piece of information and think about justice for all and equality for men, women, and children. And if that doesn't tip you over, then consider that one snotty bully in the corner does not have the right to crash everyone else's party, ruin their day, destroy the night, and then kill them. Fairness, equal opportunity, shared love—is that not what Jesus stands for?"

"If it is. . ." added Jimmy slowly, and wisely, "then that is the direction. . . we should. . . be headed."

"But for now," Sebastian asked in a hurry, "what do you know? Where's Carlotta? And if anyone asks, tell them I'm on a social visit. Tell them—oh yeah," he said with a smirk, "I've come to ask my lover to marry me and live on my farm in Wisconsin."

"True. . . true. . ." said Jimmy, bobbing his head, smiling. "We farmers. . . grow. . . sleep. . . eat. . . fun."

It takes a great deal of positive thinking, and naivety, to ignore thirty thousand bloodthirsty Nationalist killers parked on the doorstep, and even less accurate reality testing to hesitate after they have broken down the front door to plant machine guns in your living room. And yet, in Madrid, every faction had to have their say, and no one did anything, for weeks.

Trusting predictions is a flimsy excuse for lethargy. Everyone expected Franco's puny band of cutthroats to be decimated in a month. That was before Mussolini and Hitler dispatched the most war-hardened battle troops on the planet, the Army of Africa, and thousands more from Italian barracks. To those ninety thousand well-armed killing machines was added the Luftwaffe, the most technologically advanced maelstrom ever conceived, which flew over one hundred and twenty thousand warplanes supported by over three million German mechanics, who specialized in bombing apartment buildings, blanket torching, and, the latest trick, the *blitzkrieg*, which coordinated air and land attacks to overwhelm "impenetrable" defenses in hours, opening the victims' lines for tanks to annihilate resistance on the spot.

The world was confused. The pope claimed the war was religious, right before blessing the Luftwaffe and banishing the Golden Rule. Britain and France just wanted to make sure Hitler's bombers only flew over Spain. The word they used to explain their behavior was "neutrality." Along with the United States, they refused to help the best ally they had in Europe, which later cost them the lives of their youths and earned them the black badge of cowardice for repeating, "I am not my brother's keeper."

Mexico did what it could to support the Republicans, which was very little. The Soviet Union made a lot of noise, which chased commie haters away, and they did send weapons, which were soon outdated. It was rumored that Stalin was talking to Hitler. Stalin, the man who eventually murdered more Russians than enemy attacks, added his two cents behind the scenes to help fuel the most devastating sequence of human error ever to befall humanity.

And yet the numbers kept Sebastian hopeful. A half million combatants on Carlotta's side could do it. When Sebastian left Germany, he knew nothing about Hitler and Mussolini's plans to prop up the Nationalists, but they were on to his.

Franco's troops captured Spain's northern coastline within a year. It was then on to Madrid, where he ran into trouble when some of his men realized they were on the wrong side. Southern Spain, from Almeria to Barcelona, resisted capitulation, but months later, losing Seville proved costly. The port was perfect for landing Franco's African troops, who captured Cadiz immediately; but Malaga, Jaen, and Almeria remained in Republican control, even though every street was packed with spies, saboteurs, and foreign agents.

The industrial centers of Barcelona, Madrid, and Valencia resisted successfully after Jose Giral ordered weapons distributed to the civilian population. Later, he realized that if rifles had been handed to farm workers on day one, Franco would never have had a chance. The people of Spain wanted no part of dictatorship.

Mandated conscription by both sides swelled the ranks like racks of lamb on their way to the butcher. Franco managed to force a million men to do his dirty work, while Carlotta's Republic barely made half that number. George Orwell and Ernest Hemingway were among the thousands of foreigners who sped to Spain to do what they could.

At the League of Nations, whenever someone yelled "fascism," someone else yelled back "Bolshevism." No one listened when the threat of hostilities escalating throughout Europe was discussed. Meanwhile, Luftwaffe Junkers Ju87, Stukas, and Junkers Ju-52 transport trimotor bombers coordinated efforts with Operation Ursula, a U-boat search-and-destroy unit. The Wehrmacht learned a great deal—in fact, they learned all they needed to later successfully isolate England and sink ships leaving Manhattan. Germany also handed Franco half a billion dollars to pay troops. Meanwhile, the United States and the rest of the "free" world refused to send Carlotta a dime.

The British elite, always mindful of the cost of keeping up the castle, opposed those fighting for freedom and, with the help of the media they controlled, made it a crime to come to the aid of the Spanish Republic. Over four thousand Englishmen told them to go to hell as they left to join the fight alongside Americans, Canadians, and others from dozens of countries, who, like Sebastian, could not sit back and do nothing. Volunteers from the States named their troops the Abraham Lincoln Battalion. The Canadians fought in the Mackenzie-Papineau Battalion, Germans in the Thalmann Battalion, and democracy-loving Italians in the Garibaldi Battalion, which distinguished itself during the Siege of Madrid. The Irish folk musician Christy Moore was immortalized in the song "Viva la Quinta Brigada." They named their group the Connolly Column.

In 1937, Franco made a second attempt to take Madrid. He failed. His next offensive, the Battle of Guadalajara, was an even more humiliating defeat. He also failed to take Zaragoza.

In 1938, however, German and Italian air support showed up. By March, Franco had cut the Republic's territory in half and was demanding unconditional surrender. When those fighting the honorable fight refused, Franco mounted a massive campaign headed south.

That was where Sebastian finally caught up with Carlotta.

44

Carlotta was not on the roster of any fighting brigade. When she got to the front, she discovered a medical crisis, which was no medical care at all. When she lent a hand and presented her credentials, they made her captain of the medical unit. She hadn't had a good night's sleep since.

After Sebastian got nowhere with Javier, he sped to Almeria, to get nowhere again. Then he left Almeria for the front, where he joined the battle of the day. The Boadilla skirmish left a full-thickness skid-mark scar down his back from a bullet that he not quite completely ducked under. His second wound was earned jumping headfirst into a foxhole during a shelling. After that, he joked that eight toes ran faster than ten. "Thoughts of death are not what I'm here for," he told himself, trying hard to accommodate obligation, duty, and desire.

Surviving for years paid off. There was news from Almeria, of all places. A friend from the yacht club sent Sebastian a note describing a woman who had just showed up who fit Carlotta's description and who had been seen walking by *Jubilation* late at night.

The Nationalist bombing of Almeria began months before Sebastian and Jimmy got to the city. The streets were bare. Everyone was in bomb shelters. Twice, Sebastian and Jimmy got lucky. Once, the Mercedes did not. Downtown, four blocks from the tunnels, a street crater brought the car to a halt. Just after the two left on foot, they saw a bomb explode the face off of a five-story, granite building that crumbled over the car.

"May she rest in peace," said Sebastian, quickening the pace.

"And pieces," said Jimmy, looking back with wide-open eyes.

When the bombardment of Almeria began, everyone in town helped dig tunnels deep below the ground. The walls shook and leaked stone dust but never collapsed. Three full flights of stairs were chiseled at multiple entrance sites, each stairway making two right-angle turns to deter blast waves. You weren't safe until you made it around a bend. Jimmy and Sebastian did. The next two flights they took one step at a time.

The bottom of the tunnel, a healthy ten feet high and just as wide, looked like it went on forever and was everywhere lined with old people, young families, and pets. Every twenty feet, a bare bulb hung from a metal tube that ran the length of the ceiling. It wasn't just a tunnel. Sebastian and Jimmy discovered side rooms; one read "Medical Ward."

On the way in, Sebastian and Jimmy passed a dozen injured civilians. Then, when two soldiers moved to the side, Sebastian saw Carlotta, in full nursing uniform complete with bars on her shoulder. She was giving orders.

"Maria, tell Doctor Torres that I have two patients bleeding to death who won't if he can get to their amputations within the hour. And tell him that if he can't, he'll have to answer to me." Then, turning to another assistant, she said, "Amaya, get that message to Madrid at once. We need penicillin and a sterilizer, and not tomorrow. We needed them yesterday."

Sebastian and Jimmy stood waiting. Carlotta wiped her brow and looked around, trying to decide which chore to tackle next, then she looked up and saw Sebastian, who of course ballooned a smile that said it all and matched hers, which came with a joyful tear, a hasty step, and a long hug.

"Sebastian!" she cried. "You're here! With me! You shouldn't be."

"Neither should you."

Four patients and a stack of paperwork surrounded Carlotta. With drooping posture, she led Sebastian to the rear of the ward, where, behind plywood walls, she had a chair, a small table, and a bed.

"Welcome to my office and my life. Most days, there's no sense in leaving. The wounded arrive by the hour, and— " she flopped over with both arms around Sebastian— "it's horrible, Sebastian. They bomb schools, department stores, even hospitals! We haven't a single operating room left. I tell everyone out there that the doctor is making arrangements, and then they die."

"Dirty pool in a dirty business."

"Yesterday, we amputated both legs and one arm from a five-year old. What kind of monsters do such things?"

Sebastian let Carlotta cling for all the time she needed. When her breathing slowed, she pushed back, and Sebastian asked, "Is Conchita here with you? Jimmy wants to know."

Carlotta bent forward to put her head back on Sebastian's shoulder. "It was early, we were attending wounded on the other side of Casa de Campo. The French brigade took a beating. Instead of retreating when Franco ordered reinforcements, they stayed to fight it out. A single machine-gun nest wiped them out. In less than an hour, one hundred casualties showed up, and we were ordered to move at the same time. I looked over and saw Conchita loading a stretcher onto the back of one of our transport trucks. Ten seconds later, the truck blew up and Conchita disappeared. One second, she was looking at me; the next, she was—was gone forever."

Poor girls, Sebastian thought to himself, and he hugged tighter as Carlotta released grief and then straightened up.

"Sebastian, we should tell Jimmy."

They opened the door to see Jimmy emptying a bedpan into the metal barrel at the end of the room. He had a broom in his other hand. Sebastian and Carlotta said nothing from the other side of the room, but their long faces and sad eyes went right to the point.

Jimmy stopped, swallowed hard, and then mouthed, "Conchita?"

At first, no response, then Sebastian slowly moved his head back and forth and mouthed, "I'm sorry, Jimmy."

Jimmy deadpanned a look at the one lightbulb that was out, then dropped his broom and turned around. Sebastian and Carlotta watched him from the hallway. Jimmy got to the stairs and kept going.

"It's all right," said Carlotta, "that's the last bombing for the day. He'll be all right."

Carlotta tipped backward as she put a hand on her forehead. "My word, Sebastian, I think I'm getting dizzy."

"When was the last time you ate, or drank, or slept?"

"I don't remember. I was about to take a break when you came in. I have food in my office."

She ate, she drank, she said she would lay down for just a minute, then mumbled, "Sebastian, it's hell, it's over, too much. How? So much evil. . . I . . ."

Carlotta was out cold before her assistant politely opened the door. "Excuse me, we have a lot of problems out here."

"Exactly, young man. I'm orderly Sebastian. Captain Carlotta is feeling ill. I will be doing her job for now. Leave orders not to disturb her. You and I will handle the rest of the shift."

45

Carlotta opened her eyes and smiled back at Sebastian. After that, she couldn't take her eyes off the cheese omelet, home fries, and sliced oranges that Sebastian had ready. He also had the medical unit under control. The two deserved a night off. They left for the waterfront.

There wasn't a curfew, but with everything closed and nothing to do, and the blackout anyway, everyone just stayed home. The streetlights were out, the harbor's stone walkway deserted. Their way was lit by a friendly half-moon. The air was still, the temperature pleasant, and the only sound noted was the rhythmic lapping of the tide at water's edge.

Beneath the yacht club, Sebastian looked up to see the main lounge deserted. A single flickering candle lit the kitchen.

"The gang must be up there having dinner. Are you hungry, Carlotta? Filet mignon perhaps?"

"Not for me, thanks. I passed my overfed limit back in the ward; and thanks, it was delicious."

Sebastian knew everyone in the harbor. His requests, accompanied by advance payment, had *Jubilation* moored on the last ring, the one closest to an ocean getaway. Also at his request, the flag flying astern was the country of the boat's registry—Germany.

"Anything that keeps fascists away is a good thing," he said to himself.

The bow cabin was lit. Sebastian and Carlotta boarded and made their way forward. Jimmy was curled up, sleeping, in the berth he had once shared with Conchita. His pillow was damp with tears. Sebastian turned out the light. Carlotta pulled up the blanket, and behind a closed door, they tiptoed to the stern deck.

Yacht club friends had left gifts: a cheesecake, mixed nuts, and two bottles of Chardonnay. Carlotta chose salty first, bubbly second. Sebastian finger licked fresh cherries dripping sweet sauce.

"You know, Sebastian," Carlotta said, sitting back, looking up the mast and out across the universe, "clear sky, calm water, good food, great company. . . I completely forgot this world exists."

"And we are part of it, and it can be ours."

"Ours? Nothing is ours anymore. Everything belongs to the bank, the church, the state, or the army."

"But they're not here. We are. Possession is nine-tenths of the law."

Carlotta stood up to face the center of town. "Earlier this year, when other cities were bombed, our streets were jammed with refugees. I would leave the tunnel and find thousands sleeping in town square. The men had left to fight. Most of those stranded were women and children." Then, after a hesitation, she continued, "The planes came quickly. Thirty seconds after the sirens went off, the Germans dropped ten large bombs right on city square. Dead bodies were everywhere, half of them children."

"Terrorism by terrorists," Sebastian said.

Carlotta turned to hide her head in Sebastian's chest. "And Sebastian, I'm so ashamed. I freaked out. I panicked, then ran back to my room and lay in bed with a pillow over my head for three hours."

Sebastian lifted Carlotta's head as he brought his closer. "This war is not your fault, Carlotta. There was nothing you could have done."

"Oh, I don't know, Sebastian," said Carlotta, pulling away, walking to the side rail, and looking out at the sea. "Back in 1931, I was so cocky. I had it all figured out. We had won. I was to be a big shot. But it was conceit. What was I thinking?"

"You were thinking that people are basically good and no one could possibly be as nefarious as who you were up against."

"I should have known better. I should have done something. I should—"

"You should have what, Carlotta? Been perfect? Good luck with that. We all try to live a life free of remorse, but as often as not, ignorance gets in the way—sometimes ours, sometimes theirs."

"Yes, but all I had to do was—"

"Was what?" Sebastian interrupted. "Expect what wasn't expected? Listen, I heard of a man once who found a way to keep up with all those regrets and corrections that we harp on in life. His plan was to live half his life and then fill the second half catching up on all the moaning regrets from the first half."

Carlotta looked up. "That does make it sound funny, doesn't it?"

"Yes, but only because we are."

"So, we're crazy in a crazy world that does crazy things."

"I'll be kinder. I'll say we live in a poorly educated world run by those who don't understand themselves."

"And have inherited bad manners."

"There," Sebastian said, pouring a second glass, with no other intention than concentrating on the night and the love it already owned. "Did you also know that this sloop can do magic?"

"No, I did not Sebastian. Are there many tricks?"

"Oh, yes, but only one that makes headlines."

"That is?"

"Well," he said, looking around as if there were anyone to find, "on a dark night, with a fair wind, she can make dictators disappear."

"Just like that?" Carlotta said, snapping her fingers and looking around.

"It begins like that, yes, but then takes three weeks to make Canada, and then two more through the Great Lakes to get to Green

Bay, where the mayor has personally guaranteed a four-thousand-mile dictator-free radius."

"My God," Carlotta said, overdoing surprise, "how could anyone resist?"

"I know. And best of all, once you get there, no one wants to kill you, and you don't want to kill anybody. Children, free time, and a front porch. Oh, and did I mention me? I'm on that front porch."

"Is it the same front porch that you talked about on our way back from Greece?"

"Oh no, it's much bigger now. Half of your relatives moved in."

Carlotta turned to admire the sloop, then back to look ashore, where she and Sebastian heard the back door of the club close. Behind the club, from the distant sky, flashes of light were seen.

"Oh no, a night offensive!" Carlotta said, bringing out her worry wrinkles. "Not again! They aim artillery at barracks and supply tents. Then we retreat, and more Franco fascists show up the next day."

Carlotta grabbed her purse and started down the gangplank.

"Hold on a second," Sebastian pleaded, grabbing Carlotta's left hand. "You've done extra duty, and the night shift is covering. Stay right where you are. In twenty-four hours, you and I will leave Gibraltar astern on our way to meet my mother. Forget Europe. We'll be back! Please, Carlotta, look at me."

Carlotta didn't speak all the way to Sebastian's stateroom. For the rest of the night, she let nothing bother her and believed she didn't care. She even woke up smiling. Then she closed her eyes and saw the faces of the ten children she hoped to get out of town before the next bombing. She stepped on the shore, glimmering tender memories of the night. She was standing on the walkway when Sebastian finished kitchen duty.

"Sebastian, I love you. I'll be back tonight if I can get away. About the future, I hope so. For now, I can relieve suffering and save lives right here."

"You are headed for total defeat."

"Perhaps, but I have an idea that might get your damn America on our side, and then England. If they could only see who is behind this war and where it will lead and sell us the weapons we need to counter those terrible planes, we could still win this war. We'll talk later. I'm hoping you'll help."

Jimmy, barefoot and hungover, stumbled on deck just as Carlotta turned to walk away. "What? Again? What. . . happening, Sebastian?"

"This time, it might work, Jimmy. And we can sail to northern Germany to sneak Olga away if you want."

"I, yes. . . I want if she wants."

46

"How the hell did you talk me into this?" said Sebastian, panting, with an occasional grunt.

"I asked you three questions," replied Carlotta. "Do you still believe in freedom, would you bring down Franco if we could, and would you like to crawl across a field staring at my ass?"

"A setup if there ever was one. And you didn't mention that at the other end of the field was the back of one of my abandoned factories. I have a key to the front door."

"But not the ten thousand square feet that you sublet."

"To the innocuous Belgium export company."

"That's what you think. We—that is, the intelligence division of the Republican Army—are convinced it's a front for a German spy ring. Every time we try to ambush Franco, he finds out ahead of time. The dark building in front of us has the evidence we need to arrest traitors, and there are documents incriminating an alliance between Hitler, Mussolini, and Franco. In the right hands, they could convince your President Roosevelt, and England's aristocracy, that we must stop these madmen here in Spain, right now."

Northeast of Almeria, in the direction of the oceanside mountains bordering Murcia Province, Sebastian had found an area with high unemployment and local availability of quality cowhide. The cinder-block factory that he built looked more like a textile plant, and its products were worn as holsters, rifle straps, or gun cases, all shipped everywhere in Europe for weapons assembly. That was the problem. Hitler and Mussolini were on the list, which was why Sebastian had to shut it down after he lost his business permit when the war broke out.

Halfway to the black cinder-shedding wall, shrubs allowed them to crouch like monkeys, dragging their hands on the ground.

"Oh, this is fun! We can reenact evolution. What's next? And we forgot to slither through mud like snakes."

"Quiet down and get serious. I'm a member of the Republican Army. They find merit in this mission, and I obey orders."

"Okay, I apologize. And yes, spies, saboteurs, infiltrators, and double agents are everywhere. The army must be suspicious of everyone and everything."

When they reached the wall, Sebastian was allowed to stand with his back tight to it, then sidestep to the door on his side of the property, for which Sebastian, as requested, did have a key. Once inside, Sebastian's knowledge of the ceiling space helped them crawl above the rented footage. It got noisy. A stationary low slipped close enough to begin rain that clamored above their heads.

"Is dreary weather and getting soaked part of the army's plan, Carlotta?"

"Well, Mr. Authority, you might want to know that breaking and entering is recommended when other noises can add cover. We just got lucky."

"Lucky, ouch, this you call lucky?" said Sebastian, making a difficult right-angle duct turn.

"Are we getting close, Sebastian?" asked Carlotta, brushing dust off her face.

"The wall dead ahead is the back of the main office, where I used to have a safe. It might still be there."

"Shhh," whispered Carlotta. "Did you hear that?"

"All I hear is rain and splattering drops."

Carlotta was prepared, down to the rope needed to swing down from the roof beam.

"Now can I turn my flashlight on?" asked Sebastian.

Carlotta looked around, saw no trace of light, and then nodded in the dark as she said yes, which was when they found their first clue that something was fishy. An import-export business should have had file cabinets crammed with orders, receipts, and ledgers. There were none. The table opposite the oak desk was empty, and four electric outlets had been added behind it.

"Sebastian," Carlotta said, turning her light on the safe, "did you bring the combination?"

"Now why would anyone use a safe and not change the combination? Letting the world in is not how it works, and sneaking in here instead of breaking down the door didn't help either. Everything has already been cleared out. Trust me, nothing useful could possibly be here."

"Just try the combination, wise guy... please cooperate."

"That's weird," said Sebastian, feeling the rollers with his fingers. "They are dropping just—wait—yes—it's open."

"There, you see?"

"No, Carlotta, this is too easy. Germans aren't idiots. There is no way anything valuable could be in the safe."

"Oh?" said Carlotta, as she reached in and brought out several stacks of envelopes, each one with a swastika on the outside and a military warning on the jacket.

There was only one door in the room. It was on the opposite side facing the desk. When the vault door closed, Sebastian noticed a blinking light under the door, which extinguished itself in seconds.

"Carlotta," Sebastian said in a grave, low tone, "we may not be alone."

They weren't. When they turned around, they discovered they had been joined by two Lugers, one for each hand of a tall shadow wearing a black trench coat in the doorway.

"See, Sebastian, I was right," said Carlotta, as she raised her hands next to Sebastian doing the same.

"I believe," said the face beneath a black-brimmed hat, "that *dead* right is the more appropriate expression."

"By authority of the Republican Army," said Carlotta, "I arrest you for sabotage and treason, and for being a fascist spy."

"Oh, but you are mistaken, my dear. It is you who are under arrest for breaking and entering German property. You are to be transported to Germany, questioned in the most uncomfortable way, and then executed as spies." He looked directly at Sebastian. "We've had our eye on you, Herr Williamson, and as usual, the smarter soldier wins the day. Your family will be disgraced and everything you own taken over by the Third Reich. You days as a troublemaker are over."

Carlotta kept her hands up but swaggered a foot closer. "You're forgetting something. This is a Republican controlled province. You'll never get us out of here. And my superiors will be here any second."

"That might be true, my little lady, if you hadn't left your message with Chara Sanz, who works for us. But we were on to you anyway. Javier told us you were snooping around and asking questions about the plant."

"Javier," Sebastian said, with disappointed aggression.

"Yes. The bishop made him swear on a Bible, and we told him we just wanted to look for a speaker to debate you if a town meeting followed. You people are so stupid."

"That still doesn't get us out of this room and a thousand miles away. Are you going to walk behind us holding German weapons?" Carlotta continued.

"Oh no. That won't be necessary as soon as the doctor gets here."

"Doctor?" Carlotta said, voice breaking.

"Why, yes, sweetheart. He has a special medicine. You'll love it. First, you fall asleep, and then twelve hours later, you'll wake up in Auschwitz for questioning on your way to the ovens, in which you will be strapped alive, unless you cooperate fully and beg me on two knees to blow your face off."

"Oh my God, Sebastian," Carlotta said, beginning to cry. "I had no idea, I'm so sorry."

"Carlotta, like I said, if you go, I go. Where you go, I go. It was also my decision. Now we both must be brave."

A noise was heard from the door of the reception room behind the Nazi. "Ah," he said, "that must be the good doctor now. I called him when you opened the back door. The rest of our team, trucks included, are waiting outside."

The footsteps got louder, then slowed down as they neared the doorway, which the gunman cleared by moving to the side, a movement that was next exaggerated as a hand came around him to grab the gunman's left wrist and force it sideways over the gun in his right hand at the same time he was pushed out of the way.

The free hand of the intruder was in the air just long enough for Sebastian to spot a large syringe make ground zero where the sun doesn't shine. The fascist fell to the floor for twelve hours of slumber.

It was Javier, who stood without robes, more serious than ever.

"I decided," he said to Sebastian and Carlotta, "that I no longer want to be part of an organization that tortures and executes people."

Sebastian put his arm around Javier and pulled him in close. "Now would that be Nazi Germany or the Catholic Church?"

"Both. I've left the church to get closer to God."

"And God bless you for it," said Carlotta.

"And we've got trouble," Javier pressed. "There're a half dozen Nazis in the parking lot. And Sebastian, you are now a marked man everywhere in Europe. Making number one on the death wish of three dictators is not good for one's health."

"So?" Sebastian said, matter of fact.

"So," Javier said, smiling, "we escape. We run to your car out back and speed to the boat. You and Carlotta are loved at the boat club. All I had to do was mention that you guys were in trouble and they promised anything. Your boat is on the dock fully provisioned, the wind is favorable, and the fog will hide the boat for hours."

"Wow!" Sebastian said, rubbing his head.

"There are no options," Javier insisted. "Good. It's settled. You—I mean we—escape now."

"Oh yes," Sebastian said, suddenly on fire with prospects, looking at Carlotta. "We escape!"

47

The fog thickened as they approached sea level. Sebastian drove with two hands on the wheel and one eye looking out the rearview mirror for angry Germans with machine guns. Road safety was a minor consideration as he, by worrisome margin, overdrove the headlights on his Renault eight-cylinder Monastella regretting by the minute that he had not popped for the twelve-cylinder model.

If it weren't for the side rail on the hairpin turn outside of town, they would have ended up in a ditch, probably unable to walk or possibly dead on impact. Javier prayed for Sebastian to slow down. Carlotta prayed to stay alive. Sebastian thanked God that his life was finally coming into focus. All three expected gunfire any second.

What they didn't know was that Hitler's undercover SS men were preparing to break down the back door of Javier's church, who had no intention of ever returning, and enjoyed the thought of the bishop trying to talk another sap into taking over as maintenance man.

Escaping Spain, even over water in the dead of night, would not be easy. Mussolini's "pirate" subs were sinking every ship near the coast not serving Franco. Germany's Admiral Scheer had positioned four destroyers to fire hundreds of exploding shells at the city, and in addition to the fascist soldiers that were already in the fight, Hitler added his Condor Legion, twenty-six thousand Stormtroopers dedicated to frontline action. He also supplied Franco with planes, tanks, artillery, communications facilities, and thousands of officers to train and command troops.

Almeria expected that the fate of Malaga would soon be theirs. When the Republican opposition in Ronda collapsed, German and Italian planes coordinated a land and sea attack. The Italian special unit, Corpo Truppe Volontare, the most vicious of the 150,000 soldiers sent to do the devil's work, surrounded the highlands for strategic advantage. The Italian war office documented 86,420 sorties, 5,319 bombings, and 11,585 tons of explosives. Hitler boasted more dastardly numbers. Not one inch of Spain was safe.

Malaga was leveled. Those refusing to evacuate were rounded up, raped, murdered, and then dumped in mass graves. The frantic who fled for their lives were mostly elderly women, children, and those already crippled by the war. There was only one road out of town. It ran one hundred twenty-five miles north to Almeria. The civilians traveled unprotected.

Over five thousand of them, including mothers carrying children, were machine-gunned lifeless from the sky. The Luftwaffe boasted that their planes were the best terrorist weapons on earth. They studied maps of every city in Europe.

Carlotta was sent to do what she could to help those on the road to Almeria, which was nothing, unless you counted cursing and sobbing. The side of the road was littered with corpses. For decades after, skeletal remains continued to surface, thousands of little bones from thousands of tiny fingers.

While all this was going on, businessmen in America and Britain kept selling war supplies to Franco. Both democracies were prevented by law, laws they themselves had written, from selling even a single evacuation truck to the Republican Army. Their asses weren't in the sling—yet. And no one dared contradict the pope, or risk being called a commie, heaven forbid. Blacklisting took its toll.

Sebastian, Carlotta, and Javier had a lot to worry about, and Sebastian's speed didn't help. Four blocks from the harbor, the Renault fishtailed across the sidewalk before coming to rest, side-slamming a garage. It was a short run from there.

Jimmy was waiting onboard. He begged to get to sea on one knee. He already had the anchor line wrapped on the topping lift winch to pull the boat forward. The sight of *Jubilation* quickened Sebastian's pace. He was the first of the three to bounce up the boarding plank. The sea belongs to those able to float on it. In his mind, Sebastian already felt the cool wind of the North Atlantic.

Jimmy was at the bow ready to kedge off. The fog was so dense, Sebastian had a hard time making out his face, but Jimmy's smile got through. It didn't last when he spotted only Sebastian at the stern. Sebastian's grin likewise faded. Javier and Carlotta remained on the walkway.

One look is also worth a thousand hours of heartache. On the faces of Javier and Carlotta, Sebastian did not see fear or remorse, just sadness and a sense of resolve set in stone. They had dedicated their lives to something more important than themselves, something that gave their lives meaning, something that tried to warn the world, who ignored them and, worse, outright denied the problem. Mirror, mirror, on the wall, who is the fairest of them all?

Sebastian's walk down the ramp was a dirge. Not one step felt right. Carlotta moved ten feet farther away, turned to the side, and then held out her left hand, the one Sebastian always held when they walked together.

Javier stayed put, standing in front of Sebastian. So many words, so many arguments with unassailable conclusions; Sebastian had been there, over and over. So he just stood and listened.

"Sebastian," Javier said, with firmness and a look in his eyes that Sebastian had never seen before, "I love you, and I know you love me and will make sure our family in Wisconsin does not succumb to the idiocy of Europe, but you and I must part ways."

"No, we don't, Javier. You are family. Come home with me."

"My empty church left me plenty of time for reading and thinking. I finally understand Pascal, and not just the desperate wager thing. I agree with him that men never do evil so completely and cheerfully as when they do it from religious convictions."

"Convictions that change by the decade and are misguided to begin with," Sebastian insisted, hoping certainty would change Javier's mind.

"Oh, don't get me wrong, Sebastian. I've no intention of dying for a myth or spending the rest of my life resuscitating the ghost of a dead church. I also realize that just because a man says he has something to die for, that he believes is worth dying for, does not in fact mean it is. It just means that someone has talked him into it and he prefers not to be talked out of it."

"Right on, Javier. Now get on the boat. Elizabeth is waiting to see you. In America, you can start your own church, and get it right at last."

Javier nodded agreement and then took a step closer to the water, but not in the direction of the boarding plank. "Business. That's the problem with this world."

"What did you say, Javier?"

"I know now," Javier said, totally calm. "I considered Catholicism a business."

"Which it is."

"Yes, of course, Sebastian; and unrelenting devotion to business, any business, called such or not, can only be sustained by neglecting everything else in life. Sebastian, I agree with you: you don't buy heaven with pain, you support it with love. And I deserve to find love and be loved."

"Now we're talking," Sebastian said, pointing to *Jubilation*. "Let's get to it."

"Absolutely, right after I do all I can to help my people. I'm certain that's what God wants from me now. I'm sorry, Sebastian. I must go. We will meet again."

A noise from the other side of the harbor distracted them both. Then nothing. Javier hugged Sebastian, kissed him on the cheek, and disappeared into the fog.

The fog blurred Carlotta's image at the same time it made it easier to hear Javier walk away. Sebastian went to her and held the hand she had waiting.

"I too have learned much during our journey together, Sebastian. I hope America never forgets the revolution that made it possible; what one obtains too cheaply, we esteem too lightly. Don't take your freedom for granted, Sebastian. Fight for it every day of your life."

"Yes," Sebastian said, turning to hold her tightly in his arms, "with you by my side. You guide me, you inspire me, and you really turn me on."

"Likewise, big fellow," Carlotta said with a laugh, and a tender finger slid across Sebastian's lips. "But tyranny, like every evil there is, is not easily conquered. I'm convinced that humanity breaths a spirit that will survive the challenge of every hardship. We can do it, Sebastian. Our souls are godlike, eternal and indestructible."

"But our bodies aren't, and it's not a question of which serves which and why or how, we just know that, for now, we must do our best for body and soul."

Where the walkway began climbing a rock face, a wood rail lined the water's edge. Carlotta led Sebastian over to it and then had both of them turn to look back in the direction of town.

"Your Thoreau said it, Sebastian. His words remind us there are a thousand hacking at the branches of evil to one who is striking at the root. That's the root, Sebastian," Carlotta said, pointing to Spain. "This church, government, power, money-crazy mismanagement catastrophe—that is my country today, and it will be the world tomorrow if we're not careful."

"Excellent point, my dear," said Sebastian with enthusiasm, and a body bounce to liven it up. "Okay, then. Let's rid ourselves of the catastrophe by coming back with weapons that will do the job. Carlotta, listen to me, I sell weapons for a living. Your Republic hasn't a chance. *You* do not have a chance."

"Says you."

"Says logic, which also recommends a better military strategy, one that saved George Washington many times. It's called retreat, regroup, rearm, and then return for victory on your own terms."

"What?"

"You and I will fight for freedom from Wisconsin, at first."

Carlotta let go of Sebastian's hand to walk back and forth in front of him. "You know what," she said, surprising Sebastian, "I can't argue or disagree with anything you just said."

"Wonderful! So it's settled," Sebastian said, holding her closely, looking for final confirmation from eyes that kept looking down.

Carlotta's melancholy remained without hint of apology. "Sebastian, you—and for a second, me—are forgetting just one thing."

"We need haircuts?"

"Joining the Republican Army is not like buying a ticket to a bullfight. You can't just get up and leave whenever you like. In fact, they call it treason, and it is punished by a firing squad, so often that the additional loss of life is nauseating. If I go with you, I will be a deserter and a disgrace to allegiance."

"You can't desert a country that doesn't exist. Any day now, Republican Spain will be no more. As of today, it's every man for himself. And if it makes you feel any better, in 1776, the English called every American a traitor, with noose to match."

No movement, no facial change, nothing but a slow walk back to the boat. Then Carlotta mumbled, slow and soothing, "Unless everyone is equal in every way, true equality does not exist. I can't stop this war, or perhaps win it, but I can return to those who trust me to help reduce the suffering of this war. And we are sending a message to the rest of the world."

"Are you talking about our world, this world, the one with the short attention span and memory problem?"

"It's a matter of principle, Sebastian."

"And priorities, Carlotta. Spain is on the top of your list. I—that is to say, you and I—come second in your mind. I disagree. I see it the other way around. Happiness is also a duty. And I've been almost dead enough times to realize that lukewarm can eventually raise the temperature as high as need be. Burn yourself out and cold ashes will be all that's left. Give tomorrow a chance."

Carlotta said nothing. Again, there was nothing more to be said. Both felt the clock ticking. Both looked away, listening for cars approaching. They walked in silence. Sebastian showed no signs of discouragement. He had one more trick up his sleeve. When they reached *Jubilation,* he turned Carlotta around like she had done to him up the walkway. He then raised his hand to point farther south than England.

"Carlotta, first look there, see where I'm pointing, yes, right there. You are pointing at a two-hundred-acre wheat and dairy farm with three barns, one family house, and you and I on the front porch."

Carlotta closed her eyes.

"It's the end of the day," Sebastian went on, singsong. "Our day's chores, dinner, and cleanup are over because the kids did them for us, and we can hear all five playing ping-pong and games in the recreation room. For happiness, all we need is to be together. And we will help the world as I love you and you love me and we love our kids."

Carlotta looked up, grabbed a handkerchief from her purse, and began to cry in earnest. She then stood up straight and threw her hair back. Then she looked Sebastian straight in the eye—and said nothing. Then, sobbing more intensely by the second, she turned and ran away into the fog. Sebastian started after her.

Jimmy hummed the "Star Spangled Banner." Sebastian stopped when he remembered the message the Lincoln Brigade sent Roosevelt: "The bombs that are falling on Madrid will surely fall on London, Paris, and New York."

The United States of America did nothing. England did worse than nothing. Chamberlain, the prime minister, wrote a letter to King George informing him that Britain and Nazi Germany were the two pillars of European peace and a buttress against communism.

Sebastian's steps up the gangplank were slower than a death row detail. He stopped twice to look around. He had nothing. He had had it. Both shore lines were freed. The boarding plank was flipped back on the walkway. Because a winch can squeak, Jimmy used his arms at the bow to pull *Jubilation* away from the dock. Motors only make noise when they're running. It would not be turned on until they were safely around Gibraltar.

Land warmth lifted the fog high enough to see the yacht club and oceanside houses on the hill. As they drifted forward, on momentum only, the view shrunk until just the dock was seen, and then nothing but fog.

Sebastian said not a word, just stood at the stern, looking back. As they left the harbor, twice Jimmy heard a boat and changed course. Then nothing from three o'clock in the morning on, and they were in international waters obeying the rules of the road.

Sebastian was a deflated balloon. "It will be okay now, Jimmy. We're safe at sea. We can finally build the future we've always wanted. We're going home."

Jimmy was wall-to-wall grinning but felt Sebastian's loss. He put his hand on Sebastian's back.

"Thank you, Jimmy, but I'm fine. Tomorrow, I'll wake up and remind myself that we can finally live where we want to and how we want to. It's a journey."

"Olga?" was all Jimmy had to say.

"Oh, yes," Sebastian said, with a smirk of a tease. "We had that conversation. Now let's see, what did we decide?"

Jimmy put both hands on his hips and looked hard at Sebastian.

"Of course, Jimmy. I was just having fun."

"Of... of... of course."

"Jimmy, the number one priority in life is love. So yes, we will sneak into Germany, you ask the question, and then, one way or another, we put to sea within twenty-four hours. The Nazis are slow thinkers, but I don't want to take any more chances."

"Roger... that... captain."

48

Sebastian hoped for wind gusts to make hull speed. Nature tells her own story and has no sympathy for a broken heart. The cold night was followed by a bleak, windless morning. Gray was the sky of the day, and *Jubilation* went nowhere, unless you count the yo-yo course they repeated riding tidal currents.

The fog did hold and helped transmit sounds from every direction, which was something to go on when Sebastian was denied shore bearings and star sightings. Sputtering fishing boats were heard close to shore. Robust prop wash and crashing bow waves meant gunboats were getting closer, which is when they hoisted the tender over the side, attached a towline, and rowed their backs sore in the direction of the safest guess.

Only once did Sebastian risk firing up the iron horse. A giant something approached from the south, roaring props behind a bow wake that sounded like surf's up in Hawaii, and the decibels doubled by the minute from an angle that never changed—a sure sign to sailors that a collision is eminent. An hour earlier, off duty, Sebastian did not do the right thing: go below, warm up, fill up, and force sleep. Instead, he lay a blanket on the dripping wet foredeck, stared straight up at nothing, and then asked himself where he went wrong. The problem with that question is that there are always multiple answers, and human madness must have answers or make them up.

"Should life make sense?" Sebastian asked himself, loud enough to catch Jimmy's attention at the helm, who responded, "What? Sebastian?"

"Oh, nothing, Jimmy," said Sebastian, getting up and cupping his hand over one ear to augment pickup. He was paying attention; the alternative to being alive can do that. After all, who was to say that someday Carlotta might not hand Mother Elizabeth a bratwurst from their barbeque? Depression is not a prediction; it is the lack of a better one.

"Sebastian. . . Sebastian. . . another monster," Jimmy repeated with appropriate concern, "louder. . . louder. . . big ship. . . big ship!"

Sinking *Jubilation* was not part of the plan.

"Ninety degrees to starboard—or to port, Jimmy?" asked Sebastian, who ran to the stern, sending Jimmy to the bow. Both estimated the noise difference to guess the best direction to flee. Jimmy disagreed with Sebastian. Sebastian remembered Jimmy's special talents.

"Your call Jimmy, and full throttle." They had less time than expected. Twenty seconds later, fogged by mist, a three-hundred-foot Italian troop transport passed so close they could see heads through the third-level portholes. The wake that followed rocked *Jubilation* to the rail.

"Too. . . close," Jimmy said softly after their motor was shut down.

"Much too close," said Sebastian, wiping dew and sweat from his brow. "I could have hit it with a potato," a navigation trick actually used cruising the fog-bound, rock-wall shores of Maine.

By afternoon, the sun finally burned off the fog. Just in time, because from the bow, Jimmy could have hit Gibraltar with a potato. Jimmy held on tight when Sebastian turned the wheel so sharp *Jubilation* heeled to the lifelines.

They sailed north with Portugal to starboard, then east to the coast of France. Another world opened up. Just saying the word "French" brought smiles to both seamen. La Rochelle's old harbor Vieux Port added safety, and the best chocolate balls ever.

"Now this is what I call a national achievement," said Sebastian with a mouth full of dessert that night. The next morning, neither volunteered to scramble eggs. Both offered to row to shore for authentic French toast. Both ate too much.

Death only overshadows life when you face it, which is of no profit once all that can be done to avoid it has been affected. No one does that; some get close. Death had taught Sebastian the value of life. Hemingway considered life a tragedy because it always ends the same way. He had issues, and was a product of his times, like when Spain ripped his heart open as deeply as it froze Sebastian's soul. Almost to the minute, both men came to the same conclusion: "The world can go to hell. I'm going fishing as far away as I can get."

Hemingway never recovered from the cynicism of needless, unjust suffering. Sebastian almost fell down the same canyon, and twice cracked open the cashbox to buy a car for Jimmy to drive himself to the farm and back to pick up Olga. A good night's sleep and three morning crepes changed his mind. When he looked across the breakfast table at Jimmy, who no longer came across as a helpless child, more like an adult who pressed on no matter what, an experience repeated every time he opened his mouth, Sebastian realized how much he loved Jimmy and that there was no way he could send his friend in alone to face the blond beasts. At noon, two overfed sailors hoisted the mainsail.

It's been said that men walk slowly on the way to their deaths. Sailors don't raise the jib. It was a slow trip. Neither Sebastian nor Jimmy were eager to return, but they went, more fearful, less trusting, but mostly just to get it over with, the worst excuse there is for living.

"Wow, it's true," Sebastian noticed, "from here, in the middle of the English Channel, we can see the shores of both England and Germany. Jimmy, do you realize we are directly over Doggerland?"

"Dog who?"

"Doggerland. Until the ice melted seven thousand years ago, what we call England and Germany were a single connected landmass. Proto-Germanic hunter-gatherers, basically a single genetic family, shared the entire space, and to this day, the same gene is found in men of Germany, Britain, Ireland, and Scandinavia."

Jimmy raised his eyebrows before squinting out his question, "So, the English are Germans?"

"Or the Germans are English, bred as Saxons, Vikings, Jutes, or Angles, whose later language evolved into English."

"One big family," Jimmy added.

"Who take turns killing each other."

"Sebastian. . . we human beings are idiots."

"Not all the time."

Sebastian remained offshore to appear to be on their way to Norway until Marlene's uncle's harbor was directly abeam, then he fired up and darted in. They anchored in a partially exposed cove that the locals knew not to trust in a gale. Marlene's uncle Manfred's gaff-rigged schooner was one harbor down. He was not contacted. The fewer people who knew they were in Germany, the better.

Wide-brim hats, worn sweatshirts, and muddy pants made it hard to tell them from guest workers, and the walk to the family enclave was only a two-hour hike. They didn't recognize the foreman who met them at the gate, who listened to their hard luck story, which ended asking for work. It was too early to harvest, but odds and ends always needed attention. They were shown the itinerant living space and invited to dinner.

Olga jumped on Jimmy as they walked over. No one noticed. Olga was confused but did much better communicating with the limited sign language she had picked up from Jimmy. It was a short discussion. Jimmy got out three words, signed and verbally: marriage, America, and babies. Olga threw her arms around him before a sixty-second smooch. The boys took that as a yes.

"Okay," Jimmy said to Olga, "we. . . danger. . . tell no one. . . must leave now. Get your dad and mom, please. They can visit. . . or live with us. . . anytime in the future. But. . . we leave now. . . Okay, Olga. . . right now. . . this minute. . . no packing. . . no attention."

Olga knew nothing. Her dad Eberhard knew everything, and it made him nervous. As soon as he caught sight of Sebastian and Jimmy, both were rushed back to the workers' private quarters. Eberhard looked out of a window on each side of the building before opening his mouth.

"First of all, kinder," he began tensely, "I know nothing, you know nothing, and Olga actually does know nothing. Repeat not a word of what I say, and leave immediately."

The story he told was not good. Once again, Gunter had told Marlene not to go. Once again, Gunter ordered her to stay home. He even locked the door, but after he left for work, Marlene broke the door down, grabbed their two girls, Hilke and Ingeborg, and left for Lutchburg. Her plan was to stop for just five minutes behind a grocery store to pick up Winifred Hoffmann and her three boys. Winifred's husband had been shot to death shooting it out in their living room when the SS arrived. His death allowed the family to escape and disappear to the underground railroad that was helping Jews leave Germany.

They had been followed. Marlene and her daughters were arrested alongside the Hoffman family.

"And?" said Sebastian, caught between anger and consternation.

"They are locked in a freight car, one of ten, that at this moment is being connected for transportation to Treblinka, where over one hundred thousand Jews have already been murdered."

"And Gunter?" Sebastian asked.

"There is a warrant out for his arrest. He is to be shot on sight as a traitor."

"Where is Gunter now?"

Eberhard sat down, exhausted, then looked out of every window again. "I've got to get out of here, and you have to leave right now. My life, our lives, are at stake."

"What about Gunter!" Sebastian yelled loud enough to force Eberhard to open up.

"He's planning to derail the train to save his family."

"Where and when?"

"Where the tracks split outside Aurich, at midnight, when the train is scheduled to leave."

"How do you know this? How many men does he have?"

"He refused to let any of us get involved. He said he's a dead man and so is his family, but he has to give it a try."

"Gunter is a fool," Sebastian exclaimed, stamping his feet and standing up. "Eberhard, I'll need your fastest vehicle and the locked chest I left in the back of your barn."

Eberhard had helped Gunter load his truck. He also helped him do the math. The plan was to plant explosives between the engine and the freight cars, and then another set between the cars and the caboose, where half of the SS guards always resided. Gunter's plan was to blow the links one at a time. The heavy and powerful locomotive would charge ahead at the same time the caboose would explode to kill as many soldiers as possible.

"Which leaves at least a half dozen standing on top with machines gun," said Sebastian. "Gunter needs backup, Jimmy."

Sebastian and Jimmy sped off. Sitting next to Sebastian in the driver's seat, Jimmy turned for a final look at Olga, which he hoped would not be his last.

They caught up with Gunter all right, and it was a pathetic sight, but he was a smart soldier; he had planted himself, tommy guns in both hands, on top of an elevation adjacent to the tracks, making it easy for Sebastian to find him.

"What? You?" Gunter said, amazed, and also disturbed that someone snuck up without him noticing.

"Shut up and listen, Gunter. We passed the train creeping out on our way over. It'll move slow until the crossing. Jimmy is on the other side behind cover. He will fire first to turn the guards around. That's when you and I charge from this side."

"Sebastian," Gunter said with dread, "you don't have to do this. Save yourself. Get out of here. The odds don't look good."

"You're telling me. I armed the goons coming our way. But I'm staying."

Ten minutes of silence followed. In an instant they then discovered that Gunter had overestimated the charges, which exploded the caboose to smithereens and lifted a cattle car clean off the tracks, killing several inside and tipping three more cars clean over, opening the sliding freight doors on top for trapped Jews to escape.

Everyone inside got the message. A hysterical mass poured out in every direction, which, thanks to Gunter, turned out to be a complete success, thanks to Sebastian and Jimmy adding xfirepower. Only four guards survived the detonations to remain on top. They cocked their machine guns and prepared to fire.

Jimmy took one out with a single shot. When the others opened up to lay down a barrage, Jimmy laughed behind a rock. That's when Sebastian and Gunter, forty feet apart, stormed the train from the opposite side, blazing lead. Sebastian dropped one guard at the same time Gunter sprayed the last two standing. Every German hit the deck.

Gunter raised his gun and yelped, "Ya-vohl!"

But Sebastian noticed movement from one of the guards Gunter had shot. Sebastian made sure the job was done, but not before the fascist got off a round at Gunter.

Sebastian took no chances, his latest motto. All four swastika killers were treated to a half dozen more machine-gun penetrations, blowing their corpses clear off the other side of the freight cars. Sebastian loved it. "Die, you sons of bitches!"

He growled like a north woods bear, then shook himself. "Oh my God, what have I turned into? Blood, blood, blood. . . that's all I want. I want to kill. I like to kill. . . death, death, death. . . No, I must stop."

Sebastian had killed before, but never had he felt so good about it, which he figured was just about, perhaps, the worst thing that could happen to a human being. "Carnivores, carnivores, carnivores. . . we kill, we eat. . . we kill, we take. . . I kill, I live, you die!"

Sebastian looked at the ground as he paced back and forth. Then he stopped, took a deep breath, and said to himself, "You can't wrestle with wolves without getting bitten. You can't kill without turning into a killer, but that ends now. Right, Sebastian? Yes, right."

Jimmy found Marlene and the girls. It wasn't hard to do. Marlene recognized the fire pattern. She knew her man was near. She did not run. She held the hands of both her children, investigated the scene, and then proceeded slowly in the direction of friendly fire.

As soon as Jimmy reached the girls, he grabbed Hilke. Marlene lifted up Ingeborg, and they ran for the car. Jimmy looked over to Sebastian and signed, "I meet you at car, and hurry."

Sebastian expected Gunter to be at his side, but he was nowhere in sight.

"Oh my God no. . . no. . . no. . . please God, not Gunter."

"Hello, Sebastian," said Gunter, lying on his back in the grass, spitting blood. "Look at these." He pointed to three bullet wounds in his body. "Machine-gun hits no less, three vital organs bleeding internally at the same time. I'd guess ten minutes maybe, and there is no alternative."

Sebastian got down on his knees and held both of Gunter's hands after wiping blood from his face. "You're a brave man, Gunter, and a credit to loyalty and compassion. You just saved your family and hundreds more from being murdered. You're a hero, man."

"You always know just the"—and then weaker—"right thing to say, Sebastian. I always wanted to be like you, but it was confusing. I do know this, though—I love you, Sebastian. You're like a brother to me."

Sebastian leaned over for a gentle hug. Gunter didn't want to let go. Sebastian stayed until Gunter got weaker but was still conscious.

"Do you want some morphine, Gunter?"

"No, it hurts, but I'd rather be here."

"Like life, I guess."

"There you go again, Sebastian. Always the right thing. Got anything else? But make it short. You have a bus to catch, and I'm changing my address."

"Yeah," Sebastian said, sitting back, leaning on his arms in the most relaxed way. "Gunter, I've got to be honest with you. I am one-hundred-percent convinced that this identity God gives us—you know, life, a body and all—is part of a big picture. Bodies support spirits, spirits keep God company and all of us together for all times. We are eternal spirits, Gunter. We travel together, and at the rate I'm going, I'll be joining you any day now."

Both shared the laugh of irony.

"And again, Gunter, when that happens, we'll be together again buddy. So, I'll be perfectly honest—again—it's going to be a pleasure sharing eternity with a fine gentleman like yourself."

Gunter's head barely nodded up and down. His face turned pale and white as he slowly got out, "A. . . Sebastian. . . Marlene. . . Hilke. . . Ingeborg. . ."

Sebastian put his hand on Gunter's leg. "They'll have the best of everything, don't you worry. And be safe and sound, where they will be proud of their dad who saved them."

To move or not to move—and then not to move at all—Gunter became like a statue.

Sebastian collected the weapons and walked away, not in the haste the situation required, but just as he pleased, fed up with putting up with a continent of hypocrites, and committed more than ever to exit posthaste. The thought turned his gait up three notches.

Jimmy was at the wheel of the car. The engine was running. Marlene and the girls felt better huddled on the back seat floor. The world had done them wrong.

Sebastian slowed his walk when he got to the car and saw that all was well, but he didn't hesitate to jump into the back seat as he signed Jimmy to burn rubber and take chances all the way to the boat. "Olga's dad has her on the beach, waiting for us," he said.

Marlene looked up from the floor, one sobbing girl on each arm. She counted the weapons and noticed Jimmy speeding away. Then she looked at Sebastian. Sebastian looked back. Then he leaned over to get closer.

When the tears dried, the embrace that followed opened a world of joy, security, and love that had, and would, survive more than any fiddle-faddle, old, mixed-up world could throw at them.

One might have called them the four-on-the-floor family, which was actually five in the car, six on the boat, and seventy-two ten years later, if you count the three boys that Marlene and Sebastian added.

One hundred miles offshore was all it took to breathe deeply. It was decided to pass by England on the way. Europe would get not one more chance to mess up their lives, or so they thought. Between the first and second son, Sebastian was accepted for naval officer training. His knowledge of the European coast came in handy.

He also broke his own promise. He was not always as cautious as he might have been. He piloted the first Higgins boat landing craft to the beach at Normandy, and then, on his next trip, when his plywood lander was hit, he grabbed a gun, found a hole, and returned fire. Sebastian, together with a world of good people, took back Europe.

After the war, Javier visited the lake compound twice a year. After all, he was family, and so became Burt, the tailor he lived with in Greenwich

Village. Javier, on a yearly basis, whispering to avoid unnecessary politics, kept Sebastian updated on Carlotta's family, six half-French children who helped their parents run a lodge in wine country. Apparently, the French resistance was impossible to resist.

EPILOGUE

Many years later, on a rainy afternoon in the attic of 34 Stuart St., Fond du Lac, Wisconsin, Zeek, named after his great-grandfather, and Olga, who took her grandmother's name, opened a dusty trunk labeled "Europe."

In the chest was a Purple Heart, a yacht club pendant, a sailor's uniform, baby shoes, and a journal with an introduction that read, "If mankind is to become wiser and happier, we must record and remind ourselves of genuine truth. Power is a pestilence that pollutes whatever and whomever it touches. There is only one secret to morality, and that is love. Please benefit from the error of my generation." It was signed, Sebastian Williamson.

Zeek and Olga read page by page and then decided to collaborate on a book that would satisfy their fourth-year college English requirement and warn their readers that evil had not left the planet.

Sebastian described politicians and organized religion partnering to exploit the human race. One news-brief cellphone tap had Zeek and Olga wishing Sebastian was there to help, but his words taught them that good people can do confused things, like Eugenio Maria Giuseppe, who helped three sociopaths seize power, ravage Europe, and subject innocents to the cruelest war in history. And then there was Auschwitz, which was known world-wide.

Josefina Lehnert, later known as Sister Pascalina, spent forty years at Eugenio's side serving his needs as his personal housekeeper and secretary. On December 19, 2009, Rome declared Eugenio Maria Giuseppe a saint.